**dark
days
ahead**

# dark days ahead

natalie docherty

This is a work of fiction. Any references to real people, organizations, events, and places are used fictitiously for narrative purposes. Other characters, organizations, events, and places portrayed in this novel are the product of the author's imagination. Any resemblance to actual organizations, events, places, or persons, living or dead, is entirely coincidental.

Copyright © 2024 by Natalie Docherty.

All rights reserved, including the right to reproduce, distribute, or transmit in any form or by any means. Printed in the United States of America.

Pacific Books Press

(paperback) ISBN: 979-8-9915954-0-7
(ebook) ISBN: 979-8-9915954-1-4

www.nataliedocherty.com
Cover design and illustration by Clay Smith

First Edition: 2024

10 9 8 7 6 5 4 3 2 1

*For the one who eats the first pancake.
I love you, Mom.*

# stage one / technology trigger

# the apparatus

Austria
2014

The founder gazed out the window at the layer of mist covering the mountains in front of him, overlooking the Salzach River Valley. The medieval palace he sat in, an hour outside of Salzburg, was more fortress than castle, its location chosen in the eleventh century equally for its beauty and its impenetrability. It had been built by his predecessors, men like him, programmers of the future known as the Architects of the Apparatus.

The Apparatus plotted the world's path as if weaving an elaborate tapestry. Each thread represented a year of time, an event, an innovation, a war that would shape everything that followed. The work the Apparatus did was both everything and nothing at the same time, a subtle sleight of hand. If they did their job correctly, their actions would later be deemed natural human progress, a simple evolutionary force at work. The Architects were the handpicked puppet masters who pulled the strings of the Guardsmen—the world's leaders, investors, executives, economists, and scientists—who did the bidding of the Apparatus in exchange for wealth, fame, and the facade of power.

The founder looked around the room, impatient. Every Architect was there, everyone except Reinhold, the chairman, who would of course keep them waiting. He reached for his phone, only to remember that he had left it back in Salzburg as a security measure. The urge to check his emails, texts, and social media quickly blossomed into an itch he couldn't scratch. He was grateful for the technology; after all, he had played a key role in getting smartphones into the hands of over four billion people, making him obscenely wealthy in the process. Yet despite his appreciation, he still marveled at how much of his life could be bottled up and displayed on a screen no bigger than his palm, as if his whole existence were nothing more than the handheld video games he'd played growing up.

He glanced down at his watch to check the time and saw the faded outline of the ram tattoo that had been seared into his wrist years ago. Inked in blood red, it was the only symbol of his true nature that he carried, the entrance into the Apparatus that had ultimately led to a seat at this table. They called it the Mark. He moved his shirt slightly to cover it up, not wanting to think about what he had done to get it.

He was the youngest in the room, only in his second body after his first had been ravaged by cancer and gave out at the age of fifty-five. Some of the men there were hundreds of years old, having transitioned bodies several times already. He was also the newest Architect at the table. He'd replaced Leonardo a decade earlier, after the former Architect made his final transition at nearly three hundred years old. While the Apparatus had developed the technology to extend the lives of the Architects by downloading their consciousness and powers into new bodies, they couldn't live forever. Not yet.

He heard feet shuffling in the hallway and turned to see Reinhold entering the room. The chairman had dressed in the casual, refined luxury of a man who had all the money in the world but no one he deemed worthy enough to impress. The rest of the men murmured a subtle salute as Reinhold took a seat at the head of the round table. Everyone was waiting to find out why they were there. It was dangerous for all of them to be in the same location at once. Large companies had policies preventing more than two executive officers from traveling together at the same time—key man risk mitigation, the idea being that you couldn't have all the decision-makers die at once. The same was true for the Architects. After all, they were the only decision-makers in the world who mattered.

## dark days ahead

Reinhold began to address the room. "Thank you for coming today. I know many of you have traveled a long way, and as always, the safety and security of the Architects is our utmost concern. What needs to be discussed can only be communicated in person. We have an important event on our horizon, the next revolution that will shift the paradigm all of humanity operates under. As you're aware, these revolutions can only happen during specific intervals, when the crop sitting ripe on the vine is ready for a harvest.

"Think back to the paradigm shifts our predecessors facilitated in the past—the first three industrial revolutions, which introduced steam engines, electricity, and computing. Each of these stepwise advancements brought us closer to the fourth and final one we're approaching now: the intelligence revolution. Some like to call it the Singularity, but I prefer the Merge. In this stage, humans will transcend the limitations of their own biology and become one with artificial intelligence. Humanity will merge with machines and cease to exist as we know it today. The Apparatus will no longer have to resort to the trivial mind manipulations and propaganda employed in the past to achieve our goals. Instead we'll have direct control over the machine—and, in turn, humanity itself. Our wealth and power will finally be absolute and unlimited."

A few Architects pounded their fists on the table and applauded in support. When it came to power, there was no such thing as enough.

Alfred, ever the pragmatist, interjected. "With revolutions in the past, the benefit to humans was so clear that they did our work for us, acting as ushers and proponents of the shift. Think of the farmers who saved thousands of hours of backbreaking work as a result of the previous industrial revolutions. We didn't have to convince them; they were our biggest champions. But I can't see how we'll convince people to merge with machines. There would be an uprising at the mere suggestion of it. How will we get them on board?"

Reinhold laughed, a pure and giddy release that lit up his dark eyes as he spoke. "Don't you see? We've already convinced them,

## natalie docherty

and they don't even know it yet. After you leave here today, watch the people around you—their eyes glued to their phones, headphones in their ears. Soon they'll have wearable devices to track heart rate, breathing, sleep patterns, and nutrient levels. As with everything, it's a progression. The first step was to create the technology as a separate entity from humans, something they hold in their hand and use when they need it. It was imperative to change their behavior, to normalize their reliance on the technology and make them see it as a net benefit in their life, to addict them to its usefulness and entertainment so that eventually, wearing it constantly on their body became more convenient than using it periodically. This is the phase we're entering now; we've coined it 'wearable tech.'"

Reinhold paused and turned to the man on his left. "Speaking of which, Graham, can you make sure that investors start using the term 'wearable tech' in their meetings? We've spent a lot of time testing this phrase, and we're ready for it to enter the mainstream dialogue. It needs to become a big focus over the next few years to facilitate the shift."

Graham nodded and took note.

The chairman turned back to address the room. "Now, getting back to the broader point. We've made technology so integral to daily life that people feel naked without it. Think of yourselves, all of you sitting here today without your phones—how many times have you reflexively reached into your pocket even though it's empty? You feel lost without it, like a phantom limb.

"Well, phones are mere child's play. They will become as obsolete as fax machines once we introduce wearables. We're simply priming them for what's next—the stage where we'll put the technology directly inside of them. Humans and technology will become inseparable. Wearables will be replaced with a chip injected at birth that stores data, preferences, and behaviors and comes equipped with a built-in holographic retinal display. By that point, the line between biological and digital identities will already be so blurred that no one will even notice the changes.

"But as always, there will be individuals who will see the future we're moving toward long before we're there, and they'll sound an alarm. We'll need to do what we can to minimize those voices."

While the founder was the newest Architect, he knew enough about how the Apparatus operated to know what Reinhold meant by "minimizing voices." The Apparatus owned the media and the tech companies. Those who spoke out would be silenced on social platforms, smeared by the media, and canceled by society. The Apparatus would make sure the ideas of this vocal minority were grouped with other fringe conspiracies, so that the mainstream population would have no choice but to write them off as just more crazy people wearing tinfoil hats.

Reinhold continued speaking. "For the rest of the population, distraction will suffice to keep them from seeing the truth. That's what we're here for today: to identify the means and narrative we'll use to reach our goal. We'll decide which events will give us the opportunity to reimagine and rebuild a better world, one more aligned with our vision."

The founder tuned Reinhold out momentarily as he thought back to the work of the Apparatus that had played out the previous month—the bomb threat the president of the United States had received. The FBI had found texts the bombers sent to each other while planning their attack. As a result, a bill was introduced that allowed the government access to all the text message data of every US citizen. The means: a thwarted terrorist attack on American soil. The narrative: safety and protection for the country's leaders and citizens. The entire thing was nothing more than a camouflaged flex by the powers pulling the strings.

The formula was simple, really—use a crisis or event to introduce fear, then provide a solution to quell the fear that had just been created. The more fearful the population became, the more they would support the solution. The means and narrative never varied much. Problems introduced by war, terror, natural disasters, economic instability, crises, and social unrest were rectified with solutions related to national security, environmental preservation, health, personal safety, equality, and social responsibility. It was so predictable he was surprised more people didn't catch on, but Reinhold was right. It worked because everyone was too distracted to notice, too stuck in survival mode. The coming shift would require an entire destabilization of the current status quo. They'd likely need to employ multiple tactics at once, lurching society from one crisis to another. Reinhold delighted in this part of the process, designing the threads they'd use to weave their grand vision into being.

Alfred shook his head and spoke up again. "I hate to be the pessimist here, but before we even get to the means and the narrative, don't we need to discuss the elephant in the room? The technology. We don't have the tech ready for the Merge. The artificial intelligence we have is limited, so far only working on specific tasks within narrow domains. We're still at least fifty years away from artificial general intelligence that could actually replace the broad adaptability and cognitive function of the human mind."

Graham shifted his gaze and locked eyes with the founder, who understood what the look meant. The Apparatus was composed of members from varying arenas and geographies. Most of the Apparatus still came from legacy industries—banking, pharma, manufacturing, oil and gas. The proverbial "old guard." But Graham was the investor behind the other venture capitalists who had shaped the world through innovation over the past several decades. And now the founder would be working as Graham's partner and ally, representing the tech capital of the world and engineering the solutions they'd need for the Merge.

Graham spoke up. "That's no longer true, Alfred. We've recently made some critical advancements in the foundation models that will power generative AI, moving the timeline up substantially. We're talking years, not decades."

Alfred's eyes widened.

"Of course, we can't be the ones to introduce the technology directly," Graham continued. "We'll use the Silicon Valley ecosystem, just like we have over the last forty years. We'll start feeding

## dark days ahead

VCs information, encouraging them to invest in the right products and markets. They'll follow suit and fund companies that match those parameters. The changes we need will be ushered in without us lifting a finger. We won't need to create anything; their greed will do it for us."

"Do we have a more precise timeframe?" Reinhold asked, turning now to the founder.

The founder cleared his throat before addressing the room for the first time. "We need three years to train the models, then another two years to tuck the complexity of LLMs behind consumer-friendly apps. I'd say we're looking at five years, give or take."

Reinhold lit up. "This is wonderful news. It will be tight, but it sounds like we'll have all the pieces in play before our window closes."

"What window?" the founder asked hesitantly.

Reinhold smiled. "Our window of opportunity for the Merge closes in 2030."

No one spoke for a minute as the room absorbed the magnitude of Reinhold's words.

Finally, as if on cue, Alfred chimed in with the question everyone was thinking but was too afraid to ask: "And what do we plan to do about the Liminals?"

# the ex

New York City
December 12, 2030

Spencer walked out of her hotel and headed toward Washington Square Park. The Waverly was one of the few hotels still left in the formerly bustling Greenwich Village. She had lived in New York City years before, after she graduated from college in 2011, when both she and the world seemed to have their entire lives ahead of them. Anything was possible back then. Today, she was there for a meeting with the Liminals to prepare for what was coming.

New York City was now an adulterated version of what it had once been. Still concrete everywhere, but less teeming jungle and more wasteland. The major turning point for the city had been the Zero-Day War in 2020, when a coalition of Chinese, Russian, and Iranian hackers created a small digital army that decimated the city without laying a finger on a single person. In the hacking world, "zero-day" referred to an invisible point of entry, a flaw in any software that allowed hackers to exploit the vulnerability before developers had a chance to fix it.

Starting in 2016, when a group of hackers had infiltrated American intelligence agencies and leaked plans for top secret cyber weapons, the scale and quantity of zero-day attacks exploded. But that hadn't stopped Americans from plugging everything they could into the internet. Electricity, resource pipelines, hospitals, banks, cars, home appliances, and health monitors were all powered by an interconnected web of online infrastructure. In their quest to make

## dark days ahead

smart homes and smart cities, Americans had unknowingly created the largest attack surface in the world.

The coalition that hit New York in 2020 had spent months scanning the city's networks for vulnerabilities and designed malware disguised as software updates to move around undetected. The first major vulnerability they found was in the software that powered the city's transportation system. On the nineteenth anniversary of 9/11, terrorists once again struck New York City, this time with an entirely different type of warfare. The hackers cut power to subway trains, leaving thousands of people trapped underground, in some cases for days. The attacks occurred at intermittent, seemingly random intervals over the course of the year and incapacitated the entire transit system in the process. People stopped using public transportation, and the former main artery of the city, the lifeblood that had shuttled people everywhere they needed to go, withered away. New York began its slow atrophy.

Next, the hackers targeted the newly introduced driverless fleet of ridesharing cars, causing dozens of sometimes fatal accidents by overriding the networked computer systems. Without even that option for getting around, New Yorkers opted to stay home more often. To adjust for the lack of mobility, companies shifted to remote work, but New York apartments weren't designed with home offices and shared coworking spaces in mind, and the trickle of people leaving became a steady stream.

Then the cyberattacks became a full-fledged war when the hackers turned their attention to the smart meters that powered the electric grid and water supply. State and federal government agencies were shockingly ill prepared for this type of crisis. It took twenty-nine days to restore electricity and running water to residents, and the mass exodus began.

By 2023, the population of the city had halved, from eight million residents to just under four. Businesses and restaurants began to close up shop. For the first time in New York's history, real estate supply heavily outweighed demand, and prices plummeted. Hundreds of thousands of property owners were forced to declare bankruptcy, ushering in an unprecedented economic decline.

As it turned out, the attacks on New York City were just a warm-up. The coalition broadened their target and brought the United States to its knees, kicking off what would later become known as the Great Scarcity, a period marked by high inflation, food and water shortages, real estate crises, and record unemployment. What had been initiated by the Zero-Day War was made worse by ever-increasing climate change, the introduction of artificial intelligence, and the collapse of traditional financial institutions. Economists estimated the negative impact of the Great Scarcity as three times greater than that of the Great Depression and the Great Recession combined.

In New York City, vacant storefronts and properties led to a surge in homelessness, vandalism, and crime. In 2026, the population dipped under one million for the first time since the 1800s. By that point, Spencer knew enough to understand that the Apparatus had been behind it all, but it didn't matter who had caused it or why. People had died, lost their jobs, gone broke. The damage was done.

Now America was changing, and revitalization efforts were underway across the country. New York City was transformed into seven smaller Geo Cities—two in Manhattan, two in Brooklyn, and one in each of the remaining outer boroughs. These Geos, as they came to be known, were touted as enclosed areas where everything—grocery stores, theaters, restaurants, schools—could be accessed within a twenty-minute walk. Millions of cameras and sensors tracked every movement inside each Geo's radius, keeping residents safe.

The microcities got their name from the geofencing technology that guarded their perimeters, only allowing entry into the radius for those with an approved chip and an adequate social-behavior score. People flocked to exchange the personal freedoms they had grown up with for the guaranteed safety and security offered by the Geos, signing up on waitlists and going through lengthy application processes to gain resident permits. For the first time in nearly a decade, New York City was growing again. Just the previous week,

## dark days ahead

Spencer had read that the population was up above two million—a major milestone. People were coming back, but it was to a very different New York.

The areas outside of the Geos were known as Dead Zones, aptly named for both their lack of security technology and the type of residents who inhabited them. Safe passage between the Geos was provided twice a day by a new aboveground electric rail, but travel outside of these designated times was unsanctioned. There were no police or government officials who could help you in the Dead Zones. These areas were the new Wild West, with drug use, thefts, murders, and rapes known to happen in broad daylight.

Spencer was depressed to see what had become of the city she'd once loved. The land that had inspired millions of dreamers was now a tale of two cities: high-tech walled utopias sitting alongside slums. The new Geos were picture-perfect but completely artificial. Even property ownership had become nothing more than artifice. When almost everyone left the city during the Great Scarcity, a handful of investment giants had bought up every piece of available land and everything built on it. They were now the landlords of the new Geos and had collectively decided to "innovate" the real estate market by introducing a leasehold model. Residents no longer purchased properties outright. Instead, they paid the same price to enter a long-term lease agreement that gave them the right to modify the property the investment firms owned. It was nothing more than a sophisticated rental model dressed up as ownership.

Spencer was in Village Park, the Geo that had replaced the old neighborhoods of the West Village and Greenwich Village. She walked along Hudson Street, the main thoroughfare of the Geo, where an atmospheric Australian cafe sat alongside an aesthetic Scandinavian pottery shop and a charming Parisian patisserie. The shops were designed to look local and feel artisanal, but the investment firms' formulaic approach could never quite capture one important element: soul. They served their purpose, though— tactile and sensory superficialities that disguised the virtual reality the residents now lived in most of the time.

Spencer knew all of this was intentional, designed to make these cities appealing, to turn them into a sterilized movie-set version of life. So it shocked her how much she *enjoyed* it. She enjoyed the safety. She enjoyed the trivial shops. She enjoyed that it all looked like a curated social media feed circa 2018. It was like walking through a time capsule that insulated her from the memories and fear of the last decade.

Village Park included the part of the West Village where Spencer used to live, and feeling nostalgic, she decided to walk past her old apartment, the one she'd shared with three friends above an Italian restaurant and an ice cream shop at the corner of Seventh Avenue and Grove Street. She was pleased to see that the building still stood and the restaurant had been reopened under a different name. The old entrance to her apartment was now a Random Coffee, one of the first of the private equity–backed chains later emulated when designing the Geos.

She had a few minutes to spare before her meeting, so she walked in and simultaneously placed her order for a flat white using her Orb. The neural interfaces had replaced smartphones two years earlier, enabling direct communication from the brain to the neural net chip located inside. A small cylindrical device attached to the top of the earlobe projected the screen of the interface in front of the eyes of the wearer. As Spencer placed her order, her Orb flashed a warning that she had reached her monthly ration of dairy milk, so she opted for oat milk and waited for her drink.

She recognized the barista, a guy named Lucas. He had been a year ahead of her in business school, landing offers from the Big Three consulting firms. That was over a decade earlier. Now he was serving coffee. He looked up at Spencer, giving a subtle nod of recognition, then shrugged, an acknowledgement of the way the world had changed.

One of the surprising impacts of artificial intelligence had been the order in which it eliminated jobs, as if from top to bottom. The materials needed to match the exponential explosion of AI compute power—chips, voltage transformers, and electrical power

## dark days ahead

generation—were in extremely short supply, so companies had to identify how to make the most out of the limited resources they could afford. The results were always the same. AI excelled at cognitive labor, so the jobs that made the most sense to cut were the intellectually demanding, high-paying roles that could be centralized in a single location. Back-office functions like finance, accounting, marketing, and operations went first. The next wave took out software engineers, product managers, and designers. Jobs that required a presence across multiple physical locations were spared. There simply wasn't enough hardware to place AI in every truck, restaurant, coffee shop, or retail space, and physical robotics required more compute power than cognitive labor did. Within a few years, nearly all white-collar jobs had been wiped out, while many blue-collar jobs remained. The scales had shifted. Lucas had probably beaten out hundreds of Ivy League grads to get the barista job.

As Spencer thanked Lucas and gave him a five-star review on her Orb, she felt a zap at the base of her neck. It was like an electric shock, an oddly familiar sensation that made her stomach clench.

She turned slowly, already anticipating the shock's origin. There he was. Vik. The boy who'd broken her heart all those years ago, before the world fell apart.

Only now he was a man, with salt-and-pepper hair and weathered eyes. Time hadn't diminished his intensity, though. He stared right at her, an entire history shared in a single glance, and motioned her to the empty seat at his table.

Spencer walked over. As she slid into the chair across from him, she couldn't help but glance down at his hand. The ring she'd been expecting to see wasn't there. She was surprised at how, after all this time, her heart still skipped a beat. He noticed her gaze and shifted his hand.

It was in that subtle movement that she caught it: a small outline inked in blood red. A tattoo sneaking out from behind his shirtsleeve that almost no one else in the world would recognize. The Mark of the Apparatus.

Her stomach sank. Oh Vik, she thought, what have you done?

# the pitch

San Francisco
Summer 2015

Vik sat inside a glass meeting room, looking out at the water. Traffic was at a standstill on the Bay Bridge, like it always was at this hour on a Friday afternoon. He was in his firm's downtown office instead of the Sand Hill Road one he worked from during the rest of the week, to meet with founders.

He was about to turn thirty, and his career was exactly where he wanted it to be, better even than he could have imagined. When he'd graduated from Wharton in 2008, he'd planned to become an investment banker like many of his peers, but he was rejected by all the top banks. It turned out he lacked the technical quant skills required for hedge funds and private equity. He was smart, certainly, but his true skill was his ability to influence people. Vik remembered the first time he'd read Robert Greene's *48 Laws of Power*, during his senior year of college. He'd felt that Greene, instead of analyzing the power dynamics of human interactions throughout history, had reached directly into some hidden part of Vik's own psyche to find the words. Vik, pissed off about his latest job rejection and scrambling to figure out what to do next, asked his mentor, a Wharton alum named Jack whom he'd interned for two summers earlier, for advice.

"They say when one door closes, another one opens," Jack said, "but that's absolute bullshit. I got fired from my first job as a bond trader and spent the following summer investing money for friends and family. A few years later, I started my own fund. Now I have more money than I ever imagined. That rejection saved me from a lifetime of absolute mediocrity. Maybe it's doing the same for you. Take this closed door and go find a fucking window to push yourself through."

Vik liked the sentiment, but he'd been hoping for more concrete advice. "Got any ideas?"

Jack thought for a minute. "Let me introduce you to my friend. He might have just the role for you."

Two weeks later, Vik flew to Menlo Park to meet with Graham, the icon behind one of the biggest venture capital firms in the Valley. Vik walked away from the interview with an offer and moved out to San Francisco three days after graduation.

Jack was right—the investment bank rejections had been a stroke of luck. Later that fall, Lehman Brothers filed for bankruptcy, kicking off the beginning of the Great Recession. By the end of the year, half of Vik's investment banking classmates were out of jobs. Vik's career, meanwhile, was about to skyrocket.

Junior associates at venture capital firms were mostly responsible for deal flow: sourcing companies before passing them off to the firm's partners. As the managing partner, Graham was the one in charge. Vik meticulously studied what type of companies and founders Graham favored, which industries were on his radar, and how he managed deal flow. Within six months, he was consistently sourcing companies that exactly matched Graham's investment appetite. Graham was impressed. He started to give Vik more and more responsibility. A few years later, when two of Vik's companies had big exits in the same month, he became the firm's youngest partner.

Now, Vik was sitting across from Yusuf, the CEO and cofounder of a sports optimization system, for a pitch meeting. Yusuf was telling some personal story about his startup journey. He had played squash at Yale and wanted to take his skills to the next level. In order to measure and optimize his performance while training, he needed data. He started researching, and that research turned into an obsession. The following year, he built Trackkr.

This was Vik's least favorite part of the job, the contrived stories. Just more information he'd have to remember to give the impression that he had been listening. To help himself, Vik liked to keep a mental list of phrases that he could reference later in conversation.

Squash.

Yale.

Optimization.

Data.

Performance.

Vik's list never exceeded five words. This wasn't part of a system—it just happened naturally. All the talking, all the emotion, all the backstories could always be boiled down to five words or less. People were never as nuanced or unique as they believed they were.

Yusuf was now talking about the product. He had designed Trackkr to track (ha!) two proprietary metrics for elite athletes: sleep and recovery. Yusuf proceeded to show several mind-numbing charts that highlighted the correlation between sleep and recovery, apparently proving why these metrics were so important, as if it weren't obvious that the two were inextricably linked.

These graphs were pulled from part of the product—the desktop software—that the athlete's coach would use to view the results at the end of each week. Yusuf flashed a slide that showed the hardware behind the system, a sensor placed inside of an arm or leg sleeve worn by the athlete while training.

This feels really clunky, Vik thought to himself. It's subpar desktop software that doesn't even provide real-time data, combined with ugly hardware that only the most committed athlete would wear.

But then he saw it. At the bottom of the slide, an image showed custom wrist straps—a thin band that almost looked like a watch. It was a throwaway part of the presentation, the last-minute addition of an idea that wasn't fully baked yet. Next to the image were the words "flexible wearability."

Vik felt something click in his mind. He loved when this happened. He'd suffer through men like Yusuf talking about their competitive squash days if it meant he got to experience this—the feeling when all the puzzle pieces fell into place. It was like a first-time high every time.

One of the reasons Vik had continued to align himself with Graham even after he'd made partner himself was the way that Graham always seemed to be on the cusp of things—almost like he had knowledge of what was coming before everyone else did. One day a few months earlier, Graham had started talking about something he called wearable tech—sensors and devices that would collect data and communicate information to the wearer.

Up until that point, smartphones had served as both the hardware (the phone itself) and the software (the apps installed on the phone). Under this paradigm, the hardware had been the limiting factor. No one had been able to dictate to the major smartphone makers what hardware to develop, so outside innovation was strictly limited to new app development. What Graham was suggesting with wearable tech was that any device could serve as a new hardware input and still leverage a smartphone app as the software. It was ingenious. It flipped the old model on its head and removed the hardware bottleneck. The opportunities now were endless.

This Yusuf guy had no idea what he had in front of him, but Vik did. Yusuf thought this product was for elite athletes who would wear a sleeve while training. That was too niche a product, too specific a use case, too small a market. Throw away the sleeves and place the sensor in a sleek band that looks like a watch. Throw the desktop software in the garbage right next to the sleeves and develop an app that can read from the sensor in short, time-delayed intervals. *Ding ding.* You now had a very compelling wearable that could give insights to the user with a simple glance at their phone. There was even a built-in market—the Bay Area tech crowd loved any data they could use to optimize themselves.

Vik had been on the hunt for wearable tech companies ever since Graham had planted the seed. This one was perfect. Since Yusuf had no idea how big the product could really be, he'd get terrible terms, but Vik didn't feel bad. After all, he'd basically just recreated Yusuf's entire product and go-to-market strategy in under thirty seconds.

Frankly, Yusuf should be thanking him.

Vik was grinning as he walked out of the room. What a great day. He left work and dropped his bag off at home before heading out for a first date. He was meeting a gal he'd matched with on the apps, named Spencer.

# stage two /
# peak of inflated expectations

# the date

San Francisco
Summer 2015

Spencer walked toward the wine bar on Chestnut Street, a few blocks from her apartment, to meet Vik. They had matched three weeks before. Vik's profile had made him seem successful and attractive but down-to-earth at the same time. He had a perfectly assorted photo selection: one casual professional headshot, one on vacation with his nieces, one with friends at a baseball game, one cooking dinner, and one playing tennis.

Spencer appreciated that Vik had waited a respectable five messages before asking her out for a drink. He was direct but not overly eager. She'd been traveling for work when they first matched, so the date had to wait a few weeks. They'd continued to get to know each other in the meantime, sending one or two messages back and forth on the app each day before he'd asked for her number last night to finalize plans for their date over text.

Spencer had tested out a few different outfits in preparation for the night. First she'd tried a black bodysuit that made her feel confident, then a green silky blouse that made her hazel eyes pop. But there was something about trying too hard to look good on a first date that always felt mildly embarrassing to her, like wearing makeup to the gym. So instead she opted for a simple tone-on-tone look: a lightweight cream knit top and alabaster linen pants. It was neutral and casual but luxe at the same time. Like a white woman on safari, Spencer thought to herself as she looked in the mirror on her way out the door.

When she was two blocks away from the bar, she felt a buzz in her pocket.

> Vik    I'm here. I'm the only guy sitting alone at the bar, you can't miss me. See you soon.

She smiled. He was early. And thoughtful.

Spencer was nervous. She dated like she did everything else in life—in fits and spurts. She'd go after things with a sort of raw, determined focus for a period, hoping she'd found the boyfriend, or the job, or the city that would give her purpose and distract her from the nagging emptiness she often felt if she sat still for too long.

It always worked for a little bit, but inevitably, the dopamine-inducing quality of the new shiny object would wear off. Spencer would grow increasingly bored and despondent, take a rather long break from it all, and begin again a few months or, at times, a few years later. She had lived in New York City for three years after college, and moving to San Francisco last year had temporarily revitalized her like change always did, offering a fresh start with every branching path of life a new possibility laid bare before her.

Spencer saw Vik as soon as she walked into the bar. He turned as if sensing her presence, and they locked eyes. Her stomach tightened, and energy pulsed up her spine.

Vik got up from his seat, gave her a light hug, and pulled out the chair next to him. He was cute, as attractive in person as in pictures, but shorter than she'd expected, closer to five-nine than the six feet his profile claimed. When he smiled, though, Spencer felt weak, and she forgot all about the height discrepancy.

He handed her a menu as the bartender approached. "I just ordered a pinot," he said. "I wasn't sure what you'd want."

She ordered a chenin blanc.

"How was your work trip?" Vik asked.

"Great, but absolutely exhausting. We facilitated workshops in China, Romania, and Mexico. It was a lot to cram into three weeks."

"Well, I'm glad you're here now."

"Yeah, me too."

Vik was wearing a cashmere polo sweater, dark slim-fitted chinos, and expensive sneakers, with two thin gold necklaces tucked under his shirt. He was well dressed in a practiced way that Spencer recognized. She had dated this type of long-on-money, short-on-time finance guy before, and she knew from the fit of his pants and the material composition of his shirt that his outfit was the work of a stylist.

She soon realized that Vik had a way of taking control of the conversation and driving it exactly in the direction he wanted. He asked Spencer a lot of questions.

"Are you close with your family?"

"Yeah, we're close," Spencer said. "I love them, and they would be there for me through anything, but the strength of our relationship is inversely correlated with how close we live to each other. It works well that I'm here and they're back home in Chicago. I talk to my mom and sister a few times a week, my brother less so, but I've always been the closest to him in a way. My mom and sister were each other's best friend, so my brother and I formed our own little alliance."

"And your dad?"

Impressive—Vik had noticed the way she'd left him out.

She shook her head. "My parents divorced when I was young. My dad and I don't have much of a relationship now."

"I'm sorry. That must have been hard," Vik said, placing his hand lightly on her arm. Spencer felt a spark where his fingers contacted her skin.

She shrugged. "It's really all I know, and both my parents are much happier now in their new marriages than they ever were together."

Vik paused a considerate beat before changing course to something lighter. "What do you do for fun? Do you have any hobbies?"

"I tend to think hobbies are a bit overrated. They seem manufactured. I'm pretty simple. I just like walking outside, spending time with friends, and reading."

"What are you reading now?"

"I usually like to read two books at a time—one brain candy book and one that I can learn something from. Right now, I'm reading *The Girl on the Train* and Nassim Taleb."

He perked up a bit at the latter, as if surprised she might be reading something as intellectually rigorous as a thought piece on economic risk. In truth, Spencer found the book tedious and hard to follow, but she'd thought it might be impressive to mention, and it seemed she was right.

"Taleb is a good follow," Vik said. "Are you reading *Black Swan* or *Antifragile*?"

"*Black Swan*."

"What do you think of it?"

"Well, it's hard to get past his ego."

Vik chuckled.

He kept asking questions. Do you keep in touch with friends from high school? What about your college friends? What do you think of your job? What shows have you been bingeing lately?

Even when Vik was making statements, he was still asking questions. He shared how he had dated someone for seven years, and that they'd broken up when she let him know she wasn't sure if she wanted to get married or have kids. The implicit question being—do you eventually want to get married and have kids? Because if not, then this was apparently a nonstarter.

Spencer found herself unable to make sustained eye contact with him. Something about the intensity of his gaze penetrated her in ways that felt pleasurably uncomfortable. She sensed she was being interviewed, and she liked it. She had always felt strangely at home in situations that required her to prove her worth, as if she didn't exist as a person until she was judged and chosen by another. The more she noticed Vik evaluating her, the more she performed for him. Be engaging, open but not too open, honest but not too honest. She was good at first dates, good at reading the person sitting across from her and being exactly who they wanted her to be. Vik wanted someone approachable but a little shy, smart, a "good girl." So she told him about her family, her friends, her life. She threw in

## dark days ahead

little stories she knew had been crowd-pleasers in the past, ones that were sometimes self-deprecating, sometimes incisive, and sometimes vulnerable.

They got another glass of wine, and the questions continued. His eyes never left her face, and his body inched closer as the date progressed. She knew she was passing his test.

After two hours and two glasses of wine, they walked out of the bar, heading in the same direction for a few blocks before they split to make their way to their own homes.

Vik hugged her and kissed her lightly on the cheek. "I had a really great time," he said as he fixed his eyes on her once again.

Spencer looked down at her fingernails. "Me too."

It was true—she'd had a great time. She'd liked him from the second she met him. It felt like she was meeting him again, not for the first time. He seemed like a fuzzy memory that she couldn't quite place, like she had known him in another life. There was something deeply intense about him—the sustained eye contact, the nonstop questions, the subtle but repeated grazing of her arm—that made Spencer feel more alive than she had in months.

She felt lightheaded and dizzy as she walked through her front door a few minutes later. She pulled out her phone, about to order something for dinner, when a new message appeared.

> **Vik** I had a really great time today, Spencer. I'd love to see you again. I'll be in New York all week for work. Want to grab dinner when I'm back next weekend?

Spencer felt her face flush, but she didn't want to reply right away and risk appearing too available, so she responded to a few other texts first. She smiled when she saw she had twenty-five new messages in her favorite group thread, the one she shared with Narina and Rose.

> **Narina** Guys I'm so excited
> Sam and I are planning a trip to Costa Rica

## natalie docherty

Rose      I went last year
It's beautiful, you'll love it
Which part?

Narina      We're staying a few nights in Nosara and then doing a weeklong retreat
What did you think of it?

Rose      It's a really vibrant place, but it's good you're going now
Something about being there felt like watching coral reef slowly die
There will definitely be a Lululemon or Reformation there in 5 years

Narina      Why do we have to ruin everything?
Goodbye cruel world

Rose      Speaking of a cruel world—the apps are bleak
I just had an awful first date
These guys are lame

Narina      Tell me more

Rose      He started his own company—something about "innovative wearable tech that will revolutionize our lives"
He talked a lot about his cold plunge routine

Narina      Joyless

Rose      And he thinks ketamine and supplement stacking are personality traits

Narina      JOYLESS

### dark days ahead

**Rose**      It was like he was a shell of a human who was just playing the role of a tech bro with a growth mindset

**Narina**      We are truly sacrificing our happiness at the church of human "optimization"
I think Spence had a first date tonight too

**Rose**      I wonder how it went

Spencer could perfectly picture the man Rose was describing. She had gone on several first dates with guys like that herself. She laughed as she updated them on her date with Vik.

**Spencer**      I did!
With that guy I've been talking to for a few weeks now
I'm into him

**Narina**      Details please

**Spencer**      His name is Vik
He's 29, grew up in Houston, went to Penn, is a partner at a VC firm

**Narina**      Sounds like he has a great resume . . .

**Spencer**      You know I like smart and driven men

**Narina**      I know you do, you always date that kind of guy
But sometimes I wonder why

**Spencer**      What do you mean?

**Narina**      I can never tell if you actually like them or if you just want to BE like them

## natalie docherty

**Spencer** Can't I admire someone AND like them?

**Narina** Other than his resume, what did you like?

**Spencer** Well, he drove the convo and asked a bunch of questions which was super engaging
But I guess I didn't really get to know him

**Narina** So what exactly are you into?

**Spencer** It just felt really charged
He's the first guy I've been excited about in forever—
don't ruin it for me already

**Rose** Do you have plans for a second date?

**Spencer** He just texted about seeing me again

**Narina** Good, find out more about him
And see what it is you're really attracted to

Narina had strong opinions, loosely held. It was a trait that might have been a flaw if there hadn't always been an undeniable kernel of truth in her observations. Spencer was extremely attracted to Vik, but she wasn't sure why. She knew she wanted to see him again, though, so with the group thread out of the way, she replied to his text.

**Spencer** I had a great time too, Vik. Dinner next weekend sounds perfect!

# the tension

San Francisco
Summer 2015

Vik had been on Spencer's mind all week. She couldn't stop thinking about him, but she also couldn't stop thinking about what Narina had said. Did Spencer like Vik, or did she want to *be* like Vik? Was this a pattern she had with men?

Spencer thought back to her first boyfriend, Jeff. He'd been tall, attractive, popular, and the captain of her high school's soccer team. He'd ranked third in his class throughout high school, a fact his mom never failed to mention in any conversation.

Jeff was two years older than Spencer, and to Spencer's surprise, he was interested in her. He said she was pretty, but that he really liked her because she was so smart. Spencer was apprehensive—she hadn't dated anyone before—but he was respectful, never pushing her before she was ready.

She spent every waking moment either with Jeff, texting him, or talking to him on AIM. He told her he loved her two months after they started dating. One evening in Jeff's basement, Spencer lost her virginity. His parents were upstairs cooking dinner, so instead of taking their clothes off, Jeff simply tugged her Hollister jean skirt higher onto her hips and moved her underwear out of the way before he pushed himself inside her. In that moment, Spencer believed wholeheartedly that they would be together forever.

But at the end of her freshman year, as she stood by her locker and opened her report card, she felt Jeff stiffen behind her. She was ranked first in her class of nearly one thousand students. She hadn't even been trying.

Spencer sometimes thought her brain was like a giant library full of organized shelves. As she learned new information, she'd write it down in a mental book, put the book on a shelf, and note where it was filed for reference later. As she accumulated more and more knowledge, it fell into place in her library naturally. With her mental catalog, she seemed to remember everything, and by high school, academics had become easy.

Spencer had thought Jeff would be proud of her, but over the next few weeks, he slowly began to pull away. He was busy with soccer, he'd say. He put his away message on his AIM whenever Spencer came online. He canceled plans with her and hung out with friends instead. Inexplicably, Jeff never actually dumped her—he just slowly disappeared until he'd vanished completely. By the beginning of Spencer's sophomore year, he had a new girlfriend—a pretty junior who, conveniently for him, wasn't in a single AP class.

She had learned her lesson. Men, she realized, liked to have the upper hand. She could be smart, but not too smart, and certainly not smarter than the men she dated. So on tests, she started to strategically change a few right answers to wrong ones. She took easier classes. She left out her most interesting insights from her essays.

Spencer continued down this path after college, taking jobs that were good but not great, always respectable but unthreatening. And instead of being powerful herself, she dated powerful men. She upgraded from a soccer captain to an investment banker, a hedge fund manager, a venture capitalist. She was always in someone's shadow, but she didn't mind—the proximity to their increasing levels of power made her feel alive.

Sometimes, Spencer considered the way she might feel if she had the power herself, instead of as a vicarious drip through the men she dated, but then she would remember Jeff and the way he had recoiled from her, the way he had slowly faded into oblivion, the way it had seemed like she didn't even exist. It reminded her of the emptiness she'd felt when her dad left years earlier. Somewhere along the way, Spencer had unconsciously decided that being chosen by a powerful man was better than being powerful herself.

But with Narina's words popping into her mind again, she remembered something else about Jeff. The way she'd felt both attracted to him and repulsed by him at the same time—the prototypical love-hate relationship and the toxic intensity it brought with it. She'd always thought that she loved his confidence and hated his arrogance, but maybe what she'd really hated was the way she'd abandoned parts of herself to be with him. Did she date smart and successful men because they embodied some disowned part of herself?

All of this ran through Spencer's head on her way to meet Vik for their second date. When she arrived at the Mexican restaurant he'd chosen, Vik was already seated at the bar. He was writing in a notepad.

As soon as Spencer sat down, he started to ask more questions, but she held up her hand to stop him. She was determined to learn more about him this time.

"I appreciate how much you're trying to get to know me, but I feel like I know nothing about you. It's your turn to be in the hot seat."

"Well then, what do you want to know?" Vik asked, smiling.

She decided to probe. "What were you just writing down?"

"A speech. I'm going to be the officiant at my friend's wedding in a few weeks."

"Can I hear it?"

"It's not ready yet—I was just finding some quotes that I want to reference." He closed his notebook and looked back up at her. "What else do you want to know?"

She felt like they were past the pleasantries of work, family, hobbies, and interests, even though she knew none of his own answers to those kinds of questions, so she reached for something deeper instead.

"Well, speaking of couples, you mentioned you were in a relationship for seven years. Can you tell me more?"

Spencer had an easy way about her that coaxed intimacies out of people she'd only just met, a calm energy that allowed her to be direct without being invasive.

Vik nodded. "We started dating in college. After graduation, she moved to Boston and I moved to San Francisco. We did long distance for a few years before she decided to move here. We lived together, but we were always fighting. We started couples therapy, and it helped a bit, but ultimately, I wanted to get married and have kids, and she didn't. So we parted ways. I can see now that it was for the best. The whole experience really helped me realize that building a family is a resounding theme in my life right now."

"When did you break up?"

"A year ago."

It sounded like an amicable split tinged with sweetness and sadness. A college relationship that had simply expired. Two people who loved each other but had grown apart—so much time and effort invested with someone only to end up on different pages.

Spencer wanted to ask more about his ex—she hadn't even gotten a name—but felt like they had reached a natural limit on the topic. Vik had shared a lot for a second date. She was ready to transition the conversation to something lighter, but he kept going.

"Can you believe what her parting words were to me when we broke up?"

Spencer looked up at him. His voice was now tainted with bitterness, and his eyes flared with rage. The amiability was gone. Before Spencer could speak, Vik continued.

"The last thing she said to me was 'You're just a footnote in my life, but I'll always be a chapter in yours.'"

"Wow."

"I know. I couldn't believe it either." His voice was clipped.

Those were indeed particularly savage parting words, but Spencer couldn't help but wonder what truth was really behind them. "Why do you think she said that to you?"

Vik stared at Spencer as if the question had never crossed his mind. "What do you mean? Clearly, she wanted to get in one final blow—punch me when I'm already down."

"But why that comment specifically? Your ex could have said a million mean things. Why that? Why might she think that you'd be less significant in her story than she is in yours—if she actually did think that?"

Vik looked down. "I guess she always complained that I worked too much. She expected us to spend more time together once she moved here, but I was always at the office, meeting with founders, or responding to emails. She liked to say that I wasn't very present in the relationship." His voice grew a little quieter at the end.

Spencer understood now. What his ex had said was only exactly how she had felt in the relationship: like a footnote herself. She suspected the woman had thrown the insult back at Vik so that he might feel a fraction of the insignificance she'd probably felt over the years.

She didn't want to think too hard about what this meant about Vik. Better not to break the fantasy version of him she was building in her head, not yet. The daydreaming was the best part, after all. She felt relieved when the waitress approached their table, offering a diversion.

"Are you ready to order?"

"Anything catch your eye?" Vik asked Spencer.

"I think the guac, elotes, and mushroom tacos all look good. I'm a vegetarian," she added as an explanation for her menu choices.

"That sounds great." Vik turned back to the waitress. "We'll share those."

Once she'd walked away, he fixed Spencer with his penetrating gaze again. "I'm a vegetarian too," he said.

She smiled in response.

"Did you do anything earlier today?" Vik asked.

"Just yoga. I'm trying to find a studio I like near my apartment and took a class at Yoga Flow."

"I love that place. My grandma was a yoga teacher back in the day in India."

"No way," Spencer said. "What kind of yoga did she teach?"

"I don't think it really translates to American yoga. In India, yoga isn't really considered a workout the way it is here. The spiritual aspect of the practice is equally as important as the physical asanas," he explained.

Spencer nodded. "Are your grandparents still in India?"

"Yeah, both of my parents were born there and came here in their twenties."

"I heard about a study that found the children of immigrants often experience similar emotional trauma to the children of alcoholic parents," Spencer said, immediately regretting sharing it.

Vik stared at her blankly.

"Sorry, I don't mean to imply anything about you. It just seemed to make sense to me when I heard it. The children of both immigrants and alcoholics often end up parenting their parents, just for obviously different reasons."

Vik let out a breath and relaxed a bit. "Yeah, normally parents can role-model behavior for their kids, but in the case of my parents, I often found myself helping them learn the language, customs, societal norms. I remember being so embarrassed to have friends over to my house when I was younger, afraid they'd comment about the 'weird smells' from my mom's cooking or the Hindu statues on my dad's desk."

Now Spencer was glad she had brought it up. Some sort of wall seemed to lower in Vik as he spoke, and with it, a barrier of intimacy was crossed. He pressed his leg up against hers under the table as they shared a pitcher of margaritas, and his hand rested on her thigh. Spencer felt a thrum of energy pulse through her body. Her stomach clenched even though the placement of his hand, closer to her knee, made the gesture feel more sweet than sexual.

Somehow, after that initial disclosure about Vik's past relationship and then about his parents, the conversation drifted back to Spencer. His evasiveness annoyed her, but it made her feel special at the same time. He cared so much about getting to know her.

The waitress surprised Spencer when she came around to tell them it was last call. They'd been there for four hours already?

As they left the restaurant, Vik turned to her. "I'll walk you home."

He reached down, grabbing her right hand with his left, interweaving his fingers and hers. His thumb made a slow, circular motion on her palm. They walked in an easy silence for a few minutes, and soon they approached Spencer's front door. She was about to invite him up to her apartment, but before she could speak, Vik placed his hand around the back of her neck and pulled her face close to his.

"Night, Spencer," he whispered in her ear. Then he kissed her lightly on the cheek. "Sweet dreams."

The warmth of his breath lingered on her skin as he turned to walk away.

Spencer made her way upstairs, once again feeling dizzy—and completely alive.

| | |
|---|---|
| Narina | Guys, how were your dates? |
| Rose | Just as bad as the last one<br>This guy is getting his MFA<br>He spent the entire time talking about the book he's writing and said things like "my craft is the most sacred thing in my life"<br>He didn't ask me a single question |
| Narina | I know this type<br>He's probably been in the "ideation" stage of a novel for several years and is growing increasingly frustrated that his fellow classmates are getting published<br>I doubt he's written anything, he just spends his days "workshopping" other people instead of focusing on himself<br>Was he really forgettable looking? |
| Rose | Ha this is scarily accurate<br>And YES<br>I can't deal with this madness<br>Spence—how was the second date with Vik? |

## natalie docherty

**Spencer**  Ugh I'm sorry, Rose
It was great
I haven't been this attracted to a man in a LONG time
I really wanted to hook up with him, but nothing happened—just a kiss on the cheek
I did get to know him better, he shared a bit about his last relationship

**Narina**  And? Any red flags?

**Spencer**  He dated his ex for 7 years, they lived together
Seems like they really tried to make it work (they even did couples therapy)

**Rose**  Let me guess—he couldn't commit?

**Spencer**  No, actually the opposite
He wanted to get married and have kids
She didn't

**Rose**  God that is wildly refreshing

**Spencer**  Yeah, he said marriage and kids are a resounding theme in his life right now

**Narina**  Please don't tell me he used the words "resounding theme"?

**Spencer**  He did...

**Narina**  Gross
Does he always talk like such a VC?

**Spencer**  Stop
He's not gross and no

### **dark days ahead**

**Narina**   I'm sorry, it's just hard not to generalize
Every VC I've known has always been the same
Just wait for him to repurpose other people's opinions as his own

**Rose**   Narina, be nice! He sounds sweet!
I get wanting to hook up with him, but I like that he's taking things slow
When are you seeing him again?

**Spencer**   We don't have plans yet, but I'd be surprised if I don't hear from him soon

# the shock

San Francisco
Summer 2015

Spencer was disappointed when she woke up the next day and looked at her phone. There were no messages from Vik.

She couldn't stop herself from checking every five minutes throughout the day. By the time she crawled into bed that night and still hadn't heard from him, she felt a sense of dejection creeping in.

The next day, the same thing happened—constant checking of her phone, followed by constant disappointment that Vik hadn't texted her. She replayed the date over and over in her mind, wondering if she'd done something wrong, if she had misread everything.

When she woke up the following morning, she made a promise to herself not to ruin another day. As soon as she arrived at work, she put her phone on silent and vowed not to check it until she left the office.

Waiting for the elevator at the end of the day, she took it out and looked at the lock screen with trepidation. Her brain processed the name quicker than she could read it. Vik had texted her at 12:33.

I can't stop thinking about you. Come over tonight? I'll make us dinner.

She quickly typed a reply.

Sorry for the delay, busy day! That sounds great, I'll bring wine. What time?

Vik texted back moments later.

Any time after 7. See you soon.

Spencer rushed home to freshen up before heading to his place.

She picked out a black lace thong and matching bra to wear under a black silk top with jeans. On her way to Vik's, she stopped at Epicurean Trader to buy a bottle of wine.

"Hey," Vik said, a huge smile plastered on his face when he opened the front door. "Come on in."

He lived alone in a beautiful three-bedroom apartment that spanned the first floor of an old Victorian. The place was quintessential San Francisco—tall ceilings, intricate crown molding, and big bay windows. The apartment was impressive and objectively well decorated, but it felt bare. Spencer had always thought that most men lacked the ability to turn a house into a home. Vik had tried, but it was like he had bought every item from a single staged area of a popular home decor store.

"I hope you like Indian," he said. "I made my mom's famous matar paneer. I can't take any credit for the naan, though. That's from Trader Joe's."

Spencer smiled. "That sounds delicious. Where's your bottle opener and wine glasses?"

He grabbed an opener from a drawer and popped open an overhead cabinet full of glassware. Spencer got to work and poured the wine while Vik prepared their plates.

"Let's eat in here," he said, gesturing to the large island in the kitchen.

They sat side by side, Vik's leg grazing hers before she even took her first bite.

"This is actually really good," Spencer said.

"Geez, don't sound so surprised."

She laughed in reply.

"While you were so busy working today, I was finalizing my officiant speech. Want to hear what I have so far?" Vik asked.

"Sure," Spencer said, nodding.

He grabbed his notepad and stood up, spreading his legs and inflating his chest in a serious manner. Spencer noted the role-playing they were clearly partaking in and put down her fork, turning to give him her undivided attention.

"Friends and family, we're gathered here today to celebrate the union of James and Anika, two individuals who've chosen to walk together—hand in hand—through the journey of life.

"Marriage is a sacred commitment, a partnership built on respect, patience, and support. It's a journey not taken lightly but one with many light moments scattered throughout—growth, family, shared dreams.

"Before these two kindred souls embark on their new path together, I'd like to reflect on the wisdom shared by one of the most iconic couples of our time, Caleb and Rebecca Gray. Their marriage exemplifies the power of love."

Interesting choice. The Grays were a political power couple who had taken the country by storm when Rebecca became the first female president in 2012. They were a landmark couple in many ways—notably, they'd been the first interracial family in the White House. They were charming and had this whole "East Coast intellectual meets West Coast cool" air about them. Despite their popularity, Spencer thought they'd be better suited for career mentorship than marriage advice.

"Caleb once said, 'When we're sitting together, I look at her, and it's like we're two separate waves meeting at the shore. We each have our own histories, families, friends, lives—but for this moment, and hopefully many more, we're crashing and joining constructively, creating a bigger wave together than either of us could ever imagine alone.'

"This separate togetherness Caleb references is at the very core of marriage. The merging of two separate souls is where all the happiness and hardships in marriage arise. It's important to cultivate as much respect for the individual as the union; one can't exist without the other."

Vik paused. "That's what I have so far. I need to add a quote in there from Rebecca, too. What do you think?"

"It's great," Spencer replied. "Why did you choose the Grays?"

"I tried asking my parents for advice, but their quotes were terrible. The Grays are America's favorite couple, right?"

Spencer nodded. She pushed Narina's comment about VCs repurposing opinions out of her mind and focused on how heartwarming it was that Vik was putting so much effort into his role as the officiant. Clearly, he placed great value on both friendship and marriage.

"Why don't you come with me?" Vik asked.

"Sorry?"

"Why don't you come with me? To the wedding."

"Where is it?"

"In San Diego—we can fly down for the weekend."

"When?"

"In three weeks."

Spencer felt butterflies, but she also heard a voice in her head. This seemed fast. It was too soon to be taking a trip together. She felt like there was some rule that existed out there in a book like *Why Men Love Bitches* that required her to say no to an invitation like this. But then another voice spoke, louder. A voice that said, "Why the hell not?"

Spencer checked her calendar on her phone. She was free that weekend.

"Sure, I'll go with," she replied.

Vik smiled. "I'll send you all the details later."

They cleared their plates, and Vik offered Spencer a refill on her wine before they moved to the living room and sat on the couch.

The best part of his place was undoubtedly the sofa. It was one of those ultradeep ones where sitting wasn't really an option; you had no choice but to lounge. Spencer curled her bare feet up underneath her and made herself comfortable as Vik searched for a show to watch. She looked around the room and noticed a guitar hanging on the wall next to the fireplace.

"Can you play me a song?" she asked.

Vik looked at her, then followed her gaze to the guitar.

"I don't know how to play," he said, avoiding eye contact.

She couldn't quite read the expression on his face. Was that embarrassment? "Why do you have a guitar on your wall if you don't know how to play?"

He took a moment before replying. "I like people thinking I'm someone who knows how to play guitar."

Spencer just stared at him. The admission confused and startled her.

"You'd be surprised how few people ask for proof," Vik added.

A long silence passed between them as she took this in. She remembered the fib about his height on his profile, and now there was the staged guitar. How else did he manipulate his image?

Vik reached down and grabbed her big toe, pressing into it with his thumb. It was a strange and unusual first move, and it pulled Spencer out of her thoughts, sending shivers down her spine.

It reminded her of a time when she was young, maybe ten years old, on a family vacation in Tennessee. She'd been out on a bike ride with her mom. They rode for miles, passing fenced-in pastures where cattle grazed freely. It was a picturesque scene if you didn't look too closely at the electric barbed wire that lined the fences, an added security measure to keep the animals from escaping.

At one point, Spencer saw a jet-black stallion standing alone in a large field, near the edge of the fence that separated him from the road. There was something about the stallion that drew her in; he looked so lonely and so powerful at the same time. His strong, muscle-bound legs glistened in the sun. As Spencer stared, he reared up on his hind legs. She got off her bike and went toward the horse almost in a trance. Her mom, now a few hundred feet ahead, turned around and sighed in exasperation.

"Spencer, what are you doing?" she yelled.

Spencer kept walking.

"Get back on your bike!"

She reached out, ready to hurl herself over the fence.

"Spencer! Stop! That fence will electrocute you!"

She later told her mom she hadn't heard her, but really, Spencer had chosen not to listen to her warning. She reached her hand forward and felt a shock ripple through her body before she collapsed on the ground in a crumpled heap. When she woke up a few moments later to her mom standing over her, it was the stallion's churning black eyes she saw where her mother's should have been.

She thought about that day any time she drove past a suburban home with an invisible fence that trained the dog not to go outside of the yard's boundary by emitting a tiny electric shock. Spencer always wondered why the threat of shock hadn't worked on her, why she instead chose to keep moving toward the dark, mysterious horse in front of her.

The shock she'd felt then, the electric current meant to warn her, was the same one she felt now when Vik touched her.

"Can I kiss you?" he asked.

Spencer paused and looked up into his dark eyes, the current now pulling her toward him.

She nodded.

Vik leaned in immediately, his right hand moving up to her face, his left moving from her foot up the inside of her leg to her inner thigh. His lips touched hers, tender and soft at first, then with an intensity that matched his gaze. He parted her lips with his tongue and slid it into her mouth.

"Let's go to the bedroom," Vik said after a minute. He stood up and grabbed her hand to lead her down the hallway.

Maybe it was the wine-induced haze, but Spencer couldn't remember anything after that. It was the kind of sex where the specifics seemed to blur in and out. It all felt fluid. She kept moving along the electrical current that intermittently shocked different parts of her body. Her ears, her neck, her breasts, her lower back. Zap. Zap. Zap. She wasn't sure if it lasted five minutes or five hours.

She woke up the next morning with Vik curled behind her, his arm on her hip.

"You look beautiful, Spence," he whispered in her ear.

The nickname felt like he was staking a claim. Spencer tried to hide her smile as she leaned back against him.

"I need to go take a quick call for work. I'll be back in a few minutes," he said.

Spencer stayed in bed, still feeling the afterglow from the night.

Then she noticed a familiar tingling feeling. She called it her spidey sense—an intuition that had come to her at different moments throughout her life. This time, she felt a deep knowing in her gut that she was being watched.

She looked around and didn't see anything, but she couldn't shake the feeling that eyes were on her. She could hear Vik's voice coming from the kitchen; he was clearly on a call in a different room. Then it hit her. There must be a camera.

She surveyed the entire room until she saw it—a lens no bigger than her thumbnail, perched above the TV mounted on the wall across from the bed. Spencer's stomach dropped at the realization, then dropped again as she thought back to the night before. Vik had filmed them having sex.

After the initial shock wore off, however, the next emotion she felt was not anger but intrigue.

Spencer had once been told she had the type of indiscriminate open-mindedness that sometimes caused her brain to skip the logical first layer of questions one would normally encounter. When she was in high school, her boyfriend had asked her if he could dip his balls in a glass of warm milk while Spencer blew bubbles with a straw. A ballcuzzi, he'd called it. Instead of contemplating the juvenile perversity of the request, or whether she wanted to partake in the act at all, Spencer had wondered whether the smoothness of nonfat milk or the viscosity of whole milk might yield a better result. They tried both.

So now, instead of worrying if she should be afraid of the man in the kitchen who had videotaped her last night, if she might somehow be in danger, Spencer instead found herself wondering if Vik was watching her right now. Spencer knew she should leave, but she suddenly felt hot. Had Vik left the room for a call just to see what she would do?

She decided to test that theory. She took off his T-shirt, which she had thrown on at some point before falling asleep. Positioning herself face down in bed, she pulled down the sheets to her thighs so that the camera could see her lace thong and bare butt. Then she reached her hand into her underwear and lightly touched herself.

Within a few seconds, Vik came back into the room and slid into bed beside her. He was still on his work call, so he placed his phone on speaker on the nightstand and pressed mute as he inched closer to Spencer's almost naked body.

"Nice ass," he said as he moved his hand up her leg and pushed her thong aside. He started to talk about the call he was on while he slowly pushed his middle finger inside of her. "This company has been a dud. We're trying to sell but haven't had any luck. The founder is a total douche." His hot breath hit her ear.

Spencer felt disoriented. She didn't know where to focus. Vik kept talking about the douchey founder as he rhythmically moved his finger in and out. His thumb pressed down on just the right spot outside of her as his index finger joined his middle finger inside. The disorientation faded as Spencer felt something else course through her. Power. Instead of focusing on an important work call, there Vik was, focusing on her. That power was all she thought about until she orgasmed a few minutes later.

Vik grabbed a tissue from his nightstand and reached for his phone at the same time. "Shit," he muttered as he glanced down at the screen.

"What?" Spencer asked, now worried.

"We weren't on mute. Fuck. I'm fucked."

Well this is a first, Spencer thought. Then she laughed.

Vik stared at her in horror for a second before he broke out in his own laugh. "I'll deal with that later," he said, hanging up the phone and moving back toward her.

They had sex once more before he dropped her off at home.

Spencer   I went to Vik's last night for dinner and things
             escalated . . .

Narina   Did you have sex?

Spencer   Yep
             And he asked me to go with to his friend's wedding

## natalie docherty

Narina    Tell us everything

Spencer  I was not disappointed
           The attraction is crazy intense—like out of control, but in a good way
           Maybe noticed some yellow flags though

Narina    Like?

Spencer  He has a guitar hanging on the wall in his living room, but he doesn't know how to play it

Rose      Maybe it has sentimental value?
           Did you ask why he has it?

Spencer  He said he "liked people thinking he was someone who knew how to play guitar"

Narina    Well, it's really embarrassing to admit that
           I'm glad he was honest about it

Rose      Do you guys remember that guy Jason I dated?
           He had these expensive sound bowls
           One time I asked if he would play them, and he said he had no idea how to and had never actually tried

Narina    Wait, no please
           Why?
           The sound bowls
           No
           Please
           I just don't understand—how do you buy them and not even try?

## dark days ahead

Rose      He was shocked when I asked him to play

Narina      You need to describe them to me
                Were they different sizes?
                What color?
                Location?

Rose      HE HAD FOUR OF THEM
                The biggest one was pink crystal, semi-translucent
                The other three were brass with like these intricate carvings on the outside
                He kept them prominently displayed on his bookshelf

Narina      He didn't even want to try?
                I'm really stressed out

Rose      God, he was so strange in a way that now creeps me out
                I was in such a low place around dating then like I was desperate to be in a relationship

Narina      Remind me why you were so into him?

Rose      Honestly, I was sexually attracted to him in a way that felt chemical

Narina      It sounds like you and Vik, Spence

Rose      He was the first guy in SO LONG that wasn't the beer/football/golf guy
                I thought he moved to his own drum
                Then I realized he was just following the yoga guy with Birkenstocks playbook
                He even went to Eckhart Tolle retreats

Narina   Well, Burning Man with a W2 is your type

Spencer  Guys, now I'm stressed out
         Is Vik just the VC version of Jason?

Narina   What are the other yellow flags?

Spencer couldn't bring herself to tell them about the hidden camera. That wasn't a mild yellow flag; it was a literal signal of danger. She didn't want to think about it, so she pulled up the notes on her phone, where she stored her to-do list. She was determined to check off at least one item before she finished her lunch break.

*Buy new couch*, she read from the list.

She thought back to the couch at Vik's, the way she'd loved leaning back and putting her feet up on the extra-deep seat. She searched around until she found it. The "Lounge Deep" sofa from Crate and Barrel—currently 30 percent off. She added it to her cart.

Narina   I'm still not over the sound bowls
         AT ALL

# the list

### New York City
### December 12, 2030

Spencer glanced again at Vik's wrist. She couldn't take her eyes off the Mark. She caught him noticing her gaze, so she attempted a diversion. "No watch?"

Vik had always had a thing for watches, and as with any good investor, they mirrored his career progression: Rolex, then Blancpain, then Vacheron, then Patek Philippe.

"Who needs a watch when you control time?" Vik replied, his eyes glistening.

"What are you doing in town?" Spencer asked.

If he was part of the Apparatus, she could only assume he was there for the same reason she was—the Harvest.

"Work," he said, before quickly changing the subject. "Do you remember the last time we were here together?"

Of course Spencer remembered. Those nights were forever seared into her brain. It had been a few months after they started dating. They'd both traveled to New York frequently for work, and when their schedules overlapped, they met for dinner, drinks, or just a quick rendezvous. The night he was referring to, they had gone to dinner up the street from where they now stood. On the way to his hotel later, Spencer had given Vik a blow job in the back seat of a taxi. Vik had thanked her and the driver at the same time as he zipped up his pants and stepped out of the car in front of the Mercer. Her cheeks flushed at the memory.

Spencer wanted to tell him she didn't remember, that she had forgotten he existed. But he would see right through the lie, so she played along. "How could I forget?" she replied.

Vik's eyes never left her. His gaze still tugged at something deep inside of her. "I need to run for a meeting," he said. "I'm in town for a few days. Can I see you again before I leave?"

She wanted to say no, but she needed to find out how deep into the Apparatus he was and how much he knew about the Harvest. "I'd like that."

"Wine? Tonight? I know a great place," he said as he put on his coat.

Spencer nodded and walked out of the coffee shop.

She longed for the days when she could have pulled out her phone and texted Narina and Rose to tell them everything that had just happened. Texts would always be inextricably linked to her twenties in the same way that AIM messages were tied to her teens. But everything was different now, and texting her friends wasn't an option.

She headed around the corner to the meeting point. She'd been to the old church on Christopher Street a few times. It used to be St. John's, a small neighborhood Lutheran church. The current leasehold owner, Sue, had converted the first floor into a mixed-use space—part plant shop, part bar, part library. After the place opened, it became a not-so-discreet secret that Sue had some copies of censored books that she loaned out to trustworthy parties, books that had come out in the final few years before wide-reaching bans were enacted. It was through this private library that Sue came to be involved with the Network, and she allowed them to use the upstairs space as their meeting ground.

Spencer walked inside, waved at Sue behind the counter, and headed toward the curtain next to the bathroom, then up the rickety flight of stairs behind it.

Luisa was already there. She looked as exhausted as Spencer felt, but they both lit up at the sight of each other. It had been over a year since they'd been together in person. Travel restrictions implemented to combat climate change had limited cross-state air travel to twice per year. Those who needed to travel outside their allotment used black market train travel, but safe passage through the Dead Zones couldn't be guaranteed, and it was too big of a risk for them to take.

Spencer and Luisa were college friends, and they had both lived in San Francisco in the before times. Before the attacks, before the world changed, before they became part of the Network. Spencer wished she could catch up with her old friend, but they had more important things to discuss.

"I just ran into Vik," she blurted out.

"Shit. Where?"

"Getting coffee. He has the Mark."

Luisa raised an eyebrow before she spoke. "Were you surprised?"

"I don't know. The whole interaction caught me off guard. I haven't had time to fully process it yet."

The Apparatus was adept at hiding their highest-ranking members, which made it nearly impossible to confirm the identity of the Architects. The Network had worked diligently to profile and track a list of likely candidates, and Vik's name had been on their watchlist for years, but some part of Spencer had never wanted to believe it could be true.

"If Vik is in the Apparatus, and he's here now, then the intel we received about the solstice is likely accurate," Luisa said.

Spencer nodded. She'd had the same thought when she saw him.

Over the years, as the Liminals had become more in tune with their powers, they noticed the way their abilities were heightened on the solstices each year, when the veils between realms were thinnest. Powers—both light and dark—were amplified during these portal periods. A few weeks ago, the Network had heard from one of their sources that the Apparatus was planning the Harvest the night of the winter solstice, and Vik's appearance in New York now all but confirmed it.

"Which means we have *nine days* to figure out what their plan is and come up with a counterattack," Luisa continued, shaking her head.

Spencer nodded solemnly. She felt Luisa's frustration. Despite growing stronger and recruiting new Liminals every year, the Network had never managed to take an offensive position. The Apparatus was always one step ahead, which left the Network scrambling to play defense.

"If we want to have any chance of stopping them," Spencer said, "we need to get as much information as we can. That's why I agreed to meet Vik tonight for a drink—to see if I can find out anything that might help us."

Luisa's eyes widened. "I don't know if that's a good idea, Spence."

"I know what I'm doing," Spencer said. "I know him."

"You *knew* him. You dated him years ago, way before he was in the Apparatus. We have no idea what he's capable of now. We don't even know what his powers are."

Luisa's words struck something in her. When Spencer first saw Vik's name on the Network's watchlist, she had spent considerable time contemplating *if* Vik was involved with the Apparatus, but she had never contemplated *when* he would've become involved.

"How do we know he wasn't in the Apparatus then?" Spencer asked, memories crystallizing in her mind as she spoke.

Luisa looked surprised. "I never considered that. Do you think he knew all along?" she asked. "Did he know about you? About what you are?"

Spencer thought back to those pivotal few years when everything in her life had changed.

Had he known?

# stage three /
# trough of disillusionment

# the trip

Oakland
Fall 2015

Spencer and Vik had been spending all their free time together, or rather, all of Vik's free time together. Vik was often busy with work, so Spencer tried to make herself available around his schedule. She found herself canceling plans with friends and declining invites in case he might be free. Narina had made it known she was annoyed with Spencer's behavior, but Rose let it slide.

"She's in the honeymoon period! We've all been there before," Rose had said the last time Narina called Spencer out.

But tonight, Spencer couldn't bail on her friends. She and Rose were on their way to Narina's house for dinner after receiving cryptic texts the night before.

> **Narina**   We just got back from Costa Rica
> The retreat was life changing
> I need to tell you both all about it in person
> Come over tomorrow night

Rose and Narina had known each other for years, having worked at the same tech company since college. Spencer had met them both at the party of a mutual friend shortly after she'd moved to San Francisco the year before.

"I love to get people's first impressions. What's the strangest thing about living here compared to New York?" Narina had asked Spencer.

Spencer thought for a moment before replying. "Everyone here has hobbies they think they're experts at. Like I overheard some guys at Blue Bottle talking about roasting their own coffee beans at home for their Chemex pour-overs, saying things like 'the orange notes in this coffee are overrepresented.'"

Narina and Rose laughed.

"You're so right," Narina said. "That makes me think of the men who wear their cycling kits to brunch after a fifteen-mile ride in Marin, acting like they just biked the Tour de France."

"Or the women talking about sourdough starter hacks and optimal proofing temperatures while waiting for their Barry's class to start," Rose added.

The three of them had been hanging out ever since.

"I still can't get over how amazing your house looks," Spencer said to Narina as they walked through the front door.

Narina had gotten married the year before, and she and her husband, Sam, had decided at Narina's insistence to throw a dagger through the heart of their honeymoon period by immediately undertaking a gut renovation of a hundred-year-old Oakland home. The house was nestled on a side street a few blocks north of Lake Merritt and had Victorian bones. It wanted to be grand and open and eclectic and colorful, but the previous owners had painted the exterior a tinny gray and put walls everywhere, closing off rooms, hampering the flow, and blocking any natural light. Their house, like many in the Bay Area, was built close to neighbors on a long and narrow plot of land, so the only real light came in through the front and the back. To make it bright, you had to knock down every wall and open it up fully.

That was exactly what Narina and Sam had done. The resulting space felt both moody and airy at the same time. The design was minimal and slightly modern, with unique touches—acrylic chandeliers, organic shaped mirrors, and chubby furniture—scattered throughout. Spencer had been to the finished house a few times now, but she was still impressed with how her friend had transformed the space. Narina's style, like Narina herself, was naturally confident and magnetic, drawing people in like a force of gravity.

Her style was so magnetic that soon enough, Narina would probably start to see pieces of her home show up in other places. The same thing had happened with her last renovation project—a condo in SoMa that she'd sold when she got married. First a knockoff of the white oak floors she'd meticulously sourced from Malmö appeared in a friend's place in Piedmont. Then another friend bought a piece of art from the same local artist Narina had chosen to feature in her entryway. After that, a designer started to showcase her own eerily similar home on social media, introducing her "new" design aesthetic.

Twelve months after she'd put the finishing touches on the condo, Narina went to dinner at a coworker's house. The coworker was a sweet, kind woman who had a dated style that made Narina cringe. When Narina saw not one but two of the knotted-wood art pieces she had painstakingly searched through countless art fairs to find, she almost lost it. She thought back to a story she had heard about Kurt Cobain. Early in his rise to fame, he'd encountered a young, pimply-faced teen at a local mall wearing a Nirvana T-shirt. Instead of being proud of the success of the band, he was embarrassed. It physically pained him to see that Nirvana had become so mainstream, so commercial, so utterly common that this tasteless prepubescent boy knew who they were. That was how Narina felt staring at the wooden knot hanging above her coworker's dining table.

She'd called Rose on the way home. "I'm ready to burn my condo down to the ground and start from scratch," she said as she seethed.

Right now though, as Spencer and Rose sat at Narina's dining table that evening, Narina was still in the few months of post-renovation bliss, where her creation was still her own and hadn't yet been tainted by the sticky fingers of the world around her.

Narina poured them each a glass of wine, put the bottle down, and fixed her gaze on the other two. "I had the craziest experience when I did ayahuasca," she said. "Are you ready to have your mind blown?"

Narina and Sam had just returned from a seven-day transformational program meant to awaken growth and enable healing, complete with farm-to-table meals, rhythmic breathwork, somatic experiencing, and kundalini yoga. It all culminated in a three-night ayahuasca ceremony.

"I can't wait," Rose said. "I've been dying to do ayahuasca."

It still surprised Spencer how openly her friends talked about their journeys. She'd never taken a single drug before she moved to San Francisco. While she appreciated the way people in the Bay Area embraced psychedelics and had recently begun experimenting herself, she could never quite shake the shame that years of Catholic school and D.A.R.E. programming had instilled in her. But like Rose, she'd been curious about ayahuasca and couldn't wait to hear about Narina's experience.

She nodded, and Narina began.

During the first night of the ceremony, after everyone had drunk the medicine, as people were violently purging, bursting into tears, releasing lifetimes of trauma, and surrendering to the wisdom of ayahuasca known as the mother, the shaman made his way around the room. He stopped at each person to sing in their ear, singing to the spirit inside of them that activated the medicine.

As he came up to Narina, she saw a veil lift, and she began to have visions of different energetic beings. There were three stages: one that was empty and devoid of any substance, one that had a small amount of energy, like a single ray of light, and one that was a blinding blast of pure white. She knew she was witnessing a sort of magic that she couldn't fully comprehend. After the three stages of energy passed before her eyes, a veil fell, obscuring it all. Her vision became normal again, and the energy disappeared as quickly as it had arrived.

The following morning, during the day's sharing circle, Narina told the group about her experience, explaining the three different energetic states she had witnessed. Afterward, the shaman approached her privately and pulled her aside.

"Narina, what you experienced last night is special and rare," he said. "While everyone here is on their own unique journey, you are at the precipice of an initiatory phase of a profound awakening. It would be my honor to serve as your guide during the initiation, but I need to give you a warning first. If you choose to continue, you must remember there is only one direction on this path—you can't turn around and go back once you start. The journey will show you the truth hidden in plain sight, but there is a price to pay in exchange for what you will learn."

"What's the price?" Narina asked.

"The price of truth is everything," the shaman said simply. "You will have to give up the world as you know it—every friend, every relationship, every belief. Once you see things as they truly are, you can't unsee it. You can't go back to the way things were before you knew."

"Why would I want to go back?"

"Because reality as you know it so far is like one big amusement park. You get to ride a bunch of different rides that make up the experiences of life. Some rides are filled with joy, some gratitude, some sadness, some suffering. You ride the ride until it's over, then you choose another one. But to see the truth, you must leave the amusement park altogether. You must let a part of yourself die for a new part to be born."

Narina contemplated what he was saying for a moment. "Will it be worth it?"

"Worth is subjective, my dear. You'll be giving up everything for one thing, and that one thing is truth. The entire world is like an onion. Maya, the goddess of illusion, tricks us with layer upon layer of thin wispy veils, hiding the truth in plain sight. What you've known your whole life to be true will crack before your very eyes. For some people, that fractured reality is enough for them to go mad, to fall into a state of insanity from which they can never come back. For others, it sets them on a new path that becomes their destiny."

"I saw veils in my vision last night," Narina said. "Are these the same veils you're talking about?"

"The very ones, yes."

"And the three states of energy? Is this part of what I'll see?"

"Yes, you'll understand what those states of energy are. And which *one* you are."

"Which one I am? What do you mean?"

"You'll understand it all, but only if you choose to move forward. If you do, I'll give you a different medicine tonight. Last night you experienced ayahuasca, the mother, and tonight you'll experience San Pedro, the father. Ayahuasca and San Pedro impart feminine and masculine energy respectively. With the balance of the two, you'll begin to see the full picture. The part you couldn't see last night will become visible. Do you want to continue?"

"I need some time to think about it."

"Of course, take your time. But please, Narina, remember the price. Only you can decide if you're willing to pay it."

Back in her room, she told Sam about the conversation. She still didn't quite understand what the shaman meant when he said the price of truth was everything. What exactly would she have to give up? Would she lose her husband? Her family and friends? Her health?

While it ultimately was her choice, it wasn't a decision she could make in a vacuum. She'd married Sam the year before; they'd made vows to each other and had plans for a family. They both had been on the same path since they met: a path to life at the center of being, stripped away from the false layers of self created over time. They supported each other through their own personal inner work. That was why they were there now, participating in the ceremony.

Sam understood the gravity of what the shaman had said and how it might affect his and Narina's relationship, but he also understood something deeper, something that was at the heart of the shaman's words.

"Narina, let's think this through," he said. "If what the shaman is saying is right and you see the truth, and because of it, our relationship ends—doesn't that mean our relationship was a lie? And if that's the case, isn't that ultimately for the best?"

Narina just stared at him.

"Look," Sam continued, putting his hands up in the air, "that's obviously not what I want to happen. What I want to happen, and what I *believe* will happen, is that you'll see the truth, and as a result, our relationship will be stronger than ever. But no matter what the outcome might be, I think you have to do it. We've been on this path of awakening to the truth since we met—can we really stop now?"

Narina felt relief. She would never have admitted it to Sam, but she'd made her decision the second the shaman asked her if she wanted to continue. Narina's parents had been born in a remote village in Tunisia with no running water, no electricity, and no access to groceries or healthcare. After her father lost his brother to malaria at a young age, he'd vowed to give his own family a different life than the one he'd been born into. The village had a small collection of old books, the only remnants of the well-meaning but terribly misguided missionaries that had visited over the years. Narina's father read the books until he'd memorized every word. He taught himself how to read and write, developing his own process of inquiry in the margin of every page, filling them with notes and questions.

Narina's father married her mother in a small village ceremony when they were both fifteen years old, and the following year, he applied for two scholarships to attend a small college just outside of Washington, DC. Once her parents arrived in the US, they never left. By the time he was thirty, her father was an advisor for the African Development Bank and her mother taught economics at American University.

Her parents had fought for their freedoms and passed that same mentality down to their daughter—it was in Narina's blood. But having grown up with easy access to the physical freedoms her parents had been denied, Narina craved a different kind of freedom. Freedom from lies. Freedom from illusion. She'd never really had a choice—she had to know the truth.

So she went back to the shaman, and that night, she had a different experience than the rest of the group. She was given San Pedro, and two hours into the ceremony, after the most profuse bout of purging she'd ever experienced, she saw Maya, the goddess of illusion, approach. Narina walked toward her, and as she got closer, Maya started to lift the veils.

The first veil showed Narina the same three energetic states she'd witnessed the night before: one devoid of any light, one with a glimmer of light, and one of full-blown brightness.

As Narina observed each state, Maya spoke their names: Empty, Ray, and Liminal.

Narina kept walking toward Maya. The second veil was a mirror that Maya held up to Narina's face. As she looked into the mirror, Narina saw a single ray of light beam into her head. A sheen of orange and red shimmering flecks skittered across her face, like glitter had blossomed from within and touched her skin from the inside out. She understood what it meant. She was a Ray. She possessed some life force inside of her that lit her up. It was pure and beautiful, as if she was connected to a source of energy deep within her being. Tears streamed down her face. She wanted to hit pause and wait there forever, but the medicine wouldn't let her.

Maya continued her approach.

The third veil was upon Narina. It was another mirror. This time it showed her a reflection of her sister, Leila. Instead of a ray of light beaming into her sister's head, a rotting necrosis crept up her neck. Within seconds, Leila's face was nothing more than a corpse's, as if the life had been sucked out of her. There was no marrow, no blood, no energy. She was all skin and bones. She was Empty—alive, but dead inside. There was no life force at all; she was nothing more than a husk. Narina felt something break inside of her as she looked at Leila.

She couldn't move forward anymore. It felt like she was standing in a vat of quicksand that was slowly pulling her under, but Maya didn't stop.

The fourth veil was yet another mirror. This time, Narina saw in quick succession the faces of every person she had ever held close—her family, friends, coworkers. Each individual was shown as either withered away or glowing. Dead or alive. Empty or Ray. Of the hundreds of faces that passed before the mirror, only a handful were Rays. Everyone else was Empty.

The final face was Sam's.

Please don't be Empty, Narina implored. Please.

The reflection darkened momentarily, and then suddenly a beam of light hit Sam's head. His face glowed with vitality.

Narina fell to her knees and placed her head on the ground, as if in prayer.

"Thank you," she managed to get out before the first sob escaped. She cried the rest of the night for the life she had lost. She was mourning for each and every one of the Empty people she had seen, mourning for her own state of innocence, which she knew would never return.

The shaman was right—Narina could never go back to how she had seen the world before. She had entered a new reality.

# the stage

Oakland
Fall 2015

A timer went off, interrupting Narina's story. "Shit, food's ready," she said. "Let's take a break and eat."

Spencer needed the intermission. She was trying to make sense of everything she'd just heard.

"Wow. Just wow." Rose shook her head. "Narina, I'm still processing all of this. I imagine that must have been a really difficult experience. Thank you for sharing this with us."

Narina brought over dinner, and they sat in silence for a few minutes as they ate.

Spencer spoke first. "I have so many questions," she said.

"I figured you would," Narina said.

"What do you mean—they were dead? Like does this mean those people are going to die?"

Narina shook her head. "I think you'll understand more when I tell you about the third night, but no, they aren't going to die. They are already dead inside. The closest analogy I can give is that they're zombies, but you can't keep thinking in the *physical* plane—this is all happening on the *energy* plane."

What was she talking about?

"I don't understand," Spencer said. "What's the energy plane?"

"When you look around you now, you think you're seeing the world as it is. You think you're witnessing reality, but all you are really seeing is the physical plane. Think of the world as a stage instead. You're at the theater, sitting in the audience. What you view when you look at the stage are all the physical objects—the streets, the buildings, the houses, the people. It's all a bunch of matter condensed down into form.

"Now imagine the usher walks up to you sitting in the audience and hands you a pair of glasses. He tells you to put the glasses on to watch the show, and you'll see something else—a deeper version of the show happening in parallel with the physical one. You put the glasses on, and you realize that the stage has transformed into something slightly different. The buildings and houses are now subtly vibrating, each at their own frequency. The people are distinguishable not by their looks but by something I can only describe as their essence, an inner core of who they are. It looks like a pattern made from the elements, rising around and above them. When one person says hello to another on the street, a swirl of light and warmth leaves their body and enters the body of the person they addressed. When someone else leaves their house in an anxious rush and bumps into their neighbor, a cloud of darkness breaks off from them and attempts to enter that neighbor. This is the energy plane. Energy is all around us, all the time, but we don't realize it. Our mood, our emotions, our interactions are all energy."

This part made sense to Spencer. There were times when she was younger when she'd felt like she could see and sense things around her that others couldn't.

"It's a whole different world that exists, but it's not happening somewhere else," Narina continued. "It's not another dimension or realm. It's right here, right in front of our eyes all the time. Instead of putting on glasses, all you need to do is remove the veils that are hiding this subtler plane of existence. Each person has within them their own well of energy. It's our natural right, given to us at birth. But we can naturally lose connection to it over time, or it can be siphoned from us. That's why people are so drawn to children; children are the most potent source of this raw energy.

"When Maya held up the mirror and I saw those people as dead inside—Empty—it wasn't that they were physically dead. They are alive and well on the physical plane. If you look at them with the glasses off, they look totally normal. But when you look at them with glasses on, they are completely empty. There is no life force left inside of them."

Like nonplayer characters in a video game, Spencer thought. They're there, but they aren't really *there*.

Narina paused.

Rose and Spencer spoke at the same time.

"Did you see our faces? Were we dead or alive?" Rose asked.

"Did you say the energy could be siphoned? By who?" Spencer implored.

"Let me tell you about the third night of the ceremony," Narina replied.

# the future

Oakland
Fall 2015

On the third and final night of the ceremony, the shaman gave Narina both ayahuasca and San Pedro. The mother and the father in sacred union.

"Don't be afraid," he said. "You've been given this path because you can handle it. It's your destiny. Trust what you see. Your path doesn't end here tonight. This is just the beginning."

Narina drank from the cup and listened as the shaman sang in her ear once again. Nothing happened for a long time. No purging, no mandalas, no visuals. After what felt like days, a quiet calmness overcame her. She noticed a figure near the horizon in the distance, slowly walking toward her. It was Maya, approaching her once again. Narina expected to see more veils, but instead, as Maya got closer, she stopped abruptly and sat at a table that appeared out of thin air. The goddess pulled out a glass ball that fit in the palm of her hand. Streams of vibrant colored light swirled inside of it.

"Sit," Maya said, motioning to the chair now appearing in front of Narina.

"The beginning of any journey is always a single point in time," Maya continued, "but from that point, any future is possible. Think of it like an infinite set of branching paths emanating from a point of origin, each path dependent upon a series of decisions. You're at the beginning of your journey now, your point of origin, but there are only two possible paths. Only two futures exist—not just for you but for the entire world."

Maya paused. "Do you want to see?" she asked Narina.

"Yes," Narina replied firmly, "I want to see."

She looked down as Maya tapped on the top of the ball. It turned into a giant swirling globe, as if she were looking down on Earth from the moon. Only it wasn't Earth as she'd seen it a million times before—the famous blue, green, and brown sphere shown from space. Instead, she saw a bleak planet, devoid of natural beauty, dark and gray.

"Go ahead," Maya encouraged. "Go inside and look around."

Narina zoomed in over the United States and kept going into what looked like New York, then even farther into New York City. The streets were completely empty; no one was outside. The sleek steel-and-glass buildings that had been there before were replaced by what looked like millions of shipping containers stacked on top of each other. Inside each one was a mattress and a small bathroom. They were apartments, Narina realized, but where were the kitchens? Where were the windows? She looked inside a few of the containers, and in each one a single person lay on a dirty mattress, staring at some sort of holographic projection screen in front of them. They seemed strung out. Narina looked around for drugs or needles, assuming they were addicts, but she couldn't find any paraphernalia.

She watched a man in his apartment as a projection flashed in front of his eyes. It looked like a menu. The cursor scrolled back and forth across the options—a salad, a bowl of pasta, tacos. The man must have been communicating with his mind, Narina realized as he selected the pasta. Was a hologram about to magically deliver food to his container? But no one arrived.

The man leaned his head back against the wall behind him and closed his eyes. Once again, Narina felt like she was watching an addict shoot up. Then she noticed the IV going into the side of the man's neck. It was connected to a small stainless steel box behind him. She walked over to the box and opened it up, finding a refrigerator with hundreds of labeled vials. She picked one up and read the label: *Meat Lasagna—just like your mom made it!* Narina felt bile rise in her throat as she realized this was his dinner. His "meal" had been turned into its basest form, a string of lab-made nutrients liquified and mainlined into his veins.

Narina zoomed out a little bit to see what was happening in other parts of the country, and she saw the same scene everywhere. Everyone was lifeless and alone, staring at holographic screens. As she zoomed out farther, she saw what looked like a flashlight beam coming from the sky. A group of men sat at a round table at the apex of the beam. But the beam wasn't originating from the men and flashing down on the people below them; it was originating from the people, illuminating the men above. From the angle Narina was at, it almost looked like a church steeple. The congregation was humanity itself, and the men were God. The men were siphoning energy from every human on Earth.

Narina heard a whisper. It was coming from a man lying on a bed in a container in Brooklyn. She zoomed back in.

"What did you just say?" she asked the man.

"The Architects," he said, his voice hoarse from lack of use. "The men in the sky are the Architects."

"The Architects?" Narina asked. "Who are they?"

"The ones that control us and keep us here as slaves. They control the entire Apparatus. The Guardsmen work for them."

He paused, swallowing before speaking again. "Can you help us?" he asked quietly.

"I'd like to," Narina replied, "but I'm not sure how. What can I do to help you?"

"Please just help us! We've seen others like you here."

"Others like me? What do you mean?"

"The other bright ones. You all look the same, like shining lights."

The scene started to flicker out. Narina was being pulled away.

"No, please don't go!" the man yelled. "I haven't had anyone to talk to in years. Please, help us! You need to find them before the Harvest, you need—"

## natalie docherty

And suddenly it was all gone. Narina looked back at Maya; the small glass ball had returned to her hand. The entire scene she had just witnessed evaporated as if it was nothing more than a figment of her imagination. The goddess smiled.

"That's one possible path," Maya said. "Are you ready to see the other?"

Narina vomited across the table, flecks hitting Maya's cheeks.

"What kind of sick future is that?" Narina muttered.

But the goddess didn't respond. Instead, she turned the glass ball over in her hand and tapped on the top. Again a giant globe swirled, showing the planet from above. This time it looked much like Narina knew it—vibrant blue oceans, lush green forests, cities teeming with life. She zoomed into New York City once again.

She felt dizzy looking at the dimensionality in front of her. The city had somehow been built up into the sky without the use of buildings. Cars and trains drove on roads and tracks built hundreds of feet off the ground. What had previously been streets at ground level were now pedestrian corridors full of lush foliage. Where the sun was blocked out by the transportation systems built into the sky, beautiful prisms of glass were used to reflect light down. The corridors were full of people walking around. They each wore some sort of projection headset, but unlike the scene Narina had just witnessed, these people were engaged in the life in front of them and with the others around them. It was a giant, immersive augmented reality.

Narina found herself walking along the Brooklyn Bridge. She didn't realize it at first, but she was headed back toward the same container, to see the man who had asked for her help. She approached the building where his container had been, but in this version of New York, she found a meticulously restored brownstone in its place. A man stood outside, refilling a bird feeder in his garden. He was humming.

Narina stopped and stared at him.

He noticed her looking and glanced up. "Excuse me," he said. "Do I know you?"

It was him.

## dark days ahead

"You look familiar," Narina said. "How long have you lived here?"

"A little over ten years now."

"And has the place always looked like this?" Narina asked, gesturing to the house behind him.

"Not always. I spent five years and every allotment of Fed-Coin from my income sharing agreement on the renovation," he explained, "but it was totally worth it."

"It absolutely was. You've done a fantastic job. I'm Narina," she said, reaching out her hand.

"Colin," he said, shaking it.

Narina needed to know if Colin knew about the alternate reality she'd just experienced. "This might sound strange, but I'm trying to place where I know you from. Help me out here—have you always looked like this? Like you do now?"

"Uh, I mean I've lost a few pounds recently, but yes, I think so. I'm sorry. Can I help you with something? I have a busy day and need to get going."

"No, that's okay. You've already been a great help," Narina said, and started to leave.

"You look exactly the same!" someone yelled from behind her.

Narina turned around. An old woman with gray hair and glasses shuffled toward her, moving as quickly as her legs allowed.

"I'm sorry?" Narina asked, confused.

The woman reached up, gently holding Narina's face between her hands. "It's unbelievable," she said. "You look exactly the same, Fire One."

Narina scanned the woman's face, but she was positive they'd never met before. "Do I know you?" Narina asked.

The woman nodded. "You helped me. I always thought that dragons belonged in hell, but you and your friends, you were my angels."

Colin reached out to grab the old woman's hand. "I'm sorry," he said, turning to Narina. "My mom has Alzheimer's. Any time she sees a Liminal, she believes she's living back then, helping the Network defeat the Apparatus."

Narina froze. "When she sees a Liminal? What do you mean?"

"You're a Liminal, aren't you? From the size of your glow, I'd say you're a pretty powerful one," Colin said, gesturing at the air around Narina as if to point it out.

Narina looked down and saw a halo of orange light extending several feet around her body. In this world, she was no longer a Ray. She was a Liminal.

"What was it you said about the Network and the Apparatus?" Narina asked.

"When my mom has these delusions... she believes she's living thirty years ago still. Helping the Network," Colin explained.

"And did they? Did the Network defeat the Architects?" Narina asked.

Colin laughed. "Are you kidding? Of course they did. I was just a kid back then, so I only know the stories from my mom, but she has such reverence when she talks about the other Liminals. She helped the Network right here in New York before the Harvest."

As he spoke, something flickered in Narina's mind. A vision that felt like a memory. In the vision, she was standing in a different New York City. Her hands were burning. She looked down. No, they weren't burning, but they were hot, and she was the source of the heat. Fire erupted from her hand, directed toward a man standing across from her. She looked to her left and saw Spencer and Rose there with her. Spencer stood in the middle, her feet firmly planted on the ground and her hands balled into fists. Next to her, Rose raised her arms, and a torrent of wind engulfed the man she was fighting.

And then the vision was gone. Narina was back in Brooklyn, standing in Colin's garden.

"I really need to run, but it was so cool to meet you," Colin said as he waved goodbye.

Before Narina could reply, she was staring again into the eyes of Maya. They twinkled.

"The choice is yours," said the goddess.

Spencer hadn't had any idea what to expect when Narina texted about the "life-changing" retreat, but she certainly hadn't been

## dark days ahead

expecting *that*. Energy states, a dystopian future, a battle. It was, well, a lot to take in.

"Is that it?" Spencer asked when Narina paused.

"Is that it?" Narina replied, the incredulity nearly dripping from her mouth. "I just told you that the three of us are responsible for preventing the end of the world, saving humanity as we know it from an evil group of men using nothing more than magical powers that are going to sprout out of our hands? *Is that fucking it?*"

"You know I didn't mean it like that," Spencer said. "I just meant is there more to the story before we start asking questions."

"No, there isn't more to that epic story, so I guess you would say 'that's it.'"

Spencer waited a minute before speaking again. "Do you think it's real? Do you believe that's going to happen?"

"It felt more real than anything I've ever experienced in my life. It's the truth," Narina said. She took a long, deep breath. "Do you believe me?"

Spencer paused, mulling it over and wondering what Rose thought about it all.

"I believe that's what you experienced," Rose said, as if on cue. "It resonates for me that it's possible this could be real, but I'm not fully there yet."

Narina nodded and turned her gaze to Spencer.

Spencer had always liked to take everything in, to welcome every possibility. Who was she to think she knew anything? She looked at every theory with open eyes until she had reason to believe otherwise. This felt no different to her.

"I have no reason not to believe it's true," she said.

Spencer noticed Narina exhale as if relieved.

"So do you have, like, powers now?" Spencer asked.

"No, not yet," Narina said. "I know that my power has something to do with fire, but nothing has happened yet. I'm still a Ray now, or at least that's how I feel. I think there's some activation that happens to become a Liminal. Maybe that's when you get your powers? I don't know. I'm still trying to figure all this out. That's why I invited you guys here tonight. I thought since it's the three of us in the vision, we could start to make sense of it together."

"I thought you could see whether someone was a Ray or a Liminal—how are you not sure which one you are?" Rose asked.

"I could see what everyone was when I took the medicine, but when I came out of it, my vision went back to normal. I think it's more of an intuitive sensing. When someone walks into the room, I have a sense of what state they're in, but I can't see it like I could then. I guess I can't know for sure, but I remember what it felt like when I looked in the mirror and saw I was a Ray. I feel confident that right now I'm a Ray, and I'm confident that both of you are Rays too."

"So, we need to figure out how we transition from Rays to Liminals," Rose said.

"And we need to learn everything we can about the Apparatus and the Architects," Spencer added.

Narina nodded. "Agreed."

# the hacker

San Francisco
Summer 2016

When Spencer walked into the wine bar on their first date, Vik had been surprised by how quickly he liked her. He had known other people from the Midwest, and he'd always found them to hold strength and warmth in equal measure, a hard exterior that belied an inner softness. Spencer seemed to Vik to be a study in contradictions like this. She was kind but direct, shy but incisive, private but open. More importantly, she met the primary criteria on Vik's checklist—she was an intelligent and attractive white woman.

Vik had grown up outside Houston in Sugar Land, a wealthy and predominantly white neighborhood, as the only child to immigrant parents. His dad was an anesthesiologist, and while well respected within the community, the family still stuck out in the sea of born-and-bred Texans, all blond-haired cheerleaders and six-foot-tall football players. Vik didn't mind that he looked different from the kids around him—in a way, he liked being unique—but he understood power structures from a young age, and he knew that every high school had a hidden caste system ranking teenagers according to their athleticism, attractiveness, and popularity. It was a system ruled by the prevailing white majority. Vik noticed the way a smart but average-looking Vietnamese guy had somehow made his way into the upper caste. The guy was always dating popular white girls, and it seemed as if they offered him a proximity to whiteness that moved him from the periphery of the action directly into the fold.

One day, during AP Calc class his junior year, Vik made a joke about derivatives, and a cute brunette nearby looked him in the eyes and laughed. Two months later, he lost his virginity to her in the back of his dad's gold Lexus RX. The next weekend, he was invited to a party at a cheerleader's house.

The formula worked. The popular girls who indexed on intelligence over athleticism were Vik's winning ticket. He'd been dating women like that ever since.

As he got older, Vik had grown to prefer women of a more ethnically ambiguous nature, something he liked to think of as "white-adjacent." If someone asked him his dream type, his response was Amal Clooney. Spencer fit the bill. She was white, with dark brown hair, olive skin, and big eyes that looked brown or green depending on the lighting. She could have been Italian, Greek, or Persian, and like all the women Vik preferred, she was smart.

Every intelligence had a certain flavor. In the Bay Area, he saw a lot of what he thought of as factual intelligence. It was the type of intelligence present in those who studied hard science and math, learned the principles those practices espoused, and applied them rigorously to both their work and life. Vik found that type of intelligence rather boring and endlessly predictable. He was smart in a different way. Instead of seeing the world as a flat place with linear rules, Vik saw it as a ball of clay that could be molded. In his world, rules were nonexistent, everything was movable, and there was always room for negotiation. Vik could shape the world and the people in it into whatever he wanted; he just had to apply pressure to the right points. He'd give a compliment, tell a joke, share an insight, and the clay would move. Vik sometimes wondered if everyone else was just a character in a movie that he was directing.

But Spencer's intelligence was of a kind he hadn't seen before. It was quiet, just like she was. She watched and observed. Her eyes always seemed to penetrate something deeper than the surface. If the world for Vik was a ball of clay, for Spencer it was a puzzle. He would watch her as she put it together. Each time a new piece of information clicked into place, the puzzle became clearer. Vik knew he was part of that puzzle, and as he watched her watch him, he found himself both unsettled and turned on.

Their first date had been fun and easy. Vik wanted to stay there listening to Spencer talk for hours. He knew he wanted to see her again, so he had Sven find out what he could about her.

Sven was Vik's tech guy, a hacker based in Ukraine who handled every request Vik threw his way. Vik had first hired him a few years earlier. A deal Vik was working on had started falling apart when another VC firm got involved. The firm was convincing the founder to adjust terms, and if the deal went through, Vik's firm would lose a ton of money. It would tank the performance of the current fund and hamper their fundraising efforts for the next one, and it would be Vik's fault. He needed compromising information on the founder, something he could use to shift the terms back in his favor.

Vik hired Sven, and two weeks later, Sven handed him back gold. The founder had videos of children on his computer. Not child porn exactly, but equally disturbing—videos of children being terrorized. Kids being blindfolded, spanked, and whipped in a decrepit basement. When Vik approached the founder about the videos, he said something about the pure fear of children being like adrenaline pumped into his veins, that it was better than any drug. Vik found the behavior and the founder's rationale unsavory, but there was only one thing he really cared about: the deal. He walked away from the meeting with new terms that made his firm $3.5 billion when the company was acquired a few months later. Vik was promptly promoted to partner, and he'd been working with Sven ever since.

At first, he'd used Sven mostly for professional purposes. Over time, though, he realized that Sven might be useful in his personal life as well. When Vik had joined a popular photo-sharing app in 2015, he'd wanted his username to be @vik. He already had that handle on other social platforms and felt there was something iconic about being the one and only Vik. Adding a last name or, heaven forbid, a birth year at the end of a username was just so pedestrian. But someone already had that handle, so Vik, knowing that everything was always for sale, sent @vik a DM offering to purchase the name from him. @vik said he'd sell the name, but only at the steep price of $100,000.

There was no way Vik was paying that asshole a hundred grand. But he really wanted the handle, so he reached out to Sven, told him what had happened, and asked if he might be able to come up with a more creative solution.

"Tell him you'll pay him the $100,000," Sven said, "and we'll send him what looks like a wire link. The link will prompt him to enter his bank details to receive the funds. Instead of transferring money, we'll drain his bank account. The link will also have embedded code allowing me to hack into his account and change his username. Once I change his name, you'll log in and update yours. I'll route the transfer through several offshore accounts and wipe his message history to avoid a paper trail. @vik will be paying you for the honor of giving you the handle."

Vik signed off on the plan.

The next day, he logged in to see his newly minted handle, smiling at the beauty of those three simple letters. He opened his bank account—a measly $2,787.13 had been deposited. What a poor bastard, he thought. Vik had paid Sven $20,000 for this bout of ingenuity, but it had been worth every penny.

Sven had even helped him set up hidden cameras in his home and office, and now, whenever Vik started dating someone new, Sven did his homework and found out anything he could about the woman—family, background, past lovers, work history, finances, anything that might be useful.

Vik found that mirroring was always the easiest way to ingratiate himself with someone. People were hopelessly self-centered, and what they really wanted to see was just another version of themselves sitting across from them. When he'd dated a woman who worked at a nonprofit, he'd spoken about all his philanthropic endeavors. When he'd dated another woman who loved sailing, he'd joined a yacht club. Spencer was a vegetarian, so Vik became a vegetarian. She liked yoga, so he talked about his grandmother back in India, who was a yoga teacher. Spencer worked as a consultant specializing in retail companies, so Vik mentioned his involvement with the hottest direct-to-consumer companies—how he was on the board of a popular eyewear brand and had led the Series A funding round for an ecommerce luggage startup. None of it was true, of course, but that was beside the point. It had worked.

He started to spend more and more time with Spencer. Unlike most women, she was easy to be around—nothing tedious or shallow about her. They could talk for hours. While she seemed to like that Vik was successful, she appeared genuinely disinterested in his money, which was a refreshing first for him. She declined gifts and offered to split everything. Vik caught himself thinking about her all the time. Instead of focusing on work, he'd be thinking about their next date, the next time she'd be looking up at him with her doe eyes while he pushed himself deeper into her mouth.

Vik had even slipped up a few times in front of Spencer, letting his perfectly crafted veneer crack. He controlled what people saw of him, and he wanted them to see a nice guy who worked hard, but he'd let Spencer see his darker side a few times. In a moment of deep intimacy, he'd even voluntarily told her the story about @vik. To his bewilderment, she didn't balk. Instead, she asked him questions. She was neither condoning nor disapproving. She wasn't judging him at all, just trying to understand. It was in those moments Vik felt himself falling hard.

In July, a year after they'd started dating, Vik and Spencer went to Graham's fiftieth birthday party. Graham had invited the guests to his one-hundred-acre estate in Healdsburg. As they drove through the vineyards on the property up to the main home overlooking the valley below, Vik looked at Spencer and kissed her hand.

"I've never been this happy," he said.

Spencer beamed.

At the party, Graham pulled Vik aside for a cigar. They headed over to his office, which was located in another wing of the house. Graham pushed open a set of French doors in the back, letting in fresh air from the terrace outside. Across from the terrace stood the wing they had just come from, giving the two men a perfect vantage point from which to watch the party.

As they lit their cigars, Graham nodded over toward Spencer. "She's a real firecracker."

Vik laughed. "I know—she doesn't miss a thing."

He thought back to earlier in the night, when he'd walked up to Graham and Spencer in the middle of a heated conversation. Spencer had just responded dryly to Graham in that sassy way she did when men thought they were being insightful, but really they were just being trite. It was her playful way of calling them out on their bullshit.

"Have your fun now, but the time will come soon that you'll need to end it," Graham said.

Vik turned to him, suddenly confused. "What do you mean?"

"The path I have planned for you doesn't have room for a woman like that."

"What path? And what does Spencer have to do with it?"

"You've been working hard, Vik. You're smart, calculating, cunning. You understand that power isn't something that's given to you—you must take it for yourself. But you're still just touching the surface. There is a world of power beyond what you can imagine. I'd like to show it to you, to bring you into the Apparatus, but there are rules that must be followed—and loose ends that must be tied up before you can be initiated. Spencer is a loose end."

"I still don't understand what you're talking about, or what Spencer has to do with any of this."

"Spencer is a liability. You said yourself that she doesn't miss a thing. It won't be possible for you to be with someone like that and do the things you'll need to do."

"What are you talking about? What things will I need to do?"

"Meet me at city hall tomorrow morning at ten. I'll show you."

# the tour

San Francisco
Summer 2016

Vik walked up to city hall promptly the next morning. He was surprised by the meeting place—it was a breathtaking building, spanning two blocks and built in the Beaux-Arts style popular during the American Renaissance, but its former glory had been wiped away by present circumstance. City hall sat squarely on the edge of the Tenderloin, an area known for its homelessness crisis and open-air drug use. It wasn't uncommon to see someone shooting a needle into their arm or defecating on the street nearby. The city, at a loss for what to do with the neighborhood, had opened the doors of city hall as a shelter for those in need. Government offices like the county clerk, state's attorney, and DMV now sat alongside rows of cots, sleeping bags, and tents.

Graham was already waiting for Vik at the top of the steps near the building's entrance. After they'd gone through security, Graham walked up to a man in a navy-blue shirt with a *City Hall Tours* logo stitched where a pocket might have been.

"We're taking a tour," Graham said as he handed the docent two tickets.

Vik was perplexed, but he nodded.

They walked behind the docent as he gave his practiced speech for the group. "The building we're currently standing in replaced an older city hall that was destroyed by the 1906 earthquake," he explained.

As they walked through the giant rotunda toward a staircase,

Graham pulled Vik over to the side and pressed a panel hidden in the wall. A door popped open, and Graham pushed Vik through.

What the hell? Before Vik's brain could process the scene in front of him, he was hit by a smell. The stench was revolting. He looked around. Hundreds of homeless men and women were lying on beds, hooked up to machines.

Before he had a chance to speak, Graham turned to him. "Why do you think the city has let the homelessness crisis get so bad?" he asked.

"Well," Vik replied, struggling to focus on the conversation with Graham instead of the scene in front of him, "I think it's a complicated problem. Homelessness is primarily a function of housing unaffordability, which has been exacerbated by government regulation around new construction. When you layer in mental health issues and addiction, it gets even more complicated."

Graham laughed and patted Vik on the back. "Exactly!" he said. "That's exactly what we want you to think."

"What do you mean?" Vik asked.

"That's the exact narrative we've pushed. A plausible explanation for why there are thousands of homeless people littering the streets in one of the richest cities in the world."

"It's a narrative?" Vik asked, blinking. "Then what's the real reason why the crisis is so bad?"

"Don't you see?" Graham implored, gesturing around him. "It's not a crisis at all. Tell me what you see when you look around."

Vik glanced around the room before speaking. "I see homeless people. It looks like they haven't showered or eaten in days. They're hooked up to machines. There are people taking care of them—doctors and nurses. I assume the government or some nonprofit is trying to help them get clean and healthy."

"You see the power of the narrative?" Graham asked, smiling. "You think homelessness is a crisis, a problem to be solved, so you think the city is trying to fix it. Now throw that narrative away, wipe it clean from your mind, and look again. Do you see anything different?"

Vik looked around the room again. He watched a man in a white coat who appeared to be a doctor walk over to a homeless man. The homeless man had a long white beard, a red bandana wrapped around his head, and a sleeve of tattoos on his left arm. The doctor reached into his pocket and pulled out a small black device. He held it over the homeless man's head, and it emitted a pulse. The man cried out in pain.

"That's not enough," the doctor said, then pressed a button.

The homeless man released a bloodcurdling scream.

The doctor shook his head. "It's still not enough," he said, and pressed the button again.

The homeless man didn't have time to utter another sound before falling unconscious.

"Excellent! It's working. Let's keep optimizing to find the right level." The doctor turned to address a woman in a white coat next to him. "Administer the dose."

The woman pulled out a needle, found a vein, and injected a substance into the homeless man's arm. Then two men in security shirts came in and rolled the bed away.

The doctor looked up, noticing Graham. He smiled and waved as he walked over. "Graham, I'm so glad you're here. We've just had a major breakthrough with the device. I'll send the full results over later today."

Graham shook the doctor's hand and thanked him, then turned to Vik. "Do you see now? It's not a crisis. It's an opportunity. These aren't patients, they're subjects."

"Subjects for what?" Vik asked.

"Experiments," Graham replied with another grin.

Fifteen minutes later, as Vik left city hall, he saw two police officers resuscitating a man lying on the ground.

One officer lifted the radio from his right pocket and pressed a button before speaking. "We have another fatal fentanyl overdose," he reported into the radio.

Vik saw something red sticking out behind the officer's hand. He took a few steps forward to get a better look. It was the bandana. He noticed the sleeve of tattoos and long white beard next.

Vik froze as he stared at the now dead subject.

# the invite

### San Francisco
### Summer 2016

The following Monday, after he'd had a weekend to process everything, Vik still felt sick to his stomach as he walked into the office. If what he'd seen at city hall was the work of the Apparatus, he wanted nothing to do with it. Then again, Graham was someone he deeply admired, someone whose career path Vik wanted to emulate. Plus, Vik wanted the private jet, the Yellowstone Club property, the invite to Davos. He owed Graham a chance to at least explain himself.

He knocked on Graham's office door. "Can we talk?" Vik asked as he peeked his head around the corner.

"I've been waiting for you," Graham said. "Come in and shut the door behind you."

Vik closed the door as Graham grabbed a small cylindrical object from his drawer. He pulled the two ends of the object apart and placed it on his desk. "Just in case," Graham said. "It blocks any signals."

Vik nodded. It seemed he wanted to make sure no one could hear the conversation they were about to have.

"I have a lot of questions," Vik said.

"I figured you would. Go ahead."

"Well, for starters, what exactly is the Apparatus?"

"On the surface, the Apparatus is a centuries-old secret order that exists to improve the character of men and their communities. Education is at the core of the Apparatus, with the lofty aspiration to enlighten the world through philosophy. Ceremonies and rituals are a core part of the fraternity and are used to initiate members, transfer knowledge, and recognize status."

"And beneath the surface?" Vik asked.

"There's only so much I can tell you before you're initiated. Secrecy is a critical tenet of the work we do. Suffice it to say that like everything else in the world, there are levels to the game. The Apparatus has two levels: Guardsmen and Architects. All Guardsmen would describe the Apparatus exactly as I just did to you, as an exclusive society with philanthropic aims, but the Architects know another Apparatus. An elaborate global network designed to infiltrate, and ultimately own, the financial system, politics, media, oil and gas, pharma, tech. Basically, the Apparatus controls everything that matters."

"This sounds like the Illuminati," Vik said, rolling his eyes.

Graham chuckled. "I'm glad you bring that up. The Illuminati was a clever solution to a pesky problem. You see, there are certain rules we're required to follow. Rules that we agree to in exchange for the powers bestowed upon us. One of those rules is disclosure. We have to publicly share what we're doing, drop Easter eggs for people along the way, little hints and clues so that anyone really paying attention could see exactly what was happening. Disclosure is tricky—how do we tell people the truth and maintain our secrecy at the same time? Over the years, we've devised ingenious ways to hide the truth in plain sight. In the eighteenth century, an Architect came up with a devilish solution. Create another organization *like* the Apparatus and have their statues and goals mirror ours. Then find prominent royals, politicians, and artists to join, and slowly leak information about this mirror organization to the public. We told the world bits and pieces of what the Apparatus was doing, but we linked it to a different organization—the Illuminati.

"We took a two-pronged approach. For every piece of truth we told, we mixed in a lie, something that could be easily disproven—the truth to satisfy the disclosure requirement, and the lies to discredit the whole thing. Over time, the Illuminati became nothing more than a giant conspiracy theory. We layered in other related organizations to grow the web of lies and create more confusion around the truth lying at the center. Now the web is so infamous that it's well documented as the 'Conspiracy to Rule the World.'"

Graham handed Vik a piece of paper that detailed the intricate network. The web started with the Order of the Illuminati and branched into many paths, including government-sponsored enterprises, global organizations, and intelligence agencies. There must have been over a hundred well-known organizations listed.

"There is, of course, a group of men ruling the world, but their secrecy is all but guaranteed behind the illusion this convoluted web of lies offers."

Vik's head was spinning. "What does any of this have to do with the experiments at city hall?"

"Before I can answer that, there's something you need to see. I'm having a party on Saturday—the kind of party that requires discretion. Come. And make sure you bring Spencer."

As Vik left the office, he thought it over. Graham was hosting a sex party at his house and had just invited him to come—with his girlfriend.

# the magic

San Francisco
Summer 2016

Ever since Narina had shared her vision with Spencer and Rose, the three women had spent every minute of their spare time researching.

Spencer went to the library every night, reading any book she could find that referenced a group of men in power—a brotherhood, a fraternity, anything that might match the description Narina had shared. She scoured internet forums. She got in touch with historians and scholars, those who studied black magic and occult traditions. Some mentioned the Illuminati, but Spencer always shook her head at that. "It's different than that," she'd tell them. There were a few scholars who believed that an apparatus of power like the one in Narina's vision did exist, but specific evidence of who or where they were was nonexistent.

Narina and Rose, meanwhile, spent their time reading through every religious, spiritual, and magic book they could find. They talked to mystics, master meditators, shamans, Buddhists, enlightened individuals—anyone who might have knowledge about an initiatory phase or a way to transition from one energetic state to another and tap into hidden powers. There were many such texts, experts, and practices that allowed the women to access altered states of consciousness, but they didn't transition them from Rays to Liminals.

On the weekends, they tried other methods, those of the psychedelic variety: LSD, mushrooms, DMT. Each experience offered some small piece of insight that seemed to corroborate Narina's vision, but nothing was definitive proof, and any powers they felt like they attained while under the influence of the drugs wore off when they sobered up.

None of it worked.

Rose's latest suggestion was that they try using sex magic to tap into their inner power after she read *The Magdalen Manuscript*, a book that alleged Mary Magdalene and Jesus had practiced a type of sex alchemy that allowed him to achieve immortality and everlasting life. Narina and Sam tried tantric sex, Rose had a ketamine- and sex-fueled weekend getaway in Mendocino with her then-boyfriend, and now it was Spencer's turn to attempt sex magic with Vik.

She almost couldn't believe how easily it came together.

Earlier in the week, as Spencer was lying on Vik's chest in bed, he'd asked her if there was anything she fantasized about. Not knowing where the conversation was heading, Spencer had reached for something safe and predictable.

"Well, I've never had sex on a plane. It's always seemed fun, but at this point in my life, I'd probably only do it on a private jet."

"Noted."

"Do you have any fantasies?" she asked him in return.

"I've always wanted to have sex while people watched," Vik shared.

"Like an orgy?"

"No, not exactly. I don't have any interest in an open relationship or having sex with anyone else. I just want an audience, I guess. It gets me off thinking about people watching me. Watching *us*," he corrected.

"So like having sex in a public place?"

"Well no, not like a restaurant or anything like that. I imagine something more intimate, where this type of behavior would be acceptable. You know, something like the parties that Graham throws."

Graham's organized events, known as the "parties at the end of the world," were notorious even to Spencer.

"You know," Vik continued, "Graham mentioned he's having a party on Saturday. We could go, just to check it out. No expectations or anything, of course."

Spencer glared at him. She knew she had been set up, that Vik had asked about her fantasies only to share his and then suggest Graham's party. She would have been annoyed if not for the fact that this provided the perfect opportunity for her to test out Rose's theory.

"Okay," she said. "Let's check out the party."

# the party

San Francisco
Summer 2016

Sex parties were such an open secret among the tech elite that exposés had been written about them in GQ and *Vanity Fair*. The guest lists typically included powerful investors, entrepreneurs, and executives. The hosts were often the most powerful men, Silicon Valley celebrities who invited guests to their Pacific Heights mansions, Tahoe compounds, and Napa chateaus for a night (or sometimes a full weekend) of drug-fueled debauchery. The parties themselves were another representation of the progressive mentality behind tech's unprecedented growth. The motto "move fast and break things" applied to traditional relationships and societal norms as well. A world where anything was possible included polyamory, experimentation with drugs, and sexual freedom.

Vik knew about the parties and had always been curious, but he had never attended one himself. He liked to keep his personal and professional life separate.

When he had talked to Spencer earlier in the week, he'd thought it would be impossible to convince her to go. She was open to sexual exploration with him, but she was a private person, shy even. It was one of the things Vik liked about her, so he was stunned by how quickly she'd agreed to join him.

They arrived at Graham's Sea Cliff mansion an hour after the party started. They had decided that they'd rather enter with it already in motion and act as flies on the wall. The mansion, built on one of the most coveted pieces of real estate in San Francisco, was massive. It sat directly on top of the cliff above Baker Beach, with breathtaking, panoramic views of the bay and the Golden Gate Bridge. When you looked out the windows, you felt like you were standing at the end of the world—hence the name of the parties.

As they entered the house, a waiter handed them each a much-needed glass of champagne and a pill.

"What's this?" Vik asked, holding up the little white disk.

"Ecstasy. It helps remove inhibitions and increases arousal."

Spencer shrugged and then took the pill, downing it with her champagne. She was always surprising him lately. Maybe tonight would be more interesting than he'd planned.

He pocketed his pill as he took a swig of champagne. He liked to be in full control, so drugs had never held much appeal for him. Plus, he wasn't sure where the night was headed and didn't want to risk hampering his performance if it came to that.

Vik looked around the room. Not knowing exactly what to expect, he was surprised to find that the party seemed relatively tame. People were milling about and having conversations while drinking.

Graham walked over to greet them.

"This isn't what I imagined," Vik said.

Graham shrugged. "The drugs haven't kicked in yet."

Vik nodded, and then Graham pulled him aside. "Did you take the pill?" he asked.

"No."

"Good. I have something else for you upstairs."

What was he talking about?

"Spencer," Graham said, giving her a hug and a kiss on the cheek in greeting. "Can I borrow your boyfriend? I need five minutes with him to talk about a deal."

She nodded, though she looked reluctant.

"I'll be right back," Vik promised, kissing her on the cheek.

He and Graham walked up two flights of stairs to the third floor.

Since land in Sea Cliff was outrageously expensive, the homes of even the wealthiest residents were often built up, not out. The view from this floor was even more insane than the one downstairs.

Graham reached into his desk drawer and handed Vik a different pill from the ones being passed around by the waiter.

Vik looked at it—a white capsule with red font that said *Red Pill*. He couldn't help but roll his eyes. "Clever," he said sarcastically. "Don't I have an option for a blue pill too?"

"You're already living it, and we aren't in a simulation. Yet."

"What is it?" Vik asked.

"A proprietary blend the Apparatus perfected over the years. It's like taking a little ecstasy, ketamine, and LSD. The secret ingredient is a special chemical compound."

"What does the compound do?"

"It's a powerful narcotic and hallucinogen. It acts as the activator."

"Activator of what?" Vik asked.

"Energy particles."

"Huh?"

"The real source of power is energy," Graham said.

Vik stared blankly at him, hoping for more of an explanation.

"You'll see soon enough," Graham said. "Remember that no one else will be able to see what you can, so don't point anything out or ask any questions. I'll explain everything to you afterward."

Vik took the pill.

"Consider this a preview of life as an Architect," Graham said, patting him on the back.

They headed downstairs.

The next hour passed uneventfully. Vik stood next to Spencer as she leaned against the end of the couch. They sipped champagne, talked, and watched the scene unfold around them. Unsure if it was the champagne or the pill, Vik found himself loosening up. Spencer was wearing a short green dress, his favorite color on her. Her hair was pulled into a high bun on top of her head. Vik grazed his hand slowly up and down the inside of her thigh. The sensations rippled through his fingers, and he saw something that looked like sparks. She looked at him in surprise. They'd both seen it.

Damn, he thought, shaking his head and realizing that the pill must be kicking in.

Spencer excused herself and went to the bathroom. When she came back, she put something into Vik's pocket. He reached in to see what it was and felt something soft and wet. It was her underwear. Fuck. He was instantly hard.

"Let's find somewhere to go," Spencer said quietly.

"A few of the bedrooms are empty upstairs," Vik said, assuming she would want privacy.

She shook her head. "That's not what I had in mind."

Most of the people were outside on the terrace or upstairs in two of the designated sex rooms, which were filled with toys. Spencer led Vik over to the corner of the living room, where there was a conversation pit with several large sofas built into the ground. The setup created a sense of intimacy. Next to the pit, right in front of the windows, was a large swing hanging from the ceiling. There were four couples sitting in the pit. No one was actively having sex, but they were stroking each other, enjoying the heightened sensations the ecstasy provided.

"Is it okay if we use this?" Spencer asked, pointing to the swing.

Holy shit.

A man, a founder Vik vaguely recognized, looked up and nodded. "All yours," he said.

Spencer pushed Vik onto the swing. Despite the intensity they were both feeling, she took her time. She kissed his neck as she unbuttoned his shirt and made her way down his chest with her mouth. She went achingly slow. Kneeling, she reached to unbuckle his belt, loosening the loop with her teeth instead of her hands. Then she unbuttoned his pants and pulled them down to his ankles. She started tracing her tongue slowly up his thigh. When her mouth made contact with the hard length of him, Vik was so sure he'd come that he pushed her back a little bit, needing a second to regain his composure.

Spencer stood back up and started to strip off her clothes. She walked over to Vik and turned around to have him unzip her dress. She had already given him her underwear, and she wasn't wearing a bra. He stared at Spencer's naked body in awe. All four of the other couples had abandoned their cuddle puddle and were now watching Spencer and Vik. One of the men reached over to the woman next to him and started fingering her as he watched Spencer.

Let's give the audience a good show, Vik thought.

Spencer walked toward him and sat astride him. Before she had fully lowered herself down, Vik pushed himself inside of her. "Mmm," he murmured as he felt warmth and tightness surround him. He felt like he could do this forever. And to his pleasant surprise, he could. Something about the pill, along with heightening the sensations, also gave him incredible stamina. I'm like a Greek god, he thought as Spencer rode him.

At one point, Vik glanced up and suddenly stiffened. The scene in front of him was both the same and different from before. The conversation pit was still full of plush couches, but where the couples had been, there were now corpses. No, not corpses, he realized. They were moving and alive, but they *appeared* dead. They were drained of life, like rotting husks. Zombies having sex, he thought. He glanced around and saw more zombies.

Then he saw Graham across the room, and inexplicably, Graham looked exactly like himself.

"Are you okay?" Spencer whispered.

Vik looked up at her. Holy fucking shit. Where everyone else was dead, Spencer was alive. Vibrant. Beaming. A halo of diffuse light surrounded her. Her skin glimmered. Like an angel, he thought. The erection he'd just lost staring at the corpses instantly came back as he looked at her.

"I'm getting close," she whispered.

So was he.

As Vik crested over a life-shattering peak, he watched Spencer, completely mesmerized. When she came on top of him, Vik saw a snake coil around her torso, rising in parallel with the orgasm moving through her body. When it reached her head, the snake disappeared and was replaced by a rising sun. Rays of light streamed out from her hair. Then, as quickly as it started, it was over.

"That was fun," she said as she stood up.

Vik put his clothes back on. What the fuck had just happened?

# the mirror

San Francisco
Summer 2016

Once they were fully dressed, Vik and Spencer walked into the kitchen to get something to drink. Spencer was still glowing as she gulped down an entire bottle of water. The halo of shimmering light still surrounded her, but the snake and sun that had appeared as she orgasmed were gone. Vik was still too stunned to speak.

"Is everything okay?" Spencer asked, sounding worried.

"Yeah, of course."

"I guess I just thought you'd be happier," she said, disappointment in her voice.

Shit. What had just happened with Spencer was great—amazing, in fact. He felt bad that she thought this was about her, but he just couldn't shake what he'd seen.

"I'm sorry," Vik said. "I'm insanely happy right now, I swear. I'm just feeling sick. Graham gave me something when we went upstairs, and it's not sitting well. I'll be back in a minute. I need to go to the bathroom."

Attempting reassurance, he kissed Spencer lightly before he left. Then he went to find Graham.

"We need to talk," Vik said, interrupting Graham as he pumped himself into an Asian woman while she bent over the arm of a couch.

Graham didn't stop.

"Now," Vik hissed.

Graham nodded reluctantly and followed him to the library. They sat in two leather armchairs opposite the fireplace.

"What the fuck did I just see?" Vik fumed.

"I think you know what you saw."

"Actually, I have no fucking idea," Vik said. "Please enlighten me."

"You know more than you realize. Why don't you describe it to me?"

Vik was growing tired of these games, but he needed answers. If he had to play by Graham's rules, he would. "Everyone around the room was dead, like corpses. Well, everyone except Spencer. She looked like a goddess. The sun was rising out of her fucking head, and she was glowing."

Graham nodded. "Good, you saw it."

"Saw what?" Vik huffed.

"The truth hiding in plain sight."

Vik was still confused. He looked around the room. Everyone looked like a corpse and Spencer looked like a goddess, but Graham looked totally normal. "Why do you look the same as you always do?" he asked.

"Oh! I completely forgot," Graham said. "My shield is always up for these parties." He set his drink down and reached for something in his pocket. As he did, the mask that had been in place came off, revealing nothing but bones and tendons underneath. He wasn't hollowed out like the corpses; he was alive, but he looked like a monster. A shadow came over his face as darkness swirled around him and a gray cloud settled above him.

"What the hell?" Vik asked, jumping back, genuinely terrified.

"Is it all making sense yet?"

He sat in stunned silence, shaking his head.

"C'mon, Vik. Connect the dots," Graham pushed.

More silence. Vik thought about what he had seen—the people dead inside, Spencer a being of pure light, and Graham a cloud of darkness. Something was vaguely coming into focus, a connection between Spencer, Graham, and the people at the party.

Graham, now seeming exasperated, stood up. "Maybe a demonstration would help." He motioned for a security guard to come over. "Bring one to me," he told him in a low voice.

The guard walked through the crowd of people and approached a young woman in her early twenties. She was tall, blond, and gorgeous. It was obvious she didn't work in tech; she'd been brought to the party as entertainment.

The security guard whispered something in the woman's ear, and she nodded. He gently placed his arm on her lower back, guiding her toward the library, where Graham and Vik sat. As they walked, Vik noticed how the woman stood out from the corpses around her. She had a subtle glow, her skin slightly glistening. She wasn't as bright as Spencer, but she was distinctly alive, unlike most people in the room.

"Please sit," Graham said as she approached.

She sat down nervously.

"Are you enjoying the party?" Graham asked.

As he spoke, Vik saw a scene unfold as if the world had fractured into two states. In one state, the one that was plainly happening before Vik's eyes, Graham continued to talk to the woman. They had a completely harmless conversation—friendly, warm, inviting. Graham was getting to know her. But in the other state, the one only Vik seemed to be able to see, the cloud of darkness surrounding Graham turned into a shadow. Dark tendrils of smoke came out of his chest like hands and slowly curled their way over to the woman. As the smoke reached her skin, the light started to drain from her face. Her subtle glow was replaced by dry, cracking skin. As the light left her, it moved through the shadow and up into Graham. Graham was taking her energy and giving it to himself, and the woman had no idea it was happening.

Within seconds, she was a corpse like everyone else in the room. Graham pulled back from her, finished up the conversation, and thanked her as she left.

Vik watched Graham inhale deeply and close his eyes. When he opened them, his irises were pitch-black. He blinked once, and his eyes returned to their normal shade of blue.

"Ahh," Graham said, "she tasted particularly good."

"Tasted?" Vik spat.

"Everyone's power has a distinct flavor," Graham explained.

Vik had had enough. He needed answers.

"What the fuck is going on here, Graham?"

"The pill I gave you, it activates a part of your brain that affects how you process spatial information. Normally when you look at something, your senses—like sight and sound—send signals to your brain. These signals serve as a language, communicating information that helps you understand what you're experiencing. When you took the pill, the way your brain processes the world around you changed. Instead of vision and sound transmitting signals to your brain, energy vibrates information through frequencies. You aren't seeing with your eyes; you're sensing with other, deeper faculties."

"I'm *sensing energy*?" Vik clarified.

"Yes. You're experiencing the energy plane that happens in parallel with the physical plane. It's the same world but different planes. As you can tell, it's too ephemeral for words. That's why you had to experience it directly. No explanation could ever do it justice."

"So, on the energy plane, some people look dead and others look alive? I'm still not following," Vik said.

"I know it's hard to wrap your head around at first, but you need to trust what you're experiencing," said Graham. "Most people are dead, energetically speaking. Their energy has been used up. Sometimes, they've become deeply disconnected from their own energy source, and other times, it's been taken from them."

"And Spencer? And the woman you just . . ." Vik trailed off, not knowing the word for what he had just witnessed.

"Ah yes, Spencer," Graham said as if remembering something. "I wanted you to see what she was—that's why I told you to invite her."

"And *what* is she, exactly?"

"They're called Rays. She's still connected to her own energetic source. At her age, when someone is still connected, it's usually an indication that they have the potential to become a Liminal."

Vik sat there, unsure of what questions to ask next.

Graham prompted him. "Where do you think power comes from, Vik?"

He took a moment before replying. "I guess I've never really thought about it. It seems that money and authority are the root of power."

Graham shook his head. "Those are just physical manifestations of power. Over the years, the Apparatus has hidden the true source of power behind these external objects. Money and authority must be earned. Those who haven't earned these physical objects then feel powerless in turn. But the source of power isn't external at all—it's inside every person.

"The Apparatus realized this a long time ago. In order to accumulate *real power*, they didn't need money or authority; they needed *energy*. The Apparatus found ways to take energy from people and harness it for themselves. The strongest of us can steal power directly, like I just did, but it can also be harnessed indirectly. Anytime someone disconnects from their own source energy—their own authority—they forfeit some of their power, and we can grab it. Social media has been an unexpected boon for the Apparatus. When someone mindlessly scrolls, their power slowly seeps out of their body into the ether, free for anyone to take. The expression 'paying attention' exists for a reason. Attention is just another form of energy."

Had Vik been thinking about power all wrong? If what Graham said was true, then energy was the ultimate currency.

"Think of every person like a battery. When they're born, their battery is fully charged. Everyone is born a Ray. Over time, they lose that connection, until the battery is discharged. Once the battery is empty, it can't be charged again. That's what you saw here tonight."

That didn't explain Spencer's or Graham's appearance, though. "And people like Spencer?" Vik asked.

"We're still trying to figure out why some people remain connected to their power. It's a mystery, even to us."

"And you? Instead of light, you were surrounded by darkness. What are you?" Vik asked.

"We're something different."

"We?" Vik found himself struggling to breathe.

Graham handed him a mirror.

# the high

San Francisco
Summer 2016

Vik looked at his reflection in the mirror, slowly taking it all in. Shadows glistened on his skin. Gray smoke swirled around him. A cloud settled above him. He was darkness personified. But instead of feeling terrified, like he'd felt when he saw Graham, Vik felt calm, relaxed even. He was seeing himself for the first time. He was home. I'm beautiful, he thought.

He put down the mirror, turning back to Graham. Before he could ask more questions, Graham spoke.

"Have you heard of the dark triad?"

Vik nodded, but he didn't see the connection.

"A psychologist studying the behavior of global leaders and executives, many of whom are part of the Apparatus, came up with the term," Graham explained. "The dark triad offers a clinical explanation of who we are. It's a combination of psychopathy, narcissism, and Machiavellianism—all malevolent by nature. Callous manipulation is at the core of our being. The research offered an unexpected source of disclosure, so we allowed the work to be published."

Vik was familiar with the study. Numerous books had even been written examining the presence of these traits among high-flying individuals in business and politics, a few of which he'd read.

"People hear the word 'malevolent' and assume the world would be better without men like us, but they forget that nature always maintains a balance. Day and night, light and dark, good and evil.

## dark days ahead

They are opposite poles of the same thing. None exists without the opposing force to define it. Take away darkness, and light ceases to exist at all. Goodness has us to thank—without us, it would be nothing."

As Graham spoke, Vik felt clarity. He thought back to events in his life, his behavior, the way he had been able to shape the world like a ball of clay, and he understood exactly what Graham was saying. Vik was processing it all, lost in his own thoughts, when he saw the security guard ushering another young woman toward them.

"Do you want to try?" Graham asked.

Vik hesitated. His immediate mental reaction was no. He didn't want to do to this woman what Graham had just done to the other one moments ago. He didn't want to watch her morph from a vibrant being into a desiccated husk.

Yet as his brain said no, another answer came from his body. A feeling washed over Vik, threatening to overtake him. *Hunger.* It felt raw and undeniable.

"No one will know but us," Graham said. "She'll walk out of here perfectly fine, never knowing what happened to her. Her light will be gone within a few months anyway—it's barely more than a flicker now. Take it while you still can."

Vik motioned for the woman to sit down next to him. Then, as he'd done a million times before, he started to mold the clay in front of him. He spoke to her, asked her questions, got her to relax. He subtly pushed and pulled on the clay in exactly the right spots until she started to open up, almost as if she had lain back and spread her legs right in front of him. She was his for the taking.

Without any effort at all, Vik knew exactly what to do. The smoke formed into tendrils around him. One tendril took the shape of a hand and reached inside the woman. The energy passed from her to him and entered directly into every cell of Vik's body. Euphoria. There was a taste, sweet and creamy, so saccharine it almost hurt his teeth. Vanilla buttercream frosting, he thought. He felt more alive than he'd ever been in his life.

Vik breathed in deeply and closed his eyes, savoring the moment. When he opened them, Graham was smiling.

"It's better than heroin," Graham said. He motioned for the guard to escort the woman away. "I think that's enough for tonight. Let's go enjoy the party. We'll talk more on Monday."

They stood up and walked back into the party. Vik swore he stood an inch taller as he passed his dark reflection in the mirror.

As he drove home later that night, he had one thing on his mind. A singular, intense thought. He looked over at Spencer sitting in the passenger seat, his mouth watering.

What do you taste like?

# the notice

### San Francisco
### Summer 2016

Spencer was disappointed that her attempt at sex magic had failed. She'd spent the entire day leading up to the party getting ready. She had followed Rose's advice and set intentions, practiced breathwork, and visualized sexual energy moving through her body. She even swore she had felt her chakras unblock when she orgasmed on top of Vik. She had never felt more powerful. It had been the best sex of her life, but she still wasn't a Liminal.

She was about to message the thread to update Narina and Rose on everything that had transpired at the party when some jarring texts came through.

> **John**  This is Rose's brother, John. I'm with Rose now at a hospital in Mexico.
> She's safe, but she had what the doctors are calling mania-induced psychosis. I'm still trying to piece together what happened.
> I know she would want you both to know. I'll keep you updated as I learn more.

As shocking and heartbreaking as the texts were, Spencer wasn't entirely surprised. She had noticed some changes in Rose's behavior recently.

One night a few weeks earlier, at one of their regular dinners, Rose had told them she had news.

"I'm quitting my job," she said, grinning.

"What do you mean?" Narina asked. "You were just promoted to the role you've wanted for years. You love your team. Why are you quitting? Did you get another job?"

Rose shook her head. Spencer noticed how her eyes were wider than normal, ringed by dark circles. She didn't seem to be blinking at all.

"I just have such clarity," Rose said. "This work is what I want to be doing. It's what I'm *meant* to be doing."

"This work?" Narina asked again. "I don't understand what you mean."

"The work we're doing now to transition. We're going to save the future of humanity, and this is just absolutely how I want to spend my time, and I just booked a trip to Oaxaca to meet with a shaman there who specializes in energetic transformations," Rose replied in a rush.

Narina and Spencer exchanged a worried look. The last time the two of them had been alone together, they had talked about their research. While they both believed the work they were doing was important, they didn't yet have any evidence that what Narina had seen was real. The more time that passed since her vision, the more they wondered if it was just that: a vision. They had planned to talk with Rose about it. To see her now, moving in the opposite direction with such fevered intensity, startled Spencer.

"Rose," Narina said gently. "I love how passionate you are about this, but maybe you could just take a weeklong vacation from work instead of quitting? Give yourself some more time to think this through before you make an irreversible decision."

"I put in my notice already."

She was grinning so widely that Spencer thought it must be painful.

"I can see that you're both worried," Rose continued. "But honestly, imagine the happiest you've ever been and multiply it by infinity. That's how I feel right now. I know what I'm doing, and I feel really, really good about it, okay? This is the freest I've felt in a long time. I'm finally taking control of my life."

Spencer read the texts from John again, then switched apps to run a search. Symptoms of mania included talking fast, feeling full of great ideas and important plans, having a decreased need for sleep, and feeling high or elated.

She'd noticed the changes in her friend's behavior, but Rose had always been a deeply passionate person driven by her strong emotions, and she seemed to have everything under control. At least that's what Spencer had thought. She felt guilty. Rose had gone to Mexico to do research on their behalf, and now she was in the hospital after an episode of psychosis.

"I'm sorry," Spencer whispered to no one.

# the voice

San Francisco
Summer 2016

Rose looked out the window of her hospital room. She felt completely numb. She remembered everything, and yet she still didn't understand how all of this had happened.

Rose's parents had both grown up in the Bay Area before it became the tech behemoth it was today. Back then, it was known for something completely different, the Summer of Love, a psychedelic-fueled time with everyone getting ready to "turn on, tune in, and drop out." Her parents were hippies, concerned more with love and freedom than wealth and rules. They'd thought the party would never stop, but as San Francisco's first golden era came to an end, they decided to put down roots outside of the city in Vallejo. In an area filled with jaw-dropping beauty everywhere—with places like Marin County, Napa Valley, and the Sonoma Coast—Vallejo somehow got lost in the mix. It was a normal neighborhood in a land of giants, invisible, lost in the shadows, as if people simply forgot it was there.

Rose had been told she was beautiful—tall, with natural blond hair and oceanic blue eyes like her Viking ancestors—but she didn't see herself the way others did. She had matured early, and by eight years old, she'd stood a full head taller than every boy in her class. One day, Rose's teacher handed out a copy of her third-grade class photo. Rose had cried when she saw the way she hovered over everyone else.

## dark days ahead

That night before bed, she prayed that she would magically wake up the same height as the rest of her class. It didn't work. Rose carried around the unwelcome feeling of being uncomfortable in her own skin from that day forward. Unable to make herself physically shorter, she found other ways to make herself small, to shrink into the background, like Vallejo itself.

Rose had inherited a free spirit from her father and an artistic soul from her mother, but she lived in a very different San Francisco than they had, one that had become exorbitantly expensive after the tech industry exploded. Its former motto to "make love, not money" was now nothing more than an ironic ghost of a forgotten time.

Rose knew she wanted to get out of Vallejo after high school, but she didn't yet know what her path was in the world, so she took the one she saw others taking around her. She went to Berkeley on a full scholarship and joined a sorority. She considered working at a nonprofit after graduating, something that might give her a sense of purpose, but the prospect of equity in a growing tech company lured her in, and she started working in HR at a popular startup. Her life was good, great even. She loved her friends, she enjoyed her job, she made more money than she'd ever anticipated, and she lived close to her family in what she believed was the greatest city in the world. What more could she ask for?

But in the moments when Rose wasn't with friends or working, she noticed a nagging voice in her head that she couldn't silence. A voice telling her there was a bigger life out there and that by making herself small all those years, all she'd really done was create the limits of her own confinement. Eventually, she started to listen.

One weekend when she was home visiting her parents in Vallejo, her mom handed her a copy of *Be Here Now* by Ram Dass. "This book helped me figure things out," she said as she passed it over. "Maybe it will help you, too."

As Rose read the book, which chronicled the author's journey of self-discovery, something cracked open inside of her. Mirroring her parents' footsteps before her, Rose started to explore her own spirituality and consciousness. She had incredibly profound experiences through meditation and guided psychedelic journeys, which altered her worldview. She started to learn a new way of being, taking a radical responsibility for her own life and pairing it with a deep curiosity and openness to emotion.

When Narina returned from her trip to Costa Rica and told Rose and Spencer about her vision of the future, Rose felt like she finally had a purpose that aligned with her new outlook. She threw herself into their research; figuring out how to trigger the transition consumed every second of her free time. Their work gave her life a profound sense of meaning, so when they were no closer to finding an answer after months of research, her passion turned into an obsession.

She started staying up late into the night, creating cocktails of supplements and testing different methods on her own. One of those nights, she had a vision of quitting her job and going to Mexico. It felt like what she was meant to do, so she didn't give it much thought. She put in her notice, found a shaman, and scheduled her trip.

The day after arriving in Oaxaca, Rose met the shaman to sit in a temazcal, a traditional Mayan sweat lodge known to heal mind, body, and spirit. She was full of energy afterward and went for a walk in the park near her hotel.

As she walked past an old willow tree, it danced in the wind. She heard a voice she recognized.

"It's inside of you," it said.

Rose looked around but didn't see anyone.

"Up here, Rose," the voice said again.

Rose looked up. There was an outline of something familiar carved into the trunk of the tree. She shook her head in disbelief. That can't be right, she thought to herself. The carving had an uncanny resemblance to her grandma's face.

"Don't act like you didn't hear me," the voice said.

Rose thought back to when she was a little girl. Sometimes at night, she'd sit in her room and talk to her grandma. Rose's mom said that was impossible, that Rose's grandma had died before Rose was even born, but she knew it was her grandma's voice she heard. As Rose got older, the conversations stopped, but some part of her had never doubted they were real.

"Look at me!" the voice demanded.

Rose looked at the tree trunk where the face had been moments before, and suddenly it appeared again. This time it was unmistakable—it was her grandma. Rose just stared. She felt dizzy. A strange disorientation settled over her, but she was so happy.

"Grandma?" Rose asked in a whisper as she stared at the face in the tree trunk.

"Who else would it be?" her grandma replied, smiling. "You're not listening to me. I'm trying to tell you, *it's inside of you*."

"I don't understand."

"It's inside of you. You just need to find it."

What was inside of her? She examined her hands. She didn't see anything. She looked down at the blue shirt she was wearing, grabbed the bottom of it, and pulled it over her head. She was trying to find whatever was inside of her. Then, suddenly, she couldn't get her clothes off fast enough. Whatever her grandma was talking about was underneath her clothes; she was sure of it. She took off every piece of clothing. She had to find it.

"Cleanse yourself," another voice said to her now. This one seemed to be coming from a bird perched near the fountain.

Rose looked at the bird, and it spoke again. "You need to cleanse yourself first," it said.

She walked over to the fountain and got in. She splashed her face before submerging her body into the shallow water.

"It's going to be messy," the bird said. "Show us that you can handle the mess."

Rose looked around. It had rained earlier that morning, and there were several large puddles nearby. She walked over to a puddle, sat down, and rolled in it before looking back at the bird for more guidance.

"Now show us you have patience," the bird said.

This part might be harder. Even though she hadn't slept in days, she felt buzzy and jittery, like she'd just shotgunned an energy drink. Reluctantly, she walked over to a park bench and sat down.

Rose woke up to someone shaking her. When she opened her eyes, it was pitch-black and she was shivering.

"Necesitas levantarte y vestirte ahora," a man in uniform said. There were two other police officers standing next to him.

"Hablas inglés?" Rose asked, trying to orient herself.

One of the officers in back shook his head. Rose heard him say something about "gringa" and "ayahuasca," but she didn't catch the rest.

"You need to get up and get dressed now. You can't sleep in the park like this," the officer standing in front of her explained.

Rose looked down, realizing she was naked and covered in mud. She leaned her head back and laughed. "Oh, it's okay. My grandma told me to do it. She was over there in the tree," she explained.

The men exchanged a worried look.

"Let's find your clothes," the officer said. "We'll help you get back to where you're staying."

"I can't leave," Rose said. "The bird told me to wait and show my patience."

"You can't stay here," the officer said, his voice growing firmer. He started to walk toward her.

"No!" she yelled. "No, I can't leave. The bird told me I can't leave!"

The officer in back picked up his radio and said something into it that Rose couldn't understand. All three men were approaching her now. The one who'd spoken into the radio was reaching for his handcuffs.

"It's okay," the officer said. "We're not going to hurt you. We are just going to take you to the hospital so you can get some help."

"No, please don't do this," Rose said. "I promise I'm fine. You don't understand. It really was my grandma talking to me. Please don't do this."

The officers brought her to a hospital, where she was promptly sedated. Over the next two days, Rose spent a lot of time sleeping. Doctors and nurses came in at regular intervals to check on her, ask her questions, and run tests.

She was relieved when she woke up on the third day and saw her brother sitting next to her. She wasn't sure who had contacted John or when he had arrived, but she was glad he was there.

She looked over at him.

"Hey, sis. You gave us quite the scare," he said.

Rose nodded. "I know what happened, but I don't know what *happened*."

"You were hallucinating," John explained. "You thought you were talking to Grandma. Police officers found you naked in the park."

Rose shook her head. "They weren't hallucinations—I *was* talking to Grandma. I promise, it was real."

"Rose," John said gently, "you have bipolar disorder. What you experienced was an episode of mania. The doctors are calling it bipolar I with psychotic features. The hallucinations are part of the psychosis."

"No," Rose said, "that's not right. It was real. I swear, it was all real."

"It runs in our family," her brother said. "Grandma had the same thing. She had bipolar too."

That can't be right, Rose thought. Then she started crying.

# the spectrum

San Francisco
Summer 2016

The events of the party were so vivid, the experiences so palpable, the exchange of energy so raw that Vik hadn't questioned what he saw. It had all been utterly real. But as he woke up the next morning, he was saddened to realize how distant it felt already. It was slipping away from him, and his old reality was setting back in. He glanced over at Spencer, still asleep next to him. She looked completely normal. It wasn't like being drunk, where the details blurred and you couldn't quite remember what had happened. Vik remembered everything perfectly, but a subtle haze had started to form around the feelings. The power and the high now took on the remote quality of a dream. How had he felt so alive, when now he seemed to simply exist?

As the weekend passed, the glory of that night continued to slip away from him, and by Monday morning, as he walked into Graham's office, Vik wondered if any of it had really happened.

"Come in," Graham said before he even had a chance to knock.

Vik closed the door behind him.

"Ah, the comedown," Graham said, giving him a look of recognition. "Don't worry. It will pass. You'll feel back to normal soon."

The words didn't comfort Vik; they made him more depressed. "I don't want to feel normal. Can you give me more of the pills?"

Graham shook his head. "The pills provide a temporary way to alter consciousness. They help you triangulate so you can understand. Think of your old way of seeing the world like living in a desert, and the new way you just experienced like living in a jungle. If I tried to explain the jungle to you when all you had known was the desert, you wouldn't have believed it. Your mind wouldn't have been able to fully comprehend it, and you would have doubted its existence altogether. The pills aren't the jungle. They are simply a vehicle that drove you there and dropped you off. The jungle exists all the time, and living there will become your reality if you choose to move forward with the Apparatus."

"So what I experienced on Saturday—that's what you experience on a regular basis?" Vik asked.

"Every day."

Vik's mouth watered. "How would I join? What are the next steps?"

"Joining the Apparatus is easy. I'd refer you, and by this time next week, you'd be a Guardsman. There's a welcome ceremony with simple rituals. What you're really asking about, though, is not joining the Apparatus but becoming an Architect. That's when your living reality will change."

"And what's required to become an Architect?"

"A seat at the Architect table is incredibly rare; there are only a handful of us in the world. Luckily for you, I know of a seat coming available, and I'd like for you to be the one to take it. If you choose to move forward, two acts of sacrifice are required to prove your allegiance to the Apparatus. The first act is a mental sacrifice. Think of it like a renunciation. You need to prove to the Apparatus that you can walk away from something you want deeply now. You need to show us that your will is stronger than your desire. The second act is a physical sacrifice. It will require a different type of action on your part. The transition to Architect requires energy. And blood."

Vik's stomach dropped as he saw a flash of the dead man outside city hall. He shook his head. "Are you saying I have to ki . . ." He trailed off, struggling to get the word out.

"Yes," Graham replied. "You'll have to kill someone. Your two acts of sacrifice are to end a relationship and to end a life."

Vik breathed in sharply. He had been so focused on the second act that he'd nearly forgotten the first one. End a relationship. He thought about Spencer, the sun rising out of her head, her body shuddering as she came on top of him. "Help me understand," Vik said. "Why do I have to leave Spencer to join the Apparatus?"

"You saw what she is."

Vik still didn't fully get it. "Why does it matter that she's light? A Ray or whatever you called it?"

"The temptation will be too much for you. Plus, she hasn't transitioned yet herself—we don't know what her powers will be when they manifest."

"Powers?"

Graham rolled his eyes. "For as smart as you are, you're really not getting this, are you? I thought you'd already have put the pieces together by now. Do I need to spell it out for you?"

"That would help," Vik said tersely.

"Everyone has power when they're born. It's like an energetic well located deep within. You can liken it to divinity, the Godhead, or source energy, if that's your thing. Power isn't a static, singular aspect. Think of it as a spectrum along which the energy of power travels. There are poles on either end of the spectrum: pure black on one end and pure white on the other. Dark and light.

"Everyone's internal power falls somewhere on that spectrum. For some reason, power magnifies at the poles and weakens in the middle. Consider someone who sits at the center of the spectrum. They have equal amounts of light and darkness within them. The light neutralizes the dark, and vice versa. The effect of each extinguishes the other, making their power weak, almost nonexistent. Most people fall somewhere in the middle, possessing a muted power that's easily disconnected from the source within. But the people at the poles maintain a purity and strength of power. If the power is still strong enough as they mature, they can transition into an even higher state, one that doesn't exist on the normal spectrum of light. It's as if the source of energy no longer sits quietly within them. It comes to the surface, and when it does, specific gifts manifest. A core aspect of who they are heightens and intensifies into a power that can be wielded."

What were Vik's gifts? And when would they manifest?

"Centuries ago, a small group of men realized this and created the Apparatus. The articulated purpose of the group was to educate and enlighten men. The real purpose was to find other masters of the night, men at the dark end of the spectrum who would become Guardsmen. After a while, a few of the men of the Apparatus transitioned to a darkened state of intense power, and they became the first Architects."

Vik couldn't help it—he instantly liked thinking of himself as a "master of the night."

"The Apparatus started to study those who were able to successfully enter a heightened state of power, and they learned that the transition usually happened after some pivotal life moment. Something happened that cracked these men open and gave the darkness a place to enter. The Apparatus developed rituals, ceremonies, and rites of initiation to trigger the transition. That's where the two acts of sacrifice come from. Once the transition to Architect occurs, it becomes easy to accumulate more power.

"At first, the Apparatus didn't realize that their power was just one end of the spectrum. They didn't know another group existed, equals on the opposite pole, typically women, whose powers manifested in lightness. Initially the events were isolated—a woman would cast a spell as she passed a Guardsman, and he'd be blinded, start seizing, or be left instantly dead."

Vik wasn't sure why, but as Graham spoke those words, an image of Spencer walking by him popped into his head.

"Over time, we learned about these women and began to understand how their powers worked. We developed medicines, potions really, that could help us see who they were. We tried to fight them, but they were always stronger than us in one-on-one battle. In one of our earliest and most ingenious uses of propaganda, we leaked stories about these women and their powers, calling them witches. The puritanical and religious beliefs of the time did the work for us to eradicate them from every village and city. By the eighteenth century, fifty thousand of these so-called witches had been hanged or burned at the stake. And by the twentieth century, insane asylums had replaced witch trials as the narrative device of choice. The women who manifest light powers aren't really witches or crazy, though—they're Liminals."

Graham paused before continuing. "You have power, Vik, but so does Spencer. She's your equal and opposite."

The pieces were falling into place. He was darkness, and Spencer was light.

"Now do you see why you can't be with her?" Graham asked.

Vik was almost there.

"There's only one thing that can kill darkness, Vik. Only one thing that can kill you." Graham spoke slowly now.

There it was. The final piece. Light.

Only light could kill darkness. Spencer could kill him, Vik realized.

"Now do you understand?" Graham asked.

Vik nodded.

"Good." Graham nodded in return. "Understanding doesn't make it easier. When I first learned the truth, I struggled to accept it, but that will change quicker than you expect. The things that are asked of you won't be as difficult as you anticipate, because all you are really asked is to be yourself. Darkness is at the core of who you are. It's why I hired you years ago. The sooner you accept it and let the darkness in, the easier it all becomes. Plus, the Apparatus never takes without giving. While you'll be asked to make two sacrifices, you'll also be given two gifts. Consider them bargaining chips—and in your case, they're very good ones. I know how powerful you can be, Vik. I've seen it already, so I've done my best to make the Apparatus give you an offer you can't refuse."

"What's the offer?" Vik asked, perking up.

"In return for ending things with Spencer, we'll replace her with another, more suitable woman. And in exchange for the life you'll take, you'll be able to take something he owns."

Vik waited.

"The man you'll sacrifice is a minority owner of the Golden State

## dark days ahead

Warriors. Once he's no longer in the picture, the Apparatus will help you acquire his stake."

Shit, Vik thought. There weren't many people in the world who could afford a stake in an NBA team, but access was even more exclusive than wealth, and this was the rarest of tickets. While Vik had been successful up until this point, he was still told "no" more often than he liked. Founders declined meetings, LPs were hard to get on the phone, politicians didn't return emails—but everyone loved the thrill of celebrity that the proximity to athletes, courtside seats, and an owner's lounge offered. Vik wouldn't be told no again. He could make billions over the course of his career and still never have an opportunity like this.

Vik thought through the options. As an image of Spencer started to appear in his mind, he pushed it down deep inside of him, remembering instead the smooth taste of vanilla buttercream frosting in his mouth, the power coursing through his veins. It would be hard to leave her, but the choice was easy. "How do I get started?"

"The first step is to end things with Spencer. The rest of the path will start to unfold before you. You'll be given directions as needed," Graham said before standing up to cue the end of their meeting. He opened the door for Vik. "By the way, I overheard Katie and Amelia talking in the elevator this morning. Amelia just broke up with her boyfriend."

Katie and Amelia had both been executive assistants at the firm for nearly a decade, graduating from college the same year Vik had. Amelia had started working directly for Vik a few years earlier, when he was promoted to partner. He thought she was great. She was good at her job, nice to look at, and sweet, but he didn't understand why Graham was sharing this office gossip with him.

Graham rolled his eyes, looking annoyed once again. "I told you we'd replace Spencer with another, more suitable woman."

# the replacement

San Francisco
Summer 2016

Vik was having a busy day at work—he was finalizing term sheets on two deals—so he didn't have much time to dwell on his conversation with Graham. A little after six o'clock, as he was about to head home for the night, Katie popped her head into his office.

"A few of us are going to grab a drink at Joe's. Want to join?"

"Who's going?" Vik asked.

"Me, Amelia, and Josh."

Vik liked Katie and Amelia, but he thought Josh was an absolute prick. The guy was two years behind Vik, and he was constantly overcompensating, a trait Vik found nauseating. Vik had dinner plans with Spencer and was about to decline the offer from Katie when he remembered what Graham had said. His thoughts drifted to the newly single Amelia.

"I'll meet you guys there in ten minutes," Vik told her.

"Great," Katie said. She smiled and left his office.

Vik pulled out his phone to call Spencer. As he dialed, he felt a sense of dread and decided to text her instead.

*This deal just exploded. It's going to be a late night, so I need to bail on our dinner plans.*

He quickly pocketed his phone, not wanting to feel guilty about her reply.

When Vik walked into Joe's a short while later, Katie, Amelia,

## dark days ahead

and Josh were already there, sitting at a high-top. Conveniently, the seat next to Amelia was open.

They spent the next few hours drinking, laughing, and venting about work. The bar was busy for a Monday night and louder than usual. As the conversation went on, it became easy and natural for Katie and Josh to converse among themselves on their side of the table, leaving Vik and Amelia to a private conversation.

Vik knew Amelia's personality well from years of working together, but they'd never broached topics of a more personal nature, always respectful of the invisible professional line they knew stood between them.

As Amelia spoke, he watched her and listened intently, wondering if Graham might be right that she could replace Spencer. Vik had a physical type (white brunettes) and an intellectual type (smart women who challenged him). Amelia ticked the first box completely—she was a petite brunette with brown eyes and a great ass—but she wasn't exactly the intellectual type. It wasn't that she was dumb; she was extremely competent and effective at her job, but she had the kind of simple mind that stayed at the surface. She didn't think deeply, she didn't question things, she took the world at face value. While that might not have interested Vik in the past, he thought about everything he had learned from Graham and the life he was about to embark on, and suddenly, that simplicity seemed endlessly appealing.

Vik started to ask Amelia questions. At one point, he even lightly grazed her arm as she shared a sad story about her sick grandfather. He wanted to test the waters. Amelia didn't flinch. She instead looked him in the eyes as his hand passed over her arm. Vik had always considered her off-limits given the power dynamics; he was a partner, and she was his assistant. But as he sat across from her, he found the forbidden nature of their relationship exciting. Unavailability always added to the thrill of the chase. He'd have to handle the optics, of course, but this wouldn't be so bad. It might even be fun, he thought, as he pictured Amelia going down on him beneath his desk at work, her head hidden just out of sight, Josh walking by the glass windows of his office, waving at Vik as Vik came in her mouth.

When Vik got into his car two hours later, he opened his phone to Spencer's reply.

Hope it's not too bad. It's been a rough day over here too, I got some bad news about Rose.

He sat in his car for a minute before turning the ignition on. He knew he should feel bad, especially when Spencer was going through a hard time, but he was still turned on just thinking about Amelia.

Come over? I'm on my way back to the city now and have been thinking about you all night.

Spencer was waiting on his front porch as Vik pulled into his garage thirty minutes later.

I'll end things with her tomorrow, he thought as he buried himself inside of her that night. Twice.

# the ghost

San Francisco
Summer 2016

The next day, when Spencer brought home bagels for breakfast after her morning yoga class, Vik couldn't bring himself to end it. He found it easier to avoid it entirely—and in turn, he started avoiding her.

He used work as an excuse at first. Things were crazy, he'd say as he canceled plans with Spencer. They started spending only two or three nights a week together instead of the six nights they'd grown accustomed to. Then Vik started becoming less responsive. Instead of replying to her texts as he read them, he'd wait a few hours. By the end of the month, he'd sometimes wait a few days.

He'd thought Spencer would be so upset by his behavior that she would take the initiative to end things. But instead, she was impassive and seemed preoccupied with something going on with her friends.

Vik just couldn't stop seeing her entirely. He'd go a few days without contact, then crave being with her. She was like a drug he couldn't quite kick. But over time, the longer he went without seeing her, the easier it became, like he was slowly building a muscle of restraint.

Spending time with Amelia was a nice distraction. They continued to hang out with each other, always near the office after work. At first, Katie or some other coworkers would join them, but after a few weeks, Vik and Amelia started to go by themselves. Their texts went from strictly professional to subtly flirtatious. While they didn't cross any physical lines, it was clear they both knew a dangerous and delicate boundary had been breached.

For Katie's thirtieth birthday, some women from the office were planning a trip to Cabo.

"You should come with us," Katie said to Vik in the elevator one morning.

A weekend getaway with Amelia under the guise of a friendly trip with coworkers sounded great. And a foreign country was just like Vegas—what happened there stayed there. He agreed to join them.

A few months prior, before the night of the party at Graham's house, Vik and Spencer had talked about taking a trip to Cabo together. There was no way he could tell her he was going there without her, so he lied and said he was headed to Mexico City. He told her he was trying to sell a company there and the founder was being difficult, so Vik needed to meet him in person. He warned her he'd be mostly out of touch while he was there, but on Saturday, after a night filled with drinking and dancing, his phone buzzed from the nightstand next to where he lay in bed. It was a text from Spencer.

Hope everything went okay with the founder. Thinking of you.

Vik didn't even have a chance to feel guilty before he set his phone back on the nightstand and looked down at Amelia, who was sliding her tongue up the full length of him, then wrapping her entire mouth around him. He moaned and forgot about Spencer's text entirely.

He and Amelia had officially crossed a line, and it felt good. The thrill of an illicit office romance was enough to distract him from Spencer. Any time he felt the urge to text her, he reached out to Amelia instead. She quickly became the salve to the ache Vik sometimes felt inside.

Vik could feel things with Spencer coming to a close. They barely spoke while he was out of town on a three-week work trip in Europe. For the first time, she didn't reach out to him either. She was finally catching on, it seemed. Vik felt both relief and dejection every time he checked his phone and there were no messages from her.

When he got back in town, Spencer asked if she could come over to talk. This is it, Vik thought, she's going to end things.

They sat on his couch in the exact spot where they'd first kissed over a year before. Please don't cry, he thought as she sat across from him, readying herself to speak.

"I know something has been going on, something more than just work," Spencer said. "I'm not sure what it is, and I honestly don't care. I love you, Vik. I want to be with you. Do you want to be with me? If you do, we can forget about whatever has been going on the past few months."

Well, that wasn't what he'd been expecting. No anger, no malice, no blame. Despite everything he'd done, Spencer still wanted to be with him. She loved him. Vik had been hoping this would be easier, that he wouldn't have to say the words himself.

He looked at her—really *looked* at her. Even without the red pill Graham had given him, he could see it. The subtle glow, the shimmering skin, the way she looked so alive even in moments of defeat like this. Vik imagined another parallel universe that might exist right next to this one, one where he was a different man and Spencer was a different woman, but they were still in love. He pictured walking up behind her in the morning, kissing her cheek as she made them coffee. He imagined coming home from work, Spencer cooking in the kitchen, pulling him in close as he hugged her after a long day away. He saw her standing on the side of a stage behind a curtain, holding their daughter in her arms, looking on adoringly as Vik received an award. And then, instead of imagining a different future, he remembered the first time he'd seen Spencer at the wine bar. The way she had smiled at him and how her eyes sparkled. It's like I've known you my whole life, he'd thought as he locked eyes with her for the first time.

Despite it all, he knew what he had to do. He wasn't a different man in a parallel universe. He was this man, here right now, and the path he had chosen didn't include her.

"I think you're great and we have crazy intense chemistry, but I really don't see a future here. I'd love to stay friends, but I understand if you're not open to that," he said.

His words were painfully direct but also completely true. He knew she deserved more than that, something that didn't sound so generic, something that honored the time they had spent together instead of treating her like he barely knew her, but he couldn't give her anything else. The more he opened his mouth, the more room for error he allowed. Quick is always less painful, he thought. He saw a wave of sadness flash through Spencer, but she didn't cry.

She nodded, stood up, and walked over to the front hallway to put on her shoes.

"Bye, Vik," she said as she turned to give him one final hug.

He kissed her cheek, and as she backed away to leave, he pulled her in one more time. He kissed her again, and something in him cracked. He watched her walk down the block until she was out of sight.

She never looked back.

# the comeback

San Francisco
Fall 2016

When Rose first returned home to San Francisco after the episode in Oaxaca, she'd been confused. She still believed she'd seen and heard her grandma, but she could also recognize how her behavior had been dangerous and erratic. She had slept naked in a park in a foreign country. She was scared, scared of what she'd done and scared of the bipolar diagnosis. She stayed on the prescribed medicine, moved back home with her mom in Vallejo, went to an outpatient treatment center, and slowly, she started to feel more "normal."

A month into her recovery, looking for ways to fill her now unemployed days, Rose met Michelle, a friend from college. Over lunch, Michelle shared some of her struggles and frustrations at work. She felt like she had reached an upper limit and wasn't progressing in her career.

Rose had been part of many similar conversations in the past working in HR and found herself falling back into that role. She helped Michelle navigate her work situation, only this time Rose offered advice she never would have been comfortable giving in a professional setting. Advice that centered around her conscious approach to life, which she'd perfected over the past few years during her own period of growth. Rose asked Michelle deeply personal questions and forced her to be honest. By the end of lunch, she had mapped out a plan for her friend.

Rose left the meal feeling invigorated. The following week, she checked in with Michelle for an update.

**Michelle** I talked with my manager yesterday and just found out I'm being promoted with a substantial raise and equity grant.

**Rose** Wow—you deserve it!
How did you feel during the conversation with your manager?

**Michelle** Honestly, I've never felt more empowered.
And it was all because of your help. THANK YOU! You should really charge for this!

As Rose read the words, she felt a puzzle piece fall into place. I could do this *and* get paid? Holy shit.

Still not fully believing it was possible, she dipped her toe in to test the waters. She sent an email to an HR community listserv she'd been a part of for years, sharing that she would be doing some freelance work consulting clients on how to bring consciousness into the workplace. By the end of that week, she'd had ten consultations scheduled, and within two months, she had a roster of clients she met with regularly. Earlier that morning, she had filed the paperwork for her LLC, marking the official start to her new endeavor.

Rose had even made enough money to replace her old income, and now she was in the middle of touring an apartment in NoPa. The thought of living on her own after everything that had happened made her nervous, but her doctor was insistent that she was more than ready to take full ownership of her life again.

Rose looked around at the dated linoleum floor in the kitchen and the flickering fluorescent boob light in the bathroom. She knew at least half of the original windows were painted shut, but she didn't care. It was a proper one-bedroom apartment with a backyard in her favorite neighborhood in the city. It was a place she could afford with the income she earned doing what she loved. She was home.

"I'll take it," she said to the real estate agent, grinning.

# the hunt

San Francisco
Fall 2016

**Rose**   It's official, I'm starting my own coaching business

**Narina**   GAHHH THIS IS AMAZING NEWS
It could not be a more perfect blend of your experience and passions
How do you feel?

**Rose**   BEYOND EXCITED
And I loved the apartment I toured so I signed the lease!

**Spencer**   I'm so proud of you Rose—what a huge day!

It was true, Spencer was immensely proud of Rose, but she couldn't help but notice the way it made her feel less than great about the state of her own life. She had always considered strength to be one of her greatest attributes, so she was surprised by how weak she felt after her relationship with Vik ended. It was like he had taken all her energy with him, and now she was nothing. In the time it had taken Rose to put herself back together after her diagnosis, Spencer had completely fallen apart.

Spencer had never been one to showcase her emotions externally—even now—but internally she was drowning. Two months

## dark days ahead

after the breakup, when she was still waking up with a dark cloud over her head, she started seeing a therapist, Cynthia. At first, the sessions weren't particularly productive. Spencer liked to spend the time obsessively replaying the final few months of the relationship, trying to figure out where it all went wrong—"ruminating," Cynthia would say.

But Spencer was onto something. She'd always been hypervigilant to the emotional states of others. She could pinpoint exactly when Vik's behavior had changed, the moment he'd started to pull away—the night of Graham's party.

The realization confused her, though. Wasn't that exactly what Vik had wanted? He had told her that his fantasy was to have sex in front of an audience, and they had. In Spencer's estimation, it had been pretty great sex, too. So there must have been something else, something she was missing. She became preoccupied with figuring out what that something might be. Had she upset him? Had she been too forward? Had it all been too much for him?

Every few hours, she'd explore a different hypothesis for Vik's withdrawal. She couldn't leave any stone unturned; her mind wouldn't let her. Nothing was too trivial. Some rational part of her knew she was spiraling, but she couldn't stop it. It was a compulsion, really. Her latest theory was that her areolas were disproportionately large compared to her nipples, a trait Vik must have found too embarrassing for the public domain.

That had to be it. Spencer felt momentarily relieved. Vik could get over that. He just needed time. He'd come back around.

But then another distressing thought came into her mind. What if it wasn't something else but *someone* else?

Spencer had analyzed endlessly, but she had never even considered that possibility. She'd avoided looking at his social media since he'd dumped her as a defense mechanism, but now she had to know.

She pulled up his profile. She felt stunned as she looked at his most recent post.

And then she felt nothing.

**Spencer**  Vik is engaged

**Narina**  How is that even possible?
You literally just broke up

**Rose**  Oh Spence, my heart is breaking over here for you
How did you find out?

**Spencer**  He posted a photo

**Narina**  What an absolute asshole
I hate him
SEND ME THE PIC

Spencer took a screenshot of the post. Vik had proposed while on vacation in Kauai during a beachside dinner overlooking Hanalei Bay.

**Narina**  It's all just so predictable

Spencer knew Narina was doing that thing friends do: trying to make Spencer feel better by bringing Vik down. Spencer wanted to hate everything about the photo, to agree that it all looked boring, but Vik looked nice, and his fiancée looked pretty, and the location where he'd chosen to propose was breathtaking. She didn't have a bad thing to say.

**Narina**  Do you want to hurt hunt?

Spencer had first heard the term "hurt hunting" in a blog about attachment styles after Vik dumped her. It characterized the decision to consciously do things you knew would hurt, like picking a scab. She'd shared the expression with Narina and Rose, and now the three of them used the phrase any time they picked unnecessarily at an emotional wound they knew would hurt so good.

## dark days ahead

Spencer understood Narina's question: Do you want to stalk Vik online to see what we can find out about the woman and his impending nuptials?

**Spencer**  I know I'm going to be curious at some point, let's just get it over with now

Within a minute, Narina found out who the woman was and shared the links to her professional and personal profiles.

**Narina**  Her name is Amelia
Looks totally boring
She's iceberg lettuce

Narina had a sandwich theory she liked to employ. The theory was that every woman could be aptly described as a sandwich topping. Rose was a cucumber—light and refreshing and never offensive to anyone. Spencer was an avocado—rich and smooth but hard to open before it was ripe. Narina was corned beef—salty and spicy, with a polarizing effect. The sandwich theory was simple and crude, but it was effective.

**Narina**  Goes with everything
Totally harmless
But too bland to ever eat alone

Spencer zoomed in on the woman's face to see if the lettuce analogy held. As she got closer, her stomach dropped, her photographic memory kicking in. She went into the library in her brain, all the way back to Vik's dating app pictures.

**Spencer**  That's weird, she was in one of his dating app photos
I remember seeing her

**Rose**  You're joking

**natalie docherty**

Spencer  I wish I was, but I can picture it perfectly
He was standing with a group of friends at a baseball game—she was in the bottom right of the photo wearing a white top, a green jacket, and jeans
He knew her
He was hanging out with her before we even started dating

Rose  Maybe she was just a friend?

Narina  UHHH NO
Look at her work history please
She was his fucking assistant

Spencer  Please stop
I know you're trying to help, but I feel sick just thinking about this
Was he cheating on me with his assistant?

Narina  I'm coming over with a bottle of whiskey right now

Rose  I'll bring pizza

# the news

San Francisco
Winter 2016

Spencer was taken aback by how much Vik's engagement hit her. It wasn't so much that he'd moved on as the speed with which he'd done it that made Spencer wonder if she even existed at all.

She started seeing Cynthia twice a week, and they'd been making real progress.

"Your relationship with Vik sounds like a trauma bond between an empath and a narcissist," Cynthia had said during their last session. "Are you familiar with that?"

Spencer shook her head.

"A narcissist usually starts a relationship with love bombing," Cynthia explained. "They'll move things along quickly and give their partner a lot of attention. Sometimes, the narcissist will even mirror the interests of their partner to give the appearance of compatibility and strengthen their connection."

Spencer thought back to the way Vik had asked her so many questions, the way he'd invited her to his friend's wedding on their second date, the way they seemed to have so much in common.

"It creates a strong and often toxic bond between the two," Cynthia continued. "Narcissists like to feed off the energy of others, and empaths make particularly good targets. But if the narcissist's needs aren't being met or they no longer find the empath useful, they'll begin to discard them. During the discard phase, the narcissist will distance themselves through emotional withdrawal and the silent treatment. They can become distant, cold, unresponsive. Often, it's because the narcissist has found a new source of supply."

Spencer still felt sick thinking about the engagement photo. "That's not the first time a man has discarded me," she said quietly.

Cynthia continued. "The breakup can be particularly hard for the empath, not because they were in love with the narcissist but because the empath derived their worthiness from them. You see, empaths often have weak boundaries, so they easily lose their sense of self. It's common that empaths adopt traits of the narcissist or form their identity around them."

While Spencer recognized some truth in Cynthia's words, she didn't believe she was an empath. She had always been rather self-contained. "Aren't empaths really emotional?" Spencer asked.

Cynthia shook her head. "Not necessarily. Empaths are highly intuitive and sensitive. They tend to notice everything. They're attuned to the energy and emotions of those around them—so much so that at times, they can even feel the pain of others. Sometimes this makes them feel out of place, like they're different from everyone else. Is this something that resonates for you?"

Spencer nodded. "I always felt so different from my family," she said. "It seemed like I could see and understand more of the world than they could. I even remember them making fun of me when I refused to go to the zoo as a kid. I told my mom I could hear the animals crying in their cages, but she just rolled her eyes and dragged me inside."

Cynthia nodded. "How did you cope with everything you felt?"

Spencer thought for a minute before replying. "School. School was something I could control. It was something I excelled at. It was a good distraction, at least for a while."

"Your mind became the rock that kept your emotions at bay," Cynthia affirmed.

Spencer nodded.

"You said that's not the first time a man discarded you. When was the first time?"

"My dad."

When she was in second grade, Spencer had come home from school and found her mom standing on the front lawn, screaming at someone on the phone.

"Your dad's moving out," she'd told Spencer later that night. "We're getting divorced. He was cheating on me with multiple women, paying their rent while we were in debt. The first time I had evidence of his affairs was when I was pregnant with your brother. That was ten years ago! Can you believe when we were on our family vacation last year in Florida, he flew in hookers to meet him? Hookers!"

Spencer had been seven. She didn't know what hookers were, but she could tell her mom was devastated. She wanted to help her but didn't know how. She felt powerless. That night, as her mom sobbed in bed, Spencer crawled in beside her and held her hand, feeling like comfort was the only thing she could offer.

"My parents got divorced after my dad cheated on my mom," Spencer told Cynthia.

"And how did your dad discard you?"

"Well, he bought a house a few miles away from where we lived and agreed to take us every other weekend as part of the custody arrangement, but that didn't happen. He never made any effort to see us. We'd get together once a year around the holidays, and that was it. When I was in college, he moved to North Carolina, and I haven't seen him since."

"And how did that make you feel?" Cynthia asked.

"I'm not sure I thought about it much at the time."

"Notice that I didn't ask what you *thought*. I asked how you *felt*. We've talked about the way you tend to intellectualize your feelings. I'd like you to try again. This time, envision yourself at that age. What did you feel?"

Spencer considered this. "I guess I felt like I didn't exist, like I was invisible. Every parent says that their kids are the best part of their life, so I never understood why that wasn't true for my dad. Why didn't he want to see us?"

"The loss of a parent is always hard," Cynthia empathized, "but sometimes an optional departure can cut deeper than a forced departure, like death. I imagine it was a difficult experience for you. Did you find yourself turning to school again to keep you distracted?"

Spencer thought back to that period and shook her head. "I think school was so easy by that point that it no longer offered much of a distraction."

"Did you find another outlet?"

Spencer swallowed and nodded. "Food," she said. "If I ate enough, I could make myself completely numb, and sometimes that numbness felt like bliss. But I didn't like feeling out of control, so after I binged, I would purge."

"And did you ever share that with anyone or get help?"

"No, it just kind of naturally stopped after a few years when I started dating my high school boyfriend. I no longer felt numb. I felt alive. It was like a sensory overload."

"And that was a good thing?"

"It seemed like it. After years of feeling nothing, the thrill of feeling anything at all was amazing."

"Looking back, would you say that was a healthy relationship?"

"No, not really."

"Why not?"

"I started to change myself for him."

"In what ways?"

"I made myself less intelligent."

Cynthia nodded. "It sounds like you whittled away parts of yourself so the men around you could shine. And did you feel 'alive' with Vik too?"

Spencer nodded. "More alive than I'd ever felt with anyone. He just seemed so powerful. It was completely intoxicating."

"And how do you feel now?"

"Like an empty shell."

"It seems like you pared yourself down so much that now you feel like there's nothing left," Cynthia said. "You lost your sense of self."

"Yeah, that feels accurate."
"What are some ways you can reclaim yourself?"
"What do you mean?"
"We talk a lot about your feeling of powerlessness in our sessions and the way you find power through the men you date. I'd like you to work on finding your source of power within and identify a few actions you can take that will allow you to reclaim your sense of self."

Spencer spent the next week contemplating ways to reclaim her power. Since school was the place she had lost it—or rather, where she had given it away—she figured that it might be a good place to get her power back. She decided to go back to business school and got to work submitting applications.

She was nervous—not about the applications but about breaking the news to Narina and Rose at dinner that night. After Rose's episode, Narina and Spencer hadn't been able to help but wonder if the research they were doing had been the cause of her diagnosis. They began to question how much they really believed in the vision and decided to take a break from it all. Spencer's decision to leave the city felt like a nail in the coffin, and she wasn't sure how Narina or Rose would react.

As Narina poured them wine, Spencer was about to share her news, but Narina spoke up first. "I have some life updates," she said.

"I can't wait to hear," Spencer said, "and I have news too. But you first."

"I'm pregnant," Narina shared. "I'm almost four months in now. We've had some trouble in the past, and I wanted to be absolutely certain before I shared the news."

"What!" Rose exclaimed. "I didn't even know you were trying! That's so exciting."

"You and Sam will be amazing parents," Spencer said.

Narina beamed. "We're so incredibly happy," she gushed.

She and Rose both looked at Spencer expectantly, waiting for her news now.

"I'm going back to business school. It won't be until next fall, but I wanted you both to be the first to know."

"Stanford?" Rose asked.

Spencer shook her head. "I only applied to places far away from San Francisco," she said, looking down.

"I understand the desire for a fresh start right now, but I can't believe you're leaving us," Rose said sadly. "Between pregnancy and a cross-country move, I can't help but think this feels like the end of an era."

# the trophy

**Switzerland**
**Spring 2017**

Graham was so pleased with the news of Vik's engagement that he offered to host the bachelor party in the Swiss Alps. They flew into a small airport, just ten minutes outside St. Moritz, on Graham's private jet for a luxurious weekend of skiing. Graham never liked to leave anything to chance, so he brought plenty of drugs and women with them on the plane. The twelve-hour flight turned into another one of his parties.

"The party on top of the world!" Graham yelled as he popped a bottle of champagne and let the entire contents drip down the body of the naked brunette in front of him.

Ten hours into the flight, Vik checked off two bucket list items at once—a threesome and the mile high club, as he and Graham Eiffel-Towered a blond model.

*I wonder if we're flying over Paris right now,* Vik thought as he came inside of her.

In addition to Vik's friends, Graham had invited several Guardsmen. They spent the weekend in a castle owned by an Architect. The thirty-thousand-square-foot masterpiece was built into the side of the Engadin Alpine valley and spanned seven levels. A grand reception room with forty-foot floor-to-ceiling windows framed the view of the snowcapped mountains. The library walls and ceiling were covered in gold leaf. The suite Vik stayed in had an enormous black onyx master bath with a 360-degree glass shower. The owner of the fortress, an executive of the world's largest private equity firm named Brian, joined in the festivities for the weekend.

On Saturday night, after a long day on the slopes, the group decided to stay in. Graham would bring the party to them. Before their guests arrived, Vik stood by the bank of windows, overlooking the valley beneath him, and truly felt on top of the world.

Graham walked over and placed a drink in one of his hands and a pill in the other.

Vik glanced at the pill, his mouth immediately watering. "Is that the same pill I took at your house?"

"Yup—no better time for you to feel like a king than at your own bachelor party," Graham said.

"Can I, um, I guess I don't exactly know the word . . . can I take another taste again?" Vik asked.

"I handpicked the women just for you, Vik. All of them are Rays."

Vik sat on the couch to relax, readying himself for what he knew would come next. Forty-five minutes later, he started to feel a trickle in his veins, the low thrum of power as darkness coursed through him. He looked around in awe at the women, who were now glowing and glittering like goddesses served up on a platter just for him.

Vik watched one of the men, the young CEO of a social media giant, reach his hand up the thigh of the model straddling him. As he touched her, a cloud of smoke reached out toward her chest. A flash of light pulsed quickly as energy moved from the model to the CEO, and then suddenly, the model shriveled up. Her hair faded to straw. Her skin turned ashen, her life force now gone. The CEO pushed her off his lap and stood up. His eyes were crazed as he turned to speak to the man next to him, another exec at his company. "I just had a genius idea," he said. "Let's go."

It wasn't so much that he'd had a genius idea, Vik realized—genius had *entered* him in that flash of light. He'd taken something from the model that he could use for himself.

Vik glanced around the room, noticing the dozen men with clouds of smoke swirling around them. Some clouds were bigger and darker than others—a direct correlation to the depth of power they held, Vik now understood. Graham's cloud was the most impressive. It was dark as night and extended six feet around him in every direction.

Vik found a mirror and looked at the cloud of smoke swirling around his own body. It was midnight black, but it wasn't very large. It extended a mere inch or two around him. Vik felt a bolt of anger at the recognition that his power was weaker than that of the other men. He would need to fix that.

He walked over to the woman closest to him. She was standing alone and drinking a cocktail. She had auburn hair and impressive legs. Her black minidress left little to the imagination. Before Vik even said hello, his smoke reached out to grab a hold of something inside her chest. It tasted salty, like a Castellano olive. The light in her dimmed, but it didn't go out completely. For some reason, he'd only been able to grab a small piece of her energy, not all of it.

Vik tried again, and the same thing happened.

What the fuck? He wanted more. He thought back to Graham's house, when he'd had the sweet taste of vanilla buttercream frosting coursing through his veins. That woman had opened right up for Vik after he warmed her up.

That was it. He had skipped the foreplay. He took a step back from the auburn-haired woman and offered to get her a new cocktail. When he returned with her drink, he asked her to come join him on the couch. Vik tried again. This time, they talked first. He asked questions about where she was from and how long she'd lived in St. Moritz. She answered, slowly making more eye contact with him as her shyness evaporated. She leaned in toward Vik, and he reciprocated by lightly placing a hand on her thigh. She laughed at a joke he told and moved in closer. He inched his hand higher up. He took his time, slowly building up tension, his hunger now undeniable. He reached higher up, just beneath her dress, and delicately pushed her lace thong out of the way. She breathed in sharply as he traced a slow finger up and down. She was dripping wet. Bingo, he thought. She spread her legs wider, and Vik reached inside of her—both physically and energetically at once. The taste of salt entered every cell of his body as he watched the light in her go out. He closed his eyes and breathed in, letting the energy ripple through him. The high was just as good as the first time.

Vik went back to the mirror. His shadow seemed bigger, but only marginally so. He was pleased. But he needed more.

He looked back around the room. There were at least thirty Rays at the party. He walked up to another woman standing alone—a striking six-foot-tall Ethiopian. She was more reserved than the last woman. It took longer to open her up, but Vik relished the challenge. After her, there was a group of three brunette women, his favorite. Then a petite Korean. As Vik tasted her, he felt the urge to push a politically incorrect thought out of his mind, afraid that someone might hear him. She had the exact bold and spicy flavor of Gochujang sauce.

He felt exhausted and utterly high at the same time, with more power than he'd ever felt circulating through his body. It didn't matter that the power had originated from somewhere else; it was *his* now. He looked in the mirror—the cloud of smoke had definitely grown. He smiled in satisfaction.

It was almost five in the morning by the time Vik had made his way through the Rays. The sun was about to rise over the Alps behind him. The rest of the party was finally dying down as well. He walked into the gold-leafed library, where the bookshelves were made from mahogany dating back to the seventeenth century. Graham stood in the corner near a modern glass case full of awards and trophies.

Vik walked over to him, scanning the contents of the case as he approached. His eyes caught on a large basketball trophy in the middle. He recognized it: the Larry O'Brien Trophy, the one awarded to the team that won the NBA championship.

Brian walked up behind Graham and Vik, patting each of them on the back. "I see you've found my hardware," he said, nodding toward the trophy. "Pretty impressive, isn't it? Nearly sixteen pounds of sterling silver with a twenty-four-karat gold overlay. We won it a few years ago. It was the best night of my life."

Vik's stomach dropped.

## dark days ahead

"I own a stake in the Warriors," Brian continued. "Hopefully we'll win another one this year. What a party, Graham! Do either of you want a coffee?" he asked as he walked toward the kitchen.

They both nodded.

Graham turned to Vik. "Do you understand why I brought you here?"

Vik nodded again. The realization nearly took the air out of him.

Graham said it anyway. "He's your mark. The second act of sacrifice."

# the birth

### Oakland
### Spring 2017

Narina went into labor right on schedule. She woke up on the morning of her baby's due date and felt a splash of water hit her feet while she was brushing her teeth.

"Sam," she yelled, "it's time!"

Narina had known from the moment she saw the positive pregnancy test that she wanted a natural birth, and she'd worked with both a midwife and an OB on her plan. From the beginning, the OB had been annoyed with her. He was annoyed that Narina asked questions, that she advocated for both her and her baby, that she'd opted to work with a midwife. As much as Narina hated the clinical setting of the hospital, she also liked the assurances it provided in the event there were any complications. One of her friends had been so determined to bring her baby into the world naturally that she had decided to give birth swimming alongside dolphins off the coast of Washington. Things didn't go according to plan, and she had to be airlifted by helicopter to Seattle for an emergency C-section. After that, Narina and Sam decided on a water birth inside the safety of a hospital.

Things started smoothly. Her contractions were manageable and coming at regular intervals, but by the evening, she started to feel like something might be wrong. She was in a lot of pain, and it was getting worse.

After twenty hours of labor, Narina's contractions started to intensify, but her cervix still wasn't fully open. The midwife helped her move from the water bath to the hospital bed, suggesting that lying down might help her relax. Shortly after, the midwife called the OB into the room. He did a quick and unnecessarily rough exam, pushing his hand inside of Narina with absolutely no warning.

She cried out in agony. "What the fuck!" she screamed.

The OB ignored her. "We need to do a C-section, now."

Narina tried to remain as calm as possible for the sake of the baby as she replied. "Help me understand what's going on. I'd like to avoid surgery unless it's absolutely necessary."

"It is *absolutely necessary*," the OB spat. "Your cervix isn't opening. The baby is stuck in the birth canal and soon won't have enough oxygen. Time is critical. We need to prep you for surgery now."

"Let me try something first," the midwife interjected, putting her hand on the doctor's arm and pushing him aside. She looked Narina calmly in the eyes as she spoke. "I'd like to do a manual adjustment, if that's okay. It might help the baby start moving and relax your cervix enough for it to fully open. I'll need to reach rather far up and then move the baby. You'll feel a sharp pain that should dissipate quickly. Would you like me to try?"

"Absolutely," Narina replied.

As the midwife reached up and twisted, something happened. The pain was sharp and intense, but Narina felt something else too, like something had shifted at the base of her spine and was now moving slowly up her back, one vertebra at a time. As it rose, it moved in a circular motion, like a coil. The pain intensified, and she saw the head of a snake in her field of vision before a new wave of contractions hit.

"Good!" the midwife yelled in her ear. "The baby is moving now. It will only be a few more minutes—some intense contractions followed by a few pushes."

As Narina labored, she realized she wasn't thinking about the birth at all but rather about her own childhood. Images of her life flashed before her eyes, images she wasn't even aware she remembered until that moment—her mother smiling down at Narina as she held her for the first time, her father whispering in her ear that he would always protect her, her sister handing her a shovel while they built sandcastles on the beach, her high school boyfriend staring down at her as he pushed her hair behind her ear and kissed her neck, her husband locking eyes with her as they shared private vows before their wedding. She was watching a montage of her entire life from above. It was all so beautiful. I was so lucky, she thought, tears streaming down her face.

She was no longer in any pain.

The same energy that was rising up Narina's spine pulled her higher now. And so, she watched from above as she gave birth to her baby girl. Love poured out from every part of her soul as she looked at Sam holding the baby. He was already so in awe of the daughter he had just met.

Then Narina heard the OB yell, "She's losing a lot of blood. Her pulse is too low."

The machine hooked up to her started to beep. She was flatlining. Was she dying?

The doctor and nurses brought over a different machine and pressed it to her chest.

Narina looked down at Sam, at his heart breaking in half as he was torn between worlds: the pure joy of holding his daughter in his arms offset by the terror of his wife dying on the table in front of him.

He pushed his way toward Narina. "Do something! Please, just do anything!" he screamed, looking around at the doctor and nurses in dismay.

Sam kissed their daughter on the forehead and handed her to a nurse, turning his full attention to Narina. Their daughter, Narina thought, smiling. Their daughter.

It hit her suddenly then. Narina stared down, stunned. She had never touched her daughter's beautiful face. She had never looked into her eyes.

No, she thought.

No. No fucking way.

She would not die before she held her daughter.

Anger and love pumped through her veins in equal measure. She yanked against the force pulling her upward; she clawed and fought until she had nothing left. Then everything went black.

And suddenly Narina was no longer watching the scene from above. She was back in her body. Sam was holding her hand and sobbing against her chest.

"I'm sorry," the OB said to him. "There's nothing else we can do."

It's okay, Narina wanted to tell Sam. I'm right here.

But she couldn't talk because something else was in her body with her. Something climbing up her legs, her back, her chest.

She couldn't breathe.

She coughed.

She was suffocating from the heat.

Sam shouted out. "She's burning up!"

The OB ran back and started checking her vitals. "What the hell?" he muttered in confusion. "She's alive!"

Narina felt a searing pain on her wrist and glanced down. She swore she saw the outline of a dragon form in white ink before it disappeared completely.

And then she understood.

*Fire.* She'd transitioned.

The shaman had been right—she had to die to be reborn.

# the liminal

### Oakland
### Spring 2017

By the time Narina's due date approached, the women's lives had pulled them in such different and new directions that the break in their research became a more permanent hiatus. Narina was prepping for life as a mom, Rose was building her new business, and Spencer was getting ready for her move.

Spencer planned to spend the summer traveling before heading to Chicago in the fall for classes. She was in the middle of packing, fantasizing about the distractions her new life might offer, when her phone rang. Narina was calling.

Strange. Even though she talked to Narina and Rose daily, it was always over text or in person. The only reason she'd call would be—

Spencer picked up her phone in a rush. "Oh my god. Hi!"

"I'm a mom!" Narina gushed.

"Tell me everything."

"Sam is holding our beautiful, healthy baby girl as we speak. I honestly can't describe how happy I am right now, but we did have a little bit of a scare. I need to tell you and Rose all about what happened after I recover a bit. Let's plan a night for dinner in a few weeks."

Two weeks later, Spencer and Rose were at Narina's. She glowed as she held her daughter.

"Can I hold her?" Rose asked.

## dark days ahead

"Of course," Narina said. She stood to hand over the baby.

"Are you finally going to tell us what you named her?" Spencer asked.

She didn't understand why Narina had been so cagey about her daughter's name. Narina and Sam had wanted the sex of the baby to be a surprise, so they had chosen two names in advance—a name from Sam's family if they had a boy and a name from Narina's family if they had a girl.

"Yeah, I thought you were going to name her Farah after your grandmother," Rose said. "What happened?"

"That was the plan," Narina said, "but things didn't go exactly as planned."

"So what's her name?" Spencer asked again.

"Maya," Narina said. A small smile formed at the corners of her mouth.

Rose and Spencer raised their eyebrows.

"Like the goddess of illusion?" Spencer asked.

Narina nodded. "Like I said, things didn't go according to plan," she replied, grinning.

Then she started to tell them about her daughter's birth. And her own death.

"Wow," Rose said when Narina finished the story. "Just wow. The thought of losing you is too much to bear—my mind hasn't even started processing the rest of the story yet."

Spencer just stared. "So, it's all real," she said flatly, not a question but a statement.

"Yes," Narina replied.

"Shit."

"I know."

"But if you got your powers after nearly dying, does that mean . . ." Rose couldn't seem to bring herself to finish the question out loud, but Spencer knew they were all thinking the same thing. Did they all have to die to transition?

"I have no idea," Narina replied. "The shaman told me I had to die, but I don't know if there is another way. Maybe that was just my path."

"So, you're a Liminal now?" Spencer asked.

"Yes."

"How do you know?"

"I just know. Plus, I can do this," Narina said.

Nothing seemed to happen at first, but then Spencer felt warmth spread across her face. It reminded her of standing in front of a bonfire.

"Holy fuck," Rose said.

She had felt it too.

"What do we do now?" Spencer asked.

Both Spencer and Narina looked at Rose, waiting for her to give an indication of what she might be comfortable with, given what had happened the last time they'd gone down this path.

"I think we need to take this seriously again," Rose said cautiously. "Let's make a plan."

# the tech

San Francisco
Spring 2017

When they returned to San Francisco, Vik planned to confront Graham in his office and demand answers, but before he had the chance, he opened his phone to a text.

**Graham** Meet me at city hall tomorrow at noon.

The next day, they once again bought tickets for a walking tour, and as the docent brought them through the rotunda, Graham waved a badge in front of the small sensor and pushed the hidden door open.

The scene was the same: hundreds of hospital beds hooked up to monitors, paired with the overwhelming stench of human bodily fluids. The same doctor, the one who had ordered the administration of the lethal dose of fentanyl after running an experiment, stood in the middle of the room. He looked up as Graham and Vik entered and walked over.

"Graham, it's a pleasure as always," the doctor said, reaching out to shake his hand.

"Dr. Grady, I'd like you to meet Vik. We're bringing him into the experiments here. Can you bring him up to speed on the work we're doing?"

Dr. Grady reached out to shake Vik's hand as well. "Of course. It would be my pleasure. Let's head over to my office."

They moved toward the back of the room. As Dr. Grady led the way, they passed a glass wall of windows that separated them from another, larger room. Behind the glass, doctors and nurses were working, reading over notes, and running tests. "This is our lab," Dr. Grady explained, gesturing to his right at the windows. "My office is just over there, down the hall."

He ushered them into his office and shut the door as Graham and Vik sat down. "Where should we start?" he asked.

"Tell him everything," said Graham.

"Wonderful." The doctor turned to look at Vik. "I'll start all the way at the beginning of our work, then. Are you familiar with the experiments done on concentration camp inmates during World War II?"

Vik shook his head.

"The Apparatus was looking for ways to test some of our theories on real subjects. We needed a variety of genetic profiles, so taking individuals at random—kidnapping, you might say—wasn't really getting us the sheer volume of subjects required for a proper sample. And those types of activities were too risky; they made the Apparatus too visible. One of our German Guardsmen, an SS officer who helped design the concentration camps, offered a creative solution. He suggested that the Apparatus purchase inmates from the camps that matched the criteria they needed for testing."

Vik felt sick at the thought. "What exactly were the experiments?"

Dr. Grady turned to Graham. "Does he know about Rays and Liminals?"

Graham nodded in reply.

The doctor turned back to Vik. "We were trying to learn more about their powers. We needed a scientific way to identify Rays and Liminals. We thought maybe they possessed certain traits or biological markers, something unique that would help us understand them or help us learn what triggered the transition."

"Did you find anything?" Vik asked.

"Not exactly. We were chasing our tails. Until one day, when

## dark days ahead

an SS officer walked into the lab after taking a rather large dose of methamphetamine. It's no secret that the Nazis loved popping speed to increase their performance during the war. When the officer entered the lab that day, high out of his mind, he walked around the room, pointing out the Rays and Liminals to the scientists. Apparently, the psychoactive compounds of the drug had activated something in his brain that allowed him to see the energy plane. We realized we didn't need biological markers—we just needed a method to identify Rays and Liminals, and we got it. We spent the next few years perfecting the drug compounds that guaranteed the best results and developed a proprietary blend."

The pill, Vik realized, thinking back to the night at Graham's Sea Cliff home and then at Brian's Swiss chalet.

"As we learned more about Rays and Liminals," Dr. Grady continued, "the next phase of research shifted from identification to treatment. How might we make them weaker? How might we disconnect them from their power? We had some interesting theories, but once the war ended, our readily available supply of test subjects dried up. Over the years, we found other sources of supply, usually near humanitarian conflicts and wars, sometimes ones we initiated for that very purpose. Russian gulags, the Khmer Rouge, the Syrian Civil War, the Rwandan genocide—all of these furthered our interests and provided valuable test subjects. But it was hard to build the state-of-the-art facilities we needed abroad, and it became harder to hide them in plain sight. We needed something here in America that we had full control over, a place that we could use for decades, not just for months during a crisis. So here we are." He gestured at the space around them.

"I don't get it—why set up an operation here and focus on homeless people?" Vik asked. "We have a supply of inmates already in prison—why not use them?"

Dr. Grady shook his head. "We tried prisons, but it turns out criminal behavior and light powers are negatively correlated. Then we studied patients institutionalized at psych wards and mental hospitals, and the results were better than we could have imagined."

Vik stared, waiting for him to explain.

"While correlation between criminal behavior and light power is negative, correlation between mental health issues and light power is shockingly high. As an individual's power intensifies, they experience visions, oneness with God, and superhuman abilities. Their old reality fractures and morphs into something new. They can now interact with a world that no one else can access. Clinically speaking, a doctor will diagnose those powers as delusions, hallucinations, and disordered thinking. At best, it's considered a temporary psychotic break, and at worst, schizophrenia.

"When we started running experiments on these patients, the results were astonishing. Work that had previously taken years could now be accomplished in weeks. In the '90s—when Silicon Valley started to blow up—there was a desire to move the labs closer so that the brightest minds in tech could oversee the experiments."

"So, why not find mental hospitals in the Bay Area?" Vik asked.

"Mental hospitals weren't foolproof, and the administrative procedures put in place became more restrictive. It became harder and harder to make someone 'disappear' when medical records were involved. By definition, a homeless person often lives outside of the system. They are unhoused and have no credit cards or IDs, nothing to prove who they really are. There is the added benefit that homeless people often have mental health issues. It's a filtered subset of the population that meets our exact needs."

"And the fentanyl?" Vik asked, thinking back to the bearded man he'd seen die on the street outside the last time he was here.

"Test subjects with little power are usually allowed to live. Their presence helps maintain our narrative around the homelessness crisis. Before we discharge them, we give them enough crystal meth to induce a prolonged state of psychosis. No one would ever believe anything they said, and they usually can't remember it anyway. Test subjects with heightened powers, though, are seen as a threat. There's always the possibility that if we don't drain their powers fully, they could transition to a Liminal state later. We always take them out."

"With fentanyl?" Vik asked.

"Or a variety of other street drugs. We try to vary the signature to avoid a specific pattern."

"So, is there even really a drug problem in San Francisco, or has it been completely fabricated by the Apparatus as a byproduct of these experiments?"

"You'll learn soon enough that it's often hard to know where narrative ends and truth begins." Dr. Grady shrugged. "By now, it's all rather convoluted—it would be like trying to determine whether the chicken or the egg came first. The work we do here is more important than anything. It's what keeps the Apparatus in power, and it's giving us the tools we need for the Harvest."

Vik was about to ask what the Harvest was when Graham interjected. "Why don't we show Vik an experiment?"

They walked over to a bank of ten hospital beds. Dr. Grady handed each of them a headset to put on, similar in appearance to the VR headsets Vik had seen some of the top tech companies developing.

"We developed these after years of using the pills," the doctor explained. "We needed a way for doctors and nurses to see and measure the light power of their test subjects without having to get high all the time."

Vik put the headset on. It reminded him of the night vision goggles he'd seen the military use. Everything in front of him turned dark except for the energy. Graham and Dr. Grady had a diffused, silvery light surrounding them. The doctor's was small and fixed, extending no farther than an inch around him, but Graham's was nearly two arm's lengths outside of his body, churning in all directions. Vik realized he was looking at the difference in energy between a Guardsman and an Architect.

He looked at the bank of beds in front of him. Each test subject was surrounded by vibrant swirls of green, purple, and blue. The light wasn't static; it moved, shimmering around them. It reminded Vik of the year before, when he had been at Slush, one of the world's biggest startup conferences, held in Finland. He had spent a night at an arctic resort where glass-igloo hotel rooms were built into the snow-covered forest. He had slept under the stars, in awe of the northern lights dancing above him the entire night.

Vik watched as Dr. Grady pulled a small device out of his pocket, the same one Vik had seen him use the first time he was at city hall. The doctor turned the device on. At first nothing happened. Then he slowly started turning a dial in the center of the device. As he moved the dial clockwise, the people on the beds froze, their light freezing with them, as if time had stopped. Dr. Grady moved the dial even farther, and suddenly, in a flash, the light transferred from the people on the beds and moved toward the device, like a vacuum creating an inescapable vortex. The device sucked every ounce of light from them.

Vik's mouth watered. He wanted the power for himself, but Dr. Grady pocketed the device.

"Take care of them," he said to the nurses standing around him.

The nurses began injecting the bodies with syringes filled with what Vik now realized was a random assortment of street drugs. When they finished, security guards came over to roll the beds away.

"I'm impressed," Graham said. "Ten bodies at once—is that the most we've been able to do simultaneously?"

"Yes, ten is the max so far, but it's really a device limitation. We believe it's totally scalable. We're working on a larger one to test out that theory."

"What exactly is the device doing?" Vik asked.

"Siphoning power," Graham said. "Do you remember how exhausted you were in St. Moritz after taking power from a handful of women?"

Vik nodded.

"Human bodies have inherent limitations. Siphoning power drains our energy; we can only hold so much of it at one time. The device can siphon and hold more power than we ever could, and we can draw on it as needed."

"Why do we need to siphon so much power at once?"

"For the Harvest," Graham replied. "We need to harvest energy from millions of people at the same time."

As they walked out of city hall a few minutes later, Vik asked Graham quietly, "What does any of this have to do with Brian and the sacrifice?"

After St. Moritz, Vik had instructed Sven to investigate Brian. Sven could find no reason that the Apparatus would want the man dead. Brian was a hugely successful founder turned investor, working primarily in Africa. While in college at Stanford, he'd founded a hydroelectric power company. After selling the business a decade later, he'd tried his hand on the other side of the table. He'd led an investment to dam the Nile River to power Ethiopia's burgeoning economy, backed a sustainable palm oil plantation in Nigeria, and funded critical infrastructure developments in Kenya. He was so successful that he became a target for Greenpeace activists, who painted him as a greedy investor trying to rule the African continent from a boardroom in New York City.

"There's been an emergence of a new energy pattern coming out of Africa," Graham explained. "It's a new type of power that we're trying to understand. We need to set up labs there for experiments, and we've identified a few villages that meet our criteria. We tapped Brian to execute this vision, but as the work progressed, he got cold feet. Mentally ill patients were one thing, but he said running experiments on healthy women and children was going too far."

"Children?" Vik clarified.

"Yes," Graham said. "Children have the strongest and purest form of power. It's a grim but necessary reality. We need to include them in experiments to develop the tech we need for the Harvest."

Vik swallowed.

Graham continued. "At first, Brian simply refused to complete the work required, but over time, he started to sabotage our efforts by involving government officials and the press. We tried our usual tactics to suppress him, but nothing worked. He's a liability and needs to be taken care of."

Vik felt sick. Experiments on concentration camp prisoners, the mentally ill, and children—he had a hard time stomaching it. He was unsure if he was allowed to ask the question he wanted to. "What happens if I say no? If I refuse to complete the second sacrifice?"

"You won't," Graham replied. "You've experienced the power firsthand. You won't be able to live without it for long. Once you're initiated into the Apparatus and become an Architect, that state of pure power will become your living reality every single day. I know you, Vik. You need power just like I do." He paused, letting that sink in before continuing. "But just in case your conscience decides to get the best of you, we've taken precautionary measures."

Graham took his phone out of his pocket and pulled up an article from a Swiss newspaper. He handed the phone over, and Vik quickly scanned it. A sixteen-year-old girl had been found dead in a St. Moritz resort after she'd been brutally raped.

Vik's stomach dropped as he continued reading. Beneath the article was a photo. It was the Korean woman—no, Korean *girl*, Vik realized, remembering the spicy taste of her. "She—she was alive when I left her," he stammered. "I didn't do this."

"I know," Graham said, "but there are videos of you with her at the party. You were the last person seen with her, and your DNA would certainly be found in the rape kit they administered. If those videos were to make their way into the hands of Swiss authorities, I can't imagine what types of conclusions they'd draw."

Vik was floored, rage rising through him. He'd been set up. The bachelor party, the handpicked Rays, the pill—all of it had just been a ruse to get blackmail on him.

"If you complete the sacrifice and take care of our Brian problem, then this all goes away."

Vik only thought for a second, imagining his career, his upcoming wedding, his entire life gone in an instant as he sat rotting in a Swiss jail. "I'll do it. What do I need to do to complete the sacrifice?"

"You need to eliminate him. I don't care how you do it," Graham said, "but you must do it yourself. The act will complete your initiation into the Apparatus, and you'll take over Brian's seat as an

Architect. Once you transition, you'll be branded with the Mark, and your heightened powers will become a permanent state."

"Branded with the Mark?" Vik asked.

"The Mark," Graham said, pulling his shirt sleeve up.

Beneath his watch was a tattoo Vik had never noticed before. A shark, outlined in what looked like blood.

"Consider it a signet," Graham explained, "an emblem representing the source of your power. It's inked on your skin after the transition. All Architects have one."

Vik nodded.

"You have two months. Good luck," Graham said, and walked away.

# the vow

**Napa Valley**
**Summer 2017**

Before Vik could complete the sacrifice, he had another rite of passage to focus on: his wedding. One year after he officially ended things with Spencer, Vik married Amelia in an intimate ceremony at Meadowood in Napa Valley. He smiled as he watched his beautiful bride walk down the aisle in front of their family and friends, feeling truly grateful for the life he had.

He only thought about Spencer once the whole day. The officiant asked Amelia if she took Vik as her partner in sickness and health, for richer or poorer, to love and to cherish until they were parted by death. Amelia locked eyes with Vik. "I do," she whispered proudly.

The words triggered a memory, and suddenly Vik was no longer at his wedding; he was back in a Miami hotel room with Spencer. They were there for a weekend getaway. The night before, they'd gotten into a dumb fight. They spent the entire next morning in bed—cuddling, talking, kissing, having makeup sex. They were buried under the covers, wrapped around each other for hours. The rest of the world ceased to exist. Vik had finally reached for his phone in the afternoon.

"Holy shit, I have eighty-nine new messages," he said.

"How many do I have?" Spencer asked.

Vik picked up her phone from the nightstand and chuckled. "None."

Spencer balled her hands into fists and theatrically slammed them on the bed. "Does anyone even love me?" she cried out in mock disbelief.

I do, Vik had thought to himself as he looked at her lying next to him. I do. I love you.

# the flow

### San Francisco
### Summer 2017

Rose was out walking with her dog through her favorite section of Golden Gate Park, a hidden path that ran adjacent to the botanical gardens. The last year had been a difficult but productive time for her. She was so absorbed in the life she was building—still in disbelief every morning that she was getting paid to do what she loved—that she had nearly forgotten about Narina's vision altogether until Narina transitioned.

The three of them had agreed to start researching again, but Rose implemented strict boundaries around her involvement, allocating only a few hours each week to it. She had obsessed over the transition once before, and she didn't want to slip back into that place, not when everything in her life was going so well. It was hard at first, her curiosity getting the best of her at times, but work kept her busy and life kept moving along.

That morning, before she left for her walk, Rose had achieved a big career milestone. She had been working with a mentor over the past few months, another coach she admired named Paige. They talked openly about all aspects of their business, and last week at lunch, they had started talking about their fees.

Paige was floored when Rose shared what she charged. "You're not charging enough. By, like, a lot," Paige said.

"What do you mean?" Recently, Rose had looked at her earnings for the year and was pleased to see they nearly matched the salary she'd made at her HR job. She had been hoping to break even and maintain her current lifestyle. She hadn't even considered charging more.

"You need to quadruple that," Paige told her.

"There's no way I can quadruple my rate. Who on earth would pay that much?"

"My clients do," Paige said sincerely. "It's usually coming from a corporate budget anyway, not their own pocket. Just try it. The next time you have a new client, act as if that's your normal rate. See what they say."

Rose stared at her, feeling uneasy.

"Say you'll do it," Paige encouraged.

Rose considered it. What was the worst that could happen? Losing a client? Getting laughed at? "I'll do it," she promised.

So earlier that morning, before heading out for her walk in the park, she had tested it out. She'd had a call with a prospective client, and at the end of the meeting, the woman asked about next steps.

Rose was nervous. She could never quite shake the feeling that she didn't deserve to take up space in the world the way other people did, a leftover remnant of all the years she'd made herself small. Not anymore, she thought.

She shared her rate—three times more than what she had ever charged before. She couldn't quite bring herself to quadruple it, but this would still be a big win.

The woman didn't hesitate. "Great," she said. "What's your soonest availability? I'd love to get started."

Rose had felt a surge of energy after the call and opened her notebook. Journaling had become an outlet for her over the past year, a lifeline when she felt alone. As she started writing, she was surprised to find that what came out was not her typical rambling self-reflections but something that seemed like a story.

A memory came back to Rose of something her mom used to tell her before bed—a story about a caterpillar named Lucy, who lived her life afraid to be herself. Lucy was so exhausted with pretending to be someone she wasn't that one day she gave up and went into a deep sleep. When she woke from her restful slumber, Lucy realized she was never meant to be a caterpillar. She was something else entirely: a butterfly. Rose's mom would say that it was a story her own mother, Rose's grandma, had told her when she was a young girl. And so, Rose wrote about Lucy, partly from memory and partly from flow as new infusions from her own experiences came through.

She finished an hour later and reread the words in front of her. It was a beautiful story. Maybe I'll try to publish the book, she thought as she smiled and closed her journal.

It was with the afterglow of the call and that writing that Rose went out for a walk. She hadn't felt that creative and talented in a long time. As she walked past an old willow tree, one of her favorites in the entire park, she heard a voice she recognized.

"I'm proud of you."

Rose felt her stomach drop. This couldn't be happening again. She tried to block out the voice.

"It's okay, Rose," the voice said. "This time will be different because *you're* different."

Rose glanced up at the tree and saw the outline of her grandma's face. "What do you mean—how am I different?" Rose asked nervously.

"I've been watching you this whole time. I told your mom that story about Lucy so that one day she would tell you. I'm glad you finally remembered it. I tried to tell you in Mexico, but you weren't ready yet. You didn't understand what I was saying."

"Ready for what?"

"Your own power. I love you so much, Rose. Remember, I'll always be with you," her grandma said, and then her face vanished from the bark.

Leaves began to stir on the ground by Rose's feet even though the air around her was completely still. Dozens of birds circled overhead. A single butterfly landed on her cheek, as if to whisper some final clue in her ear.

But Rose didn't need a clue—she knew what to do. She knew it like it was the thousandth time she was doing it instead of the first. She lifted her hands out to the side as she remembered. Wind started to move in every direction, blowing faster and harder. Leaves formed like a tornado around her; she was the vortex. Energy coursed through her body and moved up her spine, unlocking something that had been blocked her whole life. Now unobstructed, it ran all the way from her feet through the crown of her head and up into the air above her. The butterfly flew and landed on her wrist as she held her arms out. It flapped its wings and then dissolved into a cloud of glitter, each speck landing on her wrist in the perfect outline of a butterfly tattoo. The tattoo glowed white momentarily before it was gone completely.

Rose looked up at the sky and let out a little laugh as the realization hit her.

Her grandma had been trying to tell her.

Her power. It had been inside of her all along.

# the sacrifice

San Francisco
Summer 2017

Vik's deadline was approaching, and he felt sick to his stomach. He didn't want to kill anyone, but he did want to keep his life intact. He brainstormed every minute of the day, trying to find another solution. He talked to Sven about deleting the videos of Vik with the woman in St. Moritz and about finding dirt on Graham to blackmail him back—anything instead of the option laid out in front of him. He spent a month looking for a way out of the sacrifice, but he couldn't find any alternative. As more time passed, resignation set in. He had to kill Brian to protect himself, to preserve his own life.

With that certainty, he started to consider how he'd do it. There were obvious methods—a gun or a knife—but any altercation like that required him to overpower Brian physically. Vik's real strengths were mental, not physical. And Brian had five inches and sixty pounds on him.

Then Vik considered an accident, a carbon monoxide leak in Brian's house or cutting the brake line in his car, but accidents left too much room for error. Brian might end up with serious injuries but survive. Vik needed another way.

He remembered when Graham first told him about the sacrifices. "The rest of the path will unfold before you," he had said. Where the fuck is the path? Vik thought as he sat in his office. It was now five days before the deadline, and he felt his frustration and fear growing.

## dark days ahead

Katie popped her head in. She'd taken Amelia's place as Vik's assistant when Amelia left the firm so that they could go public with their relationship. "I'm going to grab lunch—want anything?" she asked.

A chicken salad sounds delicious right now, Vik thought to himself. He opened his mouth to speak, but Katie cut him off. "Chicken salad it is," she said, and walked off.

That was strange, Vik considered. It was like she read my mind.

Then the same thing happened later that day in a meeting with Josh. And again that night with Amelia. Specific moments where, before Vik could speak a response, the person he was talking to seemed to magically read his mind.

He knocked on Graham's office door the next day. "Can we talk?" Graham motioned for him to come in.

"Something strange is happening," Vik said as he shared the mind-reading events of the past day.

Graham nodded. "You're getting close to the transition. Your powers are getting stronger," he explained.

"But how are they reading my mind? Do they have powers too?"

Graham shook his head. "It's your power, not theirs. They aren't reading your mind. You're putting thoughts into theirs."

Vik understood. The path had just unfolded before him.

He stopped by Brian's office later that day over lunch, hoping to catch him in person. He wanted to avoid any paper trail, so texting or emailing were out of the question. Holding a rare box of Cuban cigars, he knocked on the door.

"Hey man, I've been meaning to thank you again for the epic weekend in St. Moritz," Vik said once inside, handing Brian the box.

"Anytime. How have things been? Did you close that deal?" Brian asked. They had talked about it on their trip.

"I did. Things have been going well. I have an interesting deal I'd like to bring you in on, if you're interested. A company based in Africa."

"I'm intrigued. Want to chat now?"

Vik shook his head. "The company is in stealth mode. I'd prefer to speak somewhere more private."

"Stop by my place tomorrow night for a drink then, so you can tell me all about it."

"How's seven o'clock?" Vik asked.

"Sounds great. See you then. We can have one of these," Brian said, holding up the box of cigars.

Vik arrived the following night at Brian's Pacific Heights mansion and parked in front. The eleven-thousand-square-foot, Tudor-inspired design stood in contrast to the rest of the Victorian homes lining Broadway. The house seemed modest in comparison to the castle in St. Moritz. Vik reached into his pocket and pulled out an assortment of pills. In preparation for tonight, he had procured ecstasy, ketamine, and LSD. It was risky; he didn't know the dosage or ratio he would need to reproduce the red pill, but he needed full access to his power for what he was about to do.

He downed the pills in one gulp and placed a tab under his tongue. Other than the drugs, Vik had arrived empty-handed. If his plan worked, he wouldn't need a weapon to kill Brian. In fact, he wouldn't have to lay a finger on him at all. He waited until he felt the thrum of power from the drugs begin to course through his veins, then walked up to Brian's front door.

Brian escorted Vik to his home office, a small, cozy room decorated with lots of leather and dark wood. His desk faced a panoramic view of the Golden Gate Bridge.

He poured them each a glass of whiskey, and they started talking shop. On the surface, Vik was telling Brian about a drone company he was looking at investing in that would revolutionize delivery in Africa. Just like Africa had skipped over generations of legacy technology like landlines and banks with the advent of smartphones and mobile payments, so too would they bypass the need for massive physical infrastructure development with the introduction of drones.

But while they talked about the deal, Vik was thinking about something else entirely. He imagined the blood of African children dripping from his hands. He envisioned looking into the eyes of crying mothers living in poverty as he flew on his private jet. He felt deep self-loathing for the greed and power that had driven his actions, a hatred so deep that he no longer deserved to live. He thought about the letter he'd leave for his family, explaining why he couldn't go on anymore; the pain was too unbearable. He built up the images and emotion until they were so large that they threatened to overwhelm him.

Then, with every fiber of power in his body, he pushed the thoughts into Brian's mind.

The two men talked for a few more minutes, and then Brian stood up. "I'm sorry, Vik. I'm suddenly not feeling well. Can we finish this conversation later?" he asked.

"Of course. I'll reach out to you next week, and we can pick it up then. I hope you feel better, man."

After leaving, Vik sat in his car for a few hours, waiting. Finally, a little after midnight, he felt a sensation move through him, something uncoiling around his spine. Then a blast of power hit him as a cloud of midnight smoke enveloped him.

He'd transitioned.

A searing pain shot through his arm. He looked down at the blood red ink branding his wrist.

The Mark of a wolf.

That Sunday, Vik picked up a copy of the paper and read the headline.

*The Life and Death of a Master of the Universe:*
*Billionaire Investor Found Dead in His Pacific Heights Home*

According to the article, Brian Nash's body had been discovered by his maid early Friday morning. Police had found him hanging from a chandelier with a note near his body, a suspected suicide.

As Vik finished reading, he thought back to the final thought he'd slipped into Brian's mind just before he walked out the front door: an image of a red rope followed by an image of the chandelier in his foyer.

Shit, Vik thought as the gravity of his power hit him. He could manipulate minds.

The following Sunday, Vik saw another article, hidden further in the paper, at the bottom of the first page of the sports section. He read the headline.

> *Golden State Warriors Welcome New Minority Shareholder:*
> *Midas List investor Vikram Agarwal purchases stake in the*
> *coveted franchise following Brian Nash's untimely death*

# the return

San Francisco
Summer 2019

It had been nearly two years since Spencer had been back in San Francisco. She still talked to Narina and Rose regularly, still spent her free time researching the Apparatus, but she had made the conscious decision to keep her distance for a while, hoping that it might help her finally move on from Vik.

Spencer had thought going to business school might be a way to reclaim her power, but what she found there—not power, but the quiet desperation of those searching for it—only depressed her more. Watching Narina and Rose both step into their own abilities in quick succession while Spencer remained powerless herself added another source of pain. She left business school $250,000 in debt, twenty pounds heavier, and none the wiser.

She debated moving back to New York when she finished school, but she loved her life in San Francisco and missed her friends. She knew that leaving to escape the memory of Vik had been just one more way in which she'd abdicated her power to him.

She moved back to San Francisco after graduation, landing a job at a small startup in the burgeoning blockchain space and moving into a light-filled corner apartment in Pacific Heights, around the corner from Alta Plaza Park. Coming back on her own terms seemed to finally dissolve the dark cloud lingering around her, and slowly but surely, Spencer started to come back to life.

Instead of the bleak futility of nothingness that had enveloped her over the past few years, Spencer now felt like an empty cup, ready to be filled. This is my chance at a fresh start, she thought to herself as she woke up one morning in August.

Her phone vibrated on the nightstand next to her. Her stomach dropped. The text was from Vik. They hadn't talked at all in the nearly three years since they'd broken up. After she had seen photos of his wedding, she'd blocked him on social media. It was too hard to watch him move on. By now, Vik was a stranger to her, a ghost that still haunted her dreams but no longer took up much space in her waking hours.

Hey! It's been a minute. I heard you're back in the bay! Coffee soon?

She wanted to say no. She hated him for how he had treated her, but she couldn't.

I'm back! Blue Bottle in Pac Heights on Saturday?

She could have punched herself for what popped into her head next. I wonder if he's divorced, she thought.

He wasn't. Vik was still married, living with his wife in a beautiful home in Atherton. His first child, a daughter, had been born in the spring. Spencer learned all of this when she sat across from him that Saturday morning.

As she held back tears, Vik took a sip from his almond milk latte. Dairy had always upset his stomach.

It was like he had reached out to her just to rub it all in her face. As if their history meant absolutely nothing to him. As if she meant absolutely nothing to him.

*Nothing.* She was nothing. She didn't exist. That feeling she had experienced throughout her life popped back up to the surface.

But then, completely out of nowhere, an image appeared in Spencer's mind. It was just a flicker, but she recognized it. She was a little girl, maybe five years old, wearing a pink leotard and a ballerina skirt. She was dancing in her family room, full of vibrancy, full of life. Not nothing, Spencer thought as she watched her younger self. That little girl dancing was something special. As if on cue, the girl turned and looked at her.

## dark days ahead

"Hi, I'm Spencer!" she said as she curtsied. Adult Spencer reached out her hand, and little Spencer stepped forward. As their palms touched, she felt a ripple of energy, and the girl dissolved into her. It was like she had finally reclaimed some long-abandoned part of herself.

Spencer was *someone*. She let that thought sink in before she looked back up at Vik.

I'm someone special. Who the hell are you? she thought to herself in indignation as she stared at him.

The corners of her vision began to blur, and a hazy fog spread to the center. For a minute, she couldn't see at all, but when her vision came back, she was looking at something else entirely. It was the same coffee shop, but everything was different. It was all more alive—humming and vibrating. All the feelings she'd numbed out as a kid came rushing back in, speaking to her in a language only she could understand. They whispered up her spine. "Look," they said. "Look at him."

Spencer looked up at Vik. The skin on his face had disappeared. She stared at the blood and tendons in its place and had the distinct feeling that she was glimpsing a monster with his mask removed. Vik was talking to her as if everything were normal, as if they were still having the same conversation as before. He didn't know what Spencer could see.

As he spoke, a gray plume advanced from his body and moved toward her. The tendril of smoke reached into her chest, broke off a small piece of her heart, and placed it back in his hollow chest, where his own heart should have been. The piece clicked into place, and the gray cloud lightened a shade, brightened by what he'd stolen from her. Then the smoke reached back out to her again.

He was coming back for more, Spencer realized.

Before she could think, her body reacted. It knew how to protect itself. Something clenched deep inside of her. She felt movement along her spine as if a caged animal was suddenly breaking free. Energy moved up through her, sprouting out from the crown of her head and down around her as a bubble of safety enclosed her. She looked in awe at the shield of glittering armor now surrounding her.

This time, as Vik's cloud of darkness reached back out to grab a piece of her again, it hit the shield and the smoke fizzled out.

Spencer felt pain on her wrist and looked down. Is that an owl? she thought, looking at the tattoo that formed in glittering white ink before it disappeared.

She told Vik she felt sick and left the coffee shop without another word. She pulled out her phone.

**Spencer** I just met Vik for coffee

**Rose** OMG how was it?

**Narina** Is he still jerking off to billionaires?

**Spencer** I transitioned in front of him

**Narina** Well shit

**Rose** What's your power?

**Narina** Not over text, come to my house tonight

Spencer wasn't sure what her power was. Was it some type of energy vision or the ability to protect herself with a shield?

It was both, she realized. While Spencer was the last of the three to get her powers, she was the first to experience the wholeness of their gifts. It turned out the powers weren't singular—rather, like everything else in nature, they had duality.

# the power

San Francisco
Summer 2019

As they sat around Narina's dining table that evening, Spencer recounted what had transpired at the coffee shop earlier.

"Why do you think Vik reached out to you in the first place?" Rose asked.

"I'm embarrassed to admit that when I first saw his name pop up, I thought he might be divorced."

Rose nodded. "For the record, that's a totally normal response."

"But he's not divorced," Narina interjected. "He cut you off completely when you broke up, so why did he reach out now?"

Spencer thought back to the way Vik's smoke had tried to grab a piece of her, and she heard Cynthia's words about a narcissist's source of supply. "It sounds weird, but I think he wanted to feed off my energy."

"Sounds like he could be part of the Apparatus himself," Narina quipped.

"Don't even joke about that," Spencer said. "I'm finally over him. I can't handle any more Vik-related trauma."

"Fine," Narina said. After a moment's pause, she changed course. "So, we've all transitioned. We're all Liminals."

"I guess so," Spencer said.

Rose was grinning from ear to ear. "I'm so happy for you, Spence."

Spencer smiled too. Rose's good energy was always contagious.

"It's cool that you have two aspects to your power," Narina said. "I wonder why Rose and I only have one."

Spencer shook her head. "We all have two aspects."

"What makes you think that?" Narina asked.

"I don't think it. I just know it. I can't explain why. We just need to figure out how to activate yours."

"Did you do anything to activate your second power?" Rose asked.

"I'm not even sure which one is my 'first' or 'second' power—I don't think that's the right way to think about it. They both sort of happened naturally. First, I used my vision to see what Vik was doing, then I dropped a shield to protect myself from it. It was like a balancing weight on a scale, like once I could see what was happening, then I could respond to it. I know that it seems like two separate powers, but when it happened, the powers felt *whole*, like the one only existed in relation to the other."

"Now that you have vision, if I use my powers on Rose, will you be able to see what's happening on the energy plane?" Narina asked.

"I think so."

"Okay, let's try that. Maybe you can see something that we don't realize is happening, and it will give us a clue."

"That's a good idea," Rose said.

They went into the backyard, and Spencer watched as Narina stood in front of Rose and raised her arm. Rose took a step forward, and Narina blasted her with a furnace of heat.

"Ouch!" Rose yelled.

Narina laughed. "Oops."

"Wait a minute," Spencer said. "Do it again."

As Narina raised her hand once more, Spencer tapped into her own power, activating the vision that allowed her to see the energy plane. This time, as Narina looked at Rose, Spencer saw a shimmering flame reach out, like a beckoning finger. Rose took a step forward, and Narina struck her with fire again.

"Rose," Spencer said, "why did you step toward Narina before she blasted you?"

Rose gave her a blank look. "I'm not sure. I didn't realize I had."

"Narina"—Spencer turned toward her—"why did you call Rose closer to you?

Narina furrowed her brow. "I wasn't calling her to me," she said. "I just wasn't sure if I could reach her. I wished she was standing a little closer, and then, suddenly she was."

Spencer explained to them what her vision had revealed. "You pulled her to you," she said, "like a moth to a flame."

"That makes perfect sense. The dual aspect of your power is your magnetism," Rose said. "You can draw people to you before you burn them alive."

Narina smiled. "That's pretty cool. Now your turn."

Rose turned to face Narina. She put her hand out beside her and summoned the energy of the air around her. Spencer felt a breeze touch her skin but didn't notice anything unusual.

"Hmm, didn't see anything. Maybe try again, and this time call on more of your power?"

As Rose looked at Narina again and clenched her fists, Spencer saw two small butterflies rise from behind Rose's shoulders. One butterfly went up to Narina, and the other came over to her. The butterflies each shook a wand filled with what looked like fairy dust over their heads. As the dust landed on her face, Spencer felt her power intensify. The dust had magnified something inside of her. When Rose struck this time, the wind took Spencer's breath away.

"Shit, that's impressive," Narina said, struggling to breathe.

"What were you thinking about before you wielded?" Spencer asked.

"Well," Rose said, "I always feel the most powerful when I'm helping other people, so when you said to make my power stronger, that's what I thought about."

Spencer told them what she'd seen, how Rose had given them some of her power first.

"Of course! You selfless bitch," Narina muttered, "your power multiplies when you give some of it away. It boomerangs back to you even stronger."

Spencer smiled, thinking about how perfectly each of their powers matched their true nature.

# the taste

San Francisco
Summer 2019

Since Vik had become an Architect, he had tasted hundreds of Rays, but he'd still never witnessed anyone glow quite like Spencer had at Graham's party. He often found himself wondering what she might taste like, so when he heard that Spencer had moved back to the city, he couldn't help himself—he reached out.

The morning they planned to meet for coffee, Vik took a little bit of his special concoction: his homemade version of the red pills. He had long since abandoned his need for control in favor of clarity. He liked to *see* the way he influenced the energy around him, not just feel it. The drugs gave him that sight, and he took them more often than he liked to admit. He'd heard the term "chasing the dragon" used in reference to drugs, the elusive pursuit of the first-time high. Vik didn't feel that way about the drugs themselves—they were a nice purifier that refined his senses. The real high came from the power. Nothing could compare to the way a Ray tasted on his tongue, the way their glitter coursed through his veins. That was the dragon Vik sought every time.

When Spencer first walked into Blue Bottle, Vik was disappointed to see that her glow had diminished. She was still alive, but it was as if someone had hit the mute button and turned down the volume of her radiance. But even in her diminished state, she was still the brightest Ray he'd ever encountered. There was a part of Vik that didn't want to touch her. He wanted to keep her in this pristine state of luminosity forever.

## dark days ahead

Until his mouth started watering.

Just a little bit, he thought to himself as a plume of his shadow reached toward her. He grabbed a piece of her. The flavor wasn't strong, but it was delicious. It was rich and creamy, with hints of sweetness and earthiness. Images of Spencer naked in bed, his head between her thighs, came rushing back into Vik's mind. Was that avocado? he wondered as he reached back out for more.

This time, though, as his smoke reached Spencer's body, it fizzled out on contact. What he saw next almost knocked him off his chair. The same snake he had seen coiling around her spine when she orgasmed on top of him at the party was again rising through her body. It slithered from the lower part of her stomach all the way to her head, a giant cobra that grew bigger the higher it traveled. The snake was lit up, glowing from the inside, with fast-moving currents of green and purple lights. When it arrived at the crown of her head, it burst open. Millions of tiny, glittering flecks landed on Spencer, her entire skin covered by shimmering scales. Light moved and danced around her. She was so bright he almost couldn't look at her, but he couldn't take his eyes off her either.

A white owl landed on her wrist and then merged with her body before completely disappearing. The glow around her didn't dissipate.

Then the realization hit him. Spencer had just transitioned in front of his eyes. She was now a Liminal. The owl was the Liminal version of her Mark.

She left in a rush. After that, Vik couldn't get a thought out of his head, something he'd seen in her when she transitioned that unnerved him.

Spencer was more powerful than he was. But not for long.

# the memory

### New York City
### December 12, 2030

The last time Spencer had seen Vik before running into him that morning was a decade earlier, at another coffee shop across the country. It seemed so obvious to her now in hindsight. Of course Vik had been an Architect that day. She had seen the dark shadows around him. She had glimpsed the monster behind the meatsuit. But whenever she had thought back to her transition, she'd always been so focused on her own power. Any time she considered Vik's role in it all, Cynthia's words would pop into her head, and Spencer would chalk his behavior up to that of a narcissist looking for a fix. Her brain had always glossed over one critically important detail: Vik had power too.

When Spencer walked into the wine bar to meet him, he was already there, sitting in the corner secluded from the rest of the patrons, with a candle lit on the table in front of him. Great—cozy and intimate was just what she needed.

Vik stood as Spencer approached. Unsure of how to greet each other, they exchanged a glance and took their seats.

"It was such a pleasant surprise to run into you earlier today," Vik said. "I wasn't sure you'd show up tonight."

"Neither was I."

"What made you come, then?" Vik asked, tilting his head slightly to the side.

"Curiosity."

"You know what they say about curiosity . . ."

A threat.

"Let's order," he said.

They each took a second to quickly scan the menu on their Orbs, then placed their orders. A waitress brought their drinks over a few minutes later.

Spencer surveyed the man sitting in front of her. It sank in—*a man*. Even though Vik had been thirty years old when they dated, Spencer had always thought of him as a boy. The boy she fell in love with. The boy who broke her heart. But he was no longer a boy. She'd noticed it over the years when she saw articles about him or listened to him on podcasts—the way he had slowly morphed, the way he had matured. His power had matured too.

Spencer shivered.

But she had grown up too. She was no longer the invisible woman who wondered if she existed in the world. When she'd dated Vik, she'd desperately wanted an identity, a place to belong. She thought she'd finally found someone to make her whole. But Vik hadn't done that, Spencer had. At the lowest point in her life, when everything else had fallen away, there was only one thing left: her power. The power that had brought her back to life.

She looked at him again, and this time, instead of feeling scared of the power she felt emanating from him, she decided to match it. She let her stomach relax, unclenched her jaw, and allowed her energy to flow. Her shield came out around her, a shimmering bubble of protection. The black smoke around Vik tried to reach out and grab a piece of her, but as the smoke hit her shield, it fell away. He tried again and again, sometimes fast, sometimes slow. A caress, then a whisper. Every time, he met the same resistance.

"I'm impressed," Vik said.

Spencer remained impassive.

"Let's quit pretending, Spence. We both know why we're here."

Spencer paused, not wanting to show her hand first.

"I know who you are. Or rather, *what* you are. I've known for a long time."

Vik was about to continue, but Spencer cut him off. "Yes," she said, "a lot longer than I realized. You knew that day we met for coffee. You had already transitioned by then."

He nodded.

"And you tried to steal my power from me," Spencer added, her voice now carrying an edge.

"I couldn't help myself. I didn't have the restraint I do now. But I was never going to steal it. I just wanted to taste it."

Spencer shook her head in disgust.

"I know my past actions might indicate otherwise," Vik continued, "but I don't want to see you get hurt. I can't imagine you dying. That's why I invited you here tonight, Spence. You think you can stop the Harvest, but you can't. You're not strong enough, even with the network you've built. You're no match for the technology the Apparatus has developed. You don't stand a chance of winning, not without my help."

Spencer felt confused. His help? "Like I would trust you to help us."

"I helped you once before," Vik said.

He'd helped her? When?

He stared at Spencer, imploring her with his eyes to understand. Then the smoke reached back out, but this time, it didn't reach toward Spencer's heart. It went for her head instead. She realized he wasn't trying to take anything; he was trying to give her something. She hoped she wasn't making a terrible mistake as she let down her shield.

Suddenly, she was lost in a memory, but it wasn't *her* memory. She looked down and saw Vik's brown hands. He was looking through a door at Spencer, Rose, and Narina lying in hospital beds—their arms strapped down, their bodies sedated, their powers neutralized. He entered, walked up to Spencer, and whispered something in her ear. Then he slipped something into her pocket before he left.

"You were there? You saw us?" Spencer asked, looking deep into Vik's eyes, searching for the truth.

He nodded.

Her mind was racing. She had thought she was going to die that day. She had never really known how she'd gotten out.

Her heart stopped as two realizations hit her at once.

Vik had just inserted a memory into her head. He had the power to manipulate minds.

And he'd helped her escape all those years ago. Vik had saved her life.

# stage four / slope of enlightenment

# the warning

### San Francisco
### Winter 2019

Spencer's transition was the tipping point. Before that, they'd still thought of the whole thing as a vision, a possibility. But afterward, it became something more concrete: a destiny.

The future Narina saw was now half-true, which meant it was only a matter of time before the rest of it materialized. A battle with the Apparatus loomed in their future.

They spent their free time at Narina's house, practicing. They wielded their powers on each other, learning how to turn them on and off and adjust their strength. Their research picked up a feverish intensity. Despite their hard work, it seemed like every step forward with their powers was met with an equal step backward in their research. They were still no closer to learning about the Apparatus or the Harvest.

One night, Spencer left work and walked to an Indian restaurant a few blocks away. She was meeting Rose at Narina's house for dinner and had offered to pick up takeout from their favorite place on her way. She left the restaurant with two bags of the best curry in the city and turned right to walk up Market Street.

A homeless man with a blanket wrapped around his shoulders and unzipped pants hanging down around his waist ambled toward her. He was talking to himself, clearly on some sort of drugs. Spencer slowed down and moved closer to the buildings, hoping to inch her way out of his line of sight. She hated that her natural reaction was to move away from him, but there had been too many stories of strung-out people doing crazy things.

He looked up and made eye contact before she could look away. "Be careful or they'll kill you," he said, leering at Spencer as he walked closer to her.

She noticed a syringe in his hand, blood mixed with the other liquid in the vial. She started to run. Right as she turned the corner, she heard him yell from behind her.

"Watch out! The Apparatus is going to kill you!"

"Why didn't you go back and talk to him?" Narina demanded when Spencer told them the story over dinner.

"Why didn't I go back and talk to someone high on god knows what, standing in front of me with his dick hanging out and a needle in his hand? Geez, I don't know," Spencer retorted.

"Fair point."

They sat in silence for a minute. They'd talked to hundreds of people, and no one had ever heard of the Apparatus. No one except a homeless man walking down Market Street. They needed to find out whatever they could from this man, Spencer realized.

"We need to find him," Narina said, as if reading her mind. "All of us will go together. He's our only lead."

Rose, Narina, and Spencer spent the next two weeks walking up and down Market Street and the surrounding blocks every night after work. Spencer had even drawn a sketch of the man from memory. They talked to every homeless person in the area, offering food and drinks in exchange for some of their time, showing the sketch, and asking if anyone had seen the man. A few recognized him, but no one knew where he was now.

"That's Paulie," a man said.

"He's batshit crazy," a woman shared. "What do you want with him?"

They even started asking about the Apparatus, wondering if

others might have heard about them or, at the very least, heard Paulie talking about them.

They walked up to a woman who looked like she was the same age they were, her head poking out from a small tent. Inside were two candles, a book, and a stuffed animal.

A home, Spencer thought. She has a home. Why do we call them homeless? From her smell and her knotted hair, Spencer could tell it had been weeks since the woman had showered, but underneath the grime, she was beautiful.

"Have you seen this man?" Narina asked, holding up the sketch.

The woman shook her head. Her pupils were dilated.

"Okay, thanks."

"Am I in heaven or hell?" the woman asked as the three of them were about to walk away.

"Neither," Rose replied gently, "you're in San Francisco."

"I thought dragons were only in hell," the woman said.

Spencer froze, wondering whether it was just a coincidence that the tattoo on Narina's wrist was a dragon. She glanced over at Narina and Rose, who seemed to be thinking the same thing.

"What do you mean?" Rose asked.

"The Fire One," the woman said pointing at Narina. "She's a dragon."

The words felt familiar to Spencer. Where had she heard them before?

Narina inched closer to the woman, looking her up and down. Her eyes widened. "That's not possible," she stammered. "The last time I saw you, you were . . ."

Then Narina fainted.

# the lead

### San Francisco
### Winter 2019

Spencer held Narina up as Rose ordered a ride to take them back to Narina's house. Narina had regained consciousness, but Spencer was worried she might be concussed from the fall.

"No, we can't leave," Narina slurred. "We have to talk to her."

"We can come back tomorrow," said Rose.

An hour later, once Narina had fully regained her faculties in the safety of her home, she turned to Rose and Spencer. "That was her," she said.

"Who?" Rose asked.

"The old woman I saw when I did ayahuasca. She came out running toward me and said, 'You look exactly the same, Fire One.' I remember her."

Only it wasn't a memory, Spencer realized. It was a vision of the future.

"It's the same woman," Narina continued. "I'm sure of it."

Spencer believed her.

"We'll go back and talk to her tomorrow," Rose said, seemingly on the same page. "We'll find out everything she knows."

The woman's tent was in the same place, zipped up tightly, when they returned the next day.

"Knock knock," Narina said out loud, in lieu of any hard surface to physically knock on.

## dark days ahead

The woman unzipped the tent and peered out. "I knew you'd be back," she said, smiling.

"Can we take you to dinner? We'd love to ask you some questions."

The woman nodded. "I'm Mira," she replied.

They walked to a diner around the corner. The host was clearly irritated that they'd brought in a homeless woman, but he couldn't turn them away. "Right this way," he said, ushering them to a booth hidden in the back, away from the eyes and noses of the other guests.

They each introduced themselves and ordered drinks and dinner.

Spencer couldn't wait for the food to arrive to find out what Mira knew. "Do you know anything about a group called the Apparatus?" she asked.

Mira shook her head. "Never heard of them."

"Why did you call her Fire One? And a dragon?" Rose asked.

The woman laughed. "Well obviously because she is. That's a silly question."

"What do you mean, *she is*?"

"She has fire coming out of her, and she has that dragon tattoo on her wrist." Mira pointed.

Narina's tattoo had disappeared as quickly as it had appeared on the day her daughter was born. The only one who could see it now was Spencer, when she activated her vision power.

"You can see her tattoo right now?" Spencer asked.

Mira nodded.

"Do you see any other tattoos?" she prodded.

"Of course—she has a butterfly and you have an owl."

Spencer was floored. How was it possible Mira could see the tattoos?

"What do you see when you look at us?" Spencer asked.

"She has bright blue skies around her," Mira said, pointing at Rose. "And you're like a stone covered in green moss," she said, looking at Spencer now.

Spencer couldn't believe it. Mira was seeing the same energy patterns Spencer saw with her powers—the layer of vision that allowed her to see beyond the naked eye.

No one spoke.

"I know you probably think I'm crazy," Mira said. "Everyone else does. People want me to pretend that I see something different, something 'normal,' but I don't know how to. This is just what I see."

Spencer noticed Narina looking at Mira's arm. She fixed her own gaze there to get a better look and saw what had caught Narina's attention: track marks.

"Is that why you do that?" Narina asked, pointing. "Because people think you're crazy?"

Mira shook her head. "No, not exactly."

"Why do you do it then?" Narina asked gently.

"I can't really explain it. I don't understand how this happened. One day, I had a life somewhere, a family. Then the next thing I remember, I was in a hospital. Doctors were examining me and running tests. I asked why they had clouds of black smoke around them. After that I'm not sure what happened, but I woke up in a tent on the street, confused and craving something. There were syringes lying next to me, and I realized that's what I was craving. I picked one up and put it in my arm, and, well, here I am."

She shook her head as she continued. "I know that sounds like I'm not taking responsibility, but one day I was normal, and the next day I was an addict living in a tent. I don't know how I got here. I've tried talking to people, asking them to borrow a phone and to help me find my family. I even tried talking to the police, explaining what had happened. The more I tried to talk to people, the crazier they all thought I was, so eventually, I just gave up." Mira looked down at her hands, tears welling in her eyes. "Can you help me? Please, can you help me?"

Narina, Rose, and Spencer looked at each other.

"We'll help you," Narina said. "We'll help you get clean. We'll help you find your family."

Narina found a rehab center near her home in Oakland, and the three of them agreed to cover the cost of the ninety-day program.

## dark days ahead

Rose took Mira shopping for new clothes and toiletries. Spencer went through thousands of notices for missing women across the country, trying to help find her family.

They visited Mira every Saturday during open hours at the rehab center. Spencer was pleased to see the progress she was making. When they first brought her in, the doctor said she had heroin and crystal meth in her system. The withdrawal was incredibly painful, but Mira was doing well.

The doctor warned them, though, that she was at a delicate inflection point. "Recovery is a long road. She's doing great, but she needs time to heal. She's struggling to remember what happened. It's probably her body's way of avoiding the pain that triggered her to reach for drugs in the first place. I'd ask that you honor her recovery by avoiding these triggers. Help her stay distracted for the time being. Don't bring up the past unless she does."

Spencer nodded, reluctantly. She understood the importance of Mira's recovery, but she was growing frustrated with the lack of progress they were making in their research. The doctor had made it clear, though—they'd have to wait until Mira finished the full rehab program before they could ask her anything. Spencer waited patiently each visit, secretly hoping Mira would mention something—anything—that might help them find the Apparatus.

"I had a flashback," Mira said on their third visit.

Spencer perked up.

Mira looked down. "Sorry to get your hopes up—it wasn't about the doctors with black smoke around them. It was about my life before."

"That's okay," Rose said, taking her hand. "What do you remember?"

"I was in a hospital bed. Light was streaming in the window, and I had a wristband on. I could see the name printed on it: Ascension Hospital. A nurse stood next to the bed, holding a crying baby. Then she handed the baby to me. It was a boy. I was so happy."

"Colin," Narina said, her voice almost a whisper.

A look of recognition struck Mira, and tears instantly began streaming down her face. "Colin," she repeated. "*Colin*. Yes, the baby's name was Colin." She turned to Narina in disbelief. "How did you know?"

"It's hard to explain," Narina said. "I didn't want to bring anything up until you were ready, but I saw you in a dream once. You were much older than you are now, and you were living with your son, Colin. I'm so sorry I didn't remember it sooner. I forgot that part of the vision until you mentioned a baby boy just now."

Spencer was disappointed she hadn't put it together sooner herself. She had been so focused on learning about the Apparatus that she'd failed to remember the other details of Narina's vision. She wrote down the name of the hospital and the son. "I'll look into it as soon as I get home and let you know if I find anything," she told Mira.

Mira nodded, still crying, but Spencer saw her smile through the tears. Her first real smile since they'd met her.

With the name of the hospital and Mira's son, Spencer's search took less than a minute. She found an article from *The Tennessean*, published March 13, 2019. She quickly scanned the contents.

A woman named Charlotte Evans had been missing since early March. She had given birth to a son, Colin, on January 21 at Ascension Hospital. Her husband, Sean, reported that shortly afterward, Charlotte had started to show symptoms of postpartum depression and psychosis. She had been treated in a medical facility but was released after a few days.

Then on March 6, Charlotte had disappeared. There were reports of a woman matching her description walking on the side of the road, naked and yelling. One report said that she appeared manic and delusional. By the time the police had arrived on the scene, the woman was gone.

The article included a picture of Sean holding a newborn Colin in his arms outside of the hospital. Mira was standing next to them, beaming with pride.

Spencer texted a link of the article to their thread.

**Spencer**  What do we do?

**Rose**  Holy shit
Should we call the police?

**Narina**  NO!
We still don't know how she ended up here
I don't trust the police
Let's talk to Mira first and see what she wants to do

Spencer printed out the article and handed it to Mira the next day. She'd never seen a mixture of joy and sadness quite like what she witnessed when the woman sobbed in elation.

"This is my family," she said, stunned. Then confusion set in. "I don't remember him," she said, pointing at her husband.

Mira didn't want to call the police. She wanted Spencer to find her husband and talk to him directly. "Ask him to come here," she said. "Tell him I'm okay and that I'll explain everything in person, at least the parts I can."

Sean Evans flew to Oakland the next morning and met Narina, Rose, and Spencer in the lobby of the rehab center. They told him everything they knew, leaving out the parts about their powers and the Apparatus.

"Look, it's really hard to explain in any way that will make sense," Narina said, "but your wife is telling the truth. She's not crazy. Something happened to her, and we're trying to figure out exactly what that was."

Sean nodded. "I believe you. I tried to tell the police she'd been abducted, but they wouldn't listen. They said her mental state at the time of her disappearance pointed to a runaway."

"Why did you think she was abducted?" Spencer asked, perking up.

"Weird things started happening the days before she disappeared. She started seeing lights around people—'a halo of shimmering light,' she told me. She thought she was in heaven. Then one day, she saw a man with a dark cloud of smoke swirling around him, and she believed she'd gone to hell. I wasn't sure what to do, so I took her to the doctor. He admitted her into the psych ward and said she was experiencing a type of postpartum psychosis that caused delusions. He wanted to keep her there for two weeks. I was reluctant to admit her, but he warned that in this state, she could be a threat to our son. I'll never forget his words: 'This is the type of state where a woman can drown her baby in the bathtub because she thinks the child is a doll.' I didn't feel like I had a choice, so I followed his recommendations. But two days later, the hospital discharged her. I was confused why the doctor, who had just told me a two-week stay was necessary, now deemed her well enough to go home, but I didn't argue. I wanted my wife back."

Halos of shimmering light, clouds of darkness, and a psychosis diagnosis—Spencer suddenly felt grateful for the knowledge she'd had about Liminal powers *before* she transitioned. She hadn't exactly been prepared for the energy vision, and it certainly caught her off guard, but she had understood what was happening to her. Mira hadn't been so lucky.

"Once I got her home," Sean continued, "Mira told me that while at the hospital, she'd overheard conversations between her doctor and another man. The two of them talked about including Mira as a subject in experiments. The man told the doctor to discharge her first. Then they would pick her up for the experiments. The next thing Mira knew, a nurse sedated her. Once she was home, she became convinced that someone was following her. Then suddenly, she disappeared. The police barely even launched an investigation. They were so convinced that she had lost her mind that they wouldn't take anything she'd said about the doctor or the other man seriously."

Sean paused, looking down at his hands and breathing heavily. "I feel like this is all my fault," he said. "I should have trusted her and never admitted her to that hospital."

## dark days ahead

"I have a daughter," Narina said empathetically. "There are no limits to what I'd do to protect her. You had an impossible choice to make."

"Mira's safe now. That's all that matters," Rose added.

Sean smiled at the name. "She forgot everything about her life," he said, "but she remembered that she hated being called Charlotte. Only her family and closest friends call her Mira."

Only Mira didn't remember her family, or at least she didn't remember her husband. "Sean," Spencer said, "we should warn you. Mira's memory hasn't come back fully. She remembers Colin, but other parts of her life are still a blur. Whatever they did to her, it really messed with her mind."

Sean nodded. "I understand. She'll remember when she's ready."

At the completion of Mira's rehab program, Sean flew back out to Oakland to pick her up and bring her home. Before they left, Narina invited everyone over for a celebratory dinner at her house.

After they'd finished eating, Sam and Sean went outside on the back patio for a cigar while the women continued talking at the dinner table.

"I can't thank you all enough for everything you've done for me," Mira said.

"Of course," Narina said. "We were happy to help."

Narina was right. It had felt good to help Mira and reunite her family. To Spencer, it seemed like the type of good deed that required no thank you—the outcome itself offered all the gratitude.

"Mira," Narina said, "can I tell you more about the dream I had now? The one where I saw you in the future?"

Mira nodded. "I'd love to hear it."

Narina explained about the two futures she had seen, both with Colin in them. One future was desolate and bleak, where no life existed beyond the holographic one projected in front of Colin's face. The other future, while still advanced by technology, was not so different from the current world. In that future, Colin had a life, a family, and a home he was proud of.

"In the second future," Narina explained, "you were living with him. You recognized me and came outside to talk to me. Colin said you were having issues with your memory, that you often confused the present and the past. He said you sometimes thought you were living in the past, back when you had helped the Network defeat the Apparatus. Colin said that you helped us find them. I'm sorry to push—I know the doctors said to give you time—but we need to know. Is there anything you remember about the Apparatus or any powerful men? Anything that might help us?"

Mira shook her head. "I would help you in any way I could—I owe you my life. But I don't remember anything other than what I already told you. I remember being in a hospital bed, seeing men above me with dark shadows, running tests on me. That's all," she said, and shrugged. "I'm sorry."

Spencer felt deflated. They were still no closer to unearthing the Apparatus.

Mira went home the next day. Narina, Rose, and Spencer continued with their practice and their research. Spencer spent the next few months looking into unusual experiments in hospitals but came up empty-handed.

One day, she picked up her phone and saw a text from Mira and smiled. Mira liked to send them regular updates on her life. She shared pictures from her morning walks with Colin, family vacations, and holidays. Spencer unlocked her phone, expecting to see another heartwarming picture, but as she read the texts, she froze.

> Mira   I found him—the man who talked to my doctor about bringing me in for experiments
> I saw this video, and it all came flooding back
> He's standing behind the mayor

Spencer clicked on the video link. The San Francisco mayor was standing on the steps outside of city hall, giving a speech. She was announcing a momentous bill providing funding for the introduction of a task force and community advisory council on homelessness.

Spencer zoomed in on the man nodding and applauding behind the mayor as she spoke. Her stomach dropped. She recognized him. No matter how much she tried to forget, the night she'd attended his party was seared into her memory. The ecstasy. The swing. The view. The party at the end of the world.

Graham.

Gotcha, she thought, grinning as she texted the group thread.

We have a lead.

# the bar

San Francisco
Spring 2020

Narina was emphatic that they couldn't trust anyone with details about the Apparatus, and could trust technology least of all. They were always hesitant to share too much over text, phone, or email.

The following week, as soon as Sean returned home from a work trip, Mira flew out to share what she remembered with Narina, Rose, and Spencer in person. Spencer was dying to hear what Mira recalled about Graham.

"Tell us everything," Narina said before Mira could even sit down.

"It's still bits and pieces—not a complete picture, but I remember more," Mira said. "The first memory I have is from back in Nashville. That man, Graham, stood next to my hospital bed, talking to my doctor. Graham said that anyone with energy vision was considered a threat, and the doctor had done the right thing by reporting my behavior."

It unnerved Spencer to hear this. Did Graham know about her abilities?

"Then Graham asked the doctor if I'd been able to identify something called a Liminal, and he told him yes."

"Shit," Narina replied. "I first heard the term 'Liminal' in my dream of the future. This is the first time we've heard anyone else use it since then."

"What does it mean?" Mira asked.

"It's an energy state. We believe there are three states: Empties,

Rays, and Liminals. We were Rays before, but we each transitioned to the Liminal state," Narina explained.

"You're a Liminal too," Spencer clarified, "or at least we think you are. You have powers—the ability to see the energy plane like I can—but your signature is a lot weaker, so we aren't sure."

Mira nodded, seeming to understand on some deep level. "I wondered why my light was smaller than yours," she said, motioning around her, "but I think it's because of what they gave me."

Narina, Rose, and Spencer all raised their eyebrows in silent question.

"The nurse gave me something that knocked me out, and when I woke up, back in my home with Sean sitting next to me, I was weak. Not physically weak—I could get up and walk around—but energetically weak, like my inner strength was turned down. The next thing I remember is from after the abduction.

"I woke up in a dimly lit room. It was a big open space. There must have been at least fifty beds lined up in rows. The smell was so bad that I leaned over the side of my bed and vomited on the floor. It wasn't a hospital, but doctors and nurses would walk around to check vitals, draw blood, and administer meds. Then, they would walk over to a glass-paneled room on the side. I could see them working and observing us."

Where was this? And why had the smell been so bad? Spencer started racking her brain, considering locations for a facility like the one Mira was describing.

"One day, when I woke up, Graham was there. He was talking to a doctor. He asked the doctor how I was doing, and he replied that I was stronger than any of the Liminals they'd seen. The doctor said my power was like a battery, that they kept using the device to siphon it, but by the next morning I'd be back to full strength."

Shit. They had a device that could drain Mira's powers. Would it work on any Liminal?

"Before Graham left, he told the doctor to get as much data as possible so that they could start figuring out if there were others like me. He said to siphon all my energy until I was dead."

Spencer felt a sense of relief. Graham didn't know if there were others like Mira. Maybe he didn't know about Spencer or her friends. But she also felt afraid. It seemed Liminals were completely disposable to these men.

"That's the last thing I remember before I woke up in the tent. I have no idea how I got there. I don't know how I'm still alive."

"Do you remember anything about the room or the building? Anything that might help us identify where they were holding you?" Spencer asked.

Mira shook her head. "No, they used badges to get in and out of the room. There were no windows. I have no idea where it was."

"Did any of the doctors or nurses ever say anything?" she pushed. "Maybe mention where they lived?"

"No," Mira said, "nothing." Then she shook her head again. "Wait a minute. Does Smuggler's Cove mean anything to you? One of the doctors said they were going there for a drink after work."

Narina nodded. "Bingo. I've been there more times than I'd like to admit. It's a bar near the Opera House and city hall."

# the terms

San Francisco
Spring 2020

Vik looked at the sheer chaos around him. A three-year-old boy was squirting bright red juice onto Vik's brand-new Mario Bellini sofa. Two little girls were fighting over a doll, ripping the head off the body as they tugged. At least three children were sobbing in unison somewhere in the distance, as if orchestrating their performance. It was his daughter's first birthday party.

He and Amelia had hired a popular influencer-turned-designer to reimagine their Spanish-style home in Atherton. The transformation was stunning. The house, now a bohemian-meets-modern villa, had been featured in a recent print issue of *Architectural Digest* after the influencer's renovation post went viral. *The epitome of effortless luxury* read the caption on the pinned post, which had since amassed 23,437 likes.

During the interview for the feature, the reporter asked Vik how he'd found the designer. Vik thought back to a night lying in bed with Spencer as they shared dreams about a future together. "Oh my god, let me show you this designer," Spencer had said. "I'd love to have her design a home of mine one day, a Spanish home surrounded by olive trees. How amazing would that be?" she'd asked Vik, smiling as she scrolled through the photos on the designer's profile.

It was Amelia who had suggested they host Sophia's birthday party at home so that everyone could see their new #spanishrevival house. Vik looked over at his wife, who was bouncing Sophia on her knee, sitting in a chair in front of the fireplace. They both looked so beautiful. He felt lucky, happy even. Amelia was a wonderful wife, even more kind, loyal, and subservient than she'd been as his assistant, and she was an amazing mother to Sophia.

Vik enjoyed being a father more than he had anticipated. He remembered the first time he'd looked down at his daughter, as the doctor handed the newborn baby to him, and he felt something he couldn't remember ever feeling before. Joy. When it came to matters involving Sophia, Vik no longer had to pretend to empathize; he actually cared and felt deeply about her well-being. Fatherhood was an expansive experience, with new highs and lows every day, but luckily, Amelia took the brunt of the child and home labor. Her support gave Vik the ability to focus on work, his career now accelerating even more after his initiation into the Apparatus.

It was a subtle but profound change—introductions multiplied, deals closed quicker, and it seemed like he was always in the right place at the right time. To Vik's surprise, he wasn't asked to make any other sacrifices. Occasionally the pesky memory would surface, sometimes as he sat courtside at a Warriors game, sometimes as he rode on his private jet, sometimes as he skied in Tahoe. He'd see an image of Brian's troubled face as he asked Vik to leave his Pacific Heights home hours before he was found hanging from his chandelier. But all Vik had to do was look at the life around him, and the memory would go away, at least for a little bit.

Vik got up as he saw Graham enter the room with his new wife. "Thanks for coming," Vik said. "I know it means a lot to Amelia."

"I wouldn't miss it. Can we talk for a minute?"

Vik pulled Graham into the hallway that led toward his office.

"I need you in Chicago first thing Monday morning," Graham said.

Vik nodded. "I'll have to move around a few things, but that shouldn't be a problem."

"Good," Graham replied. "Tell Katie to talk to Caroline about the travel details. We'll spend one day in the suburbs of Chicago and one day in southern Illinois. I need your specific skill set there."

Vik inhaled slowly before speaking. "What for?"

"I'll brief you on Monday morning."

"Okay," he said hesitantly. "I'll tell Katie now; she's here."

Graham nodded. "Good," he said again, gesturing Vik out of the hallway and back toward the party.

Vik met Graham for breakfast the following Monday morning. They were staying at a hotel in Deerfield next to a suburban office park. The accommodations were a far cry from the boutique luxury stays he had grown accustomed to. Graham clearly felt the same.

"I think these eggs were poured from a carton and microwaved," Graham said. His face blanched as he glanced at the sad melon on his plate. He set his fork down and turned his gaze to Vik. "We're here to meet with Assurio."

Vik racked his brain for any context that might be useful here. Assurio was a Fortune 500 company and one of the largest insurers in the country, but it was a decades-old publicly traded business. Vik and Graham's firm invested in early- to mid-stage startups with high growth potential. Insuretech was a hot area, but the firm had passed on investing in many of the companies they saw. The legacy insurance giants had been quick to digitally transform policies and claims in home and auto markets, so startups in the space competed mostly on cost. Plus, in the insurance game, you either needed to be the underwriter or the broker, making it a hard market to disrupt entirely.

"What are we doing with Assurio?" Vik asked, coming up empty.

"We need to make a sizable investment and get a board seat."

"Why?"

"We need to make some changes to policy terms, and it will be easier to do that from the inside."

"Since when does the firm care about something as specific as policy terms?"

"It will all make more sense as things unfold," Graham replied. "And this isn't for the firm." He took a breath. "More will be asked of you over the next few months. The Apparatus is readying for the next phase of our plan. The Architects are beginning to put everything in motion. You were lucky that you had a cooling-off period after your initiation, but that's all about to change."

"I need more than that to go on," Vik said. "What exactly is happening? What is the next phase?"

"Unfortunately, I can't share the details yet. I'm just going to ask that you trust me. Look at your life over the past few years, Vik. Look at what you've received in exchange for your loyalty. Hasn't it been worth it?"

Vik nodded. "What exactly do you need me to do?"

"The CEO hasn't been interested in any of the offers we've made. He's worried about being ousted by activist investors. We need to reassure him and convince him that won't be the case."

"Is he right to think he'll be replaced?" Vik asked.

"That depends on how well you can convince him," Graham said. "If he does what we want him to, we'll have no reason to get rid of him."

An hour later, they were sitting with the Assurio CEO, Frank Johnston. He was a tough but friendly man from Wisconsin. Graham had been doing most of the talking since they arrived. While he gave a practiced speech about how their strategic investment would make Assurio more competitive, Vik went to work molding clay, his shadows reaching into Frank's mind. He imagined Frank sitting in a meeting, getting hounded by the other board members, while Graham defended Frank and sang his praises. Then he pictured Frank looking down at a check in his hands—a discretionary cash bonus of three million dollars and a grant of stock options worth another fifteen million.

Vik saw a small smile tug at Frank's lips and knew his work was done. He couldn't help but feel deflated. He'd been hoping for more of a challenge, something to give him a thrill. He was disappointed by the simple predictability. Ego, power, and money were the main motivators of almost everyone Vik manipulated.

After the meeting, Vik and Graham got into their car. "We should be all set," Vik said.

"Great. This next meeting is just going to be a rinse-and-repeat."

"Where are we headed?" Vik asked.

"A few hundred miles south to Springfield, Illinois. That's where HavenGuard is headquartered."

Vik nodded.

"By the way, I obviously can't take this board seat as well. Conflict of interest. You'll need to take it," Graham said.

Hopefully that meant he was going to fill Vik in on what the hell was going on.

The trip to Springfield and the work Vik had to do there turned out to be equally predictable. Two weeks later, they both had their board seats.

"Can you tell me what the plan is now?" Vik asked the following Monday morning. "What are these policy changes?"

"Extreme weather events due to climate change are causing many of the large insurance companies to rethink their coverage. They're talking to regulators about no longer writing policies in areas with the most extreme weather—making exclusions based on specific weather events and raising premiums and deductibles. Most of the exclusions being discussed are specific to the risks of hurricanes and tropical storms near the coastline in the Southeast and wildfires in high-hazard zones on the West Coast."

"Okay," Vik said, "those policy changes seem reasonable to me. I've seen some of the climate catastrophe models, and the risk of those events is simply too high now to make standard policies possible."

"Right," Graham said. "We're on board with the policy changes. We just need to make the exclusion clauses less specific." Vik's confusion must've shown, because Graham continued. "We need to make sure those regions are excluded from coverage for any type of natural disaster, not just hurricanes or wildfires. We just can't predict how climate change is going to influence extreme weather patterns."

Vik nodded.

"Oh, and one other thing. We need to make the exclusions apply retroactively to any existing policies."

# the door

### San Francisco
### Spring 2020

Spencer and Rose spent the next few weeks alternating on what they called "surveillance duty." They detailed a four-block radius around Smuggler's Cove, identifying any building that might be big enough to house a large open room with hospital beds. There were hundreds of possible buildings, most with doormen or security systems that were hard to get past. Spencer was able to find floor plans from public permits and zoning registrations that allowed them to eliminate a number of buildings that simply didn't have the space required. Then they found clever ways to enter the remaining ones. They identified what companies were located there and scheduled appointments to gain entry, or they dressed as delivery drivers and pretended to have packages that required signatures.

Spencer took off work one Friday to schedule back-to-back appointments. She was able to eliminate eleven possible buildings in a single morning. She had a few more appointments scheduled in the afternoon, so she grabbed a sandwich and headed over to sit and eat in the plaza across from city hall. She was midbite when she saw a black Mercedes pull up in front of the building. Graham stepped out of the car.

After Mira's revelation about Graham's identity, the three women had considered tailing him to see if they could learn anything based on where he went. But they all had full-time jobs, and following a man who had a private driver to escort him to countless

## dark days ahead

meetings around the city wasn't a viable option. They focused on finding a building near Smuggler's Cove instead.

But there Graham was, right inside the Smuggler's Cove radius, entering city hall. They hadn't even considered city hall, Spencer realized, but it certainly had the space for a large room.

He walked up the steps and into the building.

Spencer quickly stood up, threw away her food, and crossed the street to follow him in, but she was stopped by a security guard.

"Appointment or tour?" he asked.

"Excuse me?" Spencer replied, confused.

"Are you here for an appointment or tour? Those are the only two ways to get into the building," the guard explained.

Spencer shook her head. She had never been good at thinking on her feet and worried the guard would ask for a ticket or proof of appointment if she tried to lie. She'd already lost Graham anyway.

She walked back out and saw his car still parked at the curb. The driver must be waiting for him. She sat down on the steps near the door, hoping she'd catch Graham when he left.

Thirty minutes later, she saw him out of the corner of her eye, walking down the steps toward his car. He was on the phone. She couldn't hear what he said, but she swore she saw him mouth the word "experiments."

She pulled out her phone and texted the group.

I think I found the building—dinner tonight?

They made a plan. Spencer would go to city hall on Wednesday to take a tour. Rose would go on Thursday to get something notarized for her business at the Office of the County Clerk. Narina would go on Friday to renew her license at the DMV. They'd each discreetly take as many photos and videos as they could, anything that might offer evidence about what Graham was doing inside the building.

It was easier than they'd anticipated. On Wednesday, while Spencer looked at the map in the center of the rotunda, waiting for the tour to start, three men in white, knee-length coats walked past her. Doctors. They headed toward a wood-paneled wall. At first she was confused, but then one of the doctors waved a badge in front of a barely visible black sensor. He placed his hand on one of the panels and pushed, opening a hidden door. The other two doctors followed quickly behind the first.

Rose and Narina saw the same thing when they went—doctors shuffling in and out, always scanning a badge before entering the room.

"We need to get in there," Narina said.

They were at Spencer's apartment this time. Rose and Narina were lounging on the deep velvet sofa, the one Spencer had copied from Vik's place. She was sitting on the bay window seat opposite her friends, with pillows pushed against the windows behind her, propping her up.

She and Rose both stared at Narina, open-mouthed.

"Get in there? Are you completely out of your mind?" Rose asked. "We think they are running experiments in there. Experiments on people *like us*."

"What other option do we have?" Narina asked. "This is our first real lead on the Apparatus in four years. We have to find out what they're doing."

"And how exactly will we do that?" Rose asked.

"We can pretend to be doctors."

"With what badges?"

Narina was silent.

"The doctors weren't the only ones with badges," Spencer said quietly from her seat at the window.

Narina and Rose turned to her.

Spencer had had back-to-back meetings all day at work the Wednesday she had booked her tour, so she'd signed up for the last one of the day, at four in the afternoon. An hour later, as the tour ended and the building was closing for the day, after a steady stream of doctors had filtered out of the room, a group of women walked up to the hidden door and swiped a badge.

## dark days ahead

    Now, Spencer spoke nervously, already dreading what she knew they were about to do. "I saw cleaners go in," she said. "The cleaners come on Wednesdays."

# the badge

**San Francisco**
**Spring 2020**

The following Wednesday, Spencer once again booked the last tour of the day. She confirmed that at a little after 5 p.m., a group of cleaners entered. She found a cleaning van parked in front of the building when she left—Angie's Cleaning Service.

Rose went again the week after. This time, she parked outside the building the entire day, counting the number of doctors and nurses who arrived in the morning and left in the evening, making sure no one stayed overnight to monitor the experiments.

They devised a plan. The following Tuesday, Narina would call Angie's Cleaning Service and pretend to be a woman from city hall's administration office. "We have an event going on tomorrow, so we need to cancel our scheduled weekly cleaning," she'd tell Angie. Then the trio would go in place of Angie's Cleaning Service and scope out what was happening behind the hidden door.

"I think you're forgetting something," Rose said as Narina shared the plan with them. "The badges."

Narina shrugged. "You're forgetting something too. We have powers now."

"Oh what, you're going to burn the hidden door down with your powers?"

She shook her head. "We'll use our powers to get a badge."

Spencer gulped. They'd only ever used their powers on each

other, practicing in Narina's backyard. They weren't even sure how they would work on "normal" people.

"We can't hurt anyone," Rose said.

"We won't," Narina said. "At least I hope we won't."

They both looked at Spencer.

Spencer shrugged. "I don't see any other option," she said. "And we need to test out our powers eventually."

The next Tuesday, Narina placed her call, and the following day, the three women met outside Angie's Cleaning Service in Russian Hill. Spencer hoped that the cleaning crew would be carrying any keys that they'd need to get into the buildings they cleaned every Wednesday.

Four women, each wearing a light blue vest with *Angie's Cleaning* stitched on the breast pocket, walked toward the van parked outside and got in. Narina, Rose, and Spencer tailed them in Spencer's car, following them to the Richmond, Portrero Hill, and then Noe Valley.

At each location, a larger woman with black hair and pale skin would reach into her front right pocket, fumble around for a minute, then produce a key or card to gain entrance to the building. Spencer looked for an opening, a way to use their powers, but there were too many people around everywhere they went.

A little before four o'clock, the cleaners parked their van on a quiet street in Presidio Heights and went into a home with buckets, mops, and supplies in hand.

"This is it," Narina said. "This must be their last job of the day. If we're going to make it to city hall, we need to do something now. When they come back outside, we move."

"What exactly are we going to do?" Rose asked.

"I don't know. Something will come to me."

Spencer noticed how nervous Narina seemed. The realization only made Spencer more anxious, and she was already anxious enough. Narina usually had confidence for all three of them.

An hour later, the cleaners left the house and started to load up the van. Now finished with work for the day, one of them—a tall blond woman—took off her vest and placed it in the back of the van. Then a brunette woman did the same thing, placing her vest next to the first. Another blond woman followed.

Spencer, Rose, and Narina watched and waited.

Finally, the black-haired woman took off her vest and placed it in the back of the van, closing the sliding door behind her.

"Now," Narina said, jumping out of the car. "Rose and I will create a diversion, and Spence, you'll go grab the vests."

Shit, thought Spencer. Her stomach dropped.

"What diversion?" she asked, but Narina ignored her and crossed the street, walking directly toward the van.

The cleaners were putting on their seatbelts. The black-haired woman started the engine.

Spencer smelled it before she saw it. Slow curls of smoke were coming out of the front hood of the van.

"Oh my god! Your van is on fire. Get out! Get out!" Rose yelled, running toward the cleaners' van, her arms waving, trying to get their attention before they drove away.

Damn. She was a good actress. Spencer was impressed.

Smoke started billowing and the cleaners screamed as they scrambled to get out of the van.

Rose ran toward them. "Are you okay? I'm calling 9-1-1 now," she said as she approached.

Rose was blocking their line of sight, Spencer realized. Spencer looked over at Narina. Her eyes smoldered, her focus never leaving the hood of the van. Flames started to rise alongside the smoke. This was her window.

Spencer ran toward the van door and quickly slid it open. All four vests sat on the seat near the door. She grabbed them and ran back to her car.

Narina and Rose stayed with the cleaners until the fire department arrived and put out the engine fire. Angie's Cleaning Service would need a new van, but no one was hurt.

"Holy fucking shit!" Rose exclaimed when she got back in Spencer's car. "That was amazing!"

## dark days ahead

"Did we get it?" Narina asked, looking at Spencer.

"Yep," she said with a smile, holding up a city hall access badge.

# the subject

San Francisco
Spring 2020

Twenty-five minutes later, Spencer parked her car, and they unloaded the props—a mop and bucket, rags, sponges, latex gloves, and a caddy full of cleaning products. Spencer had suggested they take a few precautions in case something went wrong. She parked five blocks away from city hall and hid her key in the wheel well, and they each left their phones in the glove box. The only things they brought with them into the building were the fake IDs Spencer had procured to use for security. She hoped that they could get in and out without anyone noticing, but just in case, she wanted to make sure no one knew who they were.

As they entered the building, they flashed the access badge to the security guard along with their fake IDs, placed their cleaning supplies on the X-ray conveyer belt, and walked through the metal detector.

They made their way to the wood-paneled wall where Spencer had seen countless doctors enter and found the small black sensor. She waved the access card in front of it, and the red light on the sensor turned green. She heard a faint click and pushed. The door opened into a dimly lit hallway.

They were in.

They started to smile at their success but were immediately hit by the smell—body odor, sweat, urine, and feces, all rolled up together.

Spencer led the way down the long hallway. When she turned the corner, she saw it before the others: rows and rows of hospital beds.

Were those homeless people in the beds? What the fuck? They were all hooked up to machines, and an IV dripped into each of their arms. They all seemed to be asleep or unconscious. The IV must be some type of sedation, Spencer thought.

On the right side of the room stood a wall of windows separating the main room full of beds from another room, which looked like a lab. Spencer walked over to the locked door. She waved the access badge, but nothing happened. She tried again. She shook her head at Narina and Rose walking toward her. "It's not working on the lab door," Spencer whispered.

To the left of the door was another hallway that led to a bathroom, several locked offices, and a supply closet. They walked into the supply closet. It was ten feet deep. The metal racks inside were filled with a mixture of office, medical, and cleaning supplies.

"I wonder if that connects to the lab," Narina said, pointing to a large vent three-quarters of the way up the back wall.

"You want to crawl through the ducts?" Spencer asked.

"Why not? We need to find out as much as we can. We might not be able to get back in here again."

She wasn't wrong, but Spencer still didn't like the idea.

Narina started rummaging through the supplies.

"What are you doing?" Rose asked.

"Looking for a drill or screwdriver, something to help us get the vent cover off the wall."

Rose blew out a deep breath and walked over to help her.

A few minutes later, Narina was balancing on a step stool, removing the bolts from the vent cover. She handed them to Rose, who carefully placed them in a small empty container she'd found so that they could put the cover back on when they were finished. Spencer and Rose each grabbed an end of the vent cover and placed it on the ground.

Narina crawled in first, and Rose followed. As Spencer stepped onto the stool to join them, Narina reached out. "Wait," she said, placing her hand on Spencer's arm. "We need someone to stay back, in case anything happens."

Spencer wasn't sure what was worse—climbing through ducts or being stuck there alone, standing guard. Still, Narina was right. "Fine. I'll stay."

Spencer walked back into the hallway. She remembered a clock hanging on the wall, so she went to check the time, wanting to keep track of how long Narina and Rose were in the ducts. It was 5:45.

She busied herself by looking through the supply closet. She checked the clock again a little later—6:05. Spencer was growing more nervous. Narina and Rose should have been back by now.

Footsteps rang out in the hallway. Feeling relieved, she moved toward the door. They must have crawled out of the ducts somewhere else and were coming back to the supply closet.

Then Spencer heard voices—male voices.

Shit.

She put her ear to the door.

"I just need to grab a few things before we run the next test," one voice said.

They were heading toward the closet. Spencer's stomach dropped. There was nowhere to hide.

She looked around and noticed extra white lab coats hanging from hooks on the back of the door. Without thinking, she grabbed one and put it on.

As the door opened, Spencer turned away, pretending to rummage through one of the bins, like she was looking for something.

"What are you doing here?" a voice behind her demanded.

"Just looking for this," Spencer said, holding up a notepad before placing it in her coat pocket. She avoided making eye contact as she moved to walk around them and leave the supply closet.

One of the men, the older one, held out his hand to block her. "Are you new here?" he asked.

Spencer nodded.

"Well, you shouldn't be here after hours," he said, "but we could use an extra set of hands. Did they train you yet on the protocol for experiments?"

Spencer shook her head.

He huffed, exasperated. Spencer glanced up for the first time. She glimpsed the badge on his coat: *Grady*. She looked toward the other man's breast pocket: *French*.

"We'll fill you in. Come with us," Grady said to her before turning to French. "Tell Graham we need help onboarding new doctors. Their training is unacceptable."

French nodded.

They left the supply closet, but instead of turning back toward the main room or the lab, they headed in the opposite direction. At the end of the hall stood a large door. Unlike the other doors lining the hallway, which were made of wood, this one was made of metal. Steel, Spencer thought. It looked indestructible.

Grady pulled on his badge, the retractable string extending until it reached the sensor near the door. It flashed green. Grady entered first, and French held the door for Spencer as he entered behind her.

They walked into a small room with a long table. One side was pushed up against the wall, and four chairs lined the other side. Above the table was a large window looking into another room, where Spencer noticed a chair with straps on the arm and leg rests. Five feet in front of the chair stood a table with a small black box resting on top.

"It's a two-way mirror," French explained to her. "The experiments work best when the subjects think they're alone."

Spencer nodded.

"We'll bring the subject in and play a recording through their headphones. Your job is to record the levels displayed on this every thirty seconds," he said, pointing to a rectangular box in front of her.

"What is it?" she asked.

"A spectrometer."

Grady reached down, leaned over, and spoke into a microphone. "Bring the first subject in."

A security guard brought in a woman. She clearly hadn't bathed in weeks. It looked like she hadn't eaten in that timeframe, either. The guard pushed her into the seat, strapping her feet and then her arms into the chair.

Grady handed Spencer a lightweight headset. "This is the best part," he said, smiling. "Put this on and look at her."

Spencer obeyed. She put on the headset, and the room turned dark. The woman glowed, a pale blue light emanating from her. Despite her haggard appearance, she was full of light. She was a Liminal. Spencer did a double take and removed the headset, getting a good look before putting it back on, comparing the two views.

"Isn't it spectacular?" Grady asked.

Clearly, he thought Spencer had removed her headset in awe of what she had seen, but she had taken it off because the resemblance was uncanny. What she saw when she had the headset on was almost identical to what she saw when she removed it and activated her vision power. The headset made everything a little darker, like night-vision goggles, but otherwise it matched her vision. It gave the wearer the ability to see the energy plane.

Grady and French each had their own headset in front of them on the table.

Grady pressed the button and leaned over again. "We're ready for the headphones," he said.

The security guard placed large, wireless headphones on the woman.

Looking at the clock in front of him, Grady wrote the time at the top of his notes: 6:13 p.m.

The doctors reached down and put on their headsets; their eyes became immediately glued to the woman in front of them. Grady nodded a signal and French pressed a button.

"Remember to record every thirty seconds," French said to Spencer, his eyes never leaving the woman on the other side of the mirror.

The experiment had started, but at first, nothing seemed to happen.

Then slowly, Spencer saw it. The halo of light around the woman started to grow, both in intensity and size. The spectrometer increased in parallel. The first reading was 0.05. Five minutes into the experiment, it read 0.62.

"What's happening?" Spencer asked.

"She's listening to something we developed. Consider it a hypnosis of sorts," Grady explained. "We've figured out how to heighten their powers. A spectrometer reading of 1.0 is the theoretical limit, but the highest we've been able to get is 0.85. We made some adjustments to the recording she's listening to, and we're hoping to top that number tonight." He leaned toward French. "What's your guess?"

Neither doctor could take his eyes off the scene building in front of them.

"Fifty dollars it's rain," French said. "She's blue, so it has to be water."

"We place a wager on what their powers will be," Grady said. "The color of their light usually gives us an indication."

Spencer glanced down at her own hands. Shades of glittery green coated her skin.

"My money is on a waterfall," Grady said.

Spencer checked the spectrometer again: 0.82.

The crown of blue light started to stutter around the woman as if faltering.

"She's maxing out," French said. "We don't have much time."

"Give it another minute."

"We might miss our window!"

"Window for what?" Spencer asked.

"To siphon the power," Grady replied.

A pit formed in Spencer's stomach as she understood what was about to happen.

"Turn the volume up," he said to French.

French turned a dial, and the woman started to shake. Suddenly, she was convulsing, a foamy saliva dripping from her mouth. It was like she was being electrocuted from the inside out.

He held his hand over a button. "Wait," Grady said, pushing back French's arm. "She's close to her edge."

Suddenly, the blue light circling around the woman pushed forward all at once. It hardened into a wall of smooth solidity, forming a blue-white marbled surface that must have been six inches thick. Her power wasn't rain or a waterfall—it was ice. She had the power to freeze things, Spencer realized.

"Now!" Grady yelled.

French slammed his palm down on the button in front of him. A light activated on the small black box sitting on the table near the woman. A beam erupted from the box, and like a vacuum, it sucked up all the light in its path. The woman was drained of every drop of energy, of power, of essence, until nothing remained. She was still alive, but she was a husk. They had turned a Liminal into an Empty. They'd sucked all her life force into a small black device with the press of a button.

Spencer felt empty herself watching the scene, completely gutted. She remembered a new mother telling her what it was like to watch someone hurt a child. "It's no different than someone hurting your own child," the woman had said, like somehow all mothers and all children were connected by a string. That was what Spencer felt in that moment—she had been connected to this woman in some way. And what happened to her? Spencer had felt it directly herself.

"What was the last reading?" Grady asked, interrupting her thoughts.

Spencer looked down to check. "It was 0.86," she replied.

"Fantastic," Grady said with a grin. He turned toward her, and his smile immediately faded. He still had his headset on. That meant he could see the green light shimmering around her. "My, my, my— what do we have here?" he asked, a sinister expression returning to his face.

French turned to look at Spencer, and his mouth dropped open.

Spencer saw Grady reach into his coat pocket and pull out a syringe. Before she realized what was happening, French's arms were around her, holding her back. Grady reached for her and stabbed her with the syringe, immediately depressing the plunger with his thumb.

Spencer felt a warm buzzing sensation creep through her body.

She tried to stop her head from tilting back, her eyes from closing, her body from going slack.

An image of Narina and Rose flashed in her mind. Please don't find them, she prayed.

Then she was out.

# the root

San Francisco
Spring 2020

Spencer woke in a blur. A steady thrum of monitors beeped around her. The room was dim. She couldn't move her arms or legs. I'm paralyzed, she thought, panicked. No wait, I'm strapped in, she realized, glancing down at her wrists as terror coursed through her.

She looked around and saw a bed on either side of her. Please no, she thought, willing a different reality from the one she knew was in front of her. She moved her eyes up toward the top of the bed on one side and saw Narina's dark hair. Turning to her other side, she saw Rose's face in profile.

The Apparatus had found them. Spencer was supposed to stand guard to keep them safe, and she'd failed. Now they were all strapped to beds. She remembered the experiment she'd witnessed, the way the life force had been taken from the woman. They would do the same to her and her friends.

How long ago had that been? She had no idea how much time had passed since they sedated her. She glanced back down at her own body. At some point, they'd removed her clothes and replaced them with scrubs. Her fake ID and the access badge they'd used to get into the building were both gone.

Spencer heard someone near the door. Realizing they were coming inside, she closed her eyes quickly and attempted to slow her breath, pretending to be asleep. She heard footsteps as someone walked into the room.

She felt a hand on her wrist, checking her pulse.

"They're still sedated," a woman's voice said. "Which one do you want first, Dr. Grady?"

"The one in the middle. Wake her up and get her ready."

Spencer felt a pinch on her arm—a needle?—and then something coursed through her body. Was that adrenaline? she wondered, suddenly feeling alert. They were expecting her to wake now, so she pretended to stir. Then she slowly opened her eyes.

A blond-haired, blue-eyed woman looked down at Spencer. She had no warmth or malice in her eyes. The woman was the epitome of objectiveness. Spencer was just a test subject to her. "She'll need a few minutes," the woman said as she turned to Dr. Grady. "I'll have the guards bring her over when she's ready."

He nodded and left the room.

The nurse stayed with Spencer, monitoring her vitals. After a few minutes, when she was satisfied Spencer was fully awake, she called a guard in. "Bring her to the observation room."

The guard nodded and reached down to undo Spencer's straps, replacing them with handcuffs.

Spencer's arms and legs still felt like jelly. Whatever they had given her had woken her, but she still didn't have full control of her limbs. Attempting to run or escape was out of the question.

The guard lifted her, placed her into a wheelchair, and rolled her down the familiar hallway and through the steel door at the end. Spencer was now on the other side of the two-way mirror. The guard lifted her again and placed her down into the chair, strapping her arms and legs securely in place. He reached down to grab headphones and put them on Spencer's ears, adjusting the strap so they were snug on her head.

She couldn't see through to the other side of the mirror, but she knew exactly what was happening. Dr. Grady and Dr. French would be there, getting ready for the experiment, donning their headsets. Dr. Grady would be noting the time, Dr. French pressing Play. Spencer wondered who was monitoring the spectrometer this time. What level was it at? How powerful was she?

Noise came through her headset.

The sound was far away at first, but it was like it was moving toward her. It sounded like a mother murmuring something sweet to a baby. This went on for a few minutes. Then suddenly, the baby was crying, wailing out in fear. It started gasping. It couldn't breathe.

"There, there, it's okay," the mother's voice said gently. "Only another minute," she murmured as the baby gasped for life. Horrified, Spencer understood now that she was listening to a mother strangle her child. Sadness and grief washed over her, and she saw the glimmering green glow on her skin intensify. As she looked at the halo of light growing larger around her, she noticed the black box sitting on the table in front of her.

Wait a minute. Spencer remembered the end of the experiment she had witnessed right before they'd knocked her out. They wanted to take her power. Siphon it. And they wanted to make it as big as possible before they stole it. That was what the headphones were for—the hypnosis elicited emotions that amplified powers.

At the thought of these men taking her powers, Spencer felt something deep at the bottom of her stomach tighten. Despite the situation in front of her, she almost smiled as a memory popped into her head.

It was a few months earlier. Narina, Rose, and Spencer had been practicing different methods to strengthen their powers. Rose was telling Narina and Spencer about the seven chakras that run through the body.

"That's your root chakra," Rose had explained. "It represents your foundation and connection to Earth. It connects to your most basic instincts of survival, security, and stability. To strengthen it, picture your root chakra tightening, and repeat this affirmation after me."

"Um, Rose, where exactly is this root chakra I'm supposed to be picturing?" Spencer interjected.

"Between your perineum and your lower spine."

Spencer smiled. "I once dated a hedge fund manager who liked his perineum stroked with the feather of a bald eagle."

## dark days ahead

"Where do you find these sick fucks?" Narina asked as all three of them laughed.

"Okay guys, let's focus," Rose said. "Repeat this affirmation after me: 'I do all acts knowing I'm protected and secure.'"

Spencer and Narina rolled their eyes.

"Try it," Rose said. "Please, just give it a chance."

Spencer heard the wailing hypnosis in her ears again, the noise pulling her from the memory back into the room.

Fuck it, Spencer thought to herself as she began to say the words in her head.

I do all acts knowing I'm protected and secure.

I do all acts knowing I'm protected and secure.

I do all acts knowing I'm protected and secure.

The halo of light around her extended and intensified to form a shield of glittering armor. She recognized it. It was the same shield that had instinctively surrounded her when Vik tried to reach inside and take another piece of her that day they met for coffee.

The noise in the headphones changed. Instead of the mother and the baby, Spencer now heard gunfire, yelling, and explosions, then someone begging for help. "Please don't," they cried, "I'll do anything. Please don't kill me."

As she listened, she saw her shield waver.

It's hypnosis, Spencer reminded herself. Block it out. She found a center point inside of her where no sound existed, and her shield strengthened in front of her.

She envisioned a tree planted firmly in the ground, roots growing deep into the soil. She focused on that, and nothing else, for what felt like hours.

Suddenly the guard was next to her, removing the headphones, placing her back in the wheelchair, wheeling her back to the bed, and strapping her in.

The blond woman came back a few minutes later. She pulled out a syringe from her pocket and walked toward Spencer. Spencer caught a glimpse of Dr. Grady storming by in a huff before the door shut.

He started yelling in the hallway. Even though the door muffled his voice, Spencer could still hear him. "Why the fuck didn't that work? The reading was 0.98! It's the highest we've ever seen, and we missed it! Figure out what the hell happened. Graham will be here next week. He's going to have questions, and we need answers. Recalibrate everything, and we'll try again with one of the other ones."

Shit—he was talking about Rose and Narina. They were going to try the experiment with them, but Rose and Narina didn't have shields.

Spencer tried to catch what Dr. Grady yelled next, but then she felt a pinch on her arm. It was only a moment before her vision blurred and her head rolled back.

When Spencer woke once more, the room was dark and quiet. She glanced over to her right and saw Rose sleeping peacefully next to her. Spencer turned her head to the left and felt instantly sick. Narina's bed was empty. They must have taken her.

She imagined Narina listening to the hypnosis, anger roaring through her and fire erupting from her body at the exact moment Dr. French pressed the button to siphon it. As she pictured her friend strapped into that chair, Spencer felt it again: the clenching deep inside of her.

She saw the glittering shield pop up around her, but she wasn't the one who needed protection. She closed her eyes and imagined Narina's face, willing the shield to protect her. Spencer found that place deep in her center where nothing else existed, and she stayed there for as long as she could, though she had no idea if it was working.

Twenty minutes later, the door opened, and Spencer dropped her focus, the shield collapsing. The security guard rolled Narina back in. She was alive, but was she *alive*? Spencer switched her vision. A halo of fiery orange light encircled Narina's body. It had worked. Relief washed through her.

Spencer pretended to sleep while the guard strapped Narina

back into bed. The guard left, and the blond woman approached the room, reaching into her pocket once again. But before she entered, something happened outside. A few doctors were in a huddle, talking low. Spencer couldn't hear what they were saying, so she turned to Narina. "Are you okay?" she whispered.

Narina nodded.

"Did they take you into the room with a mirror and put headphones on?"

Narina nodded again, confused.

Spencer explained it all in a whispered rush. "They're running experiments. I saw them do one before they caught me. There are doctors on the other side of the mirror, wearing special headsets that give them energy vision. They can see our powers. They play a hypnotic track from the headphones that makes our power grow. When the power gets big enough, they steal it all and put it in the tiny black box sitting on the table. The woman I saw, she was a Liminal at the beginning of the experiment and an Empty at the end. They took it all from her."

Narina's eyes widened.

"When they brought me in, I was able to activate my shield," Spencer continued. "I think it protected me from the siphon. They tried to do it on you too, but when I woke up and realized you were gone, I sent my shield to you. Did you see anything?"

"No," Narina said, shaking her head, "but I felt it."

"We need to get out of here," Spencer said.

Narina nodded. "They'll kill us if we don't."

Spencer saw the blond woman outside the door and flashed her eyes at Narina, signaling for her to be quiet.

The woman entered the room and gave Narina an injection, then walked straight over to Spencer.

# the thesis

San Francisco
Spring 2020

Over the next few months, Graham had other requests for Vik. Namely, he wanted Vik to focus his efforts on cybersecurity.

One day, he came into Vik's office with a question.

"I've been running different scenario analyses," he said as he walked in, "and exploring what it might look like if there were large-scale cyberattacks. Consider a major metropolitan area like New York City—what products and technology might become more relevant if New Yorkers were faced with an onslaught of hacks on critical infrastructure?"

"Why would people in New York *specifically* be faced with cyberattacks?" Vik asked in response, not fully understanding Graham's question.

"The reason doesn't really matter. There are a number of scenarios where attackers might be able to find vulnerabilities in the system to exploit, especially as more and more of our infrastructure becomes interconnected. It's an investment thesis I want to explore—what technology would become essential?"

Vik nodded. This line of inquiry did make sense. There were looming external threats from Russia, China, and Iran constantly on rotation, along with a host of internal threats from hackers looking to elevate and profit beyond phishing scams and traditional identity theft.

"I'll look into it."

As Vik did his research, he found that the overall cybersecurity market was already fairly mature. There were plenty of well-funded companies doing endpoint protection, threat detection intelligence, and network security analytics. He looked at cloud computing next, which was similarly well-developed. Solutions for cloud workload protection and cloud access security brokers were already established.

Then Vik thought of the growing wearable market he had helped define. The market had morphed into something bigger than either he or Graham had initially imagined. Sensors weren't just being worn on the body; they were being embedded in everything, leading to the proliferation of a giant network of interrelated devices that communicated and exchanged data. This device connectivity would only explode further once artificial intelligence advanced. The attack surface for a cyber threat was no longer just computers, phones, and tablets—it was exponentially bigger.

This new attack surface gave Vik several ideas. He developed a roadmap for an investment thesis, which he presented to Graham a few weeks later. He focused on two critical markets: nonhuman identity management and geofencing.

The market for nonhuman identity management was still relatively nascent. "Nonhuman identities" referred to digital entities—machines, apps, APIs, IoT devices, bots—that continuously interacted with each other, forming a vast new ecosystem. Vik hypothesized that just like identity management had become imperative to authenticate individual users before giving them access to networks and services, so too would it become critical to authenticate these nonhuman identities before they communicated and exchanged data with each other.

The second market Vik proposed—geofencing—was a more indirect hypothesis, but one he found interesting under a certain set of circumstances. Geofencing was already a popular investment area, but it was mostly being used for location-based services and marketing purposes. Vik thought it offered more compelling future applications around asset management and monitoring, something that might become critical in the event of attacks. By establishing boundaries around infrastructure, data repositories, and even individual devices, geofences could track asset movement and trigger warnings when those boundaries were breached.

Vik proposed a Tel Aviv–based nonhuman identity management platform and a Brooklyn-based geofencing company.

Graham looked pleased. "I like it," he said. "Go make it happen."

On a Wednesday night in June, Vik got a call from Graham, who was in Bali on a belated honeymoon with his wife.

"Vik," he said, "I need you to do me a favor. There have been some developments at city hall. It's something Grady has never seen before. There are three women with unusual abilities. Melinda will kill me if I cut our trip short. The soonest I can get back there is next week. Can you go there tomorrow?"

"Sure," Vik said, "but what exactly is it that you want me to do?"

"Confirm what their abilities are, and make sure they don't leave the building alive. I'll text photos of their IDs. See what you can find on each of them."

After the call ended, Vik's phone buzzed. The text included three photos.

An ID of a woman with dark skin, black hair, and brown eyes named Luma Aayari.

An ID of a woman with pale skin, blond hair, and blue eyes named Anna Lindgren.

An ID of a woman with olive skin, brown hair, and hazel eyes named Blair Doyle.

Huh, Vik thought. The last photo almost looked like Spencer.

He forwarded the names to Sven, along with a text.

Find anything you can on these women.

An hour later, Sven replied.

These are fake IDs and doctored photos. There are plenty of women with these names. But I hacked the California DMV and none are registered residents.

Vik put down his phone. Interesting.

He had a busy morning with meetings the next day, so by the time he made his way over to city hall, it was two o'clock in the afternoon.

A nurse greeted him. "Dr. Grady and Dr. French are running an experiment. You can join them in the observatory," she said.

Vik had been to city hall with Graham several dozen times over the past few years to check in on the progress the doctors were making. He made his way over to the observatory, the room named for the two-way mirror, where Grady performed the bulk of his research.

Grady smiled as Vik entered. "Just in time. You'll never believe what we found. Three of them came in last night dressed up as cleaners. Two of them were crawling around the ducts, and this one pretended to be a doctor."

Vik looked up through the mirror where Grady pointed and froze. Spencer was sitting across from him, her eyes wide in terror.

Grady handed Vik a headset. "We're just about to get started," he said as he pressed down a button and spoke into a recording device. "We're about to begin the first session with a subject named Blair Doyle. It's 2:13 p.m."

That's definitely not Blair Doyle, Vik thought to himself as he looked at Spencer and remembered the name from the IDs Graham had sent. What on earth are you up to, Spence? You're going to get yourself killed.

Vik donned the headset, and French started playing the hypnosis recording into Spencer's headphones. Vik had watched an experiment like this one before, so he knew what came next.

As the spectrometer crept above 0.80, Vik felt Grady and French hold their breath. It kept climbing, first to 0.85, then to 0.90.

"Holy shit," French said. "We need to siphon now. This breaks every record."

Grady shook his head. "Not yet—she has more in her."

Vik looked back up at Spencer. The glittering halo around her extended nearly ten feet in every direction. It took his breath away. She was absolutely radiant. And they were going to take it all from her.

Some instinct deep inside of Vik kicked in. He wanted to protect her. He didn't totally understand the feeling that arose, but he didn't have time to think. He looked around the room for anything he could use as a weapon, but there was nothing other than pens, papers, and the experiment devices. He didn't relish the idea of taking on Grady and French physically, but he didn't see another option. He inched closer, positioning himself between the two of them, and glanced down at the screen on the spectrometer: 0.98.

"Now," Grady said to French. "Siphon it now."

Vik was about to lunge at French when the scene in front of him stopped him in his tracks. Large roots exploded beneath Spencer, branching in every direction for nearly twenty feet. A trunk rose through the center of her body. Instead of branches and leaves extending from the top, a giant, glowing canopy of glimmering light stretched out around her.

Vik was so distracted that he didn't notice French had reached down to press the siphon button until it was too late. Dread filled Vik's stomach as he waited, expecting to see all of her powers extracted into the tiny box on the table, but nothing happened.

French pressed the button again and again. "Why isn't it working?" he asked Grady.

"It's a shield," Vik whispered.

Grady nodded in agreement, staring at Spencer in awe. "She's too powerful for the siphon. That's enough for now. Take her back to the room," he said to the guard standing nearby.

Vik listened to Grady and French in a heated discussion about the different adjustments they could make to the hypnosis, the medication, and the siphon device itself. Vik was only half paying attention, thinking about what to do about Spencer and what to tell Graham. Graham didn't know who was in that room. He thought it was some woman named Blair Doyle, and Vik wanted to keep it that way.

Would Spencer be able to protect herself with her shield after the adjustments Grady and French were about to make?

Fifteen minutes later, before Vik left city hall, he stopped by the room where they were keeping Spencer and two other women. Spencer was already sedated, along with the women alongside her. Narina and Rose, Vik realized.

## dark days ahead

After a minute, he walked out of the room.
"I'll be back tomorrow," he said to Grady on his way out.

# the key

**San Francisco**
**Spring 2020**

Spencer spent the next window of time drifting in and out of consciousness. Anytime she came close to the surface of waking, some invisible force seemed to pull her back down.

A few years before, when Spencer was deep in her breakup depression, she had done a series of ketamine sessions with Cynthia. Whatever drug they were using to sedate her now reminded her of that period. It was like a soft and velvety ride underground, swimming through cozy, dark puddles. Visuals flashed into her mind, all fragments, disjointed from one another. Each a sliver of time—memories of her as a child, flashes of a place that felt like a different world, a whisper in her ear, the distinct feeling she was being buried alive, Vik's voice, reliving her own birth, something pressing against her right hip. Time seemed to move in a circle instead of a straight line. She rode a roller coaster through the hills and valleys of San Francisco. None of it made any sense.

Spencer woke up what could have been hours or days later, feeling groggy. She came to slowly and realized she was now sitting up instead of lying down. She was back in the observation room, facing the two-way mirror. The steel door opened with a creak, and she turned to see Narina being rolled in by one of the guards.

Grady entered the room and walked toward the table with the black siphon device. This time, instead of sitting behind the mirror, he pulled up a chair next to the table and took a seat facing Spencer and Narina.

## dark days ahead

Spencer glanced over at Narina, who was slowly waking up as well.

"Well, well," Grady said, "you all have been quite the surprise. We ha—"

"Where's our friend?" Narina interrupted.

Spencer sent a mental thank you to Narina for having enough sense, even in her angered and drugged state, not to use Rose's name.

"We haven't been able to wake her up," Grady replied flatly. "She's a bit more delicate than the two of you."

"Delicate?" Narina clarified.

"Your powers are all so different, it can be hard to find a standard dosage. She's like a flower. Whereas you're like a thorn. And you're like a weed," he said, to Spencer this time. "Some are easily trampled, and others, well, they just won't die no matter what we do." He smiled, his lips stretched in a tense line as his eyes passed back and forth between them.

Spencer tried to lift her shield to protect herself and Narina, but she couldn't. It was like something was numbing her, a black tar blocking her from accessing her well of power. She tried to activate her vision, and the same thing happened. She was powerless, defenseless. What had they given her?

"As I was about to say," Grady continued, "we haven't seen powers as strong as yours in a long time. It was fortuitous that you walked right in here, almost like you came to volunteer for the experiments. We thought we'd be able to siphon from you like we did the others, but you've proved more challenging for us."

"If we're so powerful, is it smart for you to be sitting here in front of us? I can light you on fire right now," Narina said.

She was bluffing; Spencer knew that. From Narina's state, it was clear she was as disconnected from her powers as Spencer was.

Grady laughed. "It took us some time to mix up the cocktail we gave you just now, but we're confident it will block your ability to access your powers. Besides, your powers can only hurt me energetically, not physically. And we have an energy shield up," he said, gesturing around.

Spencer caught on his words. Energetically, not physically? That didn't make sense. She remembered the way Narina had started the engine fire. She had affected things physically. Was Grady implying that this was something other Liminals couldn't do?

"What do you mean, an energy shield?" Narina asked.

Good work, Narina, Spencer thought. Keep him talking as much as possible. We need to find out anything we can.

"We learned it from ones like your friend," Grady said, nodding at Spencer. "We noticed there were some Liminals that could shield. It seemed immensely useful, so we studied it and made it into a technology.

"You see, nothing is ever really created; it's only observed in nature and then copied. It's how the Apparatus has worked since the beginning of time—observe a specific set of powers, find a way to create technology based off those powers, introduce the technology into the world, and then watch as the technology takes over."

"Since the beginning of time?" Narina clarified.

"Well, maybe not since the very beginning. I suppose the first story I've heard about it is the building of the pyramids."

"The pyramids were built by aliens," Narina said sincerely.

Grady shook his head and chuckled. "Humans are so out of touch with their own powers that they're willing to believe the most absurd tales instead of the truth—even when those tales include extraterrestrials or otherworldly phenomena! It wasn't aliens that built the pyramids; it was Liminals. Back then, there was a group of Liminals that could use frequency and vibration to cut and move stone with incredible precision. A group of men observed what they did and then developed the study of architecture to replicate it. The tools they designed were easier—and more importantly, cheaper. They became so popular that, within a few generations, it was all but forgotten that Liminals built them with their own powers. A few centuries later, now it's nothing more than folklore.

"Every major technological innovation has been the same since. There was a time when Liminals were telepathic. They could communicate across great distances with a simple thought. Look at you both now, only one hundred odd years after the invention of the telephone, and the two of you can't even communicate across a few feet. We've fully replaced telepathy with phone calls, emails, and texts. Later, we observed that Liminals were a networked group, all seemingly connected to each other by some invisible force, which led to the creation of the internet.

"Consciousness is the last frontier. Once we can replicate the human mind with artificial intelligence, the final shift can occur: the Merge. Technology will finally possess all the powers that humans once did. Humans will become slaves to the very tech they inspired, fully stripped of their power. The final Harvest is upon us soon. It's really such an exciting time."

Despite the situation, Spencer perked up. They had finally found someone who knew about the Harvest.

"So that's what you're doing with us? Studying our powers and then stealing them to use in the Harvest?" Narina asked. Like Spencer, she seemed to be trying to piece it all together.

Grady shook his head, confusion crossing his eyes. "Why would we use *your* powers in the Harvest?"

Spencer was completely confused as well. Wasn't that what the experiments and the siphons were for—taking their powers?

"Why else are you stealing our powers and putting them in that box?" Narina asked.

"For protection. And research," he replied flatly.

Narina stared at him.

"Liminals are the only ones who can defeat the Apparatus. We're siphoning your powers so that no one is left to stop the Harvest."

"And what about the research?"

"Liminal powers are the strongest. Using Liminals in the experiments allows us to test the strength of the siphons on the smallest number of subjects."

Spencer started to feel nauseous. A creeping thought was forming in the back of her mind about where all of this led.

"What is the Harvest, then?" Narina asked, as if sensing the same thing.

"We need a massive amount of energy, and more importantly data, to fuel the models for the Merge. We need a power source. For a paradigm shift as large as this, the power source must be equally large. We call it a Harvest because it's easier for us to do it all at once. We'll find all the ripe ones and siphon their energy simultaneously."

Narina's eyes widened.

"Rays," Grady clarified. "Anyone who still has a power source inside of them."

"How many? How many Rays do you need for the Harvest?"

"We don't know the exact calculation yet, but we estimate it to be in the millions."

Spencer gulped as she considered millions of people drained of their life force.

"Why are you telling us this?" Narina asked.

That was a good point. Grady wouldn't be sharing any of this with them if they were going to walk out of there today. He was going to kill them.

He smiled in reply.

They had to get out of here now. Spencer reached inside, trying to find any power, but she was still completely numb. Her powers were useless. She glanced at Narina, who was struggling to even hold her head up.

Think, Spencer encouraged herself. She opened the library of her mind. Help me find a solution, she said to the catalog in front of her. She thought back to everything Grady had just said, everything she had seen during the experiment, everything Narina had told her from her ayahuasca vision, everything they had learned about their powers from practicing together.

Wait a minute.

*Their powers.* Spencer and Narina had none now, but what about Rose? Spencer remembered the day they had found out about the dual nature of their gifts. The way two butterfly fairies had flown out of her and dropped dusts of power onto Narina and Spencer. She had given them some of her power.

But Rose was in another room, possibly still sedated.

They could communicate across great distances with a single thought. That was what Grady had just said about the telepathic powers of Liminals in the past.

Spencer remembered the way she'd felt when she watched the woman's powers siphoned during the experiment. It felt as if a part of Spencer had died along with the woman's energy. Grady was right; they were all connected, and Spencer was more tied to Rose and Narina than to anyone else.

She had to try something.

She pictured Rose lying in bed in the room down the hall. Spencer imagined a long telephone wire connecting the distance between them with an earpiece on either end. She pictured energy moving back and forth across the line, like whispers traveling through the air.

*Rose,* she whispered in her mind. *Rose, wake up. We're in trouble. Narina and I can't access our powers. They're about to kill us.*

Nothing.

*Rose. Rose! Wake up, please!*

Spencer could swear she felt a tug on the line. She repeated the message and waited.

Then she tried to test her powers, but she still couldn't access her vision or her shield.

A second later, it felt like something fell on her face. Small flecks landed in her eyes and mouth. She blinked and coughed. What the hell? Then the smell hit her. The dust smelled floral, just like roses.

Moments later, power started coursing through her body.

Spencer lifted her shield and threw it around herself and Narina and sent some of it back to Rose in the other room as well. Grady had no idea what she was doing. He wasn't wearing his headset because he thought their powers were muted from the drugs. He couldn't see her shield.

But Spencer's shield and vision wouldn't get them out of there— only Narina's fire could do that.

Spencer imagined a telephone hanging between her and Narina now. *Narina,* she thought. Then she yelled in her mind. *Narina! Tap your left index finger if you can hear me right now.*

Narina shook her head, looked at Spencer, and furrowed her brow, like she'd heard something but wasn't sure what it was. Spencer tried again.

Narina closed her eyes, focusing. Then she tapped her left index finger on the arm of the chair.

*Rose just sent us some powers,* Spencer said. *Can you feel them?*

Narina nodded subtly.

*We need to get out of here before Grady siphons from us. He's going to kill us. Can you do something with your fire?*

Narina clenched her mouth and made fists. Spencer saw smoke waft from the garbage can in the corner of the room behind Grady. He didn't notice.

*More,* Spencer encouraged.

The smoke turned into flames.

Grady turned to look behind him, and Narina unleashed. The garbage can erupted, the flames whirling inches away from his face.

"Shit." Grady stood up. "Fire!" he yelled.

He walked across the room, waved his access badge, and opened the door. "French!" he screamed down the hall. "There's a fire! Bring the extinguisher!"

There was no reply.

Grady looked back at Narina and Spencer, glancing down at their wrists and ankles to confirm they were still strapped in before he ran out of the room.

"I was trying to hit him," Narina said. "His shield must have diverted the fire away."

"It's okay. It still worked. We just need to think fast and get out of here."

Spencer looked down at the restraints that secured her to the chair. They were made from thick cloth bands covered with leather straps, like an industrial belt. "Can you burn through it?" she asked, looking at Narina's wrists now.

"I'll probably burn my hands off if I try."

"Focus," Spencer said. "Picture just the straps on fire and nothing else."

"Can you shield my skin?" Narina asked.

"I can try."

She pictured her shield wrapping tight around Narina's hands and feet. Seconds later, flames rose near Narina's wrists and ankles, obliterating the straps.

Narina stood up and looked down at her wrists. They were unscathed.

"No shit," she said. "Nice work, Spence."

Spencer exhaled. "My turn."

Narina nodded and moved closer. Spencer wrapped herself tight with her shield. It looked like scales the way her skin glittered from the protective bubble. Flames erupted, and suddenly she was free.

They ran to the door.

"It's locked," Narina said, pounding her fists on it. She stepped back and stared, clearly trying to use her power, but the steel door was too strong.

Spencer felt something like a memory nag in her mind. A whisper in her ear, something sliding against her right hip. She reached inside the right pocket of her drawstring pants and felt something hard and plastic. A card.

She pulled it out and looked down in awe. It was an access badge, and not the one from Angie's Cleaning Service. She didn't have time to think about how it had gotten there as she swiped it across the sensor. The door clicked, and Narina flung it open.

They peered down the hall. Grady and French were in the supply closet, yelling at each other.

"They're still looking for the fire extinguisher," Narina said. "Hurry, let's go now."

Spencer glanced up at the clock in the hallway: 6:45. She wasn't sure if it was morning or night, but she was hoping it was either too early or too late for anyone else to be there.

"We need to get Rose," she whispered, following Narina down the hall as they made their way to the room where their friend was still strapped to a hospital bed.

Rose was awake. "It worked!" she said, smiling. "I can't believe it worked."

They freed her in the same way they had themselves, using Narina's fire and Spencer's shield.

"Can you walk?" Spencer asked Rose as she stood up, her legs wobbling.

"I think so," Rose replied, holding on to Spencer for support.

"We need to go now," Narina whispered.

They were almost back to the main room. They could see the exit. But one thing stood between them and their freedom—rows of hospital beds filled with other Liminals.

"We need to save them," Rose said, reaching down to the bed nearest her, trying to shake the man awake. He didn't budge.

"They're all sedated," Narina said, shaking her head. "Even if we could free them all, we won't be able to get them out of the room."

Rose kept trying, moving from bed to bed. Spencer tried too. Maybe they could save one or two people if anyone was awake.

The fourth man Spencer shook opened his eyes. "Can you get up?" she asked him. "We're trying to get you out of here."

In the background, Narina hissed at them, "They're coming! We need to go now!"

"We need a few more minutes," Rose said. "Do something to stop them."

Spencer lifted her head to look down the hallway. Grady and French were running toward them. Narina moved in their direction, and suddenly flames erupted in front of her, blocking the hallway entrance. The men were trapped by a cage of fire.

Grady stared at the scene in front of him. "Ph-physical powers," he stammered. "That's not possible.

Spencer turned back toward the man in front of her. "You need to get up now," she said, grabbing his hand.

He shook his head. "I can't. Go! Get out while you can."

Spencer shook her head, a tear streaming down her cheek. She couldn't leave him there.

"Take it before you go," he said.

"Take what?" Spencer asked, confused.

"Take it before they take it from me." He reached toward her.

### dark days ahead

Spencer grabbed his hand, still unsure of what he meant.

When she touched his skin, she felt the warmth of his power. She looked down at him again, this time with her vision activated. A green beam of light moved from his heart down his arm and into Spencer's hand. She felt it enter her, like warm honey moving up her arm and into her heart.

The man turned into a husk before Spencer's eyes. Alive, but dead inside. Empty. He had just given her his power.

"Thank you," she whispered, tears rolling down her face as Narina pulled her away from him.

"We need to leave now." She dragged Spencer to the door as flames engulfed the room behind them.

Spencer reached for the mysterious badge one more time. It worked.

Their key to freedom, she thought, as they ran from the room and all the way out onto the steps in front of city hall.

They stood there for a minute, the sun rising in front of them. Spencer felt a mixture of energy move through her: the power from the man on the bed, the anger from Narina about everything they had just witnessed, the joy from Rose that they had escaped. Time seemed to slow as everything stilled around Spencer. The energy was building up inside of her; it was too much. Spencer planted her feet into the ground and let the power rip through her. She felt fire from Narina and breath from Rose course through every cell of her body, as if their powers were now hers. When Spencer opened her fists, an empty car parked on the street erupted in flames. Glass shattered in the windows behind them from a blast of wind.

Spencer felt a searing pain on her wrist and looked down, and her friends did as well. Next to the owl, dragon, and butterfly on each of their wrists was a new tattoo. This time, it was identical on all of them. Three dots—red, blue, and green—forming a triangle. It disappeared as quickly as it had appeared.

"What the hell was that?" Narina asked.

Rose just shrugged.

But Spencer understood. "It was a bond," she whispered.

# the escape

San Francisco
Spring 2020

Vik's phone rang at 7:23 in the morning. It was Graham.

"What the fuck happened?" he shouted, so loud Vik had to hold the phone away from his ear. "I told you to take care of the women!"

"I am taking care of it. I went there yesterday to check it out and come up with a plan. I'm heading back there first thing this morning."

"They escaped!"

Vik was surprised to notice he felt relieved.

"Get over there now and find out everything you can," Graham said before hanging up.

When Vik arrived at city hall, there were fire trucks, ambulances, and reporters everywhere. What the hell did you do, Spence? he wondered, but a part of him was impressed.

He saw two paramedics pushing someone on a stretcher toward the back of an ambulance. The man flailed his arms as he shouted. "Physical powers! They have physical powers!" he yelled as Vik got closer.

Vik looked at the man's face and turned away just as quickly to quell the nausea rising in his throat. The man's skin was completely burned off, leaving only charred and bloody fascia visible beneath it.

"Vik!" he yelled. "They have *physical* powers!"

Vik turned to get a better look, and his stomach dropped with recognition. The burned man was Dr. Grady.

He started to cough up blood. The paramedics pushing him exchanged a look, shaking their heads. Clearly, he wasn't going to make it. They pushed Grady into the back of the van and attempted CPR.

Well, at least that was one loose end Vik wouldn't have to tie up. But what had Grady meant by "physical powers"?

A reporter behind Vik was looking into a camera, speaking. "I'm Chris Falls, reporting for ABC News. We have a grisly scene this morning at city hall. Climate change has once again sparked extreme and unusual weather patterns. Onlookers say they saw a fire and a tornado outside of city hall shortly before smoke began billowing from the rotunda inside. At least three people are confirmed dead, and one is seriously injured. It's a sad day for philanthropy—the area the fire struck served as a homeless shelter, with volunteer doctors working to treat mental illness and addiction. We'll keep you updated as we learn more."

Three dead, Vik thought, feeling sick all over again. He walked over to the other ambulance. "I work for city hall. I'm part of the Homeless Initiative Program. I need to see who's dead," he said to the paramedics, the lie rolling easily off his tongue.

The paramedics nodded and opened the doors. "One doctor and two patients," one of them said. "Go ahead and take a look."

Vik climbed into the back of the van and unzipped a bag. The face was too charred to identify, but it was a man's body. He moved to the next bag. This one was a woman with brunette hair. Vik held his breath, looking her over, exhaling with relief when he realized the hair was much too short to be Spencer's. He opened the final bag. This body was completely unrecognizable except for the watch on the wrist. The watch Dr. French had worn.

Vik thanked the paramedics as he walked out, his hand in his pocket, wrapped around the metal now inside. It still felt warm to the touch. Why let a good watch go to waste?

Spencer and her friends had escaped. Graham wouldn't be happy, but Vik was.

He walked through the yellow tape now surrounding city hall, flashing his badge. He made his way into the small security room where the experiments were recorded and popped out the most recent tape, sliding it into his pocket. He'd have to ask Sven to wipe any backup data. Then he went into the observation room. The steel door had protected it from the fire outside. He looked at the black siphon device still sitting on the table and pocketed that as well.

Once he left city hall, he called Graham back. "Grady and French are dead," Vik said.

"Shit," Graham replied. "And the women?"

"Gone."

"Fuck! Can you go inside and get any recent video footage?"

"I already tried. Unfortunately, the fire destroyed it all," Vik replied smoothly.

"What about the siphon device?"

"Also destroyed."

"You've got to be kidding me."

"I wish I was."

"Well, right now we need to focus on containing the story," Graham said. "No one can find out what was going on in that room. No one can know about the experiments."

"I'm already working on it."

"And let's find those women," Graham added before hanging up.

# the totems

San Francisco
Spring 2020

The trio ran to Spencer's car. Spencer retrieved the key and drove them to Narina's house. Narina had suggested they regroup there and figure out what the hell had just happened. Rose and Spencer didn't want to go back to their apartments alone, anyway.

As Spencer parked her car in front of Narina's house, she felt a sense of relief. They were safe. They went inside and immediately collapsed onto the couch in Narina's living room.

"Sam!" Narina yelled. "Sam?"

Spencer glanced at her phone to check the time. It was a little after eight in the morning.

"He must be dropping Maya off at daycare," Narina said. "He's going to be furious. What do I tell him?"

"The truth," Rose said.

When they'd first transitioned, they'd agreed not to tell anyone, but Spencer could see that wouldn't work anymore. Narina was a wife and a mom, and she'd almost just died. Sam deserved to know what was going on. She nodded in agreement. "You should be honest with him."

They sat in silence for a while. Spencer was still processing everything they'd just been through, everything they'd just learned about the Apparatus and the Harvest.

A few minutes later, Sam opened the front door. He walked in and saw Narina on the couch first. He dropped his keys on the ground as she moved toward him. Relief and anger passed across Sam's features at the same time. He pulled Narina in tight for a hug, grabbing her head and smelling her hair like he couldn't believe she was really there. "What the fuck, Narina. Where have you been? You've been gone for two days!" As he pulled away and took in her appearance, he added, "Are you okay?"

Narina nodded. "Rose and Spencer are here too," she said, gesturing behind her.

Sam looked over Narina's shoulder and nodded to Rose and Spencer before taking a seat on the swivel chair near the fireplace. "What happened?" he asked, his voice now softer.

Narina sat in the chair across from him before she spoke. "A lot. There are a lot of things we need to tell you."

He nodded patiently. "Okay," he said, "I'm listening."

Sam already knew about Narina's ayahuasca experience and her visions of the future, but he didn't know about anything else. Narina started by retelling him about giving birth to Maya, this time adding the part about the fire and the activation of her powers. Rose told Sam about the day she had transitioned in Golden Gate Park, and Spencer shared the encounter with Vik that had triggered her own transition.

Then Narina told him about Mira and Graham and the hidden door in city hall. She paused nervously before she shared their plan to break in after hours to see what they could find. Before Sam could reply, Narina told him about the experiment Spencer had witnessed, then about their own capture, and the experiments the doctors attempted on them before they escaped.

"Holy shit," he replied when they'd finished getting him up to speed. He shook his head. "Why didn't you tell me?" he asked Narina in disbelief. "I would have helped you."

"I know you would have. I think I was scared and in denial. A part of me still didn't believe it was all real. We had no idea what we were going to find there."

Sam shook his head again. Then he suddenly stiffened. "We need to get you guys out of here. They might try to come after you."

## dark days ahead

"I don't think they know who we are," Spencer chimed in. "We used IDs with fake names and photos, and we didn't have our phones on us."

"Still," Sam said, "I think we're better safe than sorry. You guys need some quiet time away from all this to decompress."

"Shasta," Narina said quietly. "Let's go to Mt. Shasta."

Narina had been trying to convince Rose and Spencer to come with her to Mt. Shasta ever since she and Sam had taken their first trip there a few years before. The northern California town, built below the stratovolcano of the same name, was rich in spiritual folklore—some legends said that it was home to a sacred spring and a crystal city full of Atlantis descendants.

"It's always felt like a second home to me, especially after I transitioned," Narina continued. "There's something about the energy there that makes me feel more powerful. I know you guys will love it."

Rose nodded.

Spending time in a safe place sounded like music to Spencer's ears. "Okay, let's go to Mt. Shasta," she said.

"I'll find us a place to stay there," Sam said, getting up from his seat.

Spencer was surprised that he hadn't asked more questions given the magnitude of what Narina had just shared, but she was relieved he was taking the lead on getting them out of town. It was only once he walked out that Spencer noticed a huge stack of boxes in the corner of the living room.

"What's with all the boxes?" she asked Narina.

Narina let out a breath. "This is terrible timing," she said, "but Sam and I are moving. To Florida."

Rose and Spencer stared at her as if they hadn't heard correctly.

"It all happened so fast," Narina explained. "We'd been feeling the urge to leave California for a while. And I really want to be closer to my family on the East Coast. When we visited my parents a few months ago, we stopped in Tennessee, North Carolina, and Florida—just to check them out—but when we were in Florida, we absolutely fell in love with a home on the water. On a whim, we put in an offer, and it was accepted. When we came back, we decided to list our house and see what happened. We received an offer way over our asking price on the same day we listed it. It all just fell into place, like it was meant to be.

"We closed on both homes last week and have sixty days to move out. I'm sorry. I was waiting for everything to finalize before I told you both, but then it all became official right before our plan to break into city hall, and I didn't want to shift our focus. This obviously all happened before we knew what we know now about the Apparatus, but we'll figure out how to handle everything together."

They both just stared at her. Spencer felt stunned by the news.

Rose spoke first. "I'm happy that you guys are following a path that feels right for your family, but I'm heartbroken that you're leaving."

Spencer nodded in agreement.

"I'm glad we'll have time in Mt. Shasta together before we leave," Narina offered.

They left later that day. Sam drove, and Spencer sat up front so Narina could be next to Maya in the backseat. Rose sat next to her. Spencer was so deep in thought about everything that had changed over the past few days that she didn't even notice they'd spent the five-hour drive up north mostly in silence until Rose spoke up.

"Sam," she said, "I was just thinking—this all started with Narina's vision of the future in Costa Rica. You never told us what you experienced when you did ayahuasca—what did you see?"

Sam glanced up at her through the rearview mirror, and a look flashed through his eyes that Spencer couldn't discern. "What I saw is really hard to put into words," he said.

"So you didn't see the end of the world at the hands of a group of powerful men?" Rose joked.

Sam made a sound that was half cough and half laugh, startling Spencer. "Not exactly," he replied. "What I saw wasn't in this world at all."

Spencer was about to ask about that when Narina interjected, "Don't waste your time asking him questions. He still won't even tell me anything about what he experienced. It's so annoying. Sam, can we pull over at the next stop? Maya's hungry."

Sam nodded.

Narina was right—there was something special about Mt. Shasta. As soon as Spencer put her feet on the ground, it was as if the earth recharged her, sending an electrical current up through her body.

"I swear," Narina said, as Spencer sent her a knowing glance, "the mountain is an energy vortex. This place is so special."

They spent the next few days relaxing and taking time outdoors, walking through the forest. By the third day, Spencer was back to full strength, stronger even, from the energy of the mountain.

She noticed something strange. In San Francisco, she would occasionally see one or two Rays for every hundred Empties, but in Mt. Shasta, that ratio reversed. Rays were everywhere. She wasn't sure if the mountain itself charged the people who lived there in a way that strengthened their life force and turned them into Rays or if something about the energy of the place attracted Rays just like it had attracted Narina.

One morning, they walked down the main thoroughfare, Mt. Shasta Boulevard, stopping at all the local stores. They popped into a metaphysical bookstore and a crystal shop before making their way into a tiny place that sold small trinkets carved into wood. The shop owner was a Native American man who must have been about seventy years old. When Spencer saw him, she stopped dead in her tracks.

There was a small bee tattoo on his wrist in glittering white ink. A yellow light rose around him, like the sun itself. He was the brightest being Spencer had ever seen; she was almost blinded by the intensity of his glow.

"Wow," she whispered to Narina and Rose.

"What?" Rose asked, looking around blankly.

Of course—she couldn't see it. "He's a Liminal," Spencer explained. "The brightest one I've ever seen."

Rose and Narina stared too, trying to see what Spencer saw.

The shop owner looked up and saw them. He smiled as they entered. "Welcome." He walked over and introduced himself. "I'm Alo. I'm a member of the Shasta tribe. My people have called this area home for hundreds of years. My ancestors used to carve large totem poles from red cedar wood. They'd sometimes make them to tell a story or commemorate an event, but most often, they were used as a family crest to depict the powers bestowed upon a given lineage. My grandfather taught me how to carve, and now I create pocket-sized totems."

"These are so cool," Narina said, smiling at him. "I love them."

"I have the perfect one for you."

He walked over to a glass case a few feet away and grabbed a red totem, about three inches tall, from the shelf in front of him. He held out his hand to Narina, the totem resting on his palm. "Here," he said, moving it closer to her.

Narina looked at it, and her eyes grew wide. She picked up the totem and held it up in shock for Rose and Spencer to see. It was a dragon.

"And for you, Aponi," Alo said to Rose, as he plucked another totem off a different shelf.

"What?" Rose asked.

"Aponi," he said, holding up the winged totem in his hand. "It means butterfly."

"Last, but certainly not least," he said, and turned to Spencer, placing a white owl in her hand.

The three women stood there, speechless.

Alo chuckled, his eyes twinkling as bright as the sun emanating from him. "I've been waiting for the three of you," he said. "You came just in time."

"Waiting for what?" Rose asked.

"Your arrival," he said. "I'm your guide."

"For what?" Narina asked now. "What are we in time for?"

He pointed toward the calendar behind the register. It was June 18. "The summer solstice," he said. "Meet me here first thing tomorrow morning. We'll be hiking to the summit. It will take us two days, so bring hiking boots, comfortable clothes, and a pack with food. I'll bring the tent and the other gear we'll need in my pack."

"The summit?" Spencer asked.

Alo pointed out the front door of the shop to the snowcapped peak of Mt. Shasta in the distance. "The summit," he said again. "The energy of the vortex at the summit peaks on the solstice."

# the ancestors

### Mt. Shasta
### Spring 2020

They met Alo bright and early the next day.

"Morning," he said as he handed each of them a set of spiky metal chains.

"What are these?" Spencer asked.

"Crampons. You'll need them for the icy sections."

Spencer liked hiking in theory more than in practice. Her typical workout routine was to buy ten yoga classes and take three of them. As she looked up at the mountain, she realized she might be in over her head. "How long is the hike?" she asked.

"Ten miles," Alo said, "with over seven thousand feet of elevation gain."

They approached a trailhead labeled *Avalanche Gulch*. Great name. Not intimidating at all.

Her attitude quickly changed as they started to hike. The beauty was immense—immeasurable, really. The more she hiked, the more she realized she wasn't walking on a trail up a mountain; she was setting foot on the consecrated ground of a cathedral.

She thought back to when she was younger. Spencer had gone to Boston College, a Jesuit university. One night, she had been sitting in a dorm room with a few of her friends, talking, as naive women often did at that age, about their dream weddings.

"My wedding would obviously be in a church," Samantha said.

The other women murmured in agreement.

## dark days ahead

"Why would it *obviously* be in a church?" Spencer asked.

"Well, because that's where you're supposed to get married," Samantha replied with a shrug.

Spencer reframed the question. "But why do *you* want to get married in a church?"

Like all the women in the room, Spencer had grown up Catholic. She understood that weddings were sacred religious ceremonies. But she was a young woman trying to come to her own conclusions about life rather than regurgitating the dogmatic belief system that had been taught to her as a child. She genuinely wanted to understand why these women planned to get married in a church, hoping it might offer some valuable insight into her own decision one day.

Everyone looked at Spencer blankly. A few just shrugged.

She was surprised to find that no one could give her a thoughtful response. There these women were, elaborately dreaming about their future ceremonies, yet none of them had any idea why the church part was important other than the fact that a priest once told them it was.

Then Marge spoke up. "It's where I feel closest to God. I want the vows my husband and I say to each other to be recognized and heard by God, and church is where I feel closest to Him."

That struck Spencer. It was simple but profound. More importantly, it was a real answer, not a memorized one. Although she hadn't shared the sentiment back then—she'd never felt close to God in the manmade confines of a church—she understood exactly what Marge meant now. As Spencer walked up the side of Mt. Shasta, she had never felt closer to God. She looked over at Narina and Rose, both walking in complete peace, their faces glowing with a celestial radiance, and she knew they felt the same thing.

"What do you know about Mt. Shasta?" Alo asked them as they walked. "Or maybe I should ask, what theories have you heard?"

"It's known for all sorts of paranormal activity," Narina said. "Fairies, aliens, UFOs, Bigfoot. But the Lemurians are the ones people talk about the most."

"And what have you heard about the Lemurians?" Alo inquired.

"They're an ancient civilization, somehow related to Atlantis. There are some people who believe the Lemurians still live inside the mountain today in a crystal city," Narina said.

Spencer smiled as Narina spoke. Her friend was always most alive when diving down rabbit holes other people might find absurd. She had grown up watching *Beyond Belief: Fact or Fiction?*, and that love of turning the mundane into the mysterious persisted even as she grew up. She viewed reality from a kaleidoscope, not a static lens. It was one of the things Spencer admired most about her—but fairies, Bigfoot, Atlantis, and crystal cities? She turned to Alo. "Is any of it true?"

He nodded. "The legend goes that Atlantis and Lemuria were two of the most advanced civilizations that existed on Earth. Both were of a higher order of being. Their people possessed a deep connection to the soul of the earth, and that connection gave them abilities and powers. They existed peacefully alongside each other for some time, but as the years went on, they had philosophical differences about the evolution of the lesser civilizations around them.

"The Lemurians believed that these other societies should be left alone to continue to develop at their own speed. While the Lemurians knew they had higher powers, they didn't deem themselves 'better' or these other societies as 'worse,' just *different*. The Atlanteans, on the other hand, believed that the lesser civilizations should be controlled by the more evolved ones. They believed the other societies were nothing more than slaves."

Spencer noticed that she was holding her breath. Why did this story feel so *familiar*?

"The ideological differences led to many conflicts between the Lemurians and the Atlanteans, culminating after many years in a thermonuclear war, which almost wiped out the entire planet. The radiation caused the plates supporting the earth to weaken and shift. The movement created the continents and separated the elements. It was said that after the war ended, the Lemurians kept the sun and the Atlanteans kept the moon."

The hair on Spencer's arms prickled as Alo spoke.

"The Lemurians and Atlanteans both worked to spread their lineage across the newly formed continents to make their presence known in every corner of the world. Many of the ancient civilizations we know today—Mesopotamia, Egypt, the Indus Valley, Greece, Mesoamerica—were built by the powerful descendants of Lemuria and Atlantis."

"That's an interesting story," Rose said.

Alo shook his head. "Any good story is never about the characters or the plot. It's always about the listener. The reader."

Rose frowned. "I don't understand."

"I'm not telling you a story about Lemuria and Atlantis. I'm telling you a story about *you*, about where you come from." Alo paused, letting what he'd said sink in before continuing. "Where do you think the word 'Liminal' comes from?"

"Li-min-al," Rose said sounding it out slowly before it hit her. "Lemurian."

Spencer exhaled, letting it all sink in. They had descended from ancient Lemurians.

Alo nodded. "Some things morph and change over time—sometimes by accident and sometimes on purpose."

"So is there really a crystal city full of Lemurians inside the mountain?" Rose asked.

He chuckled. "Sometimes myths are created because people can't comprehend the truth. They make small changes to the story to make it fit into their version of reality. The volcano of Mt. Shasta was created during the thermonuclear war, and it's where a large group of Lemurians settled once the war ended. The settlers believed that the energy of the volcano helped to strengthen them, serving as a natural reservoir of power.

"The truth is that there are people living in Mt. Shasta who descend from the ancient Lemurians. They do have magical powers derived from light and energy, but they aren't hidden inside of some mythical crystal city in the mountain. They live right out in the open, in plain sight. I'm sure you've seen them," he said, looking at Spencer now.

She nodded. "More than I've ever seen anywhere. All Rays, though—you're the only other Liminal I've seen."

Alo nodded in return, his face saddening. "As the years passed and the storytelling faded, we've slowly lost connection to the history hidden deep within us. People need help remembering who they are."

"Do you know of the Apparatus?" Spencer asked.

Alo nodded.

"Are they the Atlanteans?"

He nodded again. "We took the sun, and they took the moon," he reiterated. "Lightness and darkness. Our ideological differences have persisted throughout time. In the battle that's upon us, we fight for freedom and they fight for control."

He knew about the battle, about the Harvest, Spencer realized. She had so many questions.

"Let's stop here for the night," Alo said. "This alcove offers good protection from the wind and elements. I'll set up the tent while you all go get us some wood for a fire."

An hour later, the tent was ready. Narina, Spencer, and Rose returned with armfuls of wood. They assembled it into a pile and sat down around it.

Alo nodded to Narina. "Can you start it?" he asked her.

Narina nodded. She stared at the wood, focusing on a specific log. Within seconds, it was fully engulfed in flames. She concentrated on another log on the other end of the pile and did the same thing.

Alo's entire face lit up in a smile. "I've waited my whole life to see physical powers like that," he said. "It doesn't disappoint. Sekhmet would be proud."

"Sekhmet?" Narina asked.

"Your ancestor. After the war, Lemuria sent the people who survived to settle across the continents. They split up the most powerful Lemurians, sending them in different directions, not wanting the Atlanteans to go unopposed in any region. The most powerful Liminals alive today each descend from a different energetic line."

He looked at Narina. "Your line descends from Sekhmet in ancient Egypt. The Egyptians couldn't understand the powers of the Lemurians and Atlanteans, so like many other cultures did, they referred to them as gods and goddesses. In Egyptian legend, Sekhmet was the daughter of the sun god, Ra. She was a warrior goddess known for breathing fire.

"Sekhmet translates literally as 'the powerful one.' In the story about the end of Ra's rule, a group of Atlanteans conspired against him. He sent Sekhmet to destroy the enemy. Her retribution was so devastating that they nicknamed her the Mistress of Dread. She was considered to be an instrument of divine retribution. In one ancient text, it's written that Sekhmet is 'she before whom evil trembles.'"

Alo paused.

"Wow," Narina said in a hushed voice.

"That tracks," Rose said.

Spencer nodded in agreement. Alo might as well have been describing Narina.

He continued. "Narina, your desire for justice and revenge is both your greatest strength and your biggest weakness. The legend says that Ra sent Sekhmet to punish the world because the laws of civilization were not being upheld. Her lust for retribution led her on a bloody rampage that almost destroyed all of Egypt. When none of the gods could get her to stop, Ra had to trick Sekhmet by turning a river into red beer. She drank it all in a bloodthirsty rage, the beer drugging her to sleep and ending her rampage."

His eyes locked on hers. "Don't let your anger overtake you," he warned.

Narina nodded in understanding.

"Show me what you can do," he said. "I want to see your power."

"Here?" she asked, looking at the forest around her. "Won't it spread?"

"You can put it out. And if you can't, she can," Alo said, pointing to Spencer.

Spencer had never considered it before, but she understood

exactly what Alo meant. She could use her shield to contain Narina's flames.

"Down there," he continued, "there's a section of dead and desiccated trees that need to be cleared away. Burn them."

Spencer looked to where Alo pointed now. It wasn't a section of trees; it was an entire forest.

Narina looked at him, her eyes wide. "All of them?" she asked.

Alo smiled. "Every single one."

Narina stared, and a few trees on the edge of the forest lit on fire.

"Not little by little," he said. "Burn all of them at once."

Narina lit a few more trees on fire.

"No," he said forcefully. "Tap into your anger. Think about something that infuriates you and reach for that feeling. Let the well of anger build up inside of you, then channel it and let it run right out through your fingers."

Narina closed her eyes, her hands in fists. Spencer knew she was focusing on some distant memory, letting it amplify inside of her. As Narina raised her arms and unclenched her fists, she opened her eyes, focusing on the trees in front of her.

Spencer watched in awe. Hundreds of trees lit on fire at once. Within seconds, the whole section of forest was up in flames.

"Holy shit," Narina said. "I did it."

The fire blazed, and then suddenly, it jumped from the section of dead trees to a living section nearby.

"It's spreading!" Rose yelled. "We need to stop it!"

"I don't know how," Narina said, looking around frantically.

"I think I can contain it." Spencer stood up, about to deploy her shield.

"No," Alo said, holding her back. "Narina needs to learn to do it herself."

"I can't," Narina said. "I don't know how."

"You can. Spencer's right, though. You need to contain it first. You're more connected to each other than you realize. You can access each other's powers, and you need Spencer's now. Anchor yourself into Spencer and then reach for her shield."

Spencer felt something tugging on her, like an invisible hand reaching out. It felt like sitting in front of a warm fireplace on a snowy winter day. She let the hand in to grab a piece of her.

She saw a glittering bubble appear around the section of trees—a dome of protection, containing the fire.

"Good," Alo said. "Now put the fire out."

"I only know how to start it, not stop it."

"The fire is just your anger made manifest. Quell your anger and the fire will extinguish naturally. Think about something that could never make you angry."

Spencer knew Narina had to be picturing Maya at that moment.

"Good," Alo encouraged. "Keep going."

Spencer watched as the flames slowly receded in front of her.

Narina exhaled, relaxing her posture.

Alo patted Narina on the back. "Good work," he said. "A controlled burn is sometimes necessary to maintain the health of the entire forest. Remember that."

Narina nodded.

He turned to Rose. "Your turn," he said. "Tell me what your power is, Aponi."

Rose stiffened a little and glanced at Spencer. Narina's power had always been the clearest, the easiest to understand. She could wield fire. But Rose and Spencer had discussed how their abilities had been a little harder to define. They knew Rose could influence the wind around her, and she could give away energy like she'd done to Spencer and Narina at city hall.

"I'm not entirely sure," Rose said. "I seem to be able to harness wind."

Alo shook his head. "It's not wind, exactly. Your power is *air*. Your ancestors settled in the Indus Valley, near what is now India. Stories of your energetic lineage can be found in ancient Hindu texts. Have you heard of Vayu?"

Rose shook her head.

"Vayu is the Hindu god of air. The divine messenger, praised as prana or 'life breath of the world.' Legend from the Upanishads says that the gods once engaged in a contest to determine who was the most powerful. When the god of vision left a man's body, the man would continue to live; he just lived without sight. When the god of hearing left, the man would continue to live; he just lived without sound. Each god took their turn to leave the body, and every time, the man continued to live with a missing faculty. Finally, when Vayu withdrew breath, the man started to gasp and wither. The man could only remain alive when empowered by air. Vayu won the contest.

"The god of air is the vital force that sustains all living beings, providing breath and vitality. His very power is in the act of giving. Vayu was often depicted as a friendly and benevolent god, but his impulsiveness was his downfall. He forgot that through him, his emotions had the ability to disrupt the balance of the entire universe. One time, after witnessing atrocities visited upon his son, Vayu cut off the supply of air to every being on Earth. Both animals and humans suffocated to death. Does that help you to understand who you are?"

"Yes," Rose replied.

It made perfect sense to Spencer. She had heard Rose being referred to as a "breath of fresh air" more times than she could count.

"Good. Show me," Alo said to Rose.

"There's already wind," she said. Spencer could feel the breeze on her arms. "Do you want me to make it stronger?"

Alo shook his head. "Giving is easy for you. I want you to take it away first, then give it back."

"I don't know how to take it away," Rose said. "Can you teach me?"

"The only thing I can teach you is about the legend of your lineage. When it comes to your powers, it's not about learning. It's about *remembering*. You have all the knowledge you need. Your power has always been inside of you; you just need to access it. Think of your emotions as the gas pedal. Find a strong emotion, or reach for Narina's anger if you need to. Tap into the intense feeling, and let your body react to it."

"I have plenty of anger. Let me send you some," Narina said to Rose, smiling.

Spencer felt a furnace blast through her veins. Narina wasn't just sending her anger to Rose; she was sending it to both of them. Spencer planted her feet, grounding herself to prevent the emotion from taking over.

But it seemed like Rose let it rip through her, and in her newfound fury, she held her breath, pulling all her power away. Everything stilled. There were no birds flying, no insects chirping, no breeze blowing. Absolute and utter silence fell on the forest, as if time had stopped.

Spencer felt disoriented. It was a strange sensory experience to feel and hear nothing.

A deer collapsed on the ground, and Rose let out a cry. She exhaled deeply, and Spencer watched a cloud of glittery dust move forward on her breath. The dust landed on the deer and then expanded to every inch of the forest canopy. Suddenly, the deer stood up. Leaves on the trees rustled, birds chirped, and insects sang.

"More," Alo said. "Reach inside for more."

The breeze intensified, whipping Spencer's face, her hair blowing everywhere.

"Concentrate it," Alo said.

Rose's eyes narrowed on a spot in front of her. A small tornado appeared and intensified, starting to suck in the branches, leaves, and dust around it.

"Good," Alo said as he held up a hand for Rose to stop. "That's enough."

Rose dropped her focus.

"It's good that you understand the limits of your power. The deer," Alo said, gesturing to the place where the animal had fallen. "Your deprivation almost killed it, and your breath brought it back from the brink. Your power can take life, and it can give it. But if you act as if you are a god, there will be consequences."

He looked between Narina and Rose. "Both of you have what

we call *atmospheric gifts*. Your powers are elemental in nature. Atmospheric gifts are incredibly strong, since they draw on your emotions, but they can become unbalanced quickly. Learning how to keep them in check is just as important as learning how to strengthen them."

He paused, letting that sink in. Then he turned to Spencer. She waited for him to speak, but he said nothing.

"What about me?" she prompted.

He shrugged. "You're a bit of a mystery. We know that you descend from Danu, the mother goddess of the Celts, but all we really know about Danu is through the name of her people. The legend has it that a group of supernatural beings arrived in Ireland in a magical mist over the isle. They were named Túatha Dé Danann, which translates to 'The People of the Goddess Danu.' She isn't mentioned in texts after that. She's considered to be a primordial goddess, a foundational figure, like the eternal force of nature itself. Others call her the matron of sovereignty and consider her to be the guardian of the land and its rightful rulers."

Spencer deflated a bit. She had been hoping to learn more about who she was and where she came from like Narina and Rose just had, but now she readied herself, curious to see how Alo wanted her to practice her powers.

Instead, he stood up from his seat by the fire. "It's time for bed. Rest up. The hike tomorrow is the most strenuous part of the journey."

As Spencer put her head down on her inflatable pillow that night, her disappointment set in, and that old nagging sensation crept into her mind.

*Nothing. I'm nothing.*

# the summit

Mt. Shasta
Summer 2020

Spencer didn't sleep well, and she woke up the next morning before everyone else. She unzipped her sleeping bag, crawled out of the tent as quietly as possible, and walked over to a lookout point a few hundred yards away.

There, she sat on the ground, pulled her knees into her chest, and stared at the rising sun in front of her. This was her favorite time of day, the slow dawn when a light mist still covered the earth around her. Alo hadn't given her much context on her lineage, but the part about coming from a group of people that appeared as a cloud of mist resonated. It was why Spencer loved her neighborhood in San Francisco. Pacific Heights sat at the top of the bay, often covered by a heavy cloud of fog. She always felt most alive walking through the veil of mist each morning.

Spencer heard noise behind her and turned to see Alo approaching. He sat down next to her, and they watched the slow advance of the sun in silence.

After a few minutes, he spoke. "You're disappointed."

Spencer shrugged. There was no reason to deny it.

"What are you disappointed about?" he asked.

Spencer paused. "It feels childish," she said, "but I'm jealous of their powers. It feels like mine are so..." She searched for the word. "...*insignificant* next to theirs. And when you told the stories of our ancestors last night, it once again felt like my story paled in comparison."

Alo nodded. "You saw my totem, right?" he asked, pointing to his wrist.

Spencer nodded. "A bee."

"I'm a pollinator," he said. "I share my knowledge and energy with those around me, and because of me, everything grows. Seeds turn into plants; Rays turn into Liminals. I'm essential for the ecosystem of the entire world, but my work is largely invisible."

He continued. "In my tribe, the highest reverence is not for the warriors. It's for the sages. The warriors go and bravely fight the battles, but the sages determine which battles are worth fighting.

"There's one story about your lineage that I didn't tell you last night. The Túatha Dé Danann were known to be a peaceful people. When another, more brutal group invaded their land, the Túatha Dé Danann fought them off twice before a final, decisive battle. The odds were stacked against the Túatha Dé Danann. On the day of the battle, they adorned themselves in their brightest colors, their flags waving proudly in the breeze, and positioned themselves at the base of the hill. As the invading troops approached, about to strike, the Túatha Dé Danann were said to have 'turned sideways into the light.' They simply *disappeared*."

"They gave up?" Spencer clarified.

Alo shook his head. "Not at all. Some view it as their departure from the mortal world and their transition to a spiritual realm in a moment of transcendence. But I like to think of it as them saying no. Faced with the reality that no one wins a war, the Túatha Dé Danann decided to reject the ground rules laid out by the invading troops. They chose another path—one that moves with the light, not against it. They made their own rules.

"The story also signifies something else. There is power in disappearing, power in becoming nothing, becoming nobody. When you realize that—when you fully become no one—the power of the universe is yours.

"There will be a day when all that power will be in the palm of your hand. And on that day, you'll need to know when all of it is *enough*. You'll see it eventually, Spencer—you're the key to it all."

"The key to what?" she asked.

"That's for you to figure out. I can't walk the path for you. It's your job to put the pieces together." And with that, he stood up and left.

A little while later, they packed up their tent and continued toward the summit. After walking for an hour, Alo motioned for them to stop and pulled out his crampons. "We'll need these for the last stretch," he said, gesturing to the snowcapped final section of the trail ahead of them.

They each strapped the spiky chains to their feet and walked on, their pace slowing substantially as they carefully traversed the ice. They were all winded and tense by the time they reached the small plateau just beneath the pinnacle of the mountain.

"I want you each to climb the summit alone, one at a time. While the three of you have a rare bond, it's important to remember that you are each strong in your own right," Alo said.

Narina went first, followed by Rose, then Spencer, each standing alone, high above the earth beneath them. As Spencer stood on the peak, she felt two conflicting truths exist at once. She was both on top of the world and infinitesimally small—everything and nothing at the same time.

She returned to the group below her, now sitting in a circle.

"Can I ask you something?" Spencer said to Alo.

He nodded.

"You said something about Narina's physical powers yesterday. It echoed something we heard from one of the men who captured us about powers being physical instead of energetic. What exactly does that mean?"

"Most Liminal powers are strictly energetic," Alo explained. "They can influence the energy plane, but they don't manifest on the physical plane. But like the volcano we're sitting on top of, power builds in cycles before it erupts. We're approaching a particularly powerful cycle, one that peaks in ten years. That power is peaking in the three of you as well, having built up over hundreds of years through your lineage. It's what allowed you to create the bond." He gestured to the invisible triangle tattoos on their wrists.

"You were right," Narina said, looking at Spencer.

Spencer nodded. "Somehow I knew it was a bond, but I have no clue how it works. Do you?" she asked, turning to Alo now.

"It's called the Triumvirate. The unique alchemy of your powers creates something much stronger than your three powers separately. The bond magnifies your abilities and connects you to each other. Legend has it that the bond acts as a sort of tipping point. It's said that as the Trium bond nears completion, all Liminal powers began to manifest physically. I'm not sure I fully believed it until I saw your powers last night. An ability like yours to influence the physical world around you hasn't been seen for centuries.

"But the Apparatus—the Atlanteans—are also stronger now. They'll use this window to once again attempt to seize control of humanity. They learned their lesson during the thermonuclear war, and instead of taking control all at once, they've slowly chipped away over centuries, winning many smaller battles. They've become the de facto rulers of the realm. And while they might rule the realm, they don't power it. At least not yet."

"What does?" Rose asked, joining the conversation.

"Humans," Alo said simply. "Human capital is the primary asset of all the world's governments. But that human capital isn't education or skills or experience. It's energy. Humans are more powerful than they realize, and the Apparatus has used innovation to externalize that power, to transfer it from humans into technology."

"Like Dr. Grady said," Narina noted, locking eyes with Spencer again.

Spencer nodded, remembering how the doctor had said that nothing was created, just observed and then copied.

"There's a reason why when tech is first introduced, it often feels like *magic*," Alo added.

Spencer thought about the first time she had scrolled on social media, ordered food from an app, or used a search engine. Alo was right—it had enchanted her.

He continued. "The Apparatus has been casting their spell for a long time now, and most humans are so under the influence of tech that they don't realize it's magic anymore. They think the technology holds the power, but they forget that it was inspired by their own forgotten abilities. Even our own intelligence, our ability to discern, is being stripped away by seemingly helpful tech—search, maps, and monitors. But that level of disembodied intelligence is the goal. Once humanity's energy and intelligence are fully externalized into technology, the Apparatus will rule *and* power the realm."

Spencer felt like it was too late. "Their tech is already too advanced. We saw the siphon devices they have. I feel like we don't stand a chance," she said quietly.

Alo nodded. "That's what they want you to think. The Apparatus has been successful for so long now that they believe their power is unmatched. Let them underestimate you. They won't anticipate your strength. Use that to your advantage."

"But how do we stop them?" Narina asked.

"The Apparatus believes they've broken down the Liminal network, and in many ways, they have. It's your job to rebuild it, to create a network of Liminals to defeat the Apparatus. You will need to reawaken the power within others. Use your vision," he said to Spencer, "to find the most powerful Rays and help them become Liminals. More importantly, identify the right Liminals to bond to create other Triums. A Trium's magnified powers make them virtually unstoppable. As far as we know, the Apparatus has no Trium equivalent."

Spencer inhaled.

"The world as you know it is about to change very soon. There are dark days ahead. The Apparatus is putting their plan into action, laying the groundwork for what's to come next.

"There will be a battle when the cycle peaks on the Harvest. The Apparatus will attempt to seize control of humanity once and for all. That battle is your destiny. Remember, as you fight, that everything is really one thing. There is no right or wrong, no good or evil, no light or dark. The illusion of duality only makes it seem so. Winning is not the goal; harmony is. The victory you desire keeps the world in balance; the one the Apparatus seeks throws the world into chaos."

Spencer felt suddenly nervous. They had been so focused on finding the Apparatus that she had forgotten about what came after that. A battle.

"Take out your totems, please. The ones I gave you in the shop," Alo said.

The women each reached into their pockets and pulled out the small wooden animals.

"Place them on the ground," he said.

Alo closed his eyes and spoke in his native language first, touching the top of each of the three totems. As he spoke, Spencer felt the ground rumble. "These totems have been imbued with the energy of the volcano beneath us, the volcano our ancestors created centuries ago combined with a touch of your own power. Keep the totem with you always."

"Does it give us extra strength?" Narina asked.

"Not exactly. It stores the essence of your energy. It will help you all stay connected to each other. Think of the totems as the antennas powering the network you're about to build."

He paused before speaking one last time. "I've done my part—now the job is yours."

Narina, Rose, and Spencer looked at each other with the weight of the world on their shoulders.

They made the descent in silence. At the base of the mountain, Spencer placed her pack in the back of Narina's car, thanked Alo, and hugged him goodbye. As Narina drove them back to the rental house, Spencer pushed the heaviness of everything she'd just learned out of her mind and attempted to focus on the warm shower and long nap she couldn't wait to take.

When she entered the small cabin, Spencer saw Sam pacing in front of the TV.

Narina and Rose walked in behind her.

Sam turned to face them. He was crying, a look of horror on his face.

Narina ran to him. "What's wrong? Is Maya okay?"

Sam just stood there, at a loss for words, staring at the TV. Tears rolled down his cheeks.

They all turned to look at what he was watching.

# the emergency

San Francisco
Summer 2020

*Stop by my office when you have some time,* Graham pinged Vik, a week after the events at city hall.

A minute later, Vik peeked around Graham's door. "What's up?" he asked.

"We found them and took care of them."

"Found who?"

"The three women from city hall," Graham said.

Vik's stomach clenched. "What do you mean? The IDs were fake. We had no leads."

"The IDs were fake, but the photos on them weren't. I had my guy run a matching algorithm on the photos against every known directory and database in the country. We sent someone to take care of them."

"Take care of them?" Vik asked.

Graham nodded, offering no additional details.

Vik felt some sense of relief. If Graham had gone after the women in the photos, then he still didn't know that Spencer and her friends were involved. But the relief was quickly washed away by the knowledge that three innocent women were now dead. Vik justified what had happened with Brian as self-protection—Vik's own life was on the line, after all—but it was harder to justify killing these women.

"I don't enjoy the decision I had to make," Graham said, "but there is too much at stake. A few pieces of the puzzle are about to fall into place that will usher in big changes. We can't take any chances now. It had to be done."

Before Vik could ask what he meant about puzzle pieces, Graham continued talking. "You've done really great work over the last few months. I'd like to bring you more into the action now. There's an important meeting happening this weekend at my place in Palm Springs. A few of the Architects will be there, and I'd like for you to join us. We're meeting Friday morning, so you'll need to fly out on Thursday. Stay through the weekend if you like, and we can golf afterward."

Vik nodded, but he knew Amelia wouldn't be happy with him—this was one of many last-minute work trips he'd taken at Graham's request.

On Thursday, Vik planned to head straight for the airport from work, but as his driver pulled up, his phone rang. It was Amelia.

Before he could even say hello, he heard Sophia wailing in the background. "What's wrong?"

"Sophia just had a seizure!" Amelia cried out. "It's over now, but she doesn't seem normal."

"Did you call Dr. Pratt?" Vik asked, jumping into action mode.

"No, I called you first. Should I call 9-1-1?"

"Let me try to call the doctor. I'll call you right back, okay?"

Luckily, Dr. Pratt was still in the office, and the receptionist put him on the line to speak with Vik. He told Vik that if Sophia wasn't actively seizing, there was no need for an ambulance, but they should get her to the hospital immediately for tests. They'd want to monitor her.

"Meet me at UCSF," Vik said when he called Amelia back. "We need to bring Sophia in for tests. I'll be there in about thirty minutes. Dr. Pratt said to ask for Dr. Everett, an attending he recommends who's on call today."

"Okay," Amelia said nervously.

Vik could tell she was crying. "Amelia, it's going to be okay. Sophia is going to be okay."

"I hope so," she whispered.

When Vik arrived at UCSF, Amelia was already sitting in the lobby, holding Sophia.

"They said it should just be a few minutes," Amelia shared.

"Good." He nodded as he sat down next to his family.

He kissed Amelia and Sophia on the forehead. It felt like they had crossed some imaginary hurdle by making it to the hospital. Now it would only be a matter of time before they had some answers.

Vik pulled out his phone and opened the airline app, changing his flight from later that night to first thing the next day. He hoped he could still make the meeting, but right now, being there with Amelia and Sophia was more important. He opened his texts next.

Vik Something came up, I changed my flight from tonight to tomorrow morning. I'll see you at the meeting.

Graham You need to be on a flight tonight.

Vik It's a family emergency. I'm at the hospital with Sophia. I'll explain more in person.

Graham Have Amelia take care of it. You're needed here.

What a prick, Vik thought as he read Graham's last text. He shoved his phone into his pocket.

They called Sophia's name a minute later. After the initial intake with the nurse, Vik was relieved to see Dr. Everett arrive.

"I just got off the phone with Dr. Pratt," he said. "He filled me in. We'll start with some lab work and do some scans and run additional tests if that's deemed necessary. Given the nature of what happened, we'll want to keep her overnight for observation regardless of what we find."

"Can we stay with her?" Amelia asked.

"Yes, of course," Dr. Everett said.

He looked at Vik and pulled him aside. "We have a suite available if you want it," he said.

"That would be great," Vik replied. The perks of being rich, he thought to himself as he imagined having to sit upright in a vinyl-covered lobby chair all night.

Nurses came in and out throughout the night, checking Sophia's vitals and taking her for various tests. Dr. Everett checked in a few times as well, but nothing was conclusive yet. He came in again early the next morning.

"My shift is about to end. Everything is looking good, but I'd like to do a final scan before we let you leave. If it looks clear, we'll be able to discharge her back into Dr. Pratt's care."

"Sounds good. Thanks for everything, Dr. Everett," said Vik. He pulled out his phone. Graham had texted an hour earlier.

Graham  Where are you?

Vik  I'm still at UCSF, we should be leaving here soon. I'm not sure if I'll make the meeting. I won't make it to Palm Springs before this afternoon.

Graham  Vik, you need to get out of the city now.

Vik  I'll be there as soon as I can.

Vik was exhausted and had zero tolerance for Graham ordering him around. He put his phone on Do Not Disturb before pocketing it again.

He sat down, leaned his head back, and closed his eyes, relaxing for the first time since Amelia had called him. She had left a few minutes before to get them coffee from the cafeteria.

Vik felt a low vibration and went to reach for his phone. Then he realized the sensation was coming from the floor beneath him. The feeling intensified, and something started to fall from the ceiling. He looked up to see dust crumbling above him. The sounds hit him next—things moving, falling, and breaking around him.

Then he felt a sharp jolt.

He realized what was happening the same moment someone in the hallway yelled it.

"Earthquake!"

# the record

Mt. Shasta
Summer 2020

Spencer turned her attention to the TV and saw an image of what looked like San Francisco, but where the Golden Gate Bridge and Alcatraz Island should have been, she instead saw water. A tall, craggy cliffside had replaced the former shoreline and beach.

A reporter was speaking now. "A record-breaking 9.7-magnitude earthquake struck San Francisco eight hours ago. Part of the city, notably Fisherman's Wharf and the Marina, have completely disappeared into the bay. Thousands are assumed to be dead."

The news channel switched to a different scene, a livestream of the mayor standing outside of what had been city hall, giving a speech. It looked like a bomb had been dropped behind her, the domed building now nothing but a heap of rubble.

The mayor spoke somberly. "The city of San Francisco and the greater Bay Area woke up this morning to a devastating reality as the largest recorded earthquake in history struck while most of us slept peacefully in bed. We're still assessing the extent of the damage, but the liquefaction zones appear to have been hit hardest. We're working with the Red Cross and several other aid organizations to rescue those currently trapped and get them urgent medical care. I'll keep you updated as the situation unfolds."

Before the newscaster came back on, the cameraman cut to a widescreen view of the mayor. Standing behind her, once again, was a man Spencer recognized. Graham.

Narina grabbed Spencer's and Rose's hands. "They've started," she whispered.

Spencer understood what Narina meant. The Architects' plan had begun.

# the break

### San Francisco
### Summer 2020

The hospital windows shook. The ceiling collapsed in the corner of the room, and items from the floor above fell through the crevice. People started running in the halls. Alarms seemed to be going off everywhere.

Sophia, Vik thought as he jumped up and sprinted down the hall toward the room where they'd taken his daughter for the scan. He ran in and stopped abruptly, his brain taking in what he saw in pieces instead of all at once. Coffee from two overturned cups was splattered all over the floor. Several doctors were trying to lift the donut-shaped section of a CT machine that had cracked and fallen during the earthquake. A nurse was holding back Amelia as an animal sob came out of her body. Dr. Everett was walking over to Vik, shaking his head, tears running down his face.

The lifeless body of a small child was lying on the bed, buried beneath the CT machine.

Before Vik could fully process everything, another piece of information entered his mind. The text from Graham. His insistence. *You need to get out of the city now*, he had said. Then Vik remembered the insurance companies and the nonspecific nature of the changes they had made to policies that would exclude coverage for natural disasters in California.

The pieces fell into place all at once.

Vik's daughter was dead. And it was Graham's fault.

Then Vik broke.

# the damage

**California**
**Summer 2020**

While they stood there in Mt. Shasta watching the news, an aftershock from the earthquake occurred in the Pacific Ocean, nearly one hundred miles off the coast of Southern California. Two hours later, the second-largest tsunami ever recorded struck land.

The waves were three hundred feet tall and decimated four hundred square miles.

Los Angeles was gone.

# the network

San Francisco
Summer 2020

In the weeks after the Trium returned from Mt. Shasta, they put their destiny aside to focus on their reality. Spencer worked tirelessly alongside other San Francisco residents, helping to clean up and rebuild the city she called home. The aftermath of the earthquake was difficult to look at—her favorite places and memories were now nothing more than graveyards of rubble. But the most shocking part of the damage was the way entire sections of the city had simply disappeared.

Much of San Francisco had been built on liquefaction zones, areas that—as the name suggested—had a high risk of turning into pseudoliquid. During the shaking of the earthquake, the loose sediment these areas were built on had combined with water, creating a saturated soil that behaved more like a liquid than a solid. It slid around, opened up, and swallowed anything above it. A neighborhood known as the Marina and sections of land from Fisherman's Wharf down to South Beach had simply vanished. There before the earthquake and gone after, swallowed by the bay.

Nearly everyone in the city knew someone who had disappeared that day. They were presumed dead, likely buried alive or drowned.

Spencer's apartment was eerily untouched by it all. She lived at the top of a hill in Pacific Heights, built on one of the strongest pieces of bedrock in the entire city. She used to spend her

Saturday mornings walking to the beach. She would leave her apartment and head north until she reached the waterfront path near Crissy Field. The journey from her front door to the shoreline took her forty-five minutes. Now, if she left her apartment and walked the same route, within two blocks she'd be stepping over the edge of a two-hundred-foot cliff, free-falling into the bay below her.

While Spencer's apartment had been spared, her friend Luisa's place in the Marina hadn't. Luisa had the type of bubbly personality that brightened every room she entered. She talked with an almost musical lilt and moved with an effervescent energy that seemed to imbue her from within. Her face was plump and dewy in that enviable natural way that women tried to emulate, first with blush and highlighter and later with injectables and lasers.

A month before the earthquake, Luisa had started dating a guy who lived over the bridge in Sausalito. She'd been annoyed it took her thirty minutes to drive to his place every time they hung out and debated ending things with him because of the inconvenience. But the night before the earthquake, they'd had a fun date at a popular bar close to where he lived, and she'd decided to spend the night at his house instead of returning to hers. When the earthquake struck early the next morning, Luisa was safe in Sausalito, while her neighbors were eaten alive by the Pacific Ocean. That single decision saved Luisa's life.

Spencer had told Luisa she could crash on her couch as long as she needed, and she'd been living there for a few weeks.

One night, as Spencer was heading out of the apartment for a dinner at Narina's—it would be one of their last before Narina and Sam officially moved to Florida—Luisa asked if she could join. Everyone was still shaken by what had happened, but Luisa was in a particularly depressed state. Her entire life had been wiped away, and she was struggling to find solid ground again. She tried to put on a brave face most days, but she couldn't hide it from Spencer. From the day Spencer had received her powers, she'd realized which of her friends were Rays. Luisa always had a bright blue light around her, but since the earthquake, it had diminished so much that Spencer wondered if it would just disappear altogether.

Spencer said yes to Luisa's request even though she knew Narina and Rose had hoped to spend the night brainstorming about how to build a network of Liminals. She quickly texted the thread about the change in plans.

The drive to Narina's house, which used to take thirty minutes, now took nearly two hours, since so many roads and highways had been structurally damaged. Rose was already sitting at the dining table when they arrived. Narina had opened a bottle of wine and had glasses waiting for them.

Narina's annoyance at the uninvited guest seemed to dissipate quickly when she saw Luisa's state. Luisa was barely able to make it through dinner, with tears welling up several times as she excused herself repeatedly to go to the bathroom.

"This reminds me of you after Vik dumped you," Narina said as Spencer and Rose brought their dishes over to the sink after dinner.

"Gee, thanks." Spencer was secretly pleased to realize the snub didn't make her sad. There had been a time when any mention of Vik had caused a pang deep in her chest. Maybe she was finally over him.

"It's hard to watch," she said. "I can see her light fading in front of my eyes."

"She's a Ray?" Rose asked.

Sometimes Spencer forgot she was the only one who could see it. She nodded. "She's blue like you."

"I wonder if we could help her transition," Rose said.

"What do you mean?"

"Alo said we were supposed to create a network," she replied. "It's our job to turn Rays into Liminals."

"But how can we just turn someone into a Liminal?" Spencer asked.

"I don't know exactly, but we were Rays before," Rose said, "and different personal circumstances triggered each of our transitions. What if every Ray is destined to be a Liminal and they just need help with the transition?"

Spencer and Narina remained quiet in thought.

"She might be right," Narina said. "Would Luisa be open to trying?"

Spencer considered it. Luisa certainly had a spiritual bent and was open to otherworldly things, if not as a real possibility, then at least as something she liked to explore philosophically. She and Spencer had bonded in college watching movies and shows centered around women with magical powers—*Charmed*, *The Craft*, and *Practical Magic* were some of their favorites. Luisa was probably as good a candidate as anyone would be.

"I think she might be open to it."

"Let's go talk to her," Narina said.

They told Luisa about their powers. They left out the part about the Apparatus and the battle, still uncertain how much of that to share, but they told her about Empties, Rays, Liminals, and each of their transitions.

When they finished explaining, Spencer turned to Luisa. "Luisa, you're a Ray. I can see your glow. We think you can become a Liminal. Do you want to try to transition?"

Luisa looked at Spencer, defeated. But there was also something else in her expression now: hope. "What do I have to lose at this point?" she asked. "How do we trigger the transition?"

Narina, Rose, and Spencer shared a glance. They hadn't really gotten that far in planning yet.

Narina spoke up. "I had my first experience with altered consciousness doing mushrooms when I was twenty-one. A few years ago, I started guiding people through journeys using a low dose of psilocybin that I grow at home. During these journeys, a few of the people have connected to a deep power within themselves—some think of it as God or Source, but really, it's just energy. We could start with a journey and see what happens?"

Luisa shrugged. "Why not?"

She met Narina the next morning for a guided journey. Narina dissolved a small dose of her homegrown mushrooms in water and

## dark days ahead

told Luisa to drink up. Luisa moved to a bed and donned an eye mask as Narina put on a playlist meant to induce theta brainwaves. She wept hysterically for the next two hours.

Later, she told them all about her experience. She'd found herself in a dream—or a nightmare, rather. She was in her apartment the morning of the earthquake. She awoke in bed as the ground shook around her. Then suddenly, she was swallowed alive by the ocean. She spent the next few hours floating underwater as entire families and homes passed by. Parents screamed and children cried. She relived the entire harrowing experience. Luisa realized in that moment that part of what she was holding on to was guilt. She felt guilty that she'd escaped the events of that morning out of sheer luck. A decision she'd made on a whim to sleep with a guy she had gone on a few dates with had saved her life. She'd survived, while every one of her neighbors, many of whom were her friends, had died.

During the journey, she let that guilt go, let it run out of her hands and feet into the cold water that surrounded her.

Afterward, Spencer could see it—Luisa's light was a little brighter, a more vibrant blue.

"I think it's working," Spencer said. "We just need to keep going."

Luisa started working with Rose. The type of coaching Rose offered focused on integrating these types of profound life experiences and allowing them to serve as a transformational bridge to a new way of being. After each session, Luisa said she felt lighter, more alive, but still no transition happened.

Until one day, six weeks after the earthquake, Spencer's phone rang.

"It worked!" Luisa yelled when Spencer answered the call.

Luisa had been out for a walk at Ocean Beach. Ever since her first journey with Narina, she'd felt a strange calmness near the water, as if the source of all her pain also offered a healing balm. She saw something floating in the water. It looked like a large piece of siding from a house. It wasn't an unusual sighting since the earthquake—dozens of crews of workers picked debris out of the water every day—but Luisa swore she saw something on top of the floating piece. A body, she realized as another pang of grief hit her. Just another casualty of that fateful morning. But then she saw a small flash of movement. It was so subtle, she thought her eyes were deceiving her. Then she saw it again—something had definitely moved. Whatever it was, it was alive.

"Someone's out there!" Luisa yelled, looking around, but no one was within earshot.

She ran into the water, attempting to swim to the body, but the waves were too strong. She kept getting pushed back, pulled underwater. The body was drifting farther out to sea with each passing wave. A giant one dragged Luisa under for almost a minute. When she finally resurfaced, she was all the way back near the shore. The makeshift raft had to be five hundred feet away from her now, beyond the breaking waves.

She stood up, and anger ripped through her.

No. Not again. I am not watching someone else disappear.

Luisa dug her feet into the ground and balled her hands into fists. She felt something move through her body. In front of her, the water started parting, as if some invisible force was reaching into the ocean and pushing it aside. The ocean gently moved out of the way, creating a path that led straight to the raft floating in front of her. She ran toward it, and as she reached for the small boy lying there, she saw the outline of a dolphin appear on her wrist momentarily.

The boy's name was Elijah.

Luisa had parted the water to save his life. She was a Liminal.

Narina, Rose, and Spencer now had a working theory about how to initiate the transition. Spencer would find potential candidates by identifying Rays with her vision. Narina would work with them to break them down and burn away the illusions. Then Rose would put them back together and help them transition into a higher state of being.

They decided to start with the Rays in their own lives first. They

## dark days ahead

approached Spencer's friend Zuri next. Zuri was a mutual friend of both Spencer's and Luisa's from college. She had a deep, intuitive intelligence that was only surpassed by her beauty. She was so statuesque—with high cheekbones, pillowy lips, and a jawline that could cut glass—that Spencer wondered why Zuri had never become a model.

Zuri had gotten married earlier that year. She and her husband had gone against their families' wishes for a traditional and elaborate Ghanaian ceremony, instead opting for a simple but elegant venue just outside the city. Spencer and Luisa had both attended, watching as their friend wed the man she loved. But that man had been ripped away from Zuri the morning of the earthquake.

The couple had favored modern luxury and bought an apartment in a new high-rise building near the South Beach liquefaction zone three months before the earthquake struck. The few blocks just east of where they lived had been swallowed by the water, and their building had collapsed. Zuri had somehow survived without a single scratch, but her husband, who had been lying in bed next to her, was buried alive in the rubble. An extraction team pulled his body out two weeks later. Spencer thought that Zuri had handled the entire thing with an astonishing level of grace, as if she refused to be swayed by the same force that had swayed the entire city and stolen her love.

Her glow was a deep, jewel-toned green, as stunning as an emerald, and Spencer noticed the way it had intensified after the earthquake. When she told Zuri about the Liminals, her friend volunteered immediately.

Zuri spent a lot of time working with Rose, processing her grief. One morning, as she and Rose went for a hike on a trail in the Marin Headlands, they talked about how powerless Zuri had felt when the building collapsed around her and on top of her husband. She wished she could have protected him, that she could have moved the heavy pieces of cement and steel that had crushed him through sheer strength of will.

"Why don't you try it now?" Rose asked.

"What do you mean?" Zuri asked, staring at the landscape around them.

"There's a rock right there." Rose pointed. "Why don't you try to move it?"

Zuri looked at the rock, channeling what she had felt the morning of the earthquake, and planted her feet into the ground. She felt something enter her and move through her. She smiled at the smell: cedarwood and bergamot. It was her husband, wrapping his energy around her, strengthening her. The stone moved in front of her, but it wasn't just one stone. Several dozen rocks moved at once, forming a huge wall in front of her like a barrier of protection.

"Holy shit," Zuri said, feeling suddenly alive. "I want to try something else."

She reached out with her mind to grab a stone. Then she used the power inside of her to hurl it twenty feet away. She lifted every one of the several dozen stones nearby and threw them with the same intensity. It was as if she were excavating her husband's body. She felt the wind of her husband kiss her cheek. When she finished with the rocks, she looked down and saw a leopard appear on her wrist.

Rose decided that the Liminal transition was so momentous, it required its own ceremony, one to honor the life left behind and to commemorate the first steps on a new path. She told Luisa and Zuri to each find a small item that embodied their new state of being. She met them at the places where they had transitioned—Luisa at the beach and Zuri in the headlands—and had them place their items on the ground.

She remembered Alo's words as she spoke. "These items have been imbued with the energy of your ancestors, combined with a touch of your own power."

Rose laughed when she saw the items they had each chosen. Luisa had brought a dolphin keychain and Zuri had found a leopard figurine from a children's toy set. They had unwittingly created their own totems.

\*

The process was working. Spencer found other Rays and Narina and Rose helped them transition. By the end of the year, they had helped five Rays become Liminals. By the time of the Harvest nearly a decade later, there were almost two hundred Liminals, and hundreds more Rays who were assisting in the work.

But it wasn't just them.

In 2020, a collective loss of innocence happened across the United States. It started with the earthquake and tsunami that devastated the West Coast in June. Then in September, the cyberattacks hit New York's subway before bringing the entire city to its knees. By the end of the year, the three hubs of industry, entertainment, and tech—the bright and shining beacons that represented the longstanding American Dream—were gone.

If the Apparatus had wanted chaos and destabilization, they certainly got it, but they also got something they weren't bargaining for. Life in the years leading up to 2020 had become a sleepwalking malaise for most Americans. Religion had been replaced by social media, content consumption, and processed food as the opiate of the masses.

When life became more fragile following the disasters and attacks, people started looking around, wondering what the hell they had been doing with their precious time. As they took in the new world taking shape around them, their focus shifted—"a grand disillusionment," one columnist had called it.

People began to notice the way the facts on the ground—the living reality of those involved in the disasters—seemed to differ from the narratives being shared by the media. In California, questions arose that demanded better answers than what the residents were being given. Why had insurance policies been changed throughout the state in the months before the disasters that allowed for exclusions of these events, leaving millions without coverage? Why were banks allowed to continue to collect mortgage payments on home loans in the immediate aftermath, leading to hundreds of thousands of defaults and bank foreclosures? Why were the cities of San Francisco and Los Angeles not approving permits for people to rebuild their homes? Why were those same city governments suing residents for trying to build temporary homes on their own properties? Why were the plans to convert these cities into Geos suddenly fast-tracked?

To some, it almost seemed as if there were people in power who had anticipated the disasters and made adjustments in advance. Adjustments that made the disasters a boon of economic opportunity for a handful of individuals and companies.

One comedian joked that the puppet masters pulling the strings had unknowingly awoken the sleeping giant, referring to middle America's generally narcotized stupor and burgeoning waist size before the crises. One popular podcast host posted a simple question on social media: *Where are the adults in the room?*

Theories attempting to explain the events ran the gamut from engineered weather to shapeshifting aliens to the simple moronic ineptitude of those in charge. Whatever the case, a slow rebellion started to build.

Then the Great Scarcity began a few years later, and many of those who awoke from their stupor were knocked back down into the mud, too busy trying to find food, water, and jobs to support their families. Surviving took precedence over rebelling for a time, but the spirit of freedom was woven into the fiber of the American psyche, and it could only be trampled on for so long before it stubbornly found its way back to the surface.

People began to hear whispers of a network forming, a group working to dismantle the power structures that many believed were behind the catastrophic events over the past few years. Spencer even hired one of the Rays to handle the thousands of inbound requests coming from people across the country, volunteers trying to find out how they could help.

And the Network was born.

# the offer

### New York City
### December 12, 2030

Spencer stared at Vik, replaying the memory he had just inserted into her mind. He had helped her escape from city hall all those years before—but why?

As if answering her mental question, Vik spoke up. "Spence, I'm on your side. I want the Apparatus gone as much as you do."

She didn't believe him.

"Do you know where I was when the earthquake hit San Francisco?" he asked.

This line of questioning threw her off. She shook her head, perplexed.

"I was right in the middle of it, at the hospital with my daughter. A machine collapsed on top of her. It crushed her to death."

Spencer inhaled sharply. The Network had kept tabs on Vik, but Spencer had explicitly told them she never wanted to hear about him, especially any personal details. She had needed distance from him for her own sanity. She had never heard about his daughter.

"I had no idea," she said honestly. "I'm so sorry."

Vik nodded. "I never recovered, and neither did my marriage. You might say I dug my own grave by becoming an Architect in the first place, but everything changed for me when my daughter died. From that moment forward, I vowed to kill Graham and dismantle the Apparatus."

Spencer looked into his eyes and saw grief. And rage.

"Let me help you, Spence," he implored.

"I need time to process all of this," she said.

Vik nodded. "Sleep on it. I'll be in touch tomorrow."

She stood outside the bar for a few minutes after Vik left. The cold air helped her focus. Spencer didn't know what to do about him, but she couldn't make this decision alone. She readied herself to send a message, feeling a sense of dread already anticipating the response she'd get.

*I just met with Vik. He offered to help us take down the Apparatus.*

She sent the message quickly down the bond. Then she waited for Narina and Rose to reply.

# stage five /
# plateau of productivity

# the whisper

### New York City
### December 13, 2030

A few weeks earlier, the Network had finalized a plan for the Harvest. Based on their intel, they believed the Apparatus would attempt to siphon energy from a handful of major US cities on the night of the winter solstice. Power was most centralized in urban areas, and the new Geos forming in New York City, San Francisco, and Los Angeles would make perfect targets.

Alo had been right about the Network but wrong about the Trium bond. Despite their best efforts, Spencer, Narina, and Rose had never been able to create another Trium. They'd tried different combinations of powers, personalities, and any other traits they could think of—astrological signs, Ayurveda doshas, Enneagram types—but none of it had worked.

With only one Trium and three target cities, they had a tough choice to make. Distance weakened the Trium's powers, but it offered one critical advantage: communication. The only way the Network could communicate across physical locations in real time outside of any Apparatus-owned technology was through Narina, Rose, and Spencer's bond, so they had decided to separate. Narina went to Los Angeles, Rose remained in San Francisco, and Spencer came to New York City.

They had all agreed this was the best plan—everyone except Sam. Sam thought separating the Trium was a mistake. He believed the Apparatus would strike a single location, and his bet was on

New York City, but the rest of the Network thought that putting everyone in one place was too big a risk. It would leave the country too exposed, so he'd been overruled. The remaining Liminals had strategically dispersed across the three locations based on their powers, and they had all arrived in their designated cities a week earlier.

But after Spencer's run-in with Vik, Narina and Rose booked a red-eye flight to New York. They needed to figure out what to do together.

Spencer walked back to the church on Christopher Street the next morning. Her confusion about how to handle the Vik situation and her dread about the impending Harvest were temporarily overridden by excitement. She couldn't wait to see her friends.

Narina and Rose were both already there when she arrived, and they quickly came in for a hug. The three of them had planned a private morning meeting before the New York–based contingent of the Network assembled later, giving them a chance to debrief on Vik first.

"I'm so happy to see you," Spencer said, feeling a momentary sense of relief for the first time in what seemed like forever.

"How are you doing? How was it seeing Vik?" Rose asked immediately.

"I can't believe you blocked us out," Narina said before Spencer could reply.

Narina was right; Spencer had blocked them out yesterday. The Trium's connection was like a telephone—both ends had to actively send and receive a signal for it to work. They generally kept the connection open unless they were dealing with something private. Spencer had kept her end of the bond closed the previous night, not knowing what might happen with Vik and wanting time to process everything.

"I'm sorry," Spencer said. She knew any attempt to rationalize her decision was beside the point. This wasn't just about her feelings and her past with Vik. It affected the entire Network.

## dark days ahead

"He's an Architect. He has the Mark," she added.

"Of course he is," Narina said. "The only person who was in denial about that was you."

"What happened when you saw him?" Rose asked.

"I ran into him, and he asked me to meet him for a drink."

"Could you get a sense for what his power is?" Narina asked, cutting straight to the point.

"He can manipulate minds," Spencer replied.

"How do you know?"

"He put a thought—a memory, actually—into my mind."

"How did he get past your shield?" Narina questioned.

"I dropped it." Her voice grew quieter. "I let him in."

"You idiot," Narina seethed. "You made yourself so vulnerable to him."

Spencer nodded. "I know, but I'm glad I did. It was the only way I would have believed it."

"Believed what?" Rose asked.

"He's the one that helped us escape from city hall. He saved our lives. And he wants to help us now."

"Over my dead body," Narina spat.

"What was the memory Vik put into your mind?" Rose asked.

"It was *his* memory, like I was in his body. He looked down at his hands and then through a door. He was looking at the three of us strapped into hospital beds. We were all sedated. He came over and whispered something in my ear and then put something in my pocket."

"The access badge," Rose said in shock. "He was the one who gave it to you?"

"I think so."

"What did he whisper in your ear?" she asked.

Spencer shook her head. "I'm not sure."

"I don't trust him," Narina interjected. "What was he even doing at city hall? He's an Architect, Spence. A powerful one. He could have fabricated the whole memory and put it into your mind."

Spencer shook her head again. "The thing is, I did have a memory of a whisper in my ear. I heard Vik's voice. When I was sedated, I had all these disjointed things come into my head, and one of the fragments was someone whispering in my ear. I remember it happening even though I can't place the specifics."

She paused, leaving out the fact that some part of the memory didn't sit well with her. It was nothing more than a pesky feeling in the back of her mind, so she pushed it down for now.

"This changes everything," Rose said.

"This changes nothing." Narina shook her head. "Even if he did help us escape, that was almost a decade ago. He's done a lot of awful shit for the Apparatus since then."

"He said that he knew the only way to take down an organization as powerful as the Apparatus was from the inside."

"I just don't get it," Rose said. "Why does he want to take them down?"

"Did you know about his daughter? That she died during the earthquake?" Spencer asked.

Rose and Narina both nodded glumly.

"You asked us not to tell you anything about him," Narina offered in explanation.

"We could never quite make sense of it. We always wondered if he had known," Rose added.

"He didn't," Spencer said. "He said that's when everything changed for him. That's when he vowed to get revenge."

"And you believe him?" Rose asked.

"I don't know. I don't know what to believe, but I do think we might have to reconsider what we think we know."

Narina shook her head, but Rose shrugged. Spencer could tell she didn't know what to make of the Vik run-in either.

"I'm seeing him again tonight," Spencer added quietly.

"You're playing with fire," Narina said. "Trust me. I would know."

"Aren't you the one who has always said that we should do anything we can to get information on the Apparatus?" Spencer retorted.

"Yes, but that didn't include you hanging out with Vik," said

Narina. "He's dangerous for you, and not just because he broke your heart once before. You said it yourself—he can manipulate minds. The more time you spend with him, the more likely it is that he can use his powers on you."

"And we don't want you to get hurt," Rose added.

"Why does he want to see you again?" Narina asked.

"He said he has something to show me."

# the map

New York City
December 13, 2030

Vik told Spencer he would pick her up, which could mean only one thing—they were going through the Dead Zones. The Geo Cities had been designed with everything a short walk or bike ride away; cars were prohibited. The mandate cited climate control, but nearly all cars were electric by that point, so people accepted it as a sort of half-truth. It was about control, not about the climate. No one could blame them, though, for accepting the conditions that were offered—living in a Geo meant safety, security, and access to creature comforts that had mostly been wiped out over the past five years. Restaurants, coffee shops, gyms, and theaters had all become rare luxuries.

Vik had given Spencer an address, and a few minutes before she arrived at the location, a ping on her Orb notified her of an incoming message.

When you arrive, take the elevator down a level to the garage. I'll be waiting for you in a black SUV.

Spencer approached the security control in the lobby of the building and placed her right hand on the sensor so that it could scan the chip in her palm. The chip stored the digital ID mandatory for entry and access throughout the Geos. She faced the camera for a simultaneous facial recognition scan. The security control in every building now was reminiscent of the automated passport machines used in Europe over a decade earlier.

Spencer remembered how, when she had traveled to London for work back then, she'd approach a set of glass doors, place her passport down on a scanner, and face a camera. After a few moments, the glass doors would pop open briefly, allowing her to pass through. It had been a welcome change at the time, shortening lines dramatically by allowing a handful of border patrol agents to oversee the entrance of hundreds of people at once. Spencer marveled at the irony of it all—how the things she'd once thought of as freedoms were now the things that kept her prisoner.

She waited a minute as the scan completed, always nervous in the moments before the green checkmark flashed. Everyone in the Network had modified chips, so there was always the chance that a new software update could make things go haywire.

Sam had been a prodigious engineer in the before times. When the chip mandate first rolled out, he'd suggested that everyone get one, and he would modify them. The idea faced resistance within the Network. Many wanted to live off the grid, completely outside the control of the Apparatus. But after a dozen Liminals died in a Dead Zone outside of Los Angeles one night, Sam's idea had gained traction.

Sam got his hands on an early prototype of the chip and spent months working to reverse-engineer it. First he gave everyone in the Network entry access to all the Geos. Then he figured out how to modify the chip so that it could still send required inputs like biometrics and payment information but couldn't receive any data (an important modification to prevent the Apparatus from influencing the Network's powers directly through the embedded hardware).

The light in front of Spencer flashed green, and she walked toward the bank of elevators. The building was eerily quiet. She rode down to the garage, and as she exited the elevator, she saw a large black vehicle. To call it an SUV would be a weird perversion of the term—this was more akin to a military-grade tank. Two armed guards sat in the front.

Vik opened the door and gestured for her to get inside. Spencer had always been sensitive to scents, and she found something unusual about the air around her. "What's with the smell?" she asked Vik.

"There's a custom ventilation system. It purifies and disinfects the air before circulating it."

"What's wrong with the air that it needs to be purified?"

Vik looked out the window, ignoring her. As it always was with him, there was more to the story than what he was willing to share.

"Where are we going?" Spencer asked

"Brooklyn."

They arrived at the location twenty minutes later and entered a vacant building. The interior was all exposed brick and duct work, as had been popular in the urban-industrial-style office craze of the 2010s.

They walked into a small room where a bunch of computers lined a table. The table faced a floor-to-ceiling wall of glass panels. On the other side of the glass was another room, much larger, filled with hundreds of servers. A massive projector screen hung in the middle of it.

Vik walked over to one of the computers and pressed a button. The projector screen came to life, showing a giant dashboard with seven small icons named *Geo1*, *Geo2*, all the way up to *Geo7*. One for each Geo in New York, Spencer realized.

Vik clicked on *Geo1*—Village Park—where Spencer and the Network had been meeting over the past few days, and the screen changed to a different view.

Now there was a navigation pane on the left side and a large map on the right. The map had a perimeter around it that Spencer recognized as the geofenced area. A bunch of different pins appeared on the map in clusters. Spencer turned her attention to the navigation pane on the left, where she saw tabs representing different slices of data with labels like *Users*, *Locations*, and *Events*. At the bottom of the screen, beneath the map, was a bar with Play, Fast-Forward, and Rewind buttons. The bar was set to the current time.

Vik started talking. "One of the first tasks the Apparatus gave me was to invest in companies that might become useful in the event that cyberattacks proliferated. At the time, it was a vague request. It was before the earthquake and tsunami, before the Zero-Day War, before the Great Scarcity. In my research, I stumbled upon this company that provided location infrastructure through geofencing by creating a virtual boundary around specific areas. The tech powered simple in-app location services for things like targeted promotions, trip tracking, and arrival detection.

"But over time, the use cases for geofencing evolved. When safety and security became the primary objectives in the changing landscape of urban life, geofencing offered the perfect solution—it provided a way to monitor those who entered and exited a virtually bounded area."

Vik paused before continuing. "At least, that's the public narrative we used. The secondary purpose was asset tracking."

Spencer had heard of asset tracking in the context of supply chain management. A company might use asset tracking to monitor the movement of a fleet of vehicles or a valuable shipment, but she suspected the assets the Apparatus wanted to track here weren't vehicles or shipments.

"What's the asset in this scenario?" she asked.

"The general population."

Spencer's stomach sank. An asset—by definition—was a resource with economic value owned by someone with the expectation it would provide future value to that owner.

"And who's the owner of the general population?"

"You already know," Vik said.

Spencer wanted to hear him say it. She waited.

"The Apparatus," he eventually let out.

Spencer was slowly putting it together. The pins on the map weren't restaurants or bars—they were people being tracked by the Apparatus.

"Smartphones and wearables enabled geofencing," Vik continued, "but once the embedded chips were introduced, the tech morphed into something else entirely. Merely tracking a location was no longer enough for the Architects."

Spencer looked at the map again, now confused. What else was the Apparatus tracking?

"What do you remember about the experiments from city hall?" Vik asked.

She thought back.

"What do you remember about the devices they used?" he prompted before she could reply to his first question.

She remembered the black box sitting on the table in front of the woman as it sucked the life force out of her. "The siphon?"

He shook his head. "Did you see the device they used to measure your power?"

"The spectrometer?"

Vik nodded. "And the headsets."

Spencer looked back at the map, noticing now that the pins—or dots, rather—were colored. There were lots of lightly shaded dots in a variety of colors, a handful of dark black ones, and dozens as vibrant as the rainbow. The dots represented Rays, Architects, and Liminals respectively.

"It's no longer just tracking people," Vik said, gesturing to the map. "It's measuring them, too. It measures the light and energy they emit."

He walked over to the touchscreen, placed his finger on the time bar, and rewound the map to earlier that day, at noon. Spencer noticed a large cluster of bright dots near the church on Christopher Street where the Network had met at lunchtime.

He then rewound to earlier in the morning, when the three largest dots—one mossy green, one fiery red, and one light blue—had been at the church alone.

Shit. That was her, Narina, and Rose.

"It still blows my mind to see how powerful you and your friends are," Vik said. He seemed to mean it as a compliment.

Spencer looked closer. He was right—the size of the dots captured the way the Trium bond had made them more powerful than the other Liminals by an order of magnitude. She knew she should be proud, but she instead found herself focusing on the way Narina's dot was the largest and most intense of the three.

Vik must have noticed her gaze, because he put his hand lightly on Spencer's arm, just like he had on their first date. She felt her skin fizzle at his touch, like water in a hot frying pan.

"I know it's hard to see someone more powerful than you," Vik said, "but she gets her strength from you, Spence. They both do. They're creators and destroyers, but you're the grounding force between them. You're the key that unlocks their powers."

Spencer felt something spark in her mind at his words. Alo had said the same thing: *"You'll see it eventually, Spencer—you're the key to it all."* This was a clue, she realized, a piece to the Trium puzzle.

"There's something else you should know," Vik said, breaking her out of her thoughts. "The same technology that helped us create the map enabled us to develop a firewall."

Spencer waited for him to elaborate.

"The firewall is our version of a shield. Once we could systematically identify, locate, and measure Liminals, we could also monitor, filter, and control their energy traffic. Think of the firewall as a gatekeeper, protecting the Architects from Liminal attacks. Your powers can't touch us when the firewall is on."

Spencer suddenly felt sick. Not only did the Architects know the location of the entire Network; they also knew the strength and type of power each Liminal possessed. And they had engineered defensive armor to keep themselves safe.

She thought ahead to the battle that would take place on the winter solstice between the Network and the Apparatus.

They didn't stand a chance.

# the clue

New York City
December 14, 2030

Spencer walked back to the church on Christopher Street the next morning. She arrived early, anxious to share everything from her conversation with Vik.

Rose and Narina arrived a few minutes later.

"I thought you might need this," Rose said, handing Spencer a coffee.

"Tell us everything," Narina insisted.

"Let's wait until the group gets here. They need to hear this too."

Narina nodded reluctantly.

The rest of the group—the portion of the Network stationed in New York for the Harvest—trickled in over the next fifteen minutes. Spencer waited until everyone had taken a seat before standing up and walking to the front of the room.

"I met with Vik last night," she shared.

Murmurs of confusion resounded. She had known it would be one hell of an icebreaker.

"He is an Architect, as we suspected. I can tell you more about the specifics of what I learned later, but right now, I want to focus on something else. I think he may have unknowingly given us a clue about the Trium bond."

Spencer took a moment before continuing. "We've always thought of the powers as three aspects of one whole—like earth, wind, and fire—but what if we've been thinking of it all wrong? What

## dark days ahead

if the powers aren't as similar as we assumed? What if each power serves a distinctive function instead?"

"What do you mean?" Rose asked from where she stood beside Spencer.

"When Vik referred to our powers, he said you and Narina were creators and destroyers. Think about it—your power of air allows you to create life, and Narina's fire can destroy anything in its path. It seemed simple once he said it, an obvious distillation. Like yin and yang, opposing but balancing forces."

"That makes sense," Rose said. "Our powers either work through addition or negation. They can amplify something good or burn away something false."

"Everyone stand up," Narina ordered. "Divide into groups—creators on the left and destroyers on the right."

Everyone in the room shuffled over to their respective side.

"Okay, now pair up," Narina said.

The room obeyed.

"Don't we need a third?" Alex, a tiny Liminal with the power to freeze people and lock them into their emotional state, asked from the front of the room. "It's a Trium, not a pair."

Rose turned to Spencer. "Spence, what did Vik say about your powers?"

"That's the thing. He said I was the key that unlocks your powers. Alo said the same thing back in Mt. Shasta too—that I was the key to it all."

"How are you the key?" Narina asked.

"Vik said I was the grounding force between you both, that your power stems from me."

Everyone looked around, unsure of what to do with that information.

"That's it!" Alex yelled.

The entire room turned to look at her.

"Spencer's a conduit!" she exclaimed.

"What do you mean?" Narina asked.

"Before all of this," Alex said, gesturing to the room around her, "I was a structural engineer. I built skyscrapers. Conduits are tubes we'd use to run electricity from one end of the building to the other. They protect and route the electrical wires throughout a space. They allow the energy—the electricity—to flow and run freely from one end of the building to the other. When conduits are made from conductive material and properly bonded, they can even act as a grounding force. Sometimes the conduits even housed transformers, taking in electricity at one voltage and redistributing it at another.

"Spencer's a conduit. That's the third power we need to complete the Trium. Creation is one pole of energy; destruction is the other. They need a force to ground and protect them, allowing them to move as one in harmony. That's why it never worked before. Look at us—we're all either creators or destroyers. When we tried to bond, we were always missing the grounding force between us."

Spencer felt annoyed. Narina could destroy anything in her path, Rose could create life, and she was a giant tube? Great.

Narina looked around the room at the pairs of Liminals. "Alex is right," she said. "We seem to be lacking conduits."

The excitement from the breakthrough was now washed away by the reality of that fact. Spencer was the only conduit standing in the room. They couldn't form more Triums without more conduits.

"Spence," Rose said, turning to her, "is there a unique element of your power? Something that might help us figure out who else is like you?"

Spencer felt a mix of emotions move through her. She had never admitted it to Narina and Rose, but she had always believed her powers paled in comparison to theirs. Her friends could wield fire and air. All Spencer could do was observe and shield. Sure, it was cool, but she couldn't really do anything impressive. She couldn't make anything happen. But now, finding out that she was the missing piece of the puzzle—the "key to it all"—made her feel special, important even.

Spencer thought about Rose's question. What made her unique? She remembered the first time they had felt the bond, the day they'd

## dark days ahead

almost died escaping city hall. She thought about how she had felt Narina's anger and Rose's joy pump through her veins, both of their powers amplified by the intensity of their feelings. Spencer had always believed that was why the bond had formed that day—because Narina's and Rose's powers were so heightened, so tied to the emotions ripping through them, that it triggered the Trium. Spencer hadn't considered her own role in the process.

What was it she had felt that day? She thought back, trying to imagine herself standing on those steps. She wasn't angry like Narina. She wasn't happy like Rose. I felt nothing—like always, Spencer thought.

But then she remembered. There was something she had felt that day: solidity. It wasn't that she had experienced no emotions; she'd just felt no *pull* from them. She had been centered. Everything had swirled around her, and there she'd stood, watching it all, unswayed.

She had anchored her feet in the ground as Narina stood to her left and Rose to her right. Spencer had slowly opened her fists, and she'd felt their energy enter her from both sides: the fire from Narina and the expansion from Rose. The energy and emotions entered Spencer but didn't touch her. She stood taller, firmer, and let it run through her. Then something clicked into place, and Narina's and Rose's powers multiplied.

"My powers aren't magnified by emotion," Spencer said. "Both of you"—she pointed to Narina and Rose—"are strongest when your emotions are heightened, but it's the opposite for me. My powers are strongest when I'm centered. In fact, I'm weakest when my emotions take hold. It throws me off balance. I think that's what makes me a conduit. The day the bond formed, I let your emotions and power enter me. I allowed them to meet in the middle. I held them steady. I protected and grounded them."

Rose and Narina nodded as the realization hit them too.

"You're right," Rose said. "Any time I reach for the bond, it's like you're the anchor."

"Do we know any other Liminals like that?" Narina asked, looking at Rose.

Rose had helped nearly every Liminal transition. She knew each of their powers as well as her own. If anyone could identify the best conduit candidates, it would be her.

"Give me some time to run through everyone, and let's regroup later."

As everyone stood up and began filtering out of the room, Spencer sent a name down the bond to Rose.

*Zuri.*

The Trium remained behind after the other Liminals left. Once the room was quiet, Narina turned to Spencer. "So, was that the only thing that happened with Vik?" she asked. "He gave you a clue about the bond, and that's it? What did he want to show you?"

"No, there's more, but I wanted to tell the two of you first before sharing with everyone."

Narina and Rose raised their eyebrows.

"He wants to meet with the three of us. He really does want to help us."

"Absolutely not," said Narina. "No fucking way. I don't trust him."

"I know, but he showed me something last night—something that wouldn't make any sense for him to show me unless he was on our side."

"What was it?" Rose asked.

"The Apparatus has a map that tracks every Liminal and Ray. It shows not just where they are located but also the size and type of power they have."

Rose and Narina both inhaled sharply.

"There's more," Spencer added. "They've also developed a firewall, a shield that protects them from our powers."

"There goes our plan," Narina said.

"I know," Spencer replied, feeling as defeated as her friend sounded.

"If he showed you the map and told you about the firewall," Rose said, "maybe it is true that he wants to help. Do you believe him?"

Spencer shrugged. "It's hard to reconcile everything about him—everything he's done. But I do believe he wants revenge. I could feel his rage when he talked about his daughter's death and Graham's responsibility in it all."

"Do you *trust* him?" Narina asked.

She shook her head firmly. "We'd be naive to ever fully trust him. I learned that lesson once before. But after what I saw, I do think we need his help. We don't stand a chance against the Apparatus otherwise."

Rose seemed more open to the possibility of working with Vik than Narina did.

"He's going to double-cross us," Narina said.

"You might be right, but why don't we at least hear him out and see if there's anything we can learn? Even if he's planning to screw us, we might get a better sense for what he's playing at when we talk to him. Right now, we're just flying blind."

"Fine," Narina said. "But we meet on neutral ground, somewhere you can shield us."

# the source

New York City
December 14, 2030

Later that afternoon, they walked out of the church and back to Random Coffee to meet Vik. They placed their orders on their Orbs and waited.

Narina cleared her throat and mimed placing a microphone in front of her mouth as she gestured toward a man sitting at a table for two nearby. "In today's episode of *Goodbye Cruel World*, I present you with: nerdy white man fulfills feline fetish with holographic girlfriend," she said.

Spencer looked over at the table. The man was sitting across from a petite, slightly pixelated woman with a catlike face. No, not a cat. A lion. Spencer thought back to a college boyfriend, a lacrosse bro named Tom, who had once told her he was sexually attracted to Nala from *The Lion King*. Spencer could never quite bring herself to orgasm with him after that unfortunate revelation and had dumped him a few weeks later.

Spencer looked again at the man and the holographic woman as they talked to each other. At one point, the man reached out to stroke her hand, and she laughed shyly in response. Spencer cringed when she considered what the man might do with her in the privacy of his own home.

"Do you think he named her Nala?" she joked.

Narina widened her eyes in amusement before replying. "Thank you for getting it," she said. "Sometimes I think we need to let the

## dark days ahead

Apparatus burn this place to the ground and hit the reset button so we can start over."

"Narina!" Rose said. "Who are we to judge someone's romantic preferences?"

Narina ignored the question and replied with one of her own. "Can humanity even be saved at this point?"

Spencer watched the man walk out of the coffee shop, holding open the door for the hologram, his hand on her lower back, and she couldn't help but wonder if Narina was right.

They grabbed their drinks and sat down, taking the table he'd just been sitting at and pulling up two extra chairs.

Vik arrived a few minutes later. As he walked toward the table, Spencer held the owl totem tightly in her pocket, strengthening her connection to Narina and Rose and the shield she had positioned around the three of them.

Vik sat down and reached for a small device in his pocket. "It's an invisibility cloak," he explained. "We won't show up on the map that I'm sure Spencer already told you about, and no data from this meeting will be recorded. We can talk freely."

Narina rolled her eyes. "And we know you're telling us the truth because . . ."

"Because my life is just as at risk as yours is in meeting you here. If the Apparatus knew I was talking to you, we'd all be dead."

"If you want to help us, then tell us what the plan is," Narina said, her voice flat.

No beating around the bush with her.

"Let's take a step back," Vik said, "and make sure we're on the same page first. What do you know about the Apparatus? About how we get our powers?"

"Why would we show all our cards by telling you what we know?" Narina asked.

It was a good bluff. The truth was, they didn't know much. They knew there was some form of ritual and sacrifice that initiated Architects into the Apparatus and gave them their own totem known as the Mark, but they didn't know much else about the source of the Architects' powers.

"Fine, I'll tell you," Vik said. "I assume you already know about Empties, Rays, and Liminals?"

They nodded.

"The Apparatus makes up the other end of the spectrum. Guardsmen are our version of Rays. They still have energy in them, but instead of light, it's dark matter. Those who make the complete transition—like Liminals—are Architects, but the way we get our power is different. Liminals seem to have some internal source of power they can draw on, but Architects are like black holes. We have no intrinsic source of energy; we need to get it externally. We siphon it, expanding our own energy source as we capture it from others."

"Like cosmic vampires feeding on the stars in orbit around you," Narina quipped.

Spencer shuddered as she thought about the power Vik must have siphoned from hundreds of people to become as strong as he was today.

Vik shrugged. "I guess that's one way to put it."

"Thanks for the science lesson, but what does this have to do with the Harvest?" Narina asked.

"Why do you think the Apparatus needs the Harvest?"

"You need a power source for the Merge," Spencer said.

"Sort of. We need a power source *before* the Merge."

They stared at Vik blankly, waiting for him to continue.

"We don't fully understand what will happen when humans merge with machines, but we think there's a very real possibility that humans will lose their consciousness once and for all."

"I'm not sure I'm following," Rose said.

"What we call consciousness, you might call life force."

"So humans will become Empty? Forever?" Rose asked, her face falling as the realization set in.

Vik nodded. "It's a possibility," he said. "It's why we need a power source before the Merge. Consider it an insurance policy."

"An insurance policy for what?" Rose asked.

They had been wrong about it all, Spencer realized suddenly. Even Dr. Grady, the Guardsman running experiments on behalf of the Apparatus, didn't know the full extent of what the Architects were really up to. The Architects didn't need the Harvest to power the Merge. They needed it to power themselves.

She turned to Vik. "If the Apparatus gets its power from siphoning, and humans lose their life force during the Merge, then there won't be any power left over for the Architects."

Vik nodded. "The Harvest is a way for us to accumulate as much power as possible before the Merge happens." He took a breath. "Have you noticed anything about the Geos here in New York?" he asked, looking directly at Spencer.

She glanced around the coffee shop at the subtle light glowing around every person there. She remembered the map filled with a sea of lightly colored dots. "The Geos are filled with Rays," she said.

Vik nodded. "Once we had the technology to identify Rays from Empties, we made sure that only Rays were accepted into the Geos."

Spencer heard Rose inhale sharply next to her. They all knew that the safety and security offered by the Geos had been in such high demand that tens of millions of people across the country had applied for resident permits. The Apparatus had handpicked the Rays from the applicants, and the Rays had voluntarily geofenced themselves into a confined area.

"Are the Geos in SF and LA filled with Rays too?" Narina asked.

"Yes, but only as a backup in case something doesn't work here."

Spencer now remembered the handful of black dots on the map. Seven of them in total. All the Architects were here, not spread across the three cities like the Network had anticipated.

"The Harvest is happening *here*," Spencer said, "in New York."

Vik nodded. "There are seven Geos. One for each Architect."

"So each Architect is going to use a siphon device in their Geo to capture the power from all the Rays there?" Spencer asked, growing quieter as she remembered the little black device sitting on the table at city hall.

"Yes. The Apparatus spent the last decade perfecting the tech. It's now powerful enough to siphon from thousands of Rays at once. The siphons can't hold all the energy, so it's transferred to the cloud and then downloaded and used as needed."

"And what about us—do you plan to siphon our power too?" Narina asked.

"No." Vik shook his head. "For a long time, the Apparatus tried to figure out a way to use Liminal power to our advantage. That was a big part of the experiments we performed, but it's like nature has a built-in defense mechanism. Our devices can siphon power from Liminals, like you saw in city hall, but the Architects can't absorb it. It's like a body rejecting an organ transplant. If we siphon from Rays and Liminals at the same time, the energy becomes hard to separate. The devices we'll use for the Harvest are designed to work only on Rays."

"What about us, then? Somehow, I can't imagine that you plan to hide behind the safety of your firewall, siphon from the Rays, and leave the Network untouched," Narina said sarcastically.

Vik's eyes glinted. "Of course not. We like to play offense more than defense."

"So what exactly do you plan to do to us?"

"Have you heard of an EMP weapon?" Vik asked.

The women shook their heads.

"An electromagnetic pulse weapon generates a high-intensity burst of radiation that destroys all electrical systems within range," he explained. "Through the experiments, we were able to identify the exact frequency of Liminal power. Think of it like a radio station that Liminals tune in to. We designed an EMP to target that exact radio station."

He paused to let that sink in before continuing. "The Apparatus plans to detonate the EMP, render the Liminals useless, then siphon from the Rays. The Harvest will be over in a matter of minutes."

Spencer's head was spinning. The years of work they'd done to strengthen the Network had all been for nothing. Their powers would be wiped out before the battle even began.

"I assume if you're sitting here, talking to us about the revenge you want on the Apparatus, then you have a different plan?" Narina asked.

Vik nodded. "I'll turn off the firewall." He paused and reached for something in his pocket. "And while the Apparatus was busy working on the EMP, I had a team of engineers building a shield against it," he said, holding up a small object and grinning.

# the blackout

### New York City
### December 14, 2030

After leaving Vik at the coffee shop, Spencer, Rose, and Narina walked over to Washington Square Park instead of meeting the Network back at the church. They needed time to think.

"We could be walking right into a trap," Narina said.

"I know," Spencer said. "That's all I was thinking the entire time—is this just a way for him to get all of the Network in the same place at once and then wipe us out?"

"I know this may be an unpopular opinion, but I feel like he was telling the truth. Although you know him better than I do," Rose said, looking at her.

Narina turned her gaze to Spencer too.

"I think what he told us today is the truth," Spencer said. "I think Vik knows I can sense when he's lying, so he would be careful to only share the parts that he can say honestly. That's not to say there aren't parts he's leaving out, but I think the parts he told us about the Architects siphoning from a specific Geo and the EMP blast are true."

"So what do we do?" Rose asked.

"If it's true that all the Architects will be in New York City on the solstice, then we need every Liminal here," Narina said. "Their powers will be wasted sitting in San Francisco and Los Angeles."

Spencer and Rose both nodded.

"I'll have Sam send out a message to the Network about the change in plan," Narina said.

They sat quietly, deep in thought. After a few minutes, Narina spoke again. "We should be able to beat them. We have hundreds of Liminals against seven Architects."

Spencer had thought the same thing earlier, noticing how differently the two groups viewed their own power. The three of them had created a vast network of hundreds of Liminals, freely giving away power to anyone who was willing to do the work to transition. In their world, energy was abundant—a renewable resource for those who understood how it worked. The more Liminals, the better. But the Architects lived in a different world. Instead of developing hundreds of Architects, they kept the power in the hands of a few, choosing to scale their strength through technology. Those who owned the tech had all the power. It was a greedy and protective mindset rooted in scarcity. Seven Architects could have the power of hundreds—thousands, even—through the devices they engineered.

"We have the numbers, but they have the tech," Spencer said, defeated.

Narina's fiery eyes blazed at Spencer's words. "Not if we take it," she said.

"Take what?"

"*Their tech.* If what Vik said is true, the Architects' entire plan rests on the ability to use technology. Technology requires electricity. What if we create a blackout?"

"And force them to fight us directly," Rose said, finishing Narina's thought.

"Exactly. We have Sam find a way to take down the grid and force them into a physical battle."

They turned to look at Spencer, waiting for her to weigh in.

"I'm thinking," she replied. And she continued to for a minute before speaking. "It could work. A blackout would incapacitate any of their networked technology—the map, the firewall, and the Orbs. But what about the siphons—weren't those battery-powered?"

How much had the siphons been upgraded from the version she'd seen in the city hall experiments?

"Shit," Narina muttered.

"Didn't Vik say that the siphons couldn't hold the energy and would need to transfer it to the cloud?" Rose offered. "Surely that wouldn't work during a blackout."

"Maybe the siphons can't store the energy without power, but can they still *capture* it?" Spencer asked. "That's the big question."

"I'm not sure it matters," said Narina. "Either way, I think it's our best option to do this on our terms. If the blackout takes out their Orbs, they'll have no way to communicate with each other across the Geos. If it takes out their map, then they'll have no way of knowing where we are. And if it takes out their firewall, then they'll have no protection. It will leave one handicapped Architect in each Geo against dozens of Liminals. I like those odds."

"You're forgetting about the EMP," Spencer said.

Narina shrugged. "Vik said it himself: all we need is a shield to protect us from the EMP."

"But the shield he developed to protect us from the blast would likely be wiped out by the same blackout you're suggesting."

"We don't need Vik's shield. We have one of our own—one that originates from an internal power source, not an external one," Narina said as she locked eyes with Spencer. "You."

"Narina, I can't protect the entire Network," Spencer replied nervously. "I'm not even sure I could protect the three of us from something as strong as an EMP blast."

"Sure you can. Dr. Grady said it himself—technology isn't created; it's observed. If Vik developed a shield to protect us from the EMP blast, all we need to do is figure out how it works and reverse-engineer it."

# the second

### New York City
### December 15, 2030

When Spencer arrived at the church the next morning, she saw Zuri standing next to Narina and Rose. Spencer ran up to greet her, hoping that her intuition about her old friend was right. Although Zuri's abilities manifested in different ways, she had the same grounded energy that Spencer did.

Luisa came up to hug Zuri too. "I'm surprised to see you here already! How did you get here so fast?"

Late the night before, Sam had sent out an encrypted communication to the entire Network about the change in plans. The Liminals who had been stationed in San Francisco and Los Angeles were currently en route to New York City.

"Rose contacted me yesterday morning and told me I was needed here," Zuri said. "Something about the Trium bond. Any idea what this is about?"

Spencer nodded. "We have a new theory about how to activate the bond, and we think you might be able to help. Let's wait for the others to get here before we test it out. The Liminals from the West Coast won't arrive until tonight, but we've called a meeting for everyone already in New York."

Zuri raised an eyebrow, intrigued.

As they waited for the meeting to start, Spencer looked around, in awe of the Liminals slowly filling up the room—the brave individuals who were willing to sacrifice their lives to defeat the Apparatus.

The way that everyone had worked so hard over the past decade was astounding. Spencer glanced over at Rose, feeling a deep sense of gratitude for the work her friend had tirelessly done. Rose had spent every second of her free time either helping people transition or teaching them how to strengthen their powers. As she started to understand the different variations of power, she devised methods to encourage their development. She led monthly seminars guiding Liminals through breathwork, meditation, and somatic experiencing, helping them map the internal territory of their energy through conscious awareness. The magnitude of Rose's work was present in all of the Liminals there—intense halos of light emanated from every body in the room.

Rose stepped toward Narina and Spencer. "I was up all night, replaying the day we first created the Trium bond. Except this time, I considered it from the perspective of creator, destroyer, and conduit. It all seems so obvious now. There's something I want to try with Zuri. I think I can help create another bond."

"Go work your magic," Narina said.

Spencer nodded in encouragement.

Rose walked to the front of the room and spoke. "I have an idea for how we might create another Trium; I'd like to try something. Zuri, can you come up to the front of the room?"

Zuri walked forward, quiet and calm like always.

"Everyone else, can you divide up into creators and destroyers again?" Rose asked.

The Liminals shuffled into two groups.

Rose turned to speak to Zuri. "We think that the bond requires one creative power, one destructive power, and one grounding power. We have plenty of creators and destroyers, but grounders—we're calling them 'conduits'—are rare. We'd like to try creating a bond with you as the conduit. Are you up for it?"

Zuri nodded. "Absolutely."

"Is there a creator here you feel a deep connection to?" Rose asked. "It's still my working theory that closeness strengthens the bond."

"Luisa," she said without hesitating.

Luisa smiled and began to walk toward the front of the room.

Spencer wasn't surprised. Luisa and Zuri had grown considerably closer after becoming the first two Liminals—other than the Trium—to officially join the Network. In the years since she had first transitioned, Luisa had become a beautiful creator of waves.

"And what about a destroyer?" Rose asked.

Zuri shook her head and laughed. "I might regret being bonded to her for life even more than we already are, but it has to be Kessie."

Kessie was Zuri's sister, a powerful destroyer who wielded lightning. They'd been born years apart but bore an uncanny resemblance, so much so that they were often mistaken for twins.

"*Sister, Sister* forever and always," Kessie replied, referencing the popular '90s sitcom. She moved to join Zuri and Luisa.

"Perfect. We need to head outside," Rose said, looking at Zuri, Kessie, Luisa and then over to Spencer and Narina. "All six of us," she clarified.

Rose turned to Sam now. "I want to test my theory out in the open where they'll have room to wield. Can you run some technical interference for us and keep people out of Washington Square Park?"

Sam nodded. "I should be able to get into the Orb system console and temporarily redirect traffic while giving the six of you access to the park. How long do you need?"

"An hour should be plenty," Rose replied.

She wasn't sure what Rose had up her sleeve, but Spencer could tell her friend was confident in her plan.

Rose turned back to the rest of the room. "We'll be back in a little bit. Alex, can you guide everyone through a power meditation while we're gone?"

Alex nodded.

The six women headed to the park. Once they arrived, they walked to the center near the fountain, where Rose motioned for them to stop.

"I want you to stand in a triangle like this," she said, repositioning them so that Zuri was at the peak of the triangle, Kessie on her left, and Luisa on her right.

"Kessie," Rose said, turning toward her, "I know in our work we've identified that the feeling of shame is most closely tied to your power. I want you to reach for a shameful memory—imagine the day it happened, what you were wearing, who you saw. Remember every detail you can. Then, imagine what you felt, and make that feeling as big as possible."

Rose turned to Luisa. "Your powers are tied to a sense of freedom. Do the same thing. Find the time in your life you felt most free and amplify it. And Zuri, your power is your calmness. Find the unshakeable center within and root yourself deep into the ground."

She waited a few minutes. "Are you all there? In the biggest form of your power?" she asked.

They each nodded.

Rose looked at Spencer to confirm. Spencer activated her vision, and her breath was almost taken away by the way their halos had grown as they tapped into their emotions. She nodded back at Rose.

"Spence, can you throw a massive shield around the park? I want to give them a space to play in so that they can wield freely."

Spencer nodded. She enclosed them all in a glittery bubble, careful to wrap every inch of the park so there would be no damage.

"We're all set," she told Rose.

Rose turned back to the three women. "Zuri, in a minute, I'm going to ask Kessie and Luisa to wield. When I do, I want you to anchor down into the ground and think of yourself as a conduit—a pipe that protects the electricity running through it. Open yourself like a valve and allow the energy to move. Don't attempt to shield yourself; that will only block the flow. Trust that you are protected by Spencer's shield and open yourself up. And trust your own power rooting you into the ground. Does that make sense?"

Zuri nodded.

"Okay, Kessie and Luisa, I want you to wield. Make your emotion as big as possible, and let it rip."

They both nodded.

"Now," Rose said.

The sky within the bubble darkened a shade, and a bolt of Kessie's lightning struck from above.

In the center of the park, the blue halo around Luisa reached over to the fountain. She slowly brought thousands of drops of water to levitate over the ground, swirling them around.

Now the attention shifted to Zuri standing in the middle. Spencer could see green, glittery roots reaching out beneath her into the ground, but no energy moved through her. She was rooted but not open. Spencer inclined her head to Rose in a whisper. "She's ready, but she's blocking the flow of energy."

Rose nodded. "Zuri, you need to open yourself up to the energy around you. Kessie, try reaching for Zuri. Let her anchor you. Reaching for her power will amplify yours."

Spencer saw Kessie's yellow light reach out to Zuri, but it stopped right in front of Zuri's chest, like armor had prevented it from moving forward. She shook her head at Rose.

"Zuri, you need to let it in. It's your sister. You can trust her," Rose said.

Zuri took a deep breath and surrendered. Suddenly, the light was inside of her, merging and dancing with her own green light. Five large thunderbolts came crashing down to the ground.

Damn. Spencer felt the lightning bounce off her shield. If it hadn't been up, Kessie would have just shattered the arch modeled after the Arc de Triomphe situated at the north entrance of the park.

"Holy shit," Kessie said, feeling the new heightened power course through her.

"Luisa, now your turn," Rose said, smiling wildly.

Luisa's blue light inched slowly toward Zuri like she was asking permission to enter. This time, Zuri let it right in. The water in the fountain was once again levitating several feet off the ground, but instead of swirling drops, Luisa hurled them into a giant tidal wave that crested near the chess tables at the southwest entrance.

Spencer sent more power through her shield to contain the waves.

"Wow," Luisa said. "That was so cool."

"Zuri," Rose said, "that was great, but the flow needs to move both ways. They've reached for your powers; now it's time for you to use some of theirs. Kessie and Luisa, remain open but don't wield. It must come from Zuri."

Spencer watched as Zuri again took a deep breath. The roots grew dozens of feet farther into the ground before long green branches reached out into the sky above her. The bubble darkened another shade as a storm ripped through it. Lightning crashed while a torrent of rain poured down on top of them.

The halos around the three women glowed in unison as the mark of the Trium, a triangle, imprinted on their wrists.

Spencer turned to smile at Rose and Narina, recognizing what they'd just witnessed and remembering their own first time. The bond had formed. Another Trium was born.

# the architects

### New York City
### December 16, 2030

Spencer, Narina, and Rose arrived at the church the next morning with a strategy in place. Spencer and Narina would continue meeting with Vik to learn anything they could about the Architects' plans for the Harvest, Rose would spend her time trying to create as many Triums as possible, and Sam would engineer a blackout. They weren't going to tell Vik about their planned counterattack. If he was really on their side, it wouldn't be a problem. And if he wasn't, then it would give the Network a leg up.

When Spencer walked into the meeting room, she was almost blinded. All the Liminals from the Network had now arrived and were crammed into the tiny space upstairs.

"Spence, why don't you fill them in on the plan?" Narina said.

Spencer walked to the front of the room, and the whispered conversations came to a halt. "We have new information about the Harvest. Each of the seven Architects will be stationed in one of the Geos here in New York the night of the solstice. They plan to use an EMP weapon that will wipe out our powers. Once we're incapacitated, they'll each use a siphon device to draw energy from all the Rays within their Geo."

"How do you know?" someone asked from the front row. It was Mira. She must have arrived last night.

"Vik," Spencer said. "Vik wants revenge on the Apparatus, and he's given us information on their plan. He wants to take them down as much as we do."

Gasps filled the room.

"How can we trust him?" Mira asked.

"We can't trust him fully. Vik proposed we use shielding technology he created to block the EMP. His shield would keep our powers intact and allow us to take down the Architects. But we've decided to take a different route. We're going to create our own shield and engineer a complete blackout to render their technology useless. That will leave us to fight them directly. We'll have hundreds of Liminals against seven Architects."

Applause erupted throughout the room, the collective dread now turning into a sense of excitement at the thought of bringing down the Apparatus.

Spencer continued, "Sam will be working on our blackout strategy. Meanwhile, Narina and I will keep working with Vik to find out as much as we can about the Architects' powers. Based on that information, we'll divide ourselves up, sending a group of Liminals to fight in each Geo. Oh, and we have another Trium," she added proudly. "Zuri, Kessie, and Luisa."

The room broke out in cheers.

"We understand the missing piece now," Spencer explained. "Rose is going to work with a handful of suspected conduits. We're hoping to have one Trium for each Geo by the solstice." She took a deep breath. "So that's the plan over the next week. Narina and I will meet with Vik to develop a strategy. Sam will focus on the blackout. Rose will work on the Triums. The rest of you will spend every minute you can training. We need you all as strong as possible for the solstice."

Narina and Spencer met with Vik later that day. "We're in," Narina said as she sat down. "We'll help you, but you need to tell us everything you know about the Apparatus."

"You'll *help me?*" Vik asked incredulously. "I'm pretty sure I'm the one helping you not get absolutely annihilated."

Narina simply stared at him with fire in her eyes. Spencer waited to see who cracked first.

After a minute, Vik sighed and asked, "Where do you want to start?"

"We want you to tell us about every Architect. We need to understand their powers and their weaknesses. Let's start with Graham," Narina said.

Vik took a slow breath before speaking. "Graham is a night whisperer. He can summon shadow creatures."

Spencer tilted her head in question.

"He invokes dark spirits of the dead," Vik explained. "The spirits take on different forms—it's a matter of preference, really. Vermin, ghosts, trolls. He can talk to the spirits and use them to do his bidding. Think of it like an energetic army he can summon at will. The spirits are quite effective. While they can't physically kill anyone, they can create fear so strong that it exterminates the will to fight, the will to live, even. If his vermin get to any of the Liminals, they can turn one of your own against you.

"Next is Reinhold," Vik continued. "He's the oldest member of the Apparatus, and the chairman. He's a shapeshifter. His shadow can take on any form—human, animal, spirit. He can even take over the form of someone near him when his shadow temporarily enters their body. For example, he could shift into Narina during battle, access her powers, and you would have no idea it wasn't really her until the damage was done.

"Alfred can plant shadow seeds—little kernels of doubt, fear, despair, sorrow. Over the years, he's found ways to speed up the development of those seeds, to water the plant, so to speak. The seeds can blossom into fully formed shadows in minutes and wreak havoc.

"Pierre manipulates darkness. He can use shadows to block access and flow. Think of it like a weapon of sensory deprivation. If he wraps his shadow around you, it can remove sight, smell, hearing. His shadows can paralyze limbs, stop a heart from beating or a brain from thinking.

"Qiang is a shadow traveler. He can teleport through darkness, traveling long distances through a shadow in the blink of an eye.

"And then there's me. I'm what they call a shadow manipulator. I can use shadows to mold and shape the things around me."

"Why don't you call it what it is?" Narina said. "Mind control."

"Yes," he said, shadows flashing in his eyes. "I can control and manipulate minds."

"And what about the seventh Architect?" Spencer asked, mentally cataloging all the powers in her library.

"He's a shadow projector," Vik said. "He can physically shape dark matter into a black liquid that solidifies as he desires. He can create weapons, tools, armor, or he can use it to constrict around objects and suffocate them."

He paused and gave Spencer a look that she couldn't quite interpret. It seemed like he was about to say something else, but he shook his head instead. "I think that's enough for today," he said. "Let's regroup tomorrow, and I'll show you the shield."

# the shield

New York City
December 17, 2030

The next day, at Vik's request, Spencer once again headed down to the garage for a trip through the Dead Zones. Narina had stayed behind to help Rose. The Trium bond had only activated one other time so far, with Mira as the conduit. They only had a few days left to create as many Triums as possible, so they needed all hands on deck back at the church.

"Where are we headed?" Spencer asked when she got into the tank SUV again.

"Same place as before," Vik replied. "It will be easier to show you there."

When they entered the control room in Brooklyn, Vik once again pulled up the map dashboard. This time, the few-block radius near the church was lit up like a Christmas tree. Well, Spencer thought, it was no secret to the Apparatus that the Network had arrived.

"Take this," Vik said, holding out his hand. In his palm was a small device that looked like one of the old USB drives you would plug into a computer to transfer files before the cloud existed.

Vik tapped on *Geo3* on the dashboard—where the two of them now stood in Brooklyn. He zoomed in on the map. Spencer saw a large green dot glowing next to an equally large black one.

"That's us," he said, pointing to the map. "Take off the cap," he told her as he gestured to the device in her hand.

Spencer looked down. There was a small line on one side of the device, like a fine crack. She gripped both sides, one in each hand, and pulled. The cap came off, revealing a tiny piece of rectangular metal beneath it. "What is this?" Spencer asked.

"Look at the map again."

She did. The black dot was still right where it had been before, but the green dot was now gone. "Zoom out," she said.

As Vik zoomed out, Spencer saw that her dot was nowhere to be found anywhere on the map. She was invisible. She turned the device over in her hands to get a better look. "The shield," she said.

Vik nodded.

"How does it work?"

"When we designed the Geos, the Apparatus had an opportunity to rebuild and reimagine what urban life might look like. Connectivity was one of the most important aspects, and a relatively new nanomaterial—graphene—was used to turn every surface of the city into a sensor. Graphene is a layer of carbon atoms arranged in a honeycomb structure that creates an intelligent skin. Think of it like a hypersensitive membrane that allows it to send and receive data. It's two hundred times stronger and six times lighter than steel, so it was easy to incorporate into our plans. Graphene replaced traditional building materials and wiring. In effect, it turns any static material into a responsive agent, creating a connected network through every inch of the city. It's like Wi-Fi on steroids. It's a bit of a wonder material, really.

"But it's also extremely conductive, a fact my engineers took into account when designing the shield. The device in your hand acts as a ground to divert energy away. It will dissipate the blast from an EMP."

Spencer thought for a moment. "So that's what will protect us from the EMP, but what makes me disappear on the map?"

"The ground in the device also acts to neutralize the energy signal emitted around it. Like I said before, Liminals operate on a specific frequency channel. I've designed a grounding technology to offset that signal. I've actually been using this technology to protect you and your friends for years."

## dark days ahead

Spencer had too much pride to say thank you, so she nodded instead. "Does every Liminal need one of these?" she asked, holding up the device.

"No, not everyone, but you'll want one in each Geo. Each device has a built-in antenna with considerable range. The shield will originate from this device that I'll be carrying," he said, holding up one of his own, "and cast a net across the antennas, protecting anyone within the area."

Spencer didn't love that. Their protection would, quite literally, be in the palm of Vik's hand.

As they rode back to Village Park a few minutes later, Spencer felt a small sense of hope for the first time since she had arrived in New York. She wasn't sure if the blackout Sam was developing would take out Vik's shield, but it didn't matter. Vik had unknowingly just given Spencer a blueprint for the Network to create their own. Reverse-engineering it would be easier than she'd anticipated. They just needed two things: antennas and grounds.

Spencer reached into her pocket, wrapping her fingers around the owl totem she always carried with her. *"Think of the totems as the antennas powering the network,"* Alo had said.

The Network already had their own antennas. And now they had conduits to act as the grounding force.

# the shadow

### New York City
### December 20, 2030

Rose and Narina's work over the past few days was paying off. The Network now had seven Triums, one for each Geo. They were perfectly matched.

Spencer spent some time working with the conduits—Zuri, Mira, Layla, Shilpa, Jordan, and Hana—to teach them how to ground and create a shield by mimicking the device Vik had shown her. Yesterday, each conduit had traveled to their specified Geo to test out the range of their shield. They couldn't ask Vik to confirm it had worked on the map, but Spencer was confident it had. During the test, she'd felt six distinct pulses come at her from every direction as a canopy of light fell over the city. The antennas were connected. Each of the conduits would be responsible for serving as the ground when Spencer cast her shield across the antennas to protect every Liminal in New York City.

They now had Triums and a shield, but Sam was still having trouble with the blackout. He hadn't been able to hack into the mainframe electrical grid that powered the city yet. He only had one more day to figure something out before the solstice, and they were all getting nervous.

Spencer wasn't able to sleep the night before. She'd been reviewing the giant whiteboard, which detailed the Network's plan, when she noticed something that didn't sit right with her. She sent a message to Vik through her Orb, telling him to meet her first thing in the morning for coffee.

She was sitting, nervously waiting, when Vik arrived. He grabbed his drink and sat down.

"Everything okay, Spence?" he said, putting his hand lightly on top of hers.

His touch still sent a not entirely unpleasant buzz through her body. She pulled her hand back.

"Sorry, old habits," he said, lifting his hands up in the air in a gesture of apology.

"I was going through the plan last night, and something is off," Spencer said. "When we talked through each Architect's powers, you listed them all—Graham, Reinhold, Alfred, Pierre, Qiang, and you—but the seventh Architect you mentioned didn't have a name. You just referred to him as the shadow projector. Who is the seventh Architect?"

"He's known as 'the founder.'"

"Okay, but who is it? What's his name?" Spencer asked.

Vik looked away before making eye contact with her again. "Right now, he goes by Sam."

"Sam who?" Spencer asked, scanning the library in her mind of all the potential Architects they'd researched over the years.

"Sam," he said again. "The seventh Architect is Narina's husband."

Spencer ran back to the church, jumping up the steps two at a time, but when she reached the second floor, she stopped abruptly. What exactly was she going to do?

They were one day away from the Harvest. If she ran into the room and told everyone Sam was an Architect, chaos would erupt, trust would be broken, and emotions would be sky-high. For a Liminal, control of emotions equated to control of powers. The Network didn't stand a chance if they couldn't keep their emotional state in check, especially Narina. She was the strongest Liminal in the entire Network. If her anger took over, she might burn down New York and all the Liminals with it. More importantly, Spencer wasn't even sure she believed Vik.

She looked around the room at everyone working together. All the Liminals were in groups—meditating, doing breathwork, and power training. She wasn't going to interrupt them.

She saw Sam huddled in the back corner with the other engineers. They'd set up a makeshift computer lab on one side of the room a week earlier, and they'd been working day and night on the blackout plan there ever since.

Spencer walked over to where Sam was standing, reviewing some lines of code on a screen.

"Hey, Spence," he said, barely looking up at her. He was fully absorbed in what he was working on, his forehead scrunched in thought.

"How's it going? Any breakthroughs yet?" she asked.

"No." He exhaled. "And we've tried everything."

Spencer stared at him with her vision fully activated. Sam had always had the subtle glow of a Ray. He hadn't been able to make the transition to Liminal, but that wasn't uncommon—they'd never been able to make it work for men. It had perplexed them for a long time. There were plenty of male Rays, in theory all perfect candidates, but they'd never been able to find the right emotional activation to trigger the transition. They knew it was possible, though; Alo had been a Liminal, and so had the homeless guy in city hall who had given his powers to Spencer. After a while, the Network gave up and focused their efforts solely on women. The male Rays who were interested in fighting the Apparatus helped in other ways—focusing on intel, tech, strategy, logistics, and planning.

Spencer looked at Sam's wrist, but there was no Mark. How could he be the seventh Architect? The same Sam who'd encouraged Narina to go through the veils, the Sam who'd developed technology to help them modify their neural chips, the Sam who'd taken care of them in Mt. Shasta after city hall. Spencer smiled, thinking back to the time they'd spent in Mt. Shasta. It would always be one of her best memories—the final few moments of her old life before everything changed when the earthquake hit.

Wait a minute—Sam was the one who had suggested they go to Mt. Shasta. It was the only reason none of them had been in the city during the earthquake. A sense of dread started to fill her. He was also the one who'd pushed Narina to move to Florida "on a whim." They had conveniently closed on the sale of their house two weeks before the earthquake. By the time the new buyer had moved in, the value of the home was down 75 percent. Could he have known what was going to happen and gotten them out just in time?

And he was the engineer-turned-founder behind a wildly successful startup. The nickname that Vik had mentioned would have been appropriate.

But then again, Sam was also the one who'd thought splitting up the Network across New York, San Francisco, and Los Angeles was a bad idea. Spencer remembered overhearing a fight between him and Narina—Sam yelling at her that she had no idea what she was doing, that her decision to separate would put the entire Network at risk. If he was in the Apparatus, wouldn't it have made sense for him to endorse the plan that had the Liminals spread out across the country?

Spencer's head was spinning.

"Sam," Spencer said, turning to him now, "I've been meaning to ask. You had always thought the Harvest was going to happen here in New York even before Vik told us the plan. What made you think that?"

"It's what I would do," Sam replied. "Liminals are strongest when they're together. We should assume the Architects' powers work the same way. It makes sense to concentrate power in one location. New York has the most residents and the most energy for the Harvest."

Sam maintained eye contact with her the entire time he spoke. He seemed so genuine and sincere. He worked on the blackout plan as if his own life depended on it. Spencer couldn't reconcile the man standing in front of her with the shadow projector—the seventh Architect. She was about to turn away when she saw something out of the corner of her eye. At the edge of the yellow glow around Sam was a smudge of gray. The shadow was only about an inch thick, but it was there, like a dark cloud peeking out behind the sun.

Spencer found Rose in the other corner of the room. She was leading a group in breathwork. Spencer pulled her aside. "I need to talk to you. Meet me in the park in thirty minutes," she said.

"Should I bring Narina?" Rose asked.

"No, just us."

Rose looked confused. They'd made a promise when they first bonded that there would be no secrets between the three of them, but she nodded. "I'll meet you there," she said quietly.

Spencer was waiting, sitting on a bench across from the fountain, when Rose arrived.

"What's wrong?" Rose asked, immediately picking up on Spencer's nervous energy.

"Block your connection to Narina," Spencer said.

Rose looked dismayed.

"Trust me," she insisted. "She can't know what I'm about to say."

Rose nodded, but she seemed hesitant.

"I had Vik meet me this morning. I was reviewing the plan last night, going over how we'd divide up Liminals based on each Architect's powers, and I realized Vik never told us the name of the seventh Architect. I asked him who it is."

Rose waited. "And? Who is it?"

Spencer shook her head, still in disbelief. "He said it's Sam."

"Sam who?" Rose asked, having the same reaction as Spencer. Her brain had totally bypassed the possibility that it could be the man they both knew.

"Narina's Sam," Spencer replied in a low voice.

A look of shock bloomed on Rose's face. "That's not possible," she said. "There's no way Sam would have lied to us this entire time. He loves Narina more than anything."

"I don't want to believe it either," Spencer said, "but there are some things that don't add up. The way they sold their home in

Oakland and the way he suggested we get out of town right before the earthquake."

"But wouldn't you be able to see if he was one of them?" Rose asked. "Wouldn't you see his shadow with your vision?"

"That's the thing—I looked at him closely just now and noticed something I'd never seen before. The edge of his glow is gray, like there's a, well, shadow. It's small, almost imperceptible, but it's there. We know from Vik that they have shielding technology. Maybe they've found a way to shield him and cloak him with light?"

Rose looked down at her hands. "There's something I never mentioned," she whispered.

"What is it?"

"Remember when we were on our way to Mt. Shasta and I asked Sam about his ayahuasca experience?" Rose asked.

Spencer nodded.

"Well, when he replied, I heard a voice that said, 'He's hiding something,' but I had no idea what it meant. This was shortly after my episode in Mexico and my bipolar diagnosis. I would sometimes hear voices, but I didn't know what to think of them. The thing is, though, for some reason, after that I never fully trusted Sam."

Spencer shook her head. "I don't know what to think. What do we do? Do we tell Narina?"

"If we block her out much longer, we won't have a choice. She'll notice something's up." Rose said, and then paused for a moment, deep in thought. "But I don't think we say anything. Think about it—if we told Narina now, she would be furious. Her emotions would be too unpredictable during the battle. Her anger might serve us, but it also might get us in trouble. I'm still not sure what I believe, either. Vik could be trying to play us, hoping to divide us before the Harvest. If it's not true, we'll have caused a bunch of emotional chaos for nothing."

"And if it *is* true?" Spencer asked.

"If it is true . . ." Rose inhaled deeply. "Then we'll find out during the battle. There's not much we can do now, anyway; we don't have enough time. It doesn't really change our plan. Our goal is to take down the Apparatus either way. If we find out he's part of the Apparatus, then we'll take him down with them."

"But our plan depends on his ability to create the blackout," said Spencer. "What if he's intentionally withholding a solution?"

Rose thought for a minute. "Well, if Sam is intentionally withholding a solution, then that means Vik is telling the truth, which might mean that we can trust Vik's plan more than we originally thought we could."

"So, we just wait and see?" Spencer didn't like that their plan hinged on one Architect or another.

"Yes. We wait," Rose said.

We're sitting ducks, Spencer thought as they left the park.

# the last supper

**New York City**
**December 20, 2030**

By the time Spencer left the church later that night, Sam still hadn't figured out a way to trigger a blackout. The entire Network planned to meet back at the church the next morning for a final brief before the Harvest.

Narina, Rose, and Spencer went out for one last dinner before the battle.

"The last supper," Narina joked. "Should I wash your feet or identify which one of you will betray me?"

Spencer exchanged a nervous glance with Rose. Had Narina noticed that they'd blocked their connection from her earlier, or was she just joking? "Convenient that you're Jesus and we're your humble disciples," Spencer retorted, trying to gauge the situation.

Narina laughed.

Spencer felt relieved. Narina was only kidding.

"Stop," Rose said. "This isn't funny. We could all be dead tomorrow."

Narina shrugged. "I know," she whispered in resignation. "Jokes aside, I've always loved our dinners. You know the last supper is where Jesus broke bread and passed a cup of wine—sharing his body and blood—and that's really what we've been doing every time we have dinner together. We share pieces of ourselves with each other. You both are a part of me. I feel immensely lucky that the two of you are the ones I get to do this with."

Tears were welling up in Rose's eyes. "I think a lot about what Alo told us that day. That we each descended from an ancient Lemurian bloodline that was forced to separate, spreading their seed across the earth, thousands of miles apart. Sekhmet in Egypt, Danu in Ireland, and Vayu in India. I sometimes wonder if we reincarnated over and over again until we finally made our way back to each other. If this epic homecoming was our destiny all along."

They both looked at Spencer expectantly. She knew they were waiting for her own sentimental addition. "I keep thinking that we're missing something," she blurted out instead. "Something right in front of us."

"Spence!" Rose said, and laughed. "Here we are, crying and sharing our deepest thoughts, and your mind is already in the battle."

"Sorry." Spencer laughed. "You know how much I love you both, but if this really is our destiny, then we need to focus on how we defeat the Apparatus."

"We've done everything we can, Spence," said Rose. "We need to let the pieces fall where they may."

"Memento mori," Narina added, lifting her glass in salute.

Narina liked to use the Latin phrase often—"Remember you must die." It was a reminder of one's own mortality, the inevitability of death. No one could escape it, so death, in a way, didn't matter at all; what mattered was that you lived before you died.

Spencer nodded.

They spent the rest of the dinner laughing and reminiscing and, more importantly, celebrating. They had lived their lives fully and were ready to face death and all the shadows it brought with it.

# the match

### New York City
### December 20, 2030

They walked to their hotel and parted ways, each heading to their own room. They wouldn't be able to sleep, but they needed to rest regardless.

Spencer changed into pajamas and was washing her face when she heard a knock on her door. She assumed it would be Narina or Rose.

She swung the door open with one hand while she dried her wet face off with a towel in the other. Vik was standing there with a bottle of wine in his hand.

He looked her up and down and smiled. "I guess I should have messaged you first," he said. "Is now a bad time?"

She felt exposed in her pajamas, suddenly wishing the tiny shorts were a few inches longer. She didn't love the idea of inviting him into her room, but there wasn't anywhere else to go this late at night. And she knew Vik. He'd shown up unannounced like this on purpose. He liked to have the upper hand, so she refused to give it to him. "No, it's okay," she replied, as casually as she could. "Come in."

Spencer was relieved her hotel room had a couch, not just a bed.

Vik made himself at home, heading over to the minibar to grab the wine opener. He poured two glasses and handed one to Spencer. "It's a Napa Valley Cab," he said. "I thought it might take us back to our first date."

Spencer looked at the bottle: a 1992 Screaming Eagle Cabernet

Sauvignon. The label meant nothing to her, but she was sure Vik would tell her its significance.

As if he'd read her mind, he started talking. "It's one of the most expensive bottles to sell at auction, considered one of the finest examples of American winemaking. They only produced 175 bottles that year."

"Cool," was the only reply Spencer could muster as she clinked her glass with his. He looked her in the eyes for longer than she liked.

"You ran away earlier today. I wanted to make sure you were okay."

"You wanted to know what I decided to do with the information you shared."

"That too." He smiled, tipping his head down in a nod.

"We decided not to do anything. The Network doesn't know about Sam."

Vik nodded. "To be honest, I'm surprised you didn't figure it out sooner. Haven't you always wondered why Narina is more powerful than you?"

Spencer shook her head. "Narina is a confident person. On the food chain of humanity, she's basically an apex predator. I'm not surprised she's the most powerful."

"That's not how the Trium bond works."

"What do you mean?" Spencer asked.

"The Trium bond forms from three equals. The natural power in you is equivalent to the strength of power in both Narina and Rose."

"Then why was Narina's dot bigger on your map? Why is she more powerful?"

"Because she has another bond."

"What are you talking about?"

"There are two types of bonds: a Trium and a Match. The Trium forms when three equals find each other—like finds like. A Match forms when two opposites find each other—dark finds light. If one Liminal in the Trium has more power, like Narina does, it's because she has another bond. Narina might not have known it at the time, but she bonded with Sam."

"How does the Match bond form?" Spencer asked, trying to understand if Narina would have known about it.

"It happens quite naturally. Once both parties have transitioned to their full state of power, they need to consummate the bond," Vik said, glancing over at the bed.

"Sex creates the bond?"

"Not just sex, but an orgasm. As the pair reaches a simultaneous climax, the energy moves up and through the body, like two snakes intertwining with each other. Their power multiplies as it weaves together."

"So Narina probably had no idea it was happening."

Vik shook his head. "Not unless she knew what to expect. She probably just thought it was the best sex of her life."

"Did Sam know?" Spencer asked.

"All the Architects know who their Match is. The Match has the most power over an Architect. Our survival depends on this knowledge."

"Every Architect has a Liminal Match?" Spencer asked.

Vik nodded.

"Who's yours?"

"Isn't it obvious?"

Spencer felt dizzy. Was she Vik's Match? In a way, she felt relieved—maybe the energetic connection between them helped to explain why he had been so impossible to get over. Maybe that was the reason she had felt so empty after he dumped her. Maybe that was why she still felt electricity run through her body every time he touched her now.

"Haven't we already bonded, then?" she asked, thinking about the countless times Vik had made her orgasm. But the last time they'd been together, Spencer hadn't transitioned yet. Had he? "When exactly did you transition?"

"After we broke up."

That's why he was there now, she realized. To trigger the Match. "So that's why you came to my room tonight? The wine, the checking in on me—it's all just an act. Of course you have another motive."

"I just thought you had the right to know," he said. "The more powerful you are tomorrow, the more likely you can take down the Apparatus."

Spencer stood up and walked toward the minibar; she needed space to think. Vik was right. She thought back to the map he'd shown her a few days before—the way Narina's dot was bigger and more intense than Rose's or Spencer's. Narina was undoubtedly more powerful than any other Liminal. Their singular goal was to stop the Harvest. She could bring herself to have sex with Vik if it meant strengthening the Network and giving them a better chance at victory.

She didn't want to acknowledge the small part of her that wanted the power for herself, the part of her that wanted to feel more significant. She remembered the day Alo taught them about their lineage and abilities, the way he'd spent time on Narina's and Rose's before ignoring Spencer's as if they didn't exist at all. She had always wanted to know what real power felt like.

She set down her glass and walked over to Vik, stopping in front of where he was sitting on the couch. She slipped her shirt over her head and pulled off her shorts, leaving nothing on but her underwear.

Inching closer to him, she lifted her right leg and slowly placed it on the couch, straddling him as she lifted her left leg to match.

He grabbed her hips and pulled her down.

Spencer felt like her body was betraying her as electric currents moved from her head to her toes. The sensation reached a heightened intensity a few inches below her belly button, like she was being shocked there.

Vik moved his right hand off her hip and grabbed a handful of her hair, pulling her face close to his. He breathed hard in her ear. The warmth felt like a caress before he gently bit the lobe.

Spencer tilted her head to give him a better angle.

She was losing control. You hate him, she reminded herself. He ghosted you and married someone else months after you broke up. He treated you like you didn't exist. You were nothing to him. It was helping. The more she remembered how he'd treated her, the less consumed by him she felt.

"Spence," he whispered in her ear, "this only works if we both orgasm. You need to relax. You need to let me in." He reached for her underwear, slowly pushing the thin material aside.

She tried to remember all the reasons she hated him, but all she could think about was how she didn't want him to stop.

He traced a finger down from her belly button, inching lower and lower. His slow pace tormented her. He paused just a second before he reached down farther.

She felt him stiffen beneath her as he touched her. She was dripping wet.

He pushed his middle finger inside of her and applied pressure just where he knew she liked it. He pumped rhythmically in and out a few times, then added his index finger.

It was just enough to make her forget about the past. She stopped fighting and gave herself over to him. She moaned in his ear, her nails gripping his back.

Then she was unbuttoning his shirt.

He tried to remove his belt and pants with his other hand, never stopping his right hand from the undulating rhythm that threatened to take her over the edge.

She reached down to help him take off the rest of his clothes, her mouth watering when she saw him. It was as if he'd grown in physical size along with his energetic powers.

He stood up, holding Spencer by the hips as he carried her over to the bed. He lowered her down and climbed on top.

She hoped he'd go straight in—she was almost at her edge—but instead, he slowed.

He kissed the tip of her nose, the sides of her neck. He put each of her nipples in his mouth slowly, tenderly, before biting down. It was never too much, just enough to send a jolt of electricity straight through her body.

He lightly caressed her stomach and thighs with his hands, then with his mouth. He kissed her belly button and then followed the same path he'd inched down earlier, now using his tongue. His head was between her knees, his mouth and his hands working at once.

He brought Spencer to the edge repeatedly. Five times in total. Each time, she was sure she would explode, but he always stopped right at the brink, pausing to let her cool down before he began again.

He was building her up.

Finally, after the fifth time, he came up for air. He moved alongside Spencer's body, lying next to her on the bed. He was still teasing her with his left hand.

"I want to hear you say it," he said in her ear.

"Say what?"

"I want to hear you beg for me."

She looked at him, feeling an equal measure of repulsion and desire. But she didn't have to lie to him—she could give him what he wanted.

She locked eyes with him, angling her face down to give him the doe eyes she knew he liked. "I need you inside of me," she said as she wrapped her hand around him. "Plea—" she whispered.

Before she could get the word fully out, he moved on top of her. Then immediately inside of her. His movement was dynamic, constantly alternating his speed. His actions were gentle but hard at the same time.

He wanted her as much as she wanted him, Spencer realized.

As he penetrated her, Spencer felt like she understood the full range of human emotion— sadness, joy, greed, lust, maybe even love—but more than anything, she felt *power*.

She felt her own power coursing through her, the grounding calm at her center. But she felt something else, too, a midnight-black smoke moving along her spine, a darkness so deep it almost engulfed her.

She moved on top of Vik to regain some sense of control, straddling him. The smoke moved up her spine higher and higher until she felt like she was sitting on the edge of fear, wonder, and ecstasy combined. And then she went over.

Her body shuddered and convulsed beneath her at the same time Vik's did.

They lay in bed for a while afterward, Vik's body pressed up behind hers as he idly stroked his finger along her hip bone.

"I'm going to send something to your Orb," he said.

A notification popped up, giving her access to an app, and she opened it.

"Look."

It was the map. The same map he'd shown her in Brooklyn, now projected in front of her eyes. She zoomed in. She saw a green glowing dot, much larger than it had been before. It was as big as Narina's had been. Next to the green dot was an equally large black shadow.

A pit formed deep in Spencer's stomach. She'd thought that having this much power would make her feel better, but instead, she felt uneasy looking at the size of the shadow next to her. All she'd done was make Vik stronger.

"When did you find out?" Spencer asked. The question had been on her mind for a while—when had he first known about the Liminals and the Architects?

"About you or me?" Vik asked.

"Both."

"I learned about you first. Graham gave me a pill at the party we went to. It allowed me to see energy. You were the most beautiful being I'd ever laid eyes on."

Spencer's stomach clenched at his words. "And when did you find out about what you were?"

"Later the same night. I saw my reflection in a mirror, and it was a dark shadow. I didn't fully understand any of it then, or for a long time, actually. The initiation into the Apparatus doesn't happen all at once. Information came in bits and pieces."

"Why did you do it?"

"Do what?"

"Join the Apparatus. You knew what they were."

"Did you feel like becoming a Liminal was a choice for you?" Vik asked. "Something you could have said no to if you wanted?"

Spencer shook her head.

"The darkness is a part of me, just like the light is a part of you. There were aspects of the initiation I didn't want to do, but it never really felt like a *choice*."

"Was ending things with me part of the initiation?"

"Yes. It was."

Spencer nodded. "Goodnight, Vik," she said quietly.

A few minutes later, when she was on the verge of falling into a deep sleep, she heard Vik whisper behind her. "I'm sorry, Spence. I'm sorry for everything."

They both woke up early the next morning. Vik was sitting on the edge of the bed, facing away from her and putting on his shirt.

"By the way," he said as Spencer rolled over and looked at his back, "the Match bonds us on more than one level."

"What do you mean?" she asked, pushing herself upright.

"If I die, you die," Vik said flatly. "The bond is only broken through death."

Spencer's stomach fell.

He stood up, buttoning his pants and fastening his belt, never looking at her.

She felt rage and hatred build inside of her. He had used her for his own protection.

Finally, as he was about to leave, he looked at her with absolutely no emotion in his eyes. "See you later, Spence," he said, and walked nonchalantly out of the room.

Spencer sat in bed, stunned. She thought back to his whispered apology last night. She had thought it was an apology for everything he'd done in the past.

But now she couldn't help but wonder if it was an apology for something he was about to do.

# the truth

**New York City
December 21, 2030**

An hour later, Spencer walked over to the church. Sam and the engineers were there. From the look of their bloodshot eyes, they'd been up all night, working on the blackout.

"Any luck?" Spencer asked.

Sam shook his head, a forlorn look in his eyes that felt familiar to her. It was the same look he'd had the day they'd found him standing in front of the TV, watching the news about the earthquake. He seemed genuinely defeated. Spencer didn't know what or who to believe anymore, but she knew they would need a new plan for today. They couldn't rely on a blackout anymore.

Narina and Rose came in a few minutes later.

Spencer smiled seeing them together. They had all been so wrapped up preparing for today that no one had thought to discuss what to wear. Spencer thought about the battle scenes in every action movie she'd ever seen, the stars outfitted in skintight black leather outfits with sheaths and holsters for weapons. Instead, the women had each engaged in their own form of dopamine dressing that morning, choosing outfits that embodied their essence and matched their light. Narina was wearing red leather pants and an orange mesh shirt that clung tightly to the skin above her black bra. Rose had on a two-piece matching set—flowing knit pants and a shirt made from a blue crochet material. Spencer had chosen her favorite olive-green turtleneck, layered a mossy suede jacket on top, and paired it with jeans.

"Morning," Rose said as she handed each of them a coffee and a croissant.

"Thanks," Spencer and Narina murmured in unison, both forever grateful that there was one thoughtful friend among the three of them.

"We need a new plan," Spencer said. "Sam hasn't made any progress on the blackout."

Rose eyed Spencer, and she knew they were both wondering the same thing: was Sam intentionally sabotaging their strategy, or could he really not figure it out?

"Shit," Narina mumbled. "At this point, we might have to hope that Vik's plan works and he doesn't screw us over."

Spencer wanted to tell them about last night, about the Match and about how she trusted Vik both more and less now than she had before, but she couldn't bring herself to do it.

They waited for the rest of the Network to file in before giving the update.

Spencer moved to the front of the room to speak. "We haven't made any progress on the blackout, so we'll revert to the backup plan—Vik's plan. He gave us the location for each Harvest site—Washington Square Park and Central Park in Manhattan, Brooklyn Bridge Park and Fort Greene Park in Brooklyn, Rockaway Beach in Queens, Pelham Bay Park in the Bronx, and High Rock Park on Staten Island. Fort Greene is Vik's site. Since Vik plans to join us at Washington Square Park, Fort Greene should see no action tonight.

"You've been divided into seven groups. The first six groups each have one Trium and thirty Liminals. You'll go to your assigned Geo at nine o'clock tonight and wait there until your Architect arrives. The seventh group—the one assigned to Fort Greene Park—will only have one Trium standing guard. You'll go to Vik's site in case he tries to double-cross us in any way, but we don't anticipate there will be any fighting there.

"The power of the solstice portal is strongest in the minutes before midnight as the veil between worlds thins, but the window of opportunity closes fully at twelve o'clock. Vik said that they'll attempt the Harvest sometime between eleven and twelve tonight.

"Our main objective is to stop the Harvest. Do whatever you

can to prevent them from siphoning power from the Rays. If you have an opportunity to eliminate your Architect, take it, but stay focused on the goal."

Sam stepped up next to Spencer and cleared his throat. "We designed these earpieces for everyone to wear," he said, holding up an example as the engineers started handing out a small earbud to every person in the room. "There are nine channels. Seven channels for each of the groups to talk amongst themselves, one channel for the Triums to communicate across the Network, and one channel for the entire Network that will basically pick up any signal within range. These channels will be invisible to anyone else, so you can talk freely. Memorize the channels before you leave. The earpieces are integrated with your Orbs—just communicate which channel you want."

Spencer looked at the bud in her hand, feeling more confused than ever. Was Sam being genuinely helpful, or was this part of a plan to help the Apparatus by sabotaging the Network? She wasn't sure what to think, but the tech might serve them. The Liminals had been able to strengthen their telepathic gifts over the years, but their abilities didn't replace real-time communication. Only Narina, Rose, and Spencer had a strong enough connection to communicate verbally through the bond. For the others, the most they could do was tug on the connection, sending pulses of emotion as signals in their own version of Morse code.

Spencer looked back at the room and spoke again. "Take some time reviewing the plan for each site, but then spend the rest of the day doing whatever activity makes you feel most powerful. There will be breathwork, meditation, and sparring sessions happening throughout the day. The whole group will meet here at eight o'clock, and Rose will lead us through a final intention before we depart."

Everyone nodded and got to work.

A few minutes before eight o'clock that night, Zuri came and took a seat next to Spencer, joining the circle she was sitting in with Narina and Rose.

"How are you feeling?" Spencer asked.

"Honestly, I'm frustrated. I hate that we're playing their game instead of our own. It feels like we've lost the battle before it's even started."

"Their game?"

"Their game is technology. The siphon devices, the EMP, the firewall—all their power is external. We aren't good at tech; external power isn't our thing. All our power is inside of us. But we had no choice but to play by their rules, trying to beat tech with tech, and we couldn't do it. I want to be optimistic, but it feels like they've already won."

Something sparked in Spencer's mind. Zuri was right. There were only seven Architects. Seven men who had little practice using their own powers because they relied on tech to do it for them. They'd done the very thing to themselves that they'd done to countless generations of humanity before—they'd replaced their own power with technology. The tech they created was nothing more than an imitation of the power that had been inside of them long before, but that same power was still inside of each and every Liminal. The Network had been thinking too small, Spencer realized. They were thinking about how to beat tech with tech when they should have been thinking about how to beat power with power.

She thought back to what Alo had told her about the way the Túatha Dé Danann had rejected the ground rules the invaders laid out before them and chosen a different path.

"What if we play our own game?" Spencer asked, her eyes lighting up as she spoke.

Narina and Rose turned their heads to listen.

"What do you mean?" Zuri asked.

"We've been trying to create a blackout using tech, but what if we create a blackout with our powers instead?"

"How?"

"Lightning. And floods."

Zuri's eyes widened. "Kessie and Luisa," she whispered in recognition.

Spencer nodded.

Zuri shook her head in dismay. "We aren't strong enough, even with the Trium bond."

"What if you had a stronger power source?" Narina chimed in, her eyes now ablaze.

They turned to look at her.

"The Network," she said. "We have hundreds of Liminals. What if we use ourselves as the power source to trigger the blackout?"

"Shit," Spencer said, "it could work." She was thinking out loud now. "We don't know how many Liminals they would need. If we send everyone, we risk leaving the Geos unprotected."

"Leave a Trium to protect each Geo and send the rest of the Liminals to power Zuri, Kessie, and Luisa," Rose said. "If the blackout works, they'll be defenseless. One Trium is strong enough to take down one Architect."

"We need to try it. Without a blackout, we have no choice but to rely on Vik's plan," Narina reminded them.

She looked at Spencer. *I still don't trust him. He's going to fuck us over, just like he fucked you last night,* Narina said to her down the bond.

Spencer looked away, her cheeks flushing in shame. Of course Narina knew. Even though Spencer had blocked their connection during it, she could probably read it all over Spencer's face. And as always, Narina wasn't wrong. Spencer hated that their plan rested on Vik, especially after his whispered apology.

Sam had wandered over at some point during the conversation and now interjected, "The server warehouse for the mainframe is at the border of Village Park, near the old Meatpacking District. The backup generators are a block away, in a different building. We identified both when we were trying to take down the mainframe. That's the origin of the city's power. If you hit that, you'll take down the whole grid and get your blackout."

Spencer looked at Sam—no trace of dishonesty anywhere on his face. Either he was an incredible actor, or Vik wasn't telling the truth.

Zuri spoke up. "If I'm channeling all that energy to Kessie and Luisa, I won't be able to shield us at the same time. It will leave the three of us—and all the other Liminals with us—completely exposed. We need another Trium there to shield us."

"That would leave one of the Geos completely unprotected," Narina said. "We can't do that; it's too big a risk."

Rose looked at Spencer.

Spencer knew what she was thinking—it depended on which side Sam was on. If he was fighting for the Apparatus, then they would need a Trium in every Geo except Vik's. One for each of the six remaining Architects. But if Sam was with the Network, then they could pull the Trium that had been assigned to his Geo and send them with Zuri. They needed to know which side he was on.

Spencer looked at Narina, sending her a silent apology through the bond before she spoke. She knew this was not the way any of this should be done, but they didn't have time.

She looked up at Sam. "When Vik first told us about the Apparatus's powers, he left out the name of one of the Architects," Spencer said. "I only noticed it a few days ago when I was prepping our strategy, so I asked him who it was." She paused before continuing. "He said it was you, Sam."

Sam's eyes fell. He shook his head, placing a hand on his forehead and running it down to the back of his neck. He let out a breath as if dropping a heavy weight he'd been carrying for a long time. Something else dropped along with it: his shield. Spencer saw black shadows swirl around him and the unmistakable outline of a ram on his wrist—his Mark.

"It's not what you think." He said it again, this time making eye contact with Narina. "It's not what you think. I promise. Everything I've done has been for you."

Narina's eyes flared in disbelief, hatred emanating toward Sam, then toward Spencer. Flames erupted in front of her. She smoldered.

Spencer contained the flames with her shield and then put them out.

"You bitch," Narina said. "*You knew.* You knew and you kept it a secret from me."

"We were trying to protect you," Spencer whispered. "We didn't know if it was true. Sam has always been so loyal, and we know that Vik can't be trusted. We figured we would wait and see what happened during the Harvest. That was the only way to know for sure without disrupting the entire Network. But it can't wait anymore.

## dark days ahead

We need to know whether we can leave another Geo unmanned. We need to know what Sam plans to do."

"We?" Narina asked, focusing on only one word out of everything Spencer had just said. Her eyes narrowed on Rose.

"I'm sorry," Rose said. "We didn't know what else to do."

Narina rose to her feet, heat blasting from her body like a furnace before she walked away.

Rose followed her.

Spencer knew she should join them, but they had mere minutes to finalize a plan before they had to leave. None of this would matter if they were all dead tomorrow.

She looked back up at Sam. He was trying to hold back tears as Narina walked away.

Spencer thought through the options. If he planned to fight for the Network, he would be in Village Park, standing alongside Narina, when they faced Graham later that night. If he planned to fight for the Apparatus, he'd be in the Bronx at Pelham Bay Park, ready to siphon from the residents there.

"Sam," Spencer said, "I don't know which side you're really on. But I believe you care about the people in this room, especially Narina. The safety of every Liminal here depends on how you answer this question. I don't care which answer you give, but I need the truth. I'll let you walk out of here regardless if it means we know what we'll be facing in a few hours. Which Geo will you be in tonight?"

Sam looked Spencer dead in the eyes. "My plan has always been to fight alongside Narina at Washington Square Park and defeat the Apparatus. That's still my plan. I'll be right there, if you let me. I can explain everything to all of you later, but please believe me. I would do anything to protect my wife. And my daughter." His voice cracked on the last words.

Spencer believed him. If nothing else was true, she believed that Sam wanted to protect Narina and Maya. That part wasn't a lie.

She nodded and turned back to Zuri, praying that her intuition to trust Sam wasn't wrong. "We'll pull Mira and her Trium from Pelham Bay Park to shield you," she said. "We'll place a handful of

Liminals in Fort Greene and Pelham Bay as a safety measure. Each of the other five Triums will go to the remaining Geos. And all other Liminals will go with you to the server warehouse to power your Trium. Once you're done there, split into equal groups and head to each of the Harvest sites in case anyone needs backup."

Zuri nodded.

Spencer noticed Rose and Narina were standing behind the group. She wasn't sure when they had returned. "Did you hear the new plan?" Spencer asked.

Rose nodded. Narina didn't acknowledge her at all.

"Rose," Spencer said, "we only have a few minutes. Did you want to say something to the group?"

"Yes." She walked to the front of the room and pulled a paper out of her pocket. "I'd like to share a verse that I find myself coming back to often. The source might be a bit unexpected: the Bible. It's from the Book of John." She looked down at her paper and began reading.

*In the beginning was the Word, and the Word was with God, and the Word was God.*

*He was with God in the beginning.*

*Through him all things were made; without him nothing was made that has been made.*

*In him was life, and that life was the light of mankind.*

*The light shines in the darkness, and the darkness has not overcome it.*

*There was a man sent from God whose name was John.*

*He came as a witness to testify concerning the light, so that through him all might believe.*

*He himself was not the light; he came only as a witness to the light.*

*The true light that gives light to everyone was coming into the world.*

She folded the paper and put it back in her pocket. "We are not the light," she said, looking back up at the group. "We're merely vessels for it to travel through. We're here tonight to testify on its behalf, to show the world that light can shine in the darkness, and that darkness has not overcome it. Not tonight."

"Not tonight," the room murmured, before they filed out the door and into the darkness.

# the solstice

### New York City
### December 21, 2030

The Triums headed to their designated locations—Washington Square Park, Central Park, Brooklyn Bridge Park, Rockaway Beach, and High Rock Park. Fort Greene was Vik's site and Pelham Bay was Sam's, so if everything went according to the new plan, those locations would see no action save for a few Liminals sitting idly by.

Zuri, Luisa, and Kessie made their way to the server warehouse, along with Mira's Trium and all the remaining Liminals who were going with them to power the blackout.

Sam stayed with Narina, Rose, and Spencer, and the four of them walked to Washington Square Park in silence. They would face Graham tonight. The plan was for Vik to join them shortly after Graham's arrival. Vik had a personal vendetta against the man. He wanted retribution for his daughter, so one of the stipulations of his information-sharing had been that he would get to watch Graham's demise.

They stood in the center of the park and waited. It was eerily quiet. Spencer connected to the earpiece Sam had given them through her Orb and switched to the Trium channel. "Is there anyone in any of your parks?" she asked.

Several replies came in quick succession, all "No."

Sure, it was getting late, but it was unusual for parks in the city to be completely empty at this hour, especially since the Geos were now so safe.

Spencer turned to Narina and Rose. "All the parks are completely empty."

"Something's up," Narina said, turning to Sam and glaring. "What's going on? Why is there no one outside?"

"I have no idea," he said. Confusion crossed his face. "There was nothing about altering the population's behavior in the plan. The siphon device is strong enough to work on anyone within the boundaries of each Geo, so there's no reason for the Apparatus to interfere."

Narina shook her head, unhappy with the response.

Zuri spoke into Spencer's ear. "We're all set up outside of the warehouse. Just give us the go-ahead when the Architects arrive, and we'll start the blackout."

"Will do," Spencer replied.

They wanted to wait until each Architect was in place before they struck to ensure they had them cornered. They didn't want to miss their opportunity to grab and destroy every siphon device.

"Sam, make sure you're out of view when Graham arrives," Spencer said. "You'll be a better asset to us as a surprise."

Sam nodded and moved several hundred feet away, hiding in the shadows.

A little before eleven o'clock, Spencer noticed some movement near the north entrance of the park. Four people were approaching. Two more were walking near the west entrance and five near the south. It was hard to make out, but it looked like they were all in pajamas. What the hell were people doing in the park in their PJs?

They stopped near the park entrances, standing still. Spencer activated her vision; they were all Rays, but that was unsurprising, given what they'd learned from Vik.

Over the next thirty minutes, dozens more people did the same thing—lingered near the entrances in what looked like their pajamas. Were they sleepwalking?

"What the hell is going on?" Rose asked. "I'm going to talk to them."

But as she was about to leave, a man wearing gray slacks and a long black overcoat walked into the park.

## dark days ahead

Spencer saw a gray storm cloud with a ten-foot circumference hiding a body in shadows. It was Graham.

She heard a voice in her earpiece.

"Alfred is approaching," Layla said from Rockaway Beach.

"We have eyes on Qiang," Jordan added from Brooklyn Bridge Park.

"What about Reinhold and Pierre?" Spencer asked.

"Reinhold hasn't arrived yet," said Shilpa, the conduit stationed in Central Park.

"Neither has Pierre," Hana added from High Rock Park.

Spencer noticed movement behind Graham. Two other men were with him. One she would recognize from anywhere: Vik. The other was an older white man: Reinhold.

"Reinhold is here with Graham and Vik," Spencer said into the earpiece, confused.

As she said Reinhold's name, Narina and Rose spun their heads toward the park entrance to look at the men they were about to face. There were now hundreds of Rays lingering behind them.

"Still no Pierre?" Spencer asked Hana.

"No—there's no one else in the park but our Trium."

Spencer steadied her gaze on the approaching men and spoke into her earpiece. "We'll deal with Reinhold here," she said. "Everyone, keep your eyes peeled for Pierre. He might be a wild card." She took a deep breath to steady herself before continuing. "It's time. Conduits, engage your shields now."

Spencer reached into her pocket and clutched her owl totem. She looked up at the stars above and saw a glittering net cascade across the sky as a protective canopy dropped over the entire city.

She turned her attention to Vik walking behind Graham, anger blurring the edges of her vision. What was he up to? This wasn't the plan they had agreed to. Vik was supposed to pretend that he was at Fort Greene Park and show up here later, after Graham. He wasn't supposed to arrive in a caravan with Graham and Reinhold.

*I knew we couldn't trust him*, Narina communicated through the bond.

The three men stopped ten feet away from where Narina, Rose, and Spencer stood in a triangle.

Vik raised an eyebrow at Spencer, moving his eyes around as if to ask, "Where is everyone?" He'd been expecting to see the thirty Liminals who had planned to join them there. He didn't know they had been sent to the server warehouse instead.

Spencer saw Vik reach into his pocket and pull out the master shield he carried. He placed the cap back on it to turn the shield off, then glanced at something in front of him. He was looking at his Orb. The map, Spencer realized—he was checking the map to see where all the Liminals were.

Spencer remembered that he had shared the map with her last night in bed to show her the way their powers had grown after bonding. Did she still have access to it? she wondered as she went to pull it up on her Orb.

She did. There were four large midnight-black dots there in Washington Square Park—Vik, Graham, Reinhold, and Sam. There was another black dot in Brooklyn and one in Queens. Every Architect except Pierre was accounted for. And there weren't any Liminals. The shield the conduits had deployed was working.

Spencer looked back at Vik. He opened and capped the shield several times, turning it on and off, trying to understand why he couldn't see any Liminals on the map when his shield was turned off. He didn't know what was going on. The Network had the upper hand.

Spencer smiled.

She still had the map up on her Orb when she noticed something strange—what must have been millions of tiny glowing dots were moving toward them. What the hell? Every Ray in the entire city seemed to be walking to Washington Square Park.

"Well," Graham said, pulling Spencer's attention from the map. "I've been so looking forward to this evening. It's been a long time in the making. You three have made quite a name for yourselves. We haven't seen a Trium this strong in centuries."

As he spoke, Spencer saw a shadow break off from Reinhold's body and move toward Narina. The shapeshifter. He was trying to access her power. Spencer dug her heels into the ground, reached for more strength, and sent it to the iridescent bubble around Narina.

Reinhold's shadow was strong—it pushed into the bubble, making a dent, almost touching her body before rebounding.

Graham tried next with his shadow creatures. He stared at the three of them, and suddenly, hundreds of small vermin poured from the back of his head in a torrent. The vermin ran up along every part of the bubble, trying to chew through it. Spencer had had a disproportionately large fear of rodents ever since a mouse once walked across her face while she slept in her New York City apartment. She felt sick to her stomach looking at hundreds of them now, but she held the shield strong. The vermin retreated.

Spencer knew this part was just a game for them, like a cat playing with its prey.

"So much for a little appetizer before the main course," Graham said in disappointment.

More Rays were moving behind the three men at the north entrance. Spencer tilted her head to get a better look. There had to be thousands of them lined up along Fifth Avenue now.

*Why the hell are all the Rays coming to Washington Square Park? We must be missing something,* Spencer said through the bond.

*It's like they're in a trance,* Narina replied.

She was right. Spencer had initially thought they were sleepwalking, but it was more like the deep hypnotic state of a trance. Hypnosis. Spencer remembered the headphones the security guard had placed on her head at city hall.

"Sam," she said quietly into her earbud, "can we see if anything is playing on their Orbs?"

There was a long pause before he replied. "Turn to channel nine."

Spencer adjusted her own earpiece to the channel Sam had designed to pick up any signal within its radius. At first, it sounded like a meditation track, with oceanic waves and birds chirping. She could almost smell the saltwater. Then she heard a voice. It was as faint as a whisper, barely audible but unmistakable. Vik's voice.

"Picture yourself standing straight with your chest open, your shoulders back, your head held high, your feet firmly planted on the ground. Take a deep breath in, and as you exhale, let the outside world fall away.

"Focus on your inner strength. Find the well of power located deep inside of you. Feel that power coursing through your body, filling you with vitality. Imagine a bright aura of light surrounding your body. With every inhale, feel the light grow stronger. With every exhale, let the light solidify around you. Remember, you are powerful. You are invincible."

Spencer felt sick as she realized what Vik was doing. She switched her earpiece back to the Trium channel. "Vik is using mind control to hypnotize the Rays. He's trying to strengthen their powers."

"Why would he do that?" Zuri asked.

Spencer, Narina, and Rose exchanged a look. The memory of city hall would be forever seared in their minds.

"If they heighten your power first, they get more energy when they siphon," Spencer said.

"Shall we begin?" Graham asked, looking at Reinhold and Vik, breaking the women out of their conversation.

Both men nodded in response.

Spencer realized Graham was referring to the EMP. She tried to see the master shield in Vik's hand. The Network's shield, which the conduits had in place through their totems, would protect them regardless, but some part of Spencer needed to know whether Vik intended to honor his plan to help them. Which side are you on? she implored, but she couldn't see his shield. She had no idea if it was turned on or off.

Graham reached into his pocket and pulled out a small stick—the detonator. He pressed his thumb down. Spencer felt something bounce off the shield she held in place, but nothing else happened. He pressed again and again.

Spencer watched Vik the entire time, looking for any sign of surprise, but his expression revealed no emotion.

"Reinhold, try yours," Graham said.

Reinhold reached into his pocket and pulled out an identical stick with a button on the end: a backup. He pressed it, and again nothing happened.

"What were you expecting?" Narina said with a bored expression on her face as she casually looked down at her nails. "That I wouldn't be able to do this?" She flicked open her hand and shot a flame fifty feet high toward them. Their shield stopped it, but it still made Graham and Reinhold jump back in surprise.

Graham muttered something under his breath to Reinhold and Vik.

Spencer saw it now: this was the Network's window to strike. She pressed on her earpiece as she spoke. "Zuri, you're up. Lights out."

The clouds above them started to glow as if lit from within. Spencer saw some fizzles and sparks before a giant bolt of lightning forked in the sky above them. Then seven bolts came down at once. Spencer smiled—one for each Architect. Kessie had always liked to put on a show, and this was her masterpiece. Brilliant streaks of light in mesmerizing shapes and patterns painted the velvety midnight background above them.

Then the lightning stopped suddenly. Spencer looked around the city. The lights were still on everywhere. It hadn't worked.

"That was a nice little show," Graham said, smiling and drawing Spencer's attention back to the Architects in front of her.

Then she saw it behind him, a poetically beautiful titan bolt that appeared to strike down in cosmic justice, as if perfectly slicing through Graham. But it didn't touch him—it hit the warehouse directly behind him, ten blocks north. The lights in the buildings around the park started to flicker.

More, Spencer thought. It's working, we just need more.

She heard something that sounded like the ocean. Turning, she saw a bright blue wave forming in the distance above the buildings. Luisa.

"Holy shit," Narina said under her breath. Even she was impressed.

The wave crested, and within a second, the entire city was thrown into blackness. Mira's shield protected the surrounding area and evaporated the water as soon as it hit the buildings and all the servers inside. But it worked. They had created a blackout.

*Now!* Spencer said to Narina and Rose through the bond. *Their firewall is down.*

Narina let out a blast of fire so quick and strong that Spencer could have sworn it came from her mouth. *She really is a dragon,* Spencer thought proudly. It scorched Reinhold and lit his dark gray wool coat on fire.

Reinhold yelled in pain and surprise. "Someone put it out!"

Graham sent a dark cloud his way that smothered the flames.

Spencer turned her attention to Rose as she raised her hands into the air behind her. It was subtle at first, the way she made the leaves dance—rising and swirling. Then the wind hit Spencer's face so hard, it almost knocked the breath out of her. *More,* she thought, sending a pulse of power to Rose through their bond. There was a loud crack and then a breaking noise that seemed to come from every direction. Spencer looked around. The windows on every single building surrounding the park shattered from the blast of Rose's wind.

Suddenly Graham was on his knees, holding his throat, gasping for breath. Rose was sucking the air out of him. He threw out his hand and released more shadow creatures, only this time, they didn't head for the Trium; they went straight to the Rays now entering the park.

Spencer felt a pulse come through the bond. The blackout had taken out the Network's earpieces too, so they had to revert to their Morse-code communication. The pulse felt like success. It had Layla's signature. Alfred was taken care of.

*One down,* Spencer thought, turning her attention quickly back to the vermin now crawling up the legs of the Rays. The creatures seemed to possess them, the eyes of the Rays turning red as their skin withered. The Rays were headed straight for the Trium, and hundreds more were entering the park from all sides.

*Can you shield us from them?* Rose asked.

Spencer shook her head. *The shield works on energetic powers. It won't stop them from physically hurting us..*

"Sam!" Narina yelled. "Sam! Do something to stop them."

Sam ran toward them, and Spencer's jaw almost dropped to the ground. The cloud of black molten liquid that oozed around him was bigger than that of any of the other three Architects in the park. Spencer saw surprise and then rage cross Graham's and Reinhold's faces as they realized Sam was not coming to their defense.

Sam threw his hand out toward the group of Rays approaching. Black lava poured from him, wrapping around them, tightening and constricting like a snake capturing prey. Suddenly the lava solidified into a circle around them. They were trapped. They weren't hurt, but they could no longer advance toward the Trium.

Sam turned and sent another bolt of liquid in another direction, repeatedly confining groups of Rays together all over the park.

Narina and Spencer locked eyes briefly as they watched Sam work. A sense of relief passed through them. Sam was an Architect, an incredibly powerful one, but he appeared to be on their side. The way his lava encapsulated the Rays was careful, gentle even. He wasn't trying to hurt anyone; he was just protecting the Trium. Narina sent a little nod to Spencer, and fire pulsed down their bond. Spencer understood. *I forgive you.* Spencer sent a pulse in reply before turning back to the three men in front of them.

Wait a minute—where was Vik?

Graham was still on his knees in front of them, gasping for air. Reinhold was removing his charred coat. But Vik was gone.

Another pulse came through the bond from Brooklyn Bridge Park. Success.

Spencer looked around again, still trying to locate Vik, and then she noticed Reinhold reaching into his pocket. He retrieved a black device. It was bigger than what they'd used at city hall, but it was unmistakable. The siphon.

"Reinhold's siphon!" Spencer yelled.

As soon as the words left her mouth, she saw a torrent of Rose's wind blow the device out of Reinhold's hand. It landed near the foot of one of the Rays, a young woman, several hundred feet away. Spencer watched as a cloud of smoke left Reinhold and headed toward the Ray.

He was going to shapeshift into the woman's body. Spencer watched the cloud slow as it neared the Ray, and then it pounced, entering through her heart before it consumed her entire body.

The woman reached down to pick up the siphon.

"It's Reinhold!" Spencer yelled to Rose. "He shifted into her body. He's going to siphon!"

Rose looked at the Ray in front of her. She couldn't see Reinhold or his black cloud like Spencer could. "I can't," Rose said quietly. "I can't do it."

Rose had to do it. Narina was off working with Sam, trying to keep the Rays at bay—Sam wrapping them in quickly solidifying lava and Narina sending lines of fire to block their path into the park.

"Rose," Spencer said, "that's not her in there. It's Reinhold. If we don't stop her, they'll siphon from every single Ray here."

But Rose just shook her head in dismay. She couldn't take the life of a Ray.

Spencer dug in her heels and tried to call on Rose's power herself. The woman started coughing, struggling to catch her breath, but it wasn't enough. She was still breathing and about to place her finger on the trigger. Spencer noticed a plume of dark, shimmering smoke enter the man standing behind her.

"No!" the man said suddenly. "She's my wife. I can't do that."

Who was he talking to? Spencer wondered.

A small object rolled toward the man. She watched him pick it up and open it. It was a pocketknife.

The man walked toward the woman—his wife—as tears streamed down his face. Without hesitating, he pulled the knife across her throat in a swift motion. Blood poured down her body, and she fell to her knees. The man picked up the siphon now lying on the ground and walked toward a bench a dozen yards away. He handed the siphon over to someone sitting in the shadows.

Spencer didn't need to see his face to know it was Vik. He'd just used mind control to have that man kill his own wife. She felt sick but also relieved. Vik had just prevented Reinhold from siphoning. Maybe he was on their side after all?

## dark days ahead

"Spencer!" a voice yelled.

She turned around, and relief washed over her. Zuri, Kessie, and Luisa were running toward her, followed by a group of Liminals.

"Narina and Sam are trying to stop the Rays," Spencer explained. "The Apparatus is using them—Graham is sending shadow creatures into them, and Reinhold just tried to shapeshift into that one."

Zuri raised a brow. "Sam?" she asked.

"He's on our side," Spencer confirmed.

"What about Vik?"

"I don't know. He disappeared for a while. But he just stopped Reinhold from triggering his siphon."

"So we have the siphon now?" Zuri asked.

"No," Spencer said, realizing only now. "Vik has it."

Spencer saw a flurry of action out of the corner of her eye. Sam was fighting Reinhold. Reinhold was jumping from Ray to Ray, shapeshifting into a different body every few seconds. Sam would close in on one, constricting his lava around them, almost suffocating them, before Reinhold's shadow would jump to the next one.

Where was Reinhold's body? She scanned the park and saw a figure in a dark gray jacket slumped over on a bench nearby.

*Narina!* Spencer sent down the bond. *Reinhold's body is on the bench while his shadow is shapeshifting. Take him out.*

Narina directed her gaze at the bench, and without a second of hesitation, an explosion of fire consumed his body. She looked over to where Sam was fighting. The Ray in front of him collapsed as the shadow inside him burned to death.

Spencer turned back to the bench and saw Graham inching forward behind Narina. *Narina, watch out. Graham is behind you!* she said down the bond.

Narina turned, but she wasn't quick enough. Graham had the pocketknife, and he held it up to Narina's throat.

Spencer froze. Her shield couldn't stop Graham from using the knife on Narina. She reached for Rose down the bond as Vik appeared out of the shadows. Spencer held her breath, unsure of what he would do next.

"I've been waiting for this moment for a long time," Vik said.

Spencer couldn't tell whether he was looking at Graham or Narina as he spoke.

She saw his shadow move toward the pair. It paused for a moment before entering Graham. Graham looked surprised, bewilderment blossoming across his face. Then Graham's left hand—the one that was tightly secured around Narina's neck—released.

"Vik, don't do this!" Graham said in agony. He raised his right hand—the one holding the knife—in front of his face and turned the blade toward himself. He plunged it into his right eye, blood spurting everywhere as he jammed the knife deeper into the socket. He let out an angry roar.

"That's for Amelia," Vik said, venom dripping off his words. "She became a shell of a woman after we lost our daughter."

Graham pulled the knife out slowly and repositioned it in front of his left eye. "Vik, please. Please don't do this. I tried to warn you. I tried to get you out of the city. You weren't supposed to be there."

"You wanted me in Palm Springs, but what about my family?" Vik seethed.

Graham plunged the knife into his left eye, again thrusting it deep inside the socket. He started to sway and fell to his knees. His roar turned into a yelp, like a little boy crying out for his mother.

"That one was for me," Vik said coldly.

Graham stopped begging now. He knew what was coming next. He removed the knife from his left eye and placed it next to his neck.

Graham stabbed himself in the throat, ripping open his jugular. He fell forward and landed on his stomach, plunging the knife deeper on impact. He coughed up blood twice before he stopped breathing altogether.

"That one was for Sophia."

Vik walked toward Graham's body and reached into his pocket, grabbing his siphon. Then he turned around, heading toward the fountain in front of him. He opened his jacket and placed the siphon he'd just stolen from Graham on some sort of metal breastplate. He reached into his pocket, grabbed the siphon he'd taken from

Reinhold, and placed it alongside the first one. Then he reached into the back pocket of his pants and found a third one: his own siphon.

Before he could add it to the breastplate, a wave of black lava flung it out of his hand. Sam. He reached down to retrieve it. Their shadows started fighting, Vik's midnight shadow reaching into Sam's head, Sam's molten shadow twirling around it, fending it off. Sam reached toward Vik's breastplate and grabbed another siphon.

He had two and Vik had one.

Narina and Rose arrived at Spencer's side.

*Who do we trust?* Rose asked. *They both helped us tonight.*

*I don't trust anyone anymore.* Narina fumed as she lit a ring of fire around both Sam and Vik. *But I trust Vik less.*

*Narina, we can't kill either of them,* Spencer said, quickly working to smother the flame with her shield as she explained. *If Sam dies, Narina dies. And if Vik dies, I die. We're bonded, each a Match.*

Narina stared Spencer down. *Maybe we should all die, then,* she replied, as anger ripped through her.

"Spence!" Vik yelled. "Put the fire out. I'm only trying to help you. The breastplate deactivates all the siphons. Graham is dead. I got what I wanted."

Sam looked at Narina in turn to plead his case now. "Narina," he said, "I was only ever trying to save you. If you believe nothing else, please believe that. I only ever wanted to help you. You're my entire world."

Something about Sam's words nagged at Spencer's brain. *Save you. Help you. My entire world.* Only, that wasn't exactly right. It was "save her," "help her," "she's my entire world." Spencer had heard those words before. But where? She closed her eyes, trying to remember.

There was beeping in the background, fluorescent lighting, a terrible smell. Her arms were strapped down. Someone was leaning over her, whispering in her ear.

"Spencer," the voice said, "I can explain everything later, but please just help get her out of here. She's my entire world. Please save her. This is an access badge that will get you out of the building.

Use your shield to protect her. The three of you have more power than you realize."

She felt something press into her pocket.

Then she heard another voice in the room. Vik's voice.

"What are you doing here?" Vik asked Sam.

Sam pulled away from Spencer. "I wanted to check in on the experiments."

"The experiments aren't in your purview."

"I know, but I heard there were new subjects with powers that we haven't seen before. I had to see for myself."

Spencer froze, letting the memory sink in. The voice that had whispered in her ear and the hand that had placed the badge in her pocket had belonged to Sam. Sam had saved them that day at city hall, not Vik. Vik had lied to her, manipulated her, used her. Just like he had last night. And he would do it again. And again.

Spencer looked at the breastplate and the siphon attached to it as it all fell into place. The breastplate wouldn't deactivate the siphon like he'd said it would. The breastplate was his version of an external hard drive. He'd anticipated the blackout. He didn't need the cloud to store all the energy he was about to take.

Every Ray in the city was there in the park, their powers heightened from Vik's hypnosis. And every Architect—except Sam—was dead. Vik *had* wanted to kill Graham and take down the Apparatus. That part was true. But the Harvest would still happen.

Spencer's stomach turned cold and rage pulsed through her as the final puzzle piece fell into place: Vik wanted all the power for himself.

*Let me be the one to do it*, Spencer said.

*Do what?* Rose asked.

*Take Vik down.*

She felt a burst of heat move up her arm. Narina was giving her power.

Then Spencer's lungs expanded as they filled with air. Rose was giving her power too.

Spencer dug her heels into the ground. For once, she wasn't grounded or calm; she was furious. She thought back to all the times she had let Vik treat her like shit. And the way she had just accepted it. Just like she had accepted that treatment from every other man in her life before him. They had broken her down until she was nothing, but she had let them do it.

Wind torrented around her, picking up debris, leaves, and broken shards of glass. A vortex formed that ripped through the park bench behind where Sam and Vik were fighting. The wind put out the flames that Narina had enclosed them in.

Sam and Vik paused to look around, trying to understand what was happening.

Spencer looked down at the ground and blasted a line of fire straight at Vik.

"Spence, don't do this!" he yelled as flames consumed him.

Spencer started burning up from the inside. She fell to her knees and began coughing.

*The fire is killing her, too!* Narina yelled to Rose. *Put it out!*

Rose sucked out all the air in the park, smothering the fire.

"You fucking bitch," Vik snarled at Spencer as he fumbled to stand back up.

He reached for the single siphon left on his breastplate.

Sam's liquid shadow moved to stop him, but he got there a second too late.

Vik pressed the button.

Spencer watched in horror as the glow around every Ray—the glow that had grown bigger and brighter as Vik's voice hypnotized them—disappeared into the siphon. Every Ray in the park was now a husk: Empty. It was the second blackout of the night, as thousands of Rays lost their light.

But the siphon didn't stop with their energy like it had back in city hall—it kept draining them. The Rays were falling to the ground, collapsing in piles.

"They must have made the siphons stronger," Spencer whispered.

They were dying.

Sam reached for Vik, pulling the siphon off him and enclosing him in molten lava that instantly solidified. "Spencer, put a shield around Vik to block his powers from getting through!" Sam yelled.

Spencer dropped a shield of glitter around him.

They had Vik, and they'd defeated the Apparatus, but not in the way they'd hoped. The Harvest had still happened. Spencer looked around at the thousands of innocent people now lying dead on the ground.

They all sat in silence for a minute, defeat setting in.

"I can bring them back," Rose whispered.

"What?" Narina asked.

"Give me the siphon," Rose said to Sam.

Sam handed the device over, looking confused. "They're dead, Rose. There's nothing we can do." His voice was full of compassion.

"Alo told me my breath can take life, and it can give it. Their power is all right here," Rose said, holding up the siphon. "I can give it back to them and bring them back to life."

"Alo also said that there would be consequences if you play God," Narina reminded her. "Even if you could give the power back, how would you know which power belongs to which person? You could be bringing back zombies."

"We have to try," Rose said, tears welling in her eyes. "We can't just let them all die."

Rose looked at Spencer now, handing her the siphon. "Spence, you ground into the siphon and channel the power to me so that I can send it out."

Spencer shook her head slowly.

"Please. Please just try," Rose pleaded.

Spencer didn't know what to do, but like Rose, she wanted to try something. She held the siphon firmly in her hands and reached into the ground, forming roots beneath her. She remembered the man at city hall who had reached out his hand to give her his powers before they had escaped, the way she had pulled them into her body.

She pulled on the energy stored in the siphon in the same way and felt it enter her bloodstream. Power coursed through her veins in a torrent. Euphoria washed through her, bringing her higher than

## dark days ahead

any high she'd ever felt before. This was the feeling she had craved for so long—real, true, unadulterated power. She wanted to keep it all for herself, to remember this feeling forever.

She heard Alo's voice in her head, telling her that she would have all the power of the universe in her hands.

But he'd said something else, too, a small voice in her head reminded her. He'd told her that she'd have to know when it was enough.

Was this enough?

She thought of the Architects' greed and lust, the insatiable thirst for power that had led them here tonight. She thought about the way Vik had used her and all the people around him as if they were disposable. Like they were each an investment, an asset he'd write off at the end of its useful life.

Spencer wasn't like the Architects. She wasn't like Vik. She could shield her friends from danger, and she was part of one of the most powerful Triums to ever exist—wasn't that something?

Wasn't that enough?

She opened her eyes to look at the faces of her friends around her, waiting expectantly as they stood in front of a sea of lifeless bodies.

This is enough. The power I have is enough. The life I have is enough. I am enough.

She opened the flow between her and Rose and pushed the torrent of energy down the bond.

Rose exhaled, and a stream of butterflies burst through the air behind her, heading toward the bodies on the ground. The butterflies deposited a breath of glittery dust on every person.

Spencer could have sworn she saw a finger move on a body to her right. Then she heard a gasp. It was working. Slowly, the lifeless Rays started to stand back up. Some even had a small glow blooming on their cheeks, a diffused halo forming around their heads.

Rose was absolutely beaming. "I need more," she said.

Zuri came to stand next to Spencer, grabbing her hand, sending her energy into Spencer. Luisa came up on her other side to do the same. Slowly, every Liminal in the park formed an interlocked circle, all sending their power to Spencer in the center. She let it flow through her and into Rose.

Every Ray was standing again now, some using their own light to break through the metal enclosures Sam had created. They weren't just Rays anymore; they were something more than that. The power the Network was channeling into them made them into something bigger.

Spencer sent every ounce of energy into Rose. When the Network's energy dried up, she didn't stop. She reached into the ground, into the plants, and pulled energy from the very earth she stood on. She used so much of her own power that she started to feel weak and dizzy.

Despite the electrical blackout, the city was absolutely glowing, lit up by power.

Liminals, Spencer realized. Rose had created thousands of Liminals.

It's so beautiful, she thought as her eyes began to close.

She caught a glimpse of him coming up behind Sam before she lost consciousness.

Pierre.

Then it all went black.

# the merge

Spencer woke up feeling disoriented and groggy, her head throbbing. The room was freezing cold. She looked down at the soft, luxurious white sheets on the bed and then around at the modern Scandinavian design of the room. Behind her, bright light streamed through the windows. She turned her head and saw a snowcapped mountain range outside the sliding glass doors that spanned the length of the wall. One of the doors was open, and frigid gusts of air billowed into the room.

She heard a click on the other side of the wall as the door opened and Vik entered. He was wearing a dark gray cashmere sweater and black trousers. The entire right side of his face was hidden behind bandages. The fire, Spencer realized. His face was burnt. The last time she had seen him, Vik had been enclosed in a steel container that Sam had created with his powers.

Vik was carrying a wooden tray holding a plate of food and orange juice. He walked over to Spencer and held the glass up to her lips.

"Drink," he said.

She tried to sit up and grab the drink, but something cold and hard stopped her arms from moving. She looked down. Handcuffs.

Vik smiled. "You think I'd trust you after what you did to me?" he asked. "I will say, I'm surprised how willingly you almost killed yourself to hurt me. You're braver than I gave you credit for."

"Where am I?" Spencer asked through gritted teeth.

"St. Moritz," Vik replied. "I inherited this place after my initiation. I lived here for a few years during the chaos of the Great Scarcity. This place has a twenty-thousand-square-foot state-of-the-art bunker built into the mountain beneath it. It's basically indestructible. And look at the view—isn't it fantastic?"

"What am I doing *here*, Vik?"

Someone knocked on the door before he could reply.

"Come in," Vik said cheerily. "What good timing."

Pierre opened the door. He made eye contact with Spencer, then turned around, bending forward slightly to grab something. Actually, to pull something. A wheelchair. Pierre backed into the room pulling the wheelchair, then turned it around slowly once he had cleared the door.

Chills ran through Spencer's body. Sam was sitting in the wheelchair, with several metal enclosures securing his arms and legs to the seat. A ball had been shoved into his mouth, secured by some sort of steel strap and lock. Both of his eyes were black and blue, and his face was completely cut open.

Pierre wheeled him over and positioned him near the foot of Spencer's bed. Then he walked over to Vik, placed a hand on his shoulder, and leaned in to kiss Vik on the mouth.

Vik put his hand behind Pierre's neck and kissed him back.

What the actual fuck?

She looked over at Sam, seeing the defeat in his eyes.

Pierre sat down in a leather Eames chair in the corner of the room. Vik walked over to the open sliding door, put his hands in his pockets, and slowly paced back and forth along the length of the glass wall.

"Spencer, Spencer, Spencer," he said, shaking his head. "Things *almost* went exactly according to plan—running into you at the coffee shop, placing the memory in your head, showing you the map, convincing you to sleep with me to trigger the Match, killing Reinhold, Graham, and the other Architects. It was so close to perfect.

"You see, I knew the truth about Sam for years. Or should I say

Matt?" Vik asked, looking over at Sam now. "I never really knew which name you preferred, and calling you 'the founder' just felt so sophomoric."

Spencer furrowed her brow. What was Vik talking about?

"I was surprised you didn't catch on, Spence. Especially after I gave you a clue," Vik said.

"A clue about what?" Spencer asked.

"I told you 'He goes by Sam.' You were so focused on the Harvest, though, that you missed that odd turn of phrase. Sam was born as Matt."

"Okay," Spencer replied. "I don't see why him changing his name is so important?"

"He didn't change *his name*. He changed *bodies*. Sam was born as Matt seventy-two years ago."

"Huh?" Her head was beginning to spin.

"Sam's body is forty-four years old. His consciousness is seventy-two."

"How?"

"The Apparatus has the technology to extend the life of our energetic force—our consciousness and powers—by transferring it into another body. We still age, but we're no longer at the mercy of biologic constraints. With each download, though, our energetic force begins to weaken. It finally reaches a point where continued transfers no longer make sense. The longest any Architect has been able to live is 324 years. That Architect lived with five biological bodies over the years."

Vik paused, giving her time to process.

"How old are you, then?" Spencer asked.

"Forty-five, same as my biological age. I'm what you might call a newbie. When an Architect's time expires, either naturally or at the discretion of the Apparatus, they are replaced by a new member entirely. That's what happened to me—I took an Architect's place when his time expired."

"So the other Architects stole bodies to continue living?" Spencer asked, trying to understand.

"Steal is a strong word. Our consciousness enters the body and takes over."

"When did Matt's consciousness take over Sam's body?" Spencer asked.

"Back in 2013, before I was a part of the Apparatus."

"That's before I even met Sam," she whispered. "So, I don't even know the 'real' Sam?"

"That's where this gets interesting." Vik seemed to be growing excited now. "Matt was an iconic founder; he pioneered the smartphone as we know it. He replaced another Architect, Leonardo, when his time expired. But after only a few years as an Architect, Matt got sick with cancer. When the time came to transfer his consciousness into a new body, he proposed something novel to the Apparatus. 'Let me take over the body of a Ray,' he said. Matt theorized that he'd be able to absorb the power of the Ray body at the time of his consciousness download, magnifying and morphing his own powers. We tested it on two subjects at city hall first.

"It worked, but neither of the subjects met Matt's requirements for a host body. He wanted another founder, someone with innovative *Zero to One* energy in their DNA. He thought those who could create something from nothing were superior beings. And Sam was the perfect candidate. Not only was he a Ray, but he was also a talented engineer who had just founded his own startup.

"It was a bold plan, but it had promise. The download went smoothly, but then four weeks later, something unexpected happened: Sam met Narina. Some might say it was love at first sight. We don't totally understand all the ways that love affects the brain, but it seemed to activate and alter dopamine pathways in unpredictable patterns that our model failed to account for. It triggered a complex neurobiological process that rewired his brain.

"For some reason, the download of Matt's consciousness into Sam's body didn't fully take. Parts of Sam remained—his love for Narina and his light being some of the critical aspects of his former self that stayed behind. But parts of Matt were also there—his memories and his shadow powers.

"At first, the Apparatus had no idea the transfer hadn't been successful, but over time, I began to suspect it. Catching Sam at city hall giving you the access badge was my first clue. I let it happen, of course. It was a good way to get you out of there. Contrary to what you might think right now, I never wanted to hurt you, Spence.

"After that, I had my tech guy, Sven, keep tabs on Sam, and we started to notice some unusual patterns. It became clear his loyalty wasn't with the Apparatus. I had planned to alert the other Architects, but then the earthquake happened, and my loyalties changed as well. I decided to let Sam continue to help you and your friends. I figured his involvement with the Network might work to my advantage when I was ready to take down the Apparatus eventually. I could never quite figure out his plan, even after years of surveilling his activities. But I knew he intended to help you, which in turn helped me, and that's really all that mattered.

"My plan for the Harvest was really so perfect that it was almost a masterpiece—my Sistine Chapel. I anticipated every detail. I even suspected that brain of yours might come up with a way to cripple the technology we planned to use. Hence the breastplate. The design included a backup power source and storage capabilities.

"I know you probably thought when I showed up with Graham and Reinhold that I had played you, but that decision was out of my control. Graham showed up at my hotel room only minutes before I had planned to leave. He told me there had been a change of plans. The three of us—Graham, Reinhold, and me—would take on Washington Square Park together instead. In truth, I think he was terrified at the prospect of facing you, Narina, and Rose alone.

"In all fairness, Spence, I didn't lie to you once. I *did* want to take down the Apparatus. I *did* want revenge on Graham. I *did* plan to shield you from the EMP. The only thing I didn't tell you, the only white lie, was the hypnosis. If I had shared that part, then my plan would have been obvious.

"The whole evening proceeded in a rather predictable fashion. That is, until you decided to light us both on fire. That part I was not expecting, but it's nothing several hundred thousand dollars of plastic surgery can't fix. That's why the Match was so critical. I knew once you figured out what I was really after, you'd be the one to kill me yourself. I hope you can understand why I had to protect myself.

"Even with the burns, I was still able to take enough energy with the single siphon I had left to last me hundreds of years. Our experiments in city hall helped us design a stronger siphon that took not just the energetic force but the entire life force. It was all going so perfectly to plan that even I couldn't believe it.

"But then"—Vik laughed at this part—"then good, pure, sweet Rose had to save all those people."

Spencer smiled, thinking back to that moment, pride welling up inside of her. She didn't care that she was locked up there if it meant they'd won, if it meant they had managed to save everyone.

"It was a shame to lose all that power," Vik continued. "I was devastated, really. Until I saw it for the gift it was."

Spencer froze. The Network had won—*right?*

"Do you remember when I showed you the shield and explained the way the graphene incorporated throughout the city's infrastructure acted as a ground to divert energy and block the EMP?" Vik asked.

Spencer nodded slowly.

"Do you remember what else I told you about graphene?"

"You said it turned every surface of the city into a sensor. That it turns any static material into a responsive agent, creating a connected network across the Geos," Spencer whispered.

"That's exactly right," Vik said. "You always remember everything, don't you, Spence? Anyway, graphene was really the breaking point for the Apparatus. Reinhold and Graham didn't have quite the same vision for the future that I did. They were stuck in a simplistic view of the Merge. They thought that we could either create robotics that displayed some level of sentience and human consciousness *or* help humans develop machine-like capacity through a combination of wearables, neural chips, and AI.

"But these options were too binary for my tastes. I found it to be an archaic way of thinking. The Merge isn't when two disparate

## dark days ahead

entities share aspects of each other. The Merge is when two things *become one*.

"You see, we didn't need neural chips and wearables when we had graphene. Graphene could turn the human body itself into an intelligent, sensing surface. With graphene, we could create our own responsive agents—human bodies ceding agency to the bodiless intelligence inside of them. We wouldn't need Orbs; humans themselves would become the GUI. I proposed we focus solely on graphene and forget about the other technology, but the Apparatus didn't agree. Only Pierre shared my vision for the future.

"When we started to create the Geos, Pierre and I decided to run a little experiment on the side. For the past two years, we've pumped graphene into the water supply, injected it into every piece of food, embedded it in every fiber of clothing, blasted it through the heating and cooling systems, and, of course, built it into every surface of the city. The concentration of graphene in the people living in the Geos is sky-high. We weren't exactly sure how to use it at first, how to test our theory and activate the sensors. That is, until your friend Rose solved the problem for us."

Spencer inhaled sharply. No, no, no. She tried to push the thought out of her mind, willing it to be wrong.

"Would you like a demonstration to help you understand how it works?" Vik asked. "It really is quite impressive."

Spencer didn't reply; the question was rhetorical.

Suddenly, her Orb was on. Vik, Pierre, and Sam were all observing the same scene on their own neural interfaces. It was a satellite image of a city. Vik zoomed in until they were at street level. Spencer recognized the place—they were looking at Seventh Avenue in Village Park.

"Do you see the man in the green jacket and jeans?" Vik asked Spencer. "He's one of the Rays Rose brought back from the dead and turned into a Liminal. He has a similar power to your dear friend Narina. Fire."

Vik pressed on something and then spoke. "See the woman walking toward you in the blue-checkered coat?" he asked into his

Orb. He paused, waiting for a reply on the other end. "Good—burn her alive," Vik said.

Spencer closed her eyes momentarily. She couldn't bring herself to look at first. When she opened them, she saw the man in the green jacket reach out his hand. Flames erupted and lit the woman on fire. She started running through the street, flailing her arms, screaming. People around her yelled for help. Several men tried to put out the fire, but it only got larger. The woman collapsed to the ground. A minute later, she was dead.

Sam shook his head in disgust. He tried to yell something at Vik. Spencer thought it sounded like "You fucking asshole."

"There, there. I was really only keeping you alive so you could see that. And so that Spencer could watch you die." Vik said as he walked over to Sam and started pushing his wheelchair toward the open door.

Spencer realized for the first time that the balcony had no railing. She thrashed in bed, trying to reach inside for her power, but she couldn't find it.

Narina's face flashed in her mind. The Match—her friend's life was tied to Sam's.

"No!" Spencer screamed, tears rolling down her cheeks. "Please, Vik. Don't do this. I'll do anything. I'll give you all my power."

Vik laughed. "I already have all your power."

Then he pushed the wheelchair forward and released it over the balcony, leaving Sam to fall thousands of feet to his death.

Spencer sat there, shocked. Several terrible realizations bubbled to the surface of her mind simultaneously.

She was Vik's prisoner.

Narina and Sam were dead.

And Vik now controlled an army of powerful Liminal robots with his mind.

Thanks for reading!

If you enjoyed this book and want to see more of the Dark Days series, please leave a review on Amazon or Goodreads.

If you'd like to be an early reader for the next book, sign up on my website or follow me on Instagram.

Website: nataliedocherty.com
Instagram: @ndocherty

Printed in Great Britain
by Amazon